Advance Praise for *The Devil's Interval*

"Murder and music, discord and harmony, guilt and innocence, domesticity and passion, smooth talk and rough sex: In *The Devil's Interval*—Linda Lee Peterson's virtuoso second novel—journalist-sleuth Maggie Fiori scores all the notes. Maggie, like thc book, is smart, stylish, and surprisingly steamy."

— Jon Jefferson (Jefferson Bass)
New York Times bestselling crime writer

"Smart and sexy, with the schemes of high society on full display, *The Devil's Interval* takes readers on a tour of everyone's favorite city, San Francisco. As Maggie Fiori attempts to solve this intricate mystery, what will happen to her damaged marriage? You'll be turning pages to discover the answers."

— Naomi Hirahara
Edgar Award-winning author of the Mas Arai mysteries

"*The Devil's Interval* is an entertaining mystery, and shines with crisp prose, layered characters, and a gripping plot."

— Jonnie Jacobs
bestselling author of the
Kate Austen and Kali O'Brien mystery series

"An intelligent and gripping novel. Maggie Fiori is a witty, feisty protagonist, and Linda Lee Peterson deftly weaves a compelling tale of how far a mother will go to save her child. *The Devil's Interval* is a roller-coaster ride through the streets and alleys of San Francisco that will evoke Robert Parker's Spenser novels with a dash of Janet Evanovich. Get out the flashlight. You'll be up late."

— Robert Dugoni
New York Times bestselling author of *The Conviction*

Praise for
Edited to Death

"Strong focus, admirable prose, and a nifty story line."

—*Library Journal*

"Brave, if blithely arrogant, character Maggie Fiori [is] a thirtysomething something Oakland writer/know-it-all sleuth/ Volvo-driving wife and mom who solves the murder of her boss, the urbane editor of a chichi regional magazine."

— *San Francisco Chronicle*

"If you are a Susan Isaacs fan, you will love Linda Lee Peterson's journalist-turned-sleuth, Maggie Fiori. This is a San Francisco and Oakland story with sparks flying as wisecracking Fiori, with her razor-sharp wit and rampant curiosity, sets out to find out who killed her editor boss. I couldn't put the book down. A very satisfying read for mystery lovers."

— Jacqueline Winspear
New York Times bestselling author of the
award-winning Maisie Dobbs mysteries

Learn more about Linda Lee Peterson at
www.lindaleepeterson.com

THE DEVIL'S INTERVAL

By
Linda Lee Peterson

This book is a work of fiction. With the exception of a few musicians, names, characters, places, and incidents are either the product of the author's imagination or are used fictitiously. Any resemblance to real persons, living or dead, is purely coincidental.

Published by Prospect Park Books
969 S. Raymond Avenue
Pasadena, California 91105
www.prospectparkbooks.com

Distributed by Consortium Book Sales & Distribution
www.cbsd.com

Library of Congress Cataloging in Publication Data

Peterson, Linda Lee.
The Devil's Interval / by Linda Lee Peterson.
pages cm
ISBN 978-1-938849-11-4 (pbk.)
1. Mothers--Fiction. 2. Murder--Investigation--Fiction. 3. San Francisco (Calif.)—Fiction. I. Title.
PS3616.E8434D48 2013
813'.6--dc23

2013017922

Cover design by Howard Grossman.

Printed in the United States of America

For Ken Peterson, my toughest and kindest critic

PROLOGUE

A few minutes before Grace Plummer died, she remembered that someone other than the regulars at the Crimson Club had called her Amazing Gracie. She was drifting, conscious of the sweat-sticky leather upholstery underneath her, vaguely wondering about the faint dome light overhead. What did it illumine, there in the back seat? Lumen, luminous, illumination.... Other, disconnected thoughts floated in and out—who had sung the "Evening Benediction" in Hansel and Gretel *at the opera last season? "When at night I go to sleep/Fourteen angels watch do keep." And was it cinnamon or something else with a "c"—cloves, cardamom—on top of the tiny holiday pastries her grandmother made? She didn't really struggle for the answers to these questions. She felt a pleasant little disconnect, like breathing deeply of nitrous oxide; feeling pain, but not really caring about what hurt or why. Or who was doing the hurting. But it was a surprise, wasn't it? The one with the cruel hands. And then, she remembered—it was cardamom, for sure. With that memory came the image of her grandmother, tall, shoulders back, one beautiful white braid wound around her head, teasing her, "Come, try one more, Amazing Gracie, just one more bite of the eplekake." And then, she felt hands on her head, like her grandfather's blessing at bedtime, and she was gone.*

CHAPTER 1

Here's a piece of useful fashion advice: Don't wear a metal underwire bra if you're visiting San Quentin Prison. They'll turn you away at the jailhouse door, when the underwire sends the metal detector into overdrive. And you can't just take the bra off, because braless ladies are not allowed inside. Those are just a couple of the things I learned when I found myself in the middle of an attempt to spring an innocent man from Death Row.

It all began when I took a break from a bookshelf purge in our family room, slapped the dust and stray dog hair from my hands, poured a cup of coffee, and sat down with *The Wall Street Journal.* Love that paper. Their editorials suck, since they perversely take political sides in opposition to my own, but wow, what great writing. The WSJ goes in for stubbornly conservative editorials, whereas I, a journalistic giant myself as editor of San Francisco's trendy, superficial, but oh-so-readable city magazine, *Small Town,* am an unreconstructed, knee-jerk liberal. Sitting there, surrounded by bags and boxes of dusty hardbacks and paperbacks that were slated to go directly to the book drive at our sons' school, I began reading a front-page story about publishers sending remaindered books to prisons. Inmates, with time on their hands and a less-than-great selection on the prison library shelves, regularly write to publishers and ask for their overstock to be donated. "Most grievously word-hungry," read the *Journal*, "are the Death Row inmates with their segregated, pitifully stocked library."

I lowered the paper and surveyed the family room floor. Our German shepherd, Raider, apparently exhausted from watching me work, had fallen asleep in the midst of the mess. Books, books, and more books. Bags and boxes of books. "Hey, babies," I said softly. "You're going to jail."

Within a few minutes, I had a polite community affairs officer at San Quentin on the phone.

"Bags of books," he said patiently. "You want to bring me bags of books?"

"Right," I said. "For the Death Row Library."

He sighed. "*Wall Street Journal* article?"

"Right again," I said.

"Prison," my husband, Michael, corrected me that evening when I told him where our extra books were going. "Jail's where you go to wait, prison's where you end up. There's a technical explanation, but it's more than you need to know." We were dawdling over coffee, enjoying the half hour between post-dinner and hardcore homework nagging. Though our three-story, sixty-plus-year-old rambling house teetered on the edge of permanent disorder, the dining room somehow managed to rise above the detritus of sports paraphernalia, pieces of electronics, and Raider's innumerable chew toys everywhere else in the house. Maybe there just weren't enough surfaces to clutter. Deep, deep forest-green walls seemed to take the noise down a notch, and my grandmother's chandelier sparkled soft light onto the table. We ate there every evening, a family agreement to slow down and feel civilized at least once a day.

"Want to split that last brownie?" I asked Michael. "And what does a tax lawyer know about jail or prison anyway?"

He pushed the plate with the lonely brownie my way. "All yours," he said. "Where do you think tax evaders go?"

"Congress," I said. "Maybe the White House. Corner office in some Fortune 500 company."

"Very amusing, Maggie. Did those bleeding-heart criminal -defense Gasworks chicks put this idea in your head?"

"They did not," I said indignantly. "I read an article in *The Wall Street Journal.* But Gasworks, that's a great idea. I'll bet they can cut through some of this red tape for me." The Gasworks Gang is an ad hoc group of stay-at-home mommy-lawyers who handle death-penalty appeals. Since the community affairs officer at San Quentin had been less than enthusiastic about my proposal to personally stock the shelves with my bags of books, I knew I'd need some insider help getting access.

"I know the Dewey Decimal System," I'd burbled over the phone. "My junior year I worked as a library aide at St. Agnes High School."

"Well, now, Mrs. Fiori," he began, "you have to understand that we have procedures," which roughly translated into, "Okay, lady, drop your books at the gate, get on with your sweet suburban life, and keep your friggin' Dewey Decimal System to yourself."

Oddly enough, Michael raised that very question.

"Maggie, why can't you just drop the books at the guard gate? You don't have to turn this into 'Avon calling' on Death Row, do you?"

I was silent.

"*Cara*?" prompted Michael, "what are you up to?" He used Italian endearments primarily when he felt I wasn't listening to him.

"I'm just curious," I said. "I've lived in the Bay Area almost twenty years and I've never been to San Quentin."

"It's not a tourist attraction," he said. "That's Alcatraz."

"Well, I know." I vacillated. "This whole thing about books and—"

"And felons. Killers," Michael completed my sentence.

"Books and desperate people," I said. "It interests me. Maybe there's a story."

Michael sighed. "Well, maybe. But they're not going to let you take a little library cart around so you can interview these guys. Which is," he muttered, "a big relief to me."

I waited a moment. "Are you *telling* me not to deliver the books, Michael?"

His face went blank. "Certainly not," he said. "Entirely your decision."

"Thank you," I said formally. "Just clarifying." I stood and began clearing dinner plates. Time to leave the room before the chill in the air froze us both into familiar conflicts. Our marriage had been tested the last year or so, and it had been my fault. Entirely. Completely. And not a day went by that I didn't regret a series of moral missteps, beginning with temporarily abandoning the whole "forsaking all others" thing, continuing through an inadvertent run at ruining Michael's career, and ending with imperiling a few lives, including my own. I did, to be perfectly fair, unsnarl the murder of my boss (and former lover) at the magazine along the way.

Since that series of misadventures, I had become painfully aware that the life Michael and I had made together, which once seemed relatively easy to navigate, had become strewn with hidden ordnance. In what felt like an endless loop, I relived every dim-witted detour I had taken off the moral high road. Turns out there's no page in the Dick Tracy Crimestoppers Notebook warning amateur sleuths about collateral damage to marriages caused by adultery or sleuthing or, worse yet, both. Which led me to remember that we'd decided to join the rest of the Bay Area's middle-class, overly self-scrutinizing couples in marriage therapy. Our first session was coming up and, all in all, I would have preferred to have an encounter with the Brazilian wax specialist.

Still, before the all-too-familiar chill had hit our conversation, Michael had innocently planted the Gasworks Gang idea in my head, and it seemed like precisely the access I might need. I had discovered the group via Edgar "the Invincible" Inskeep, a ruthless and very successful criminal attorney. We'd met when Michael introduced him to our friend, and my former managing editor, Glen. It was the climax of my *annus horribilis* when Glen confessed to murdering our former boss, Quentin Hart, the late, great—but not particularly nice—editor of *Small Town.* Edgar, in turn, had introduced me to his wife, also a criminal attorney. Unlike her money-grubbing husband, who defended drug dealers and society batterers for big bucks, Eleanor Inskeep was a public defender. Like many other women, when she became a mom, she looked for more flexible ways to run her professional life. She began doing death-penalty appeals and found it was satisfying but lonely work. To her surprise, she kept bumping into other new moms who were doing the same kind of work—and feeling the same way. Ninety percent of the time, they found themselves researching and writing, all alone by the computer and the phone. No more offices full of gossipy colleagues willing to dish fellow members of the criminal bar or commiserate when the same clients showed up for one, two, and then three strikes. Even your clients don't call—or at least, not often. And when they do, it's collect.

In the process of thanking Edgar profusely for mitigating Glen's troubles, I'd made one of those "anything I can do for you" offers we sometimes live to regret.

"Yeah," he said, "take my wife out to lunch. She's going stir-crazy at home with the new baby, and she's taken up with a posse of other new moms, death-penalty types. I think they're up to no good."

Eleanor was delighted to go out for lunch, especially when I dispatched Anya, our live-in Norwegian art student/au pair, to babysit.

"Lunch?" she said. "And you're sending a babysitter? You're my new best friend."

She explained Gasworks to me over sand dabs and chardonnay at Tadich's. Tadich's is a long, wooden bar and boothy, clubby-looking San Francisco fish house where they put mashed potatoes in the tartar sauce and the waiters are all old enough to have been honorably discharged after the War of 1812.

"Hope it's not too noisy," I said when we sat down.

Eleanor waved her hand at the room. "This is what I miss. The sound of adults eating and drinking."

"So, tell me about Gasworks. What is it and why is it?"

"It's a cross between a professional interest group and a new mom survivor society," she said. "A whole bunch of us criminal-defense types became new moms all at once. You remember what that's like, right?"

I nodded. "More or less. It fades or blurs or something. Or I guess the species would die out."

"Right," said Eleanor. "Exhaustion, isolation, days and nights on end when you can't figure out if you'll ever do a productive grownup thing again. And then you're just brought to your knees by this helpless little tyrant you worship."

"Been there," I said.

"But then," she continued, warming to her soapbox, "you're a trained professional, you're a criminal-defense lawyer. So you're trying to hold on to your self-respect and bring some money in, so you agree to accept death-penalty appeals." She buttered her sourdough bread with more vigor than necessary.

"More isolation?"

"No kidding. It takes months and years, and the only people you talk to have bad news and horrible stories. Investigators who keep turning up tales of hellish childhoods, social workers who want to let you know that your client's mother just died and that her deathbed wish was that you 'take care of her boy.'"

"Holy shit," I said softly.

Eleanor's eyes brimmed. "I was nursing Tyler when I got that particular call from the social worker." She swallowed. "I looked down at my son and thought: Once upon a time, my awful, terrible, pathetic, dumb ass violent client was somebody's baby, just like Tyler. Once upon a time, he was innocent." She took a gulp of wine. "Plus, you know, all that postpartum emotional stuff. I was falling apart. That's when I got on the phone and started calling around to my old buddies in the Women Defenders."

"Women Defenders? They sound like superheroes."

She laughed. "Well, we think we are. It's a bunch of lefty criminal-defense lawyers from all over the state. We're the daughters of the women who did sit-ins at Berkeley and Columbia. Anyway, within a few days, I'd hauled together a few of us who were new moms and did death-penalty appeals. And that's how the Gasworks

Gang got its start."

"And the name?"

"Come on, Maggie," she said. "Surely it hasn't been that long since you had babies. What did you obsess about?"

"Sleep. Getting back into a size eight. Flawless birth control."

"No, I mean about the babies?"

"Oh, colic, poop, and naps."

"Exactly," she said. "So, at our first meeting, we realized that we were talking about gas, gas, and more gas. Who's got it? Who hasn't? What do you do about it? And then, before lethal injections came along, executions took place...."

"In the gas chamber," I said. "I get it."

"Right. And by the way, they still use the same puke-green room to do their dirty work. So, we decided we were the Gasworks Gang."

After my lunch with Eleanor, I assigned a writer to research a feature on the gang for *Small Town.* I sent Calvin Bright, my favorite photographer and willing sidekick during my debut days as an amateur sleuth after Quentin's death, to shoot one of their meetings.

He showed up, contact sheets in sweaty hand, and delivered nonstop commentary as Linda Quoc, *Small Town*'s art director, and I looked through the shots.

"Those women are fine, fine, superfine," he said.

"They do very good work," I agreed. "It's thankless, but somebody's got to do it."

"Oh, loosen up, Mags. I mean, that was one sexy group of broads."

"They're all new moms, Calvin. Have a little respect. Plus, didn't they look awful? Circles under their eyes and everything?"

"I don't care. All those hormones in one room, all that 'fullness-of-womanhood' shit, cooing over each other's babies...."

"Unbuttoning to breastfeed," Linda added dryly.

"Yeah," said Calvin, "that too. Yummy icing on the cake. You know what? I think we ought to do a once-a-month follow-up for a while."

Linda and I exchanged glances. "Get out, Calvin," I said. "You've got the mind of a lecher and the maturity of a twelve-year-old."

"And that," said Calvin, on the way out the door, "is why you girls find me so irresistible. Plus, you know what they say, 'once you've gone black....'"

"No one says that, Calvin. Not one single real human being. Dream on," I said. It was too late. He was gone. And the pleasant distraction of bickering with a real person instead of staring at a screen came to an end.

But the Gasworks piece was a big hit for the magazine, and Eleanor and I became friends. So now, all these many months later, it was my turn to call for help. The Gasworks Gang, with their up-close-and-personal relationship with San Quentin, seemed like the perfect way to make sure my books got delivered to the Death Row Library.

When Eleanor answered the phone, I explained my request.

"Bring your books over," she invited promptly. "We can have coffee and catch up. Besides, there's somebody in our group who wants to meet you. I've been meaning to call."

"Advice on criminals or colic?" I asked.

"Something weird has come up," she said.

"Weird?"

"Isabella Fuentes is the member who wants to meet you. She's got an innocent client on Death Row."

I laughed. "Hey, Eleanor, isn't that what they all claim?"

"I'm not kidding, Maggie. I don't mean legally innocent; I mean *really* innocent."

"Wow."

"Yeah," she said seriously. "It's one of a kind. We could use some ink."

Interval No. 1 with Dr. Mephisto

The night before we went to our first session with Jessie McQuist, MFT, PhD, and couples counselor to every other yuppie/buppie/guppie committed twosome in the East Bay, some miserable brew of guilt and dread gave me a killer case of insomnia. Beside me, Michael snored gently, deep in the untroubled sleep of not just the guiltless but also the noble and forgiving wronged spouse. At first he'd been furious, then cold and businesslike, and slowly he'd started to return to his normal, careless, affectionate self. But therapy! Yuck. That seemed likely to reignite the whole cycle of fire and ice. To distract myself, I focused on Dante's second circle of hell, the one that was home to those who lusted. At least it was a cool club that would welcome me—Cleopatra was there, and Helen of Troy, and Guinevere. Beauties, queens, and me, a weak, slightly bored, and hassled dilettante writer-editor-mom. The irony, I realized, was that it hadn't even been lust that had tempted me into the affair with my late boss. It was curiosity about someone who seemed so elegant and elusive. It was hero worship. It was a chance to see myself as something other than the mom on the Wednesday pickup for soccer practice. It was exciting to feel seductive, to make love in the middle of the afternoon, to have a secret. But of course it was also the secret that made me miserable. And the worst moment of my life rolled around, as I should have known it would, when Michael told me he knew. It was the morning after Quentin's death, and we were jockeying for mirror and sink space in our bathroom, as we did every morning. I sniffled something about what a wonderful, irreplaceable editor and friend Quentin had been. And then Michael shut me up. "Was he a wonderful lover, too?" he asked. We were both facing the mirror, Michael shaving, his eyes cold and flat. "What do you mean?" I stammered. And then he told me. He knew. He'd known for a long time. He knew it was over, and he didn't want to talk about it. Ever.

And here we were, more than a year later, about to go sit on the couch of shame in some touchy-feely Berkeley shrink's office, and I thought, "That really will be the second circle of hell." And then my alarm went off.

Near the end of our first therapy session, I had two realizations: Michael, who could be one tough, judgmental guy about people who did what he perceived as vague things for a living, had decided he liked, or at least trusted, Dr. McQuist. Go figure. The other insight was that I didn't like her much at all. And that it was going to be oh so easy to morph her name from Dr. McQuist into Dr. Mephisto. Easy. And fun.

Just looking at Jessie McQuist made my head hurt. Black, black, black hair tipped with gold highlights, an embroidered hot pink vest, purple Lycra pants. Blue fingernails. I don't care how many initials she had after her name, I had a hard time taking a therapist seriously who had such a promiscuous relationship with color. The Craftsman bungalow that housed her office, lime-green cupola and all, should have tipped me off. Of course, I was having a hard time taking therapy seriously. Which became obvious in the first few minutes of our conversation.

"Michael, Margaret," she said, sitting cross-legged in her big chair, in that annoying way show-offy limber people do. Okay, okay, I get it! You do yoga.

"How are you?"

"I'm fine," said Michael.

"Me too," I said.

Silence.

"Weird to say, 'fine,' if we're here for therapy," I offered.

"Nothing's weird," she said.

I wanted to say that a lime-green cupola and blue fingernails on someone past the training-bra stage seemed pretty weird to me. Instead, I said, "Oh, you know, it's like the Garrison Keillor joke about the Lutheran farmer who goes to the therapist every week, and the therapist asks how he is, and the farmer always says, 'Can't complain.' And then they just sit there for fifty minutes."

More silence.

Michael sighed and not so surreptitiously sneaked a look at his watch.

"Are you Lutherans?" asked Dr. McQuist.

This was hopeless. "No," I tried to explain, "we're SO not Lutherans, but the joke is that if he's not going to complain or something, why is he there? He doesn't get the point of therapy."

"Is that why you're here?" asked Dr. McQuist. "To complain?" She took a sip from her big mug. At least it was black. Even from across the room, seated on her lavender, squishy couch, I could smell the tea. Musty, herbal, yuck. What's wrong with coffee, anyway?

"Maggie's here to complain," said Michael. "I'm here because we had some...problems last year, and they keep whack-a-moling back up."

"Whack-a-mole?"

I could see we were going to need a UN simultaneous translator to talk to Dr. McQuist.

Michael gestured, as if he were mercilessly bringing a baseball bat on targets in front of him. "It's a game. You try to hit the mole with a mallet, and he keeps disappearing into his burrow or whatever you call it. You whack him, and he keeps popping up again."

Dr. McQuist blinked. I could see the wheels turning. "Not that anyone does any hitting," I said, hoping to whack-a-mole down a misguided line of inquiry about domestic violence.

"I don't know," said Michael. "Josh popped Zach a pretty good one last night about whose turn it was to unload the dishwasher."

"Our sons," I explained. "They're eight and almost thirteen, and they don't usually hit each other." I felt my fingers creeping toward my phone, in that irresistible maternal need to just see their faces. "They're very handsome," I said. "I have photos, if you'd like to see them."

A tiny line appeared between Dr. McQuist's eyes. "Another time, thanks." No one spoke. "Okay," she said. "Michael, why don't you tell me what you meant about the—I think you called them 'problems'—last year."

Michael complied, providing a longish but very lawyerly summary of last year's events: my affair with Quentin Hart, Quentin's murder, my perseverance investigating the murder, the risks I'd created for our sons, and the *denouement*, which endangered my life.

Dr. McQuist listened. I thought I had explained all this on the phone, but oh well, I guess she can't be expected to keep all her philandering-wife/murder-investigation couples sorted out.

"Endangered," I offered brightly. "But I'm still here. All's well that ends well. Plus, our au pair, Anya, met a very nice doctor at the emergency room where I ended up, and they're still dating." I paused. "Off and on."

Dr. McQuist blinked. "He's Indian," I offered. I touched my forehead and then put two fingers up in back of my head, as Dr. Singh had done when he met me at the ER. "You know, 'dots, not feathers,' Subcontinent Indian." Dr. McQuist waited.

"I wonder if that's offensive," I said. "Do you think it is, if an Indian person says it to you?"

Dr. McQuist blinked again, then turned to Michael.

"All's well? Is that how you'd sum things up, Michael?" she asked.

Michael shifted on the couch, putting just a touch more distance between us. He shrugged. "Not from my perspective. But I may not have as finely developed a sense of happy endings as Maggie does. Otherwise..."

"Otherwise?" prompted Dr. McQuist.

"Otherwise we wouldn't be here, spending time and money we don't really have to spare," Michael snapped. The ice man was back. I glanced over at Michael, but he stared resolutely ahead. The warm, relaxed man I had married kept disappearing into someone aloof and detached. Some days I felt as if our marriage had turned into a businesslike partnership of convenience. I wanted to wave my hand, asking Teach for permission to speak, but she was refusing to catch my eye.

"Michael," she began again, "you mentioned that things keep coming back up from those issues last year. Why don't you tell Maggie what those things are? Just forget I'm here."

I could see Michael sizing up Dr. McQuist and the situation. This seemed gimmicky to him, I was willing to bet. On the other hand, this therapy had been his idea, he had scrupulously researched Dr. McQuist, and she had a number of very happy, unexpectedly effusive references among our own extended circle of pals. Straight, gay, happy, miserable, in transition, new relationships or old ones, *everyone* loved Dr. McQuist. That alone made me suspicious. But Michael was a careful consumer and he liked consensus. Plus, we were paying for the hour, so not giving her a chance felt like getting the plumber out to the house and then not inviting him to unclog the sink.

"Okay," he said. "Just tell *her*?"

"Right," said Dr. McQuist. "Talk to Maggie."

He settled back into the arm of the couch and faced me.

"After your shenanigans last year, I thought we had an agreement."

"We did," I said. "We do."

"No interruptions," said Dr. McQuist. "Listen to what Michael is saying."

"Okay, okay," I said meekly. "Sorry."

Michael turned to look at Dr. McQuist with something like wonder and admiration.

"Thank you," he said politely.

"Our agreement was, first...." He raised a finger. "No more affairs. Not ever, ever. Ever. Second, you've taken on a full-time job, and you're still—unless I missed something—a wife and mom, so no more investigating, no more poking your nose where it doesn't belong. Just—oh, Christ—cut us some slack. Enjoy what you've got."

He sat back.

"May I speak?" I asked Dr. McQuist.

"Please."

"Michael, I don't know how many ways to say it. The affair was a dumb, dumb, stupid mistake. You don't have to worry it will ever happen again. Second, you're jumping to conclusions about this Death Row story. You're right, I've got a day job. And I like that job. I'm willing to go listen to the death-appeal mommies because I've done a story on them once, and maybe there's a follow-up."

"Liar, liar, liar," said Michael.

"I'm sorry," Dr. McQuist said, "we have to end now."

CHAPTER 2

Aside from a childhood fascination with Susan Hayward's over-the-top performance in *I Want to Live!*, I'd never given much thought to the people who occupy Death Row. At the office, before I left to meet Eleanor and her Gasworks pal with the "innocent" client, I Googled up a little info.

The condemned make up quite a crowd in our country. There are 3,565 of them in the United States: 3,517 men and forty-eight women. Many are mentally ill; some have IQs that would make great golf scores but are lousy intellectual equipment for life. Some are just plain wicked. Most are guilty—of one thing or another. But not every single one. Or at least that's what the movies would have you believe—and according to Eleanor, one of the innocent was represented by a Gasworks member.

I rang the doorbell at Eleanor's just before noon. The spring bulbs were already showing some promise of color in her front flowerbed. The sun was doing its best, but March in San Francisco is still coat-and-gloves weather, even in the warm neighborhoods. The Inskeeps lived in leafy Forest Hills, an elegant but chilly part of the city, where old money and newer tech fortunes existed side by side. The Inskeeps' elegance was somewhat compromised by the large bundle on the front steps awaiting diaper-recycling pickup.

Eleanor flung the door open and pulled me inside. "Maggie! It's great you're here. Come in and warm up."

I followed her down the hall toward the living room, where I could hear sounds of chamber music drifting through the doors. Inside was a fire in the fireplace and a tray of coffee and *pain au chocolat* on the table.

Eleanor steered me to the couch, where a woman dressed in head-to-toe red raised a mug in greeting. Eleanor said, "Maggie Fiori, meet Isabella Fuentes." She gestured at the pot. "Help yourself. Peet's. Good and strong."

I poured, stirred, and settled in. No one spoke for a moment. "This is such a wonderful room, Eleanor," I said.

She grinned. "This is it. The one room free of baby clutter, work papers, and Edgar's Oakland A's paraphernalia. I just need one room that feels like this."

"I know what you mean," I said. "It's the dining room in our house. Just one room…." I glanced at Isabella. Eleanor laughed. "Isabella can't participate in this conversation. She's so tidy, so perfect, and a single mom, so there's no pile of *Sports Illustrateds* or old sweatshirts hanging around." Isabella did, indeed, look perfect. Snug red T-shirt, red jeans, red tennies. Her dark hair was piled on top of her head and skewered with a red pencil. The red was dramatic against her golden skin, glowing like a ripe Comice pear. She had the long limbs of a track star and Eurasian features. And while both Eleanor and I both had on lipstick, Isabella had what Calvin calls "twenty-minute" lips, carefully outlined in a darker color. She held a file on her lap, with not one messy spare piece of paper peeking out.

"Okay," I said. "Isabella, Eleanor hasn't told me much. Why don't you tell me about your client?"

"How much do you know about death-penalty appeals?" she asked.

"Very little. Just what I read in the piece we did on you all for *Small Town.* And what I've seen in the movies. I'm sorry. I should know more."

"Don't apologize. Most people know just what you know. And frankly, we don't talk about our work all that much with outsiders."

"How come?"

Isabella sighed. "Where do you think 'three strikes' legislation came from? Most people think our system coddles criminals."

"In the Bay Area?"

"The Bay Area is more liberal," said Eleanor. "But it's a finite piece of territory. Let's remember," she added, "what killed Rose Bird's career on the California Supreme Court."

"She was recalled, because..." I began.

"Because people knew she opposed the death penalty—and they didn't like it."

"That's our reality," said Isabella. "People don't like lawyers in general, but they especially don't like people like us. They think we're conscienceless, amoral hired guns defending the scum of the earth, and we're spending their money to do it."

"Okay, that's a basic question," I said. "Is it all taxpayer money funding your work? Don't private attorneys ever handle death-penalty appeals?"

"Maggie," said Eleanor. "Get real. Death-penalty appeals take years and years. Virtually no one is rich enough to retain counsel in a capital case."

"So it is taxpayer money funding what you do?"

"It is."

"Because," Isabella added, "if you're sentenced to death, you've got an automatic right to an appeal."

"Because sometimes people are innocent?"

"Well, first it's the law. And second, you're right, sometimes people are innocent," Eleanor said. "So it's because of that, and also it's because of the lousy counsel defendants sometimes get—there are a couple guys on Death Row in Texas whose attorneys slept through much of their trials. So there's a small but persistent movement to reexamine the cases of people currently on Death Row."

"Like those Northwestern journalism students who tracked down evidence that a guy on Illinois's Death Row was innocent?" I asked.

"Exactly. That's where the Center for Wrongful Convictions

was founded. In fact, there are Innocence Projects all over the country now, but none are willing to take on this case. Joe Kotter, the guy who defended my client, is a more-than-competent attorney, which makes it even tougher to pursue the appeal. And that's why Eleanor thought we should talk to you. We've got an innocent guy on our hands, really innocent, it's not just that flimflam stuff you think we lawyers do."

"*Small Town* is a city magazine," I protested. "We're not exactly home base for hard-hitting investigative reporters. The only things we're tough on are bad movies and unsafe sushi."

"We know that," said Eleanor. "We just want to start by asking some advice. If we go to a—forgive me, Maggie—a real reporter, somebody on the crime beat, they've got to run with the story. This is a delicate situation."

"Okay, what do we know so far? It's delicate and I'm not a real reporter. As you guys would say, 'I'll stipulate to that.' But I still don't know exactly what it is you want my advice about."

Eleanor looked at Isabella. "It's your story to tell," she said.

Isabella nodded. "My client's name is Travis Gifford. He's forty-one years old, retired from the military. Ran a couple of motor pools on big Army posts, made sure the brass got driven around. So when he got out of the service, he tried driving a taxi part-time, but he didn't like it. His mom's got a jazz club in the city, and he used to play there sometimes, but the club didn't generate enough income to support both of them. Anyway, he's a very smart, personable, presentable-looking guy, so he went to work for one of those upscale car companies. He'd do airport runs and longer-term assignments for executives. He had a license to carry a gun, so sometimes he'd do security-related driving."

"Wait a second," I said. "Travis Gifford. I remember this story. Your client's the Limousine Lothario?"

Isabella nodded. "That's what they called him. He's a handsome man, and before he went to prison, he did enjoy the company of women."

"In the limousine? Isn't that right? He used it for assignations?"

"Sometimes."

"And then he murdered a woman in the company's limousine?"

"That's what the jury concluded."

"But that's not what happened?"

Isabella pulled the pencil out of her topknot, opened her perfectly made-up lips, and began chewing on the end of the pencil.

"Isabella," prodded Eleanor, softly.

She took the pencil out of her mouth and said, "Absolutely not."

CHAPTER 3

I left Eleanor's house with two souvenirs: the leftover pastries and a thick file on Travis Gifford, the Limousine Lothario. The file included a number of society-page clips featuring Grace Plummer—a tall, ashy blond with a high cheekboned, sculpted face that either signaled great genes or extraordinary cosmetic surgery. There she was in a Rita Hayworth, put-the-blame-on-Mame black dress with a frothy white fishtail hem at the Black & White Ball, dancing cheek to cheek with Mr. Plummer; on a sailboat in the bay, leaning out over the water; barefoot at the beach, laughing directly into the camera with a live crab in each hand; making a runway twirl in tennis whites at the Junior League fashion show; holding an extravagant bouquet of roses at the San Francisco Garden Show. A breathtaking woman with what looked like a carefree, pleasure-filled life. Underneath the clips was a short stack of black and white, way too graphic police photos. Isabella warned me as I picked them up.

When she warned me, I'd looked at just one. Grace Plummer, the late Mrs. Frederick G. Plummer, lying face down, arms cinched tight, wrists bound with something that looked like a flowered chiffon scarf, on the back seat of a very spacious sedan. A limousine, in fact. Travis Gifford's limousine. I couldn't see her face, but I could see what three bullets had done to the back of her head. It was as awful a sight as I ever wanted to see.

"What happened?" I asked, turning the photograph face

down, just like the once lovely Mrs. Plummer.

"We don't really know. But here's what the prosecution said happened," answered Isabella. She took a deep breath, hugged her knees to her chest, and rocked a bit, as if she hurt, deep in her gut. "Travis met Mrs. Plummer because her husband hired him to drive on a regular basis. To and from meetings out of San Francisco, to and from the airport, frequent trips up and down Silicon Valley. When Mr. Plummer didn't need Travis's services, Mrs. Plummer often did."

"This is Frederick Plummer, venture capitalist to the once and future dot-com stars?" I asked.

"None other," said Isabella. "Travis and Mrs. Plummer became friendly. Then they became even friendlier. They became lovers. And they both had…wide-ranging tastes. A little tasteful bondage, a little playful S&M."

"Is this the prosecution talking?"

Isabella sighed. "No, up to this point, it's the defense talking, too. But this is where we part company with the DA. Nobody argues with the fact that Travis and Grace Plummer got a little adventuresome in their love life. But the night she was killed, Travis claims they made love in the limo, parked out at Land's End, and then he delivered her safe and very much alive to the Plummers' home, around 10 p.m. He drove the limo home, parked it in his garage, climbed two flights up to his apartment, and went to bed."

"And then?"

"The next morning, one of Travis's neighbors was leaving early. He parked next to Travis in the garage, and right away he saw that the limousine had been pulled in so crookedly that he was going to graze the side of it if he didn't back out really carefully. He wrote a note to leave on the windshield, complaining to Travis. But he noticed the car was unlocked, so he opened the door to leave the note on the front seat, and the smell knocked him over. Then he saw—well, you saw what he saw."

"Travis shot her?" I asked.

Isabella shrugged. "Someone shot her. But she may have

been dead already, from a broken neck. The DA argued that the gunshots were just to mislead the cops, that her neck was broken in some sex play that got out of hand."

Isabella handed the file back to me. "It's all in there. You can read it yourself."

"This sounds ridiculous. Who'd be crazy enough to kill someone in their own car and then park in the garage?"

"That's what the defense argued. But there was too much evidence. Travis's semen in Mrs. Plummer. Skin samples under her nails. No one who had seen Travis deliver her home, as he claimed."

"How about the husband? Isn't the spouse the automatic best suspect?"

"Generally, yes. But Plummer had a dinner meeting that night, and a whole crowd of young gearhead entrepreneurs and their lawyers has given him an alibi until nearly 1 in the morning. Coroner says the time of death was between 11 p.m. and midnight."

"Okay. But, going back to Gifford, why would he leave a dead body in his car, in his garage?"

Isabella shrugged. "The prosecution had an answer for that, too. The limousine had darkened windows, no one could see in. He didn't know anyone would open the door—they claimed he planned to get rid of the body later that day."

"And what about the gun? You said Travis was licensed to carry one. Did they find the gun used to shoot Mrs. Plummer? Was it Travis's gun?"

"They did find it," said Isabella, "and it wasn't his. Different caliber. It was wrapped in a pretty disgusting mess of used kitty litter in a trash can next door to Travis's apartment building. It was impossible to tell whose gun it was, because the serial numbers had been obliterated."

"What does your client think really happened?"

"He doesn't know. He figures—we all figure—that if she had something going with him, she might have had other extracurricular activities. Though he admits he didn't think she did. And it didn't much matter, because we couldn't turn anything up before the trial."

"And now?"

"Well, during the habeas process, we've got an investigator looking into everything. But frankly, people like the Plummers don't have lives that open themselves easily to the kinds of investigators we can hire."

Eleanor cleared her throat. "Which is where you come in, Maggie."

I looked at her. She had that carefully neutral expression I was used to seeing on the faces of my children when I was trying to ascertain who had fed the dog underneath the dinner table.

"The Plummers and their friends are exactly the kinds of people *Small Town* covers. You've got access to a world and information we just don't have."

Moments like this were precisely when I realized I should have gone to journalism school instead of, as a literature and piano student, lying around on rump-sprung sofas, reading 18th-century novels or scouring the music building for hunky cellists to play chamber music with. I should know how to respond, but I didn't have a clue.

I shook my head. "I don't know. This doesn't smell all that different to me than the cops coercing information out of media organizations." I held up my hand. "I know, your cause is just and all that. But, if you do it for one side, you do it for the other."

"Wait a second," said Isabella. "We're not asking you to turn over confidential interviews."

"What are you asking, exactly?" I said, as I put the file back on Isabella's lap.

Isabella put the file on the floor between us.

"Just this. I think there's more to the story that we could understand if we had access to the Plummers' lives. How does a woman like Grace Plummer spend her time? Who does she hang out with when she is doing all her socialite charity activities? Who's her hairdresser? What valet parkers does she hire if she's having a party?" She unfolded her legs, stood up, and started wandering around the living room, patting her pockets in the unmistakable tic of a recently reformed smoker.

"Look, Maggie. It's not all that different from the journalism professor at Northwestern who sent his class out to uncover evidence to have that Death Row case reopened."

"It is different," I said. "Those kids weren't working journalists, with a responsibility to a publisher and to their readers. Plus, I'm not an investigative reporter. I'm an editor. I sit in front of a computer, harass writers about deadlines, and argue with the lawyers who never want us to say one single controversial thing to anybody about anything."

Isabella stood over me, and nudged the file back toward me with one, red-tennied toe. "How about this? Take the file home, read it through, look at the clips. Talk to some people at the magazine, see if the story appeals to anybody. Mrs. Plummer was a pretty high-profile player on the social scene—that's got to be of some interest to your readers. We're not asking for any favors with the information you find. We just think that if *Small Town* stirs the pot, something might happen. Right now, we're only asking you to spend an hour reading the file. Then, give me a call."

Eleanor cleared her throat. "Travis Gifford was somebody's baby boy once upon a time," she whispered.

"Such a cheap shot," I whispered back. I closed my eyes for a moment, willing that image of Grace to go away. Suppose it was one of my boys wrongly accused. Unthinkable. Too ridiculous to contemplate. I opened my eyes, picked up the file, and stood.

"Okay, I'll look at it and I'll call you."

Isabella smiled, and pulled the red pencil out of her dark hair.

"Here's one of my lucky pencils. Just put a little check mark next to anything that puzzles you."

I looked at the pencil. It was a soft No. 1, and down its length, it read:

"*Antes que te cases, mira lo que haces.*"

"Before you get married, look what you're doing?" I asked,

puzzled.

Isabella laughed, "It's the Spanish equivalent, of 'Look before you leap.' The mom of a guy I dated in law school always used to say that. For a long time, I thought she was worried her precious *hijo* was going to marry me. Then, I figured out it was great advice for anyone nuts enough to go into criminal law."

"What do you think now?" I asked, standing up, tucking the file under my arm.

"Now I'm convinced she was very worried he was going to marry me. But it's still good counsel."

Eleanor walked me to the door.

"Thanks for coming, Maggie. We really appreciate your help."

"I've only agreed to look at this stuff, Eleanor. I haven't said yes to anything else," I reminded her.

"I know," she said. She reached over and gave my cloche a little tug, straightening it for me. "Very between-the-wars look," she said. "I love your hats. They always make me feel as if I'm in a classic movie."

"Me, too," I said. "I feel that way almost every day—only I don't have a script and have to make up my own lines. Sometimes I'm not even sure I know what character I'm playing."

"Today," said Eleanor, "you've gotten a chance to play the good guy." She put her arms around me for a hug, and put her mouth close to my ear and said, "Just remember, the habeas clock is ticking."

As I drove home, a summary of how the death-penalty appeal process works rattled around in my head. Isabella and Eleanor had explained it in brief strokes, which, as Isabella pointed out, saved me hours of boredom the rest of them had to endure in law school.

"Criminal law always looks so exciting in the movies," I'd protested.

They both laughed at my naïveté.

"It looks good in the movies because appeals only take 125 minutes, tops, from opening titles to end credits, the guy lawyers are handsome and sensitive, even when they haven't slept for several days on end, and the women get to wear great clothes," Eleanor had pointed out. "That does not happen in our world. Except for Isabella, who apparently doesn't even own sweats."

Isabella ignored the jibe and moved onto Appeals 101 for me, explaining that there are two flavors, direct and habeas petition.

"And Gifford's is?"

"Habeas," said Isabella. "And that's good. A direct appeal means that you've got to stick to issues you can identify from the trial transcript. But in habeas, you can go 'extra-record,' meaning, you can go outside the transcript and find evidence or issues that didn't come up during the trial."

"Such as?"

"Such as lots of things. Evidence the police suppressed or mishandled, a witness who wouldn't come forward during the original trial."

"Have you got any of those?"

"No," said Isabella, "not yet. But we do have one mystery we haven't been able to figure out." She'd leafed through the file again, and pulled out a few sheets fastened together with a red paper clip. "Take a look at this," she said, "when you go through the file. The police canvassed the Plummers' neighborhood during their investigation, and a neighbor insisted she hadn't seen Travis drop Grace off—which would have been nice corroborating evidence, but she did say she'd noticed two other vehicles at Grace's late that night."

"Any details?"

Isabella shook her head. "We wish. She was unclear about whether it was two cars, a car and a truck, a van, an ice cream truck! Apparently this particular little old lady was the self-appointed neighborhood watch warden. Her husband went to bed early every night, and she was a night owl. So she was constantly peering out her window late at night."

"Didn't the fact that she'd seen two other vehicles, parked at Grace's, whatever they were, support Travis's theory that someone else could have come by—another sweetheart, or a burglar or something?"

"That would have been nice," said Isabella. "But unfortunately this neighbor, Mrs. Herbert Orson Lomax—she referred to herself that way, all three names, every single time—was the quintessential elderly lady, with failing eyesight and slightly muddled recall. She was recovering from cataract surgery on the night Grace was murdered."

"They pulled a *Twelve Angry Men* discredit on poor Mrs. Herbert Orson Lomax during the trial," said Eleanor.

"Got it," I said, thinking of the Henry Fonda classic in which the busybody neighbor who insisted she'd seen the wrongly accused young man neglected to mention that she'd spied the crime at the exact moment an El train rumbled past, obscuring her view.

"Still, I guess your investigator is going back to talk to her again."

"Again, I wish," said Isabella. "Mrs. Lomax has gone to her reward since the trial."

"What about all the new DNA evidence?" I asked. "I heard Barry Scheck—the guy from the OJ criminal trial—on the news the other day, flogging his book about stuff like that."

"That's an exciting emerging area," said Eleanor. "It's one reason they reopened the Sam Sheppard case after all these years. And that may be something Isabella can pursue. But right now, the DNA evidence is hurting her case. It's Gifford's DNA that was all over Mrs. Plummer. We don't know yet if there's any other angle to pursue." Eleanor and Isabella exchanged a quick look. Neither said anything.

"Okay, so what next?"

"Now," said Isabella, "we're in the process of writing a brief and investigating the habeas. It's on a killer deadline. Because once we file our AOB—that's an appellant's opening brief—and the state responds, we file a reply brief, and then the habeas petition is due in 180 days. If we miss the deadline, the issues that are in the habeas petition are lost forever. No one can ever raise them again."

"What aren't you telling me?" I asked.

"Lots," said Isabella. "That's why we want you to read the file."

I persisted. "I mean, why did you and Eleanor give each other the big look a minute ago?"

Isabella shook her head. "Read the file. There is another possibility..."

"This mysterious possibility—is it the reason you're convinced Travis Gifford is innocent?"

The room grew uncomfortably quiet. "Maggie," said Eleanor gently. "Isabella may not want to discuss some things with you until she knows you're committed to helping."

Isabella gave me a barely perceptible nod. And I walked out the door thinking that I might be turning into a real journalist after all. The possibility of access to inside information was fueling a suddenly ungovernable hunger to be on a "need-to-know" basis with the Gasworks Gang.

CHAPTER 4

After breakfast, cold cereal and lukewarm coffee, Travis Gifford closed his eyes and tried to imagine this woman, Maggie Fiori, Isabella was bringing to visit that day. Smart for sure, he thought, careless, maybe. The way she scribbled notes in the margins of her books made him think she might be quick to judge, likely to trust her own instincts. He put his hands flat on either side of his bowl, as if he were trying to levitate right out of the chair, through the roof of his cell and into the early spring sky. What was that song his mother liked? "I remember sky/It was blue as ink/Or at least I think/I remember sky." He opened his eyes. Had Isabella said that the Fiori woman was a mother? He hoped so.

CHAPTER 5

Take a breath, Maggie," said Isabella, as she paid the toll at the Richmond-San Rafael Bridge.

She gunned the motor and zipped up the slow rise to the bridge. I looked out over the edge, into the cold, blue-gray waters. "Have I been talking too much? I guess I'm a little nervous."

Isabella took her hand off the polished burl of the gearshift and patted vaguely in the direction of my knee.

"Don't worry, *chica*. Everyone gets a little nervous on the way to Death Row. Even if you're just visiting."

"Hey," I said, "can I ask you a personal question?"

Isabella glanced my way. "Isn't that what you do for a living?"

"You speak Spanish, right?"

"I grew up speaking Spanish. I still leak the stuff, and it comes in handy once in a while."

"But you don't look..."

Isabella laughed. "Latina? I am, though. Mom was Vietnamese, Dad's family came on the run from some horrible regime or other in Nicaragua. My brother always described us as Latisians. I loved that, made it sound as if we came from somewhere else in the solar system. Instead of just being another brown-skinned, weird immigrant mix. When we were kids and went to Hawaii on vacation, I always felt it was the only place on earth people didn't stare at us and wonder, 'Where'd *you* come from?'"

"Why Hawaii?"

"Oh, because in Hawaii, everybody's a mix of something or other, so nobody wonders about your ethnicity. Everybody looks like some variation of me."

"Thanks," I said. "I didn't mean to pry."

Isabella laughed. "Oh, right. Now, I've got a question for you. What made you decide to come with me today?"

"The photos," I said. "They were haunting me."

After several sleepless nights when the *Hollywood Confidential*–style, brutal black-and-white police photos kept swimming to the surface every time I dropped off, I knew the only way to get them out of my head was to visit Travis Gifford.

"I don't get it," said Michael, over breakfast. "If this thing is creeping you out enough to keep you up at night, why do you even want to go meet this guy?" Without missing a beat, he added, "Hey, Josh, what's the rule? Drink the last of the orange juice, you've got to mix up another batch."

Josh looked guilty. "How'd you know I was drinking the end of the pitcher?"

"Your father has eyes in the back of his head," I said. "All parents do. You might as well learn it now."

Josh rolled his eyes. He was leggy and mouthy, two inches taller than me, and a poster kid for irritating adolescence. I scrutinized Josh as he hauled another can of orange juice out of the freezer with a martyred sigh. My sweet-tempered first-born was morphing into some wiseass, moody teenager. Some days, I felt as if I'd retrieved the wrong kid at school, like turning in a plaid wool skirt at the dry cleaners and coming home with a leather mini. His major sign of affection these days was absently patting me on the head as he walked by, much as he did the dog, and saying, "How ya doing, little buddy?" I was constantly confused: Was I still his mom or just a really boring playmate he'd outgrown?

Zach, on the other hand, still seemed like his real self—goofy, completely unself-conscious about his affection for Michael and me. Lately, though, I'd noted him watching Josh, and I worried that the wheels were turning. If his adored, hero-worshipped older brother thought the parents were so lame, maybe he needed to readjust his thinking as well. Soon, I suspected, Zach would just find us annoying as well. I figured we had two, three years tops to enjoy an uncomplicated relationship, and I wanted to make the most of it.

"Maggie?" said Michael. "Did you hear anything I said?"

"Sorry," I said. "You know what? I don't get why I want to go either, but I guess it's the devil-you-know theory. I mean, maybe Gifford is innocent, but right now I've got those awful police photos stuck in my head. And until I meet Gifford himself, I've got a monster pictured."

Michael tugged at the comics planted under my elbow. "If you're not reading those, I want them."

"I can't read the comics on the morning of a trip to Death Row," I said. "Take 'em."

"So, you think that if you see this guy, you'll be able to tell just by looking at him that he is—or he isn't a monster?" Michael persisted. "Gee, let's get rid of the criminal justice system, *cara*, and let you take a look at accused people. Save the taxpayers a lot of time and money, eliminate jury trials altogether." He sipped his coffee and gave me a particularly smug grin. "Why don't you explain your intuition to the warden at San Quentin, and maybe he'll send this guy home with you?"

I examined Michael while he read the comics, top to bottom. The fact that he was making wisecracks about my visit puzzled me.

I reached over and tapped my fingers on the back of his hand. Without looking up, he turned his hand over and clasped mine.

"Hey," I said. "How come you're not trying to talk me out of going to San Quentin?"

He put down the paper. "You're interrupting *Sherman's Lagoon*," he said. "Okay, remember when we were at Dr. McQuist's the other day?" he asked.

I nodded.

"You said you're interested in this as a story. I've decided I've got to believe you. I can't be second-guessing everything you're doing at work, looking for trouble. You want me to trust you, so I guess I'm going to try. If it turns into anything else, can I assume you'll talk to me?"

"I will," I said eagerly. "I promise. It's just…"

"What?"

"Well, that's great. That's wonderful. I guess that means therapy is working, it's just that I never would have thought that someone like Dr. Coat of Many Colors would work for us."

Michael sipped his coffee. "You don't think much of her, huh?"

"Do you? Look at her!"

Michael regarded me coolly. "And the great evenhanded journalist Maggie Fiori is judging people on the basis of looks again?"

"Oh, for heaven's sake. I'm not a real journalist, I was an underemployed freelance writer who fell into this job, and I'm trying to take it seriously, and yes, absolutely, I'm a terrible, shallow person and I do judge people not by how they look but by how they choose to present themselves."

"Well, if you don't give Dr. McQuist a chance, this whole thing isn't going to work," he pointed out, letting go of my hand.

Shut up, Maggie, I said to myself, just shut up. I stood, came around behind Michael and threw my arms around his neck. "I'm an idiot," I said. "Dr. McQuist is fashion-challenged, but she's a genius. I saw you light up when she made me stop talking and listen to you." I kissed the top of his head. "I've got to run. I promise not to get into any mischief today."

Michael reached up and grabbed my hand.

"One other thing you should know, Maggie."

"What? That sounds ominous."

Michael turned around to face me. "I know Frederick Plummer. Not well, but I know him."

I sank back down into the chair next to Michael.

"The widower of the murdered woman? Grace Plummer? You *know* him?"

Michael nodded. "I hadn't said anything because I didn't know if this was going anywhere. And I certainly don't know him well. He's a client of the firm, or at least, the nonprofit foundation he started is a client."

"You know him?" I repeated, a little dazed by this news.

Michael shrugged. "I've met him a few times, that's all."

"My goodness," I said. "*Small Town* all around."

"You shouldn't be that surprised," said Michael. "There are only a handful of law firms in the city that serve business-linked nonprofit foundations. And it's not like I play hockey with him or anything."

"So what do you think I should do?" I asked.

"Give the information to Isabella and, if this goes any further, to Mr. Gifford, and to your publisher. Most of all, remember that promise you just made not to get into mischief."

I thought about that promise as I chattered away to Isabella, all the way from her Berkeley office to the Richmond-San Rafael Bridge, until she suggested I slow down and take a breath. She seemed unflapped by the news that Michael had a connection, however tenuous, to Frederick Plummer. But I still couldn't stop talking. Instead of being relaxed and ready for anything as we approached San Quentin, as I assumed a seasoned journalist would be, my hands were icy and I felt the kind of breathlessness you associate with high-altitude hikes. The night before, I had asked Isabella if there were special instructions about what to wear. "No denim, no green—and make sure you don't have on an underwire bra."

"Beg pardon?"

"Metal detector," she said. "It's really sensitive, and the underwires set it off. One time, I had to go into the ladies room, cut holes in my bra and rip the wires out. Wrecked a fifty-dollar Cosabella. You don't want to screw around with that detector. They only give you three tries through, and then you're out."

"You couldn't just stash your bra?" I asked.

"Are you kidding? That's another rule. No braless women visitors. No exceptions."

As we curved off the bridge, we were at sea level, and the exit to San Quentin was ahead on our right.

We pulled off the road and up to the entry gate. Isabella said, "Look at that view. If San Quentin weren't already here, some developer could throw up some condos and get top dollar in the real estate market."

Sure enough, looking out from the parking lot, the San Francisco Bay beyond, spanned by the Golden Gate Bridge, expensive cars were wending their way from Marin County's privileged hillsides into Everybody's Favorite City. A perfectly trimmed and edged lawn stretched beyond the parking lot, and the walkway from the lot to the reception building was lined with early-blooming rosebushes. "Inmate-gardeners," said Isabella, "they're the best. They're not working on anybody's clock."

"People would kill for this view," I said, "but I guess that's an awful and old joke."

"Punch line doesn't work," said Isabella. "No view from Death Row. Say your prayers," she said to me, "we're here."

In fact, the duties and rituals associated with getting from the front gate guardhouse to sitting down across the table from Travis Gifford did remind me of a religious ceremony. There was a hierarchy at San Quentin, and you had to navigate it just right, or the indulgence you sought—an interview with Isabella's client—could be withheld. It reminded me of the first time Michael had taken me to Mass with his family. Even though I'd gone to St. Agnes, I still felt like the quintessential outsider, the Jewish girl ignorant of the language, the culture, even the scents, and the responsibilities of all those people in all those elaborate costumes. The costumes were less off-putting here than at Sts. Peter's and Paul's—khaki for the guards, denim for the prisoners, instead of all those billowy white getups the priests and acolytes went in for, but there was just as much mystery.

Isabella seemed to know most of the correctional officers, big, buffed-up guys almost without exception. It was near noon when we arrived, and many carried handled coolers on their way to and from lunch. "Why do they look like they're going on a picnic?" I asked Isabella.

"You mean the coolers? They're all into bodybuilding, so they eat massive amounts of food. No little brown sack could possibly accommodate what they've got in there."

It wasn't a regular visiting day, Isabella explained to me, so she and I had the family room almost to ourselves. "On a family day, this place is filled with people," she said. "People come with plastic see-through containers, filled with change for the vending machine."

"No cakes with files in them," I joked.

"You can't bring any outside food," she explained. "So visitors bring enough change so they can get stuff from the machines. Keeps the kids busy, and gives people a chance to feel as if they're having a meal together. It's quite a scene on visiting day with all the kids wandering around, people playing checkers, people holding hands." She gave a dry laugh. "I always think it looks a little like a Jane Austen movie. You see couples strolling around the room, the woman with her arm tucked into the man's, as if they're promenading."

Today, the room felt like an empty dining hall at camp, just the two of us, alone in a sea of tables and chairs. Suddenly, the door swung open and a correctional officer gestured Travis Gifford in. "One hour, Ms. Fuentes," he said to Isabella. She nodded. "Travis Gifford, Maggie Fiori."

We shook hands and sat down, Gifford on one side of the table, Isabella and me on the other. Pale, pale blue eyes, close-cropped graying blond hair, faint freckles across his nose and visible under the gold hairs on his forearms. He didn't look bodybuilderish like the correctional officers, but his shoulders were broad and straight, and suddenly a picture of a young Nureyev floated into my head. Muscles under artful control.

"I feel as if I know you already, Mrs. Fiori," he said.

"Isabella's been talking too much," I said.

He shook his head. "I've been reading your books. The ones

you donated to the prison library? Some of them had your maiden name in them, Margaret Stern."

I remembered the bags of books, mostly old paperbacks and some battered college texts I'd packed up and sent via Women Defenders to the Death Row Library.

"I've got plenty of time to read," said Travis, "and to pay very close attention. We get a lot of second- and thirdhand books here, so I always read everything on the page. What people underline, notes they write, everything."

He leaned back in his chair and crossed his arms.

"Want to know what I've figured out about you?"

Isabella protested, "We've got limited time, Travis..."

I put my hand on her arm; I could feel the heat radiating through the red wool. "It's okay, Isabella."

"I'll be quick," said Travis. "You don't like the romantic poets much—Byron, Shelley, those guys, hardly a mark on those pages. But you like the religious stuff—George Herbert, John Donne. If I were nineteen and trying to get you into bed, I'd send you Andrew Marvell, but not the usual, 'To his coy mistress.'"

"Travis..." began Isabella.

Travis held his hand up to stop her, and then he lowered his hand, palm cupped upward and put it in front of me. I followed his eyes, down to his palm, and he opened it slowly, as if he were setting a firefly free to twinkle away into the air. There on his palm, written in ink, it said, "Clora, come view my soul..."

"Who's Clora?" asked Isabella impatiently, looking over her shoulder to see if someone was watching this strange scene through the pane in the door.

Travis turned his palm face down on the table, leaned forward and whispered:

Clora, come view my soul, and tell
Whether I have contrived it well.
Now all its several lodgings lie
Composed into one gallery;
And the great arras-hangings, made

Of various faces, by are laid;
That for all furniture, you'll find
Only your picture in my mind.

Travis sat back and smiled. A prisoner, in a cold sterile room, with big squared shoulders and an even bigger presence. His self-confidence was palpable and seductive. It took an effort to resist. And an even greater effort not to feel invaded by the idea of a man in a cell memorizing a passage for me.

'The Gallery,' I said, coolly. "No wonder they call you Lothario. Nice parlor trick to memorize a poem I loved in college. Good thing I'm not nineteen any more."

"Why'd you give the book away?" he asked.

"I have a hardbound copy of Marvell now," I said. "I thought the paperback deserved a new home."

Isabella sighed and tapped one carmine nail on her wristwatch. "Time flies, my friends."

Travis unfolded his arms and placed his hands flat on the metal table. "Let me get this straight, Isabella. My job today is to convince Mrs. Fiori that I'm innocent so that she'll help us—before the great State of California succeeds in its goal to put me down like a stray dog. Is that about the size of it?"

"Try not to be a jerk," said Isabella. "We do want Maggie's help, and the first step was meeting you. So, here we all are."

Silence. Travis leaned forward suddenly, and it took all my self-control not to flinch. "What do you want to know?" he asked abruptly.

"I saw the police photos," I said. "I'm here because I can't get them out of my head, and because your lawyer is a pretty powerful lobby on your behalf."

"And now that you're here? Got a feeling? Got it figured out yet?" Michael's words about snap judgments based on first impressions went on replay in my head. Somehow, it was reassuring to hear Michael's voice in this particular moment.

I shook my head. "No feelings," I said. "Not yet. Look, why

don't you just talk to me?"

And so, he began talking—about the army, about learning to love anything on four wheels, about looking for work when he'd retired from the service.

"Tell me why they call you the Limousine Lothario," I prodded.

He sighed. "That's what's so crazy about being in here. I love women. And here I am in the worst kind of men's club. And it's not just about women and sex, by the way. It's everything. I love the way they talk and think and dress and smell. I'm sure some shrink would say it all goes back to my mother."

"Okay, tell me about your mother."

"It was just my mom and me when I was growing up; my dad disappeared when I was a baby. I was fascinated by my mother. She could do anything. She's the one who first taught me about cars. She could cook and she built stuff, whatever we needed when I was a kid, a go-cart for me, a kitchen table. She taught me to play poker and how to dance. I was the only guy at the senior prom who could cha-cha, mambo, and fox-trot. And she loved to read, anything and everything. In fact, she named me Travis after a character in mysteries she used to read."

"Travis McGee," I said. "John D. McDonald's character in all those mysteries with colors in the title. *The Deep Blue* something or other."

"That's the guy," said Travis. "Plus, I think she thought my name was a little trailer-trashy, seemed like the perfect way to thumb her nose at the snooty New England family she ran away from when she married my dad." He sighed. "I think she's still thumbing her nose. My mother's taste in men..." He caught himself short. "Anyway, I grew up thinking all women were remarkable—and the only real pleasure in life I'd ever had was being close to a woman. It's not..." he stopped.

"Not what?"

"It's not like I've been out looking for a woman just like my mother. It's just that I was always happy in her company. And I kind of took something in through my pores. Something women want."

Suddenly the oddest thought drifted into my head, that I hoped my boys would describe me that way when they grew up.

"Good thing no one's a Freudian in this room," I said, deliberately putting some distance in my voice. "I'll bite, what do women want?"

"They need someone to listen, to pay attention."

"To memorize a favorite poem?"

"Yeah, that was a cheap trick," said Travis. "But, let me ask you something: Does your husband know how you feel about Marvell?"

"Travis," snapped Isabella.

"No comment," I said, "he knows plenty." Inwardly I squirmed, remembering how and when I felt most disloyal to Michael. It wasn't the sex with Quentin. It was afterward, when I'd lie on his bed, both of us still catching our breath after making love, and he'd put on a scratchy 78, and we'd listen to Richard Burton reading John Donne on love. *"But O alas, so long, so far/ Our bodies why do we forbear?/They are ours, though they are not we/ We are the intelligences, they the sphere."*

"Tell me about Mrs. Plummer," I said, wanting to shift the center of the conversation back to Travis, away from me.

"What do you want to know?"

"You met her because you were driving for her husband?"

"Right. And sometimes I drove the two of them, and sometimes I just drove Grace."

"And you became involved?"

Travis shrugged. "She liked books, and I do, too. Even more than books, themselves, she liked words. When she heard a new word, she'd say it aloud as if it had some magic power or something. She loved to go to the movies, and Frederick, Mr. Plummer, was too busy. Plus, he wouldn't turn his cell phone off long enough to sit through a whole movie. So we started going to movies together."

"And one thing led to another?"

The door swung open.

"Five minutes, folks," said the officer.

Travis and I looked at each other. I could see him calculating, looking for the Hail Mary pass. "Hey," he said, "do me one favor. Go talk to my mother before you decide if you're going to help or not. Ivory Gifford, she's got a jazz joint out on Clement Street, The Devil's Interval. That's all I ask."

What the hell? Maybe the remarkable Ivory Gifford could teach me to change the oil in my car. Or mambo.

"Okay," I agreed, now more curious than scared.

Isabella stood up. "Say thank you, Travis."

He stood as well. "Thank you."

"You're welcome," I said. "And I'm glad you're enjoying the books."

"I am," he said. "Just finished *The Tragicall History of the Life and Death of Dr. Faustus.*"

"And do you identify with Faust—or with the Devil?" I asked.

He shrugged. "Sometimes neither, sometimes both," he said. "But I do remember that Faust was redeemed by the love of a good woman."

"Not his mother," I said.

"Nope," said Travis, and a wry smile lifted the corners of his mouth. "He was redeemed by a woman named Margaretta."

He inclined his head in a mock bow. "It's fate that we met, Mrs. Fiori."

"I'll go see your mother," I said briskly, "that's all I can say for now."

Interval No. 2 with Dr. Mephisto

Tell me more about this photograph you saw of the murdered woman," said Dr. Mephisto.

The room felt overheated. "Why?"

"Because there's something in it that's haunting you," she said. "You've both brought it up a couple of times."

I described it again. Briefly.

"Nice guy you're hanging out with," said Michael.

"I'm not 'hanging out,'" I said. "And don't we assume he's innocent until proven guilty?"

"A jury of his peers says he was proven guilty," said Michael.

"And courts aren't ever wrong?"

Dr. Mephisto raised her hand. "The photograph?"

"Hey," said Michael, "I'm glad to say what's bothering me. I think there's something very dark in that photo that's intriguing you. Maybe you want me to bind your hands and rough you up."

"Michael!"

Dr. Mephisto turned to me. "What do you think about Michael's observation?"

"It's ridiculous. I mean, I'm not a prude, and sure, I wouldn't mind a little more adventure now and then." The room grew very still, as if a breeze had just died down.

Dr. Mephisto cleared her throat. "More adventure? In your sex life, you mean?"

"Yes," said Michael, "why don't you tell us what you mean?"

This was not going well. How had I allowed myself to be led down this path? And what was with the "tell *us?*" Michael was aligning himself with McQuist, and I was going to be odd girl out.

"There's nothing wrong with our love life," I faltered. "It's just that sometimes it seems like one more job—like putting away groceries or folding laundry."

I was talking to Dr. Mephisto, and out of the corner of my eye, I could see Michael metamorphosing into a lawyer, coiled, strategic, ready to strike.

I was on to Dr. Mephisto's bag of tricks already, so I anticipated what was coming.

"You want me to say this to Michael, right?" I asked her.

"In a moment," she said. "First, let's hear from Michael."

I turned to him. He smiled without one ounce of warmth. "I think this is excellent news from you, Maggie," he said. "I've had several almost irresistible impulses to tie you up. And to spank you. But, I've been under the misapprehension you would find that behavior objectionable, even antifeminist. I'm happy, no, let me be more accurate, *delighted* to know you'll welcome that kind of attention."

I wished for a mirror suddenly, so I could see what this looked like. Two almost-forty-year-old educated people, parents, who went home to a mortgaged, messy house with a soccer schedule and reminder cards from the kids' dentists magneted to the refrigerator. How and why did we get to this conversation?

"Okay, Maggie," said Dr. Mephisto. "Your turn."

"Michael, this is nuts," I said. "I have absolutely no desire to turn our love life into something dark and dangerous. It's just..."

"Just what?"

"Just that it feels like one more ritual—way more fun than folding laundry or taking the kids out for pizza after soccer, but not much more surprising."

"And you *like* the idea of surprises? Like the kind Grace Plummer encountered in that photograph?" he said bitterly.

"No. I mean, yes, I like the idea of surprises, but not that kind. I think the photo obsesses me because I can't figure out how something could go that wrong between two people who love each other. And now, even meeting Travis briefly, I believe he did care for Grace. *Ipso facto*, it can't have been him. And so," I was warming to my topic, and thrilled to have steered away from the direction to which kinked-out, voyeuristic Dr. Mephisto had dragged the conversation, "when I look at that photo, I'm looking for some telltale something that will reassure me I'm right—that Travis didn't kill her. Someone else did."

Michael was not so easily dissuaded. "Uh-huh, Ms. Ipso-Dipso, I get that part. But let's get back to the surprises you're looking for in our marriage."

"Yes, let's," said Dr. Mephisto. I shot her my best "Mom-and-dad-are-talking-and-this-doesn't-really-concern-you" look that occasionally worked with the kids. She had a hyperalert glint in her eyes that made me think my tactic wasn't working so well.

But, while I was figuring out another, more effective way to tell her to back off, something clicked into focus for me, the link between our marriage and my apparently unstoppable impulse to mess around with complex, outside-my-backyard problems. "I think," I said, "there's always a surprise in how these things unravel. I mean, that's what happened with Quentin's murder. And as painful as all that was, I liked not knowing exactly what was coming next—and then figuring it out."

Silence. "And so," observed Michael, "would it be fair to say you think that looking for these surprises, these unpredictable situations, relieves me—and our marriage—from providing that kind of excitement?"

I inspected his face. It was carefully blank. "Kinda," I said.

"So, you would argue that these adventures are good for our marriage?"

Well, not exactly, but Michael had led me down some path I couldn't see my way out of. "*Nel mezzo del cammin di nostra vita…*" I said. "I am so lost right now."

Quietly, Dr. Mephisto said, "In the middle of my life's journey, I found myself in the middle of a dark wood."

More silence. "*The Divine Comedy*," she said. "Is that how you feel, Maggie? As if you're in a dark wood?"

I kept my eyes on Michael's face. "I didn't," I said, "until today."

"We have to end now," said Dr. Mephisto.

CHAPTER 6

Bars aren't usually hopeful places at 10 in the morning. Sunlight and silence bring wear and grime and smells into sharp, usually unpleasant focus. But a few bars shine when they're daylit and near-empty. The fancy places in upscale hotels, and well-loved neighborhood joints—they look clean and relatively bright, the bottles glitter in the mirror, the wood of the bar looks polished and loved and smells of lemon. Ivory Gifford's bar was of the hopeful variety, tucked in among storefront after storefront of affordable Chinese, Thai, and Vietnamese restaurants and coffee places on Clement Street.

Maybe it was because she lived "above the store" that the place had such pride of ownership. "We scraped together enough for my mom to buy the building," Travis had explained to me. "She lives in a flat above the club, so she's never far from work or home. She belongs to that building now, as much as it belongs to her."

I was expecting someone like Mae West, all bosom and bluster, with too much eye makeup and high-heeled, gold lamé mules. Oh, and maybe wearing a tool belt. The woman who answered my knock looked like a retired Bob Fosse dancer: a black tunic over black leggings, great posture, slightly reminiscent of her son's, silver-blond hair knotted at her neck and a way of cocking one hip forward that promised she could make any move any guy could imagine and then some. She wore no detectable makeup and smelled like sandalwood soap. If this was sixtyish chick-barkeep, I knew what I aspired to for my mature years.

"Maggie Fiori," I said, extending my hand. She took my right hand in her left and squeezed it. "Come on in," she said, "I've got coffee on."

I followed her across the parquet floor and hopped up on the barstool she patted. She poured coffee for both of us, pulled the cream and sugar in front of me, and then draped herself onto the adjoining barstool.

She smiled. "Travis says I need to talk you into helping out. How much talking do I have to do?"

No wasted time. I took a sip of coffee to buy a few minutes, "Why do you favor your right hand?"

She shrugged. "I had a stroke shortly after Trav was arrested. My right side hasn't completely recovered, including my hand. That's a disaster for a piano player. I'm still resting it as much as I can."

I gestured at the ebony grand at the edge of the bandstand.

"You play here?"

"I used to. So did Travis." She picked up her coffee mug. "We even did four-hand stuff when he'd drop by."

"So you're both pianists," I said. "I didn't know that."

"Pianists are the people who work Davies Symphony Hall," she said. "We think of ourselves as piano players." She waved at the piano, still with her left hand.

"Hence my name."

"Ivory?"

"Right. It's really Eugenie, but I've been Ivory since I was old enough to get on a piano bench by myself."

"Eugenie? Like the empress?"

She laughed. "Travis used to call me Mom, the Empress of the Keyboard."

With Travis's name in the air again, we both fell silent.

"All right," she said, after a moment. "Why don't you tell me what I need to say to you, so you'll help us out." She took a deep breath, "Things are getting a little desperate."

"Why don't you tell me about Travis and why you're so sure he's innocent?" I countered.

She regarded me carefully. "Why are you so sure I think he's innocent?"

"Because you're his mother," I said. "Aren't mothers always sure?"

She gave me a grin. Now that I knew about the stroke, I saw that the crookedness of her smile wasn't for effect; it was residual damage.

"You're a mother, too?" she asked, clearly not needing an answer. "You're right, I am sure he didn't do it. But frankly, the stroke did some memory damage, so I'm lousy on the events right around the time of the...murder."

"Why don't you just talk to me about Travis?"

"This place is named after him," she said.

"The Devil's Interval?"

She nodded. "Do you know anything about music?"

"I'm a piano player myself," I said.

"Well, then this is easy," she said. She slipped off the barstool, and went to the piano. With her left hand, she played two notes, "Hear that interval?"

"A fifth," I said.

"Right. Now listen while I diminish the interval a half step." She played two more notes. They sounded unpleasing, a little discordant.

"A tritone," I said.

"Right," said Ivory, "a diminished fifth or augmented fourth. It's called The Devil's Interval. It was actually outlawed in the thirteenth, fourteenth, and fifteenth centuries because the monks couldn't sing the damn notes. And they thought if they tried, they'd go mad."

"What's that got to do with Travis?" I asked.

She played a jazzy chord progression that began and ended with the restless-sounding interval. "When Travis improvised, he always ended on the Devil's Interval. It's a very unsettling sound, and it became his signature."

She played a little more, and ended again on the diminished fifth. It sounded unresolved and unhappy.

"When Travis came out of the military, he used most of his saved-up pay to help me open this place. The idea was that I'd have a home base, we'd both play here from time to time, and I wouldn't be out looking for gigs until I was far beyond the age for social security."

"But Travis was working for the limousine company."

"We couldn't take enough out of The Devil's Interval to support us both in the beginning. So, Travis had his military pension, plus the limousine work, plus..."

"Plus," I said, "he had some peace of mind knowing his mom was taken care of."

"Right," she said. "That was the plan. And a damn fine one it used to be."

She closed the lid on the piano keys.

"What else can I tell you? Isabella and Travis both say you could help if you wanted to."

"You know I'm not an investigator," I reminded her.

"I know," she said, "but you've got access to the world that Grace Plummer lived in. Through your magazine."

I protested, "It's not 'my magazine.' I'm the editor, and it's still a fairly new job for me. It's a grand title, but mostly what I do is sit in meetings and shepherd the staff into staying on schedule and budget. I'm making this up as I go along."

Ivory didn't say anything. I tried to imagine how it would feel to have a son on Death Row. I could imagine someone's son, just not one of mine. I felt myself take three careful steps away from the idea. "Tell me some more about Travis," I said, buying time.

"What do you want to know?"

"Tell me about his relationships with women," I replied. "What about this Limousine Lothario business?"

She got up from the piano bench and walked around the bar. She shook out a towel, and picked up a glass from the rack to dry.

"Travis and women. I'll tell you, from the time that boy was ten years old, he had a way with the ladies. He'd flirt with any girl, any age, any place. When he was in junior high school, he could ditch school and never get caught, because the old biddies in the attendance office would cover for him. By the time he was in high school, he knew enough to try to get all his classes with female teachers, because he could get away with murder."

The word hung in the air.

"I get your drift," I said.

Ivory picked up another glass. "I know a lot of men flirt," she says. "But Travis has some kind of gift."

"Where'd he get it?" I asked. "From his dad?"

"Who can remember? Mr. Wonderful hightailed it out of town when Travis was three. We haven't heard from him since. We stayed here partly because I couldn't go back to my family on Cape Cod. I'd burned almost all those bridges. And partly because I wanted Trav's father to be able to find him, if he ever came looking. But he never did."

"So, just the two of you, all these years?"

"Just the two of us," said Ivory. "Not that there aren't occasional gentlemen callers. I haven't led the life of a nun. But there wasn't anybody permanent." She hesitated, "Still isn't, at least not really. So Travis and I had a pretty tight relationship. And frankly, lots of guys were chased away by how tight the two of us are. Men don't like playing second fiddle."

Now or never, I thought. "So, you two talked a lot? Confided in each other?"

"You mean, did I know about Mrs. Plummer?"

I nodded. Ivory shrugged, "I didn't know much about her. I did notice that Travis seemed to look forward to his assignments driving for her."

"Did you ever meet her?"

"No. Travis would bring his lady friends to the bar occasionally, but he was private when he was seeing someone he shouldn't be seeing—like a married woman."

"And there were others?"

"That's what I read in the papers," said Ivory matter-of-factly. "The Limousine Lothario."

"What's your theory about that? About Travis getting involved with all those married women?"

"My theory? You fish where the fish are. He met plenty of bored and neglected wives. It's not as if he grew up with a lot of evidence that marriage vows were all that sacred. Or permanent."

"And he was...irresistible?"

Ivory smiled. "You have a son?"

I nodded, "Two."

"Then you know how I'd answer that. All mothers think their boys are irresistible. But, what I think isn't that important, is it? It's what all those women thought."

I flashed on Travis's careful reading of my discarded poetry book.

"He pays a rare kind of attention to women," I observed.

Ivory's mobile face went very still. "Of course," she said, "how could I forget? You've met Travis."

More silence.

"You want to know what I think?" I prodded.

"I guess I do."

For an instant, I saw Travis's hand again, darkened with the black-inked lines of poetry, opening in front of me. "It was the oddest thing," I said. "He made me think about Rudolf Nureyev."

Ivory smiled. "He moves like a dancer," she said. "Elegant, very controlled."

We sat without speaking for a long moment. "It's not the best of circumstances, meeting someone at San Quentin," I temporized.

"Just talk to me," said Ivory. "I don't have much to lose at this point."

"Okay," I said. "He's charming, all right. He's smart, and frankly, that charm makes him a little scary. But what got me here was the way he talked about you."

"We'll need more than that," Ivory said flatly. "Death Row is full of murderers who love their mothers."

"I know," I said. "But there was something very unsentimental, respectful about the way he talks about you. Which makes all this..."

"What?"

"I'm sorry to ask you about this," I began.

Ivory put down the towel and the glass and leaned on the bar. "Don't apologize. Ask anything you want. I don't give one flying fuck. All I care about right now is getting help for Travis, however I can."

"Okay, what about the S&M business with Mrs. Plummer?"

"We were close," said Ivory, "but I'm his mother. It's not as if he ever talked about that stuff with me. But, I do know there was a dark side to Travis, and I can't say it surprises me."

"Doesn't it bother you?"

"Look, I think what people do with each other sexually is their business. I've got my own little quirks and "she broke off, and looked me up and down. "I bet you've got a couple yourself."

I felt my face go warm, remembering the last session with Dr. Mephisto.

She held up her hand. "I'm not interested in yours and you're not interested in mine. We're only interested in Travis's tastes because one of his women ended up dead."

"You're something else," I said.

"No, I'm not," she shot back. "I've got a son on Death Row. You can't imagine how that enables you to cut through the nicey-nice stuff and get right down to it." She sighed. "I didn't know much about Mrs. Plummer, and I didn't know about the rough sex. But I know Travis, I know him down to my bones. He likes to have fun, he likes to take things as far as they can go. But I read the description of how they found that woman. And I cannot believe Travis would do something like that to anyone."

Neither of us spoke. I looked down at the bar, and Ivory's good hand, the one she was leaning on, was trembling. Suddenly, the door behind the bar flew open, and a burly guy pushing a hand truck loaded with cases of beer maneuvered it to Ivory's side and put his arm around her. She stiffened, then leaned into him. With his free hand, he tore off the black and orange Giants cap he was wearing and dropped it on the bar.

"Hi, babe," he said. "This was at the back door, thought I'd move it in for you." He looked at me. "Did I bust up something?"

Ivory shook her head. "No, just talking about Travis's appeal. Maggie Fiori, meet Augustus Reeves III, also known as Uncle Gus." Reeves, who had a shaved head under that cap and a nose that looked as if it had been broken and not repaired exactly the way it should have been, stuck out his hand. We shook.

"You another lawyer?" he asked. "That sounds expensive."

"Hardly," I said. "I work for a magazine."

"Oh, yeah? Anything I'd ever heard of? *Biker Mama*, say?" He barked a laugh, and hugged Ivory close to him again.

She put her hand on his impressive chest, and gently pushed him away.

"Ever the joker, Uncle Gus," she said.

"Hey," I said lightly, "I wouldn't mind an assignment for *Biker Mama* once in a while. But they never call."

Uncle Gus narrowed his eyes, as if he couldn't quite figure out if I was joking. That was okay; I couldn't figure him out either. He seemed too close to Ivory's age to be her uncle.

"You work here, Gus?" I asked.

"Not exactly," he said. "I'm a fan of Ivory's, so I try to be useful from time to time. Keep a hand truck in my van, just to help my favorite proprietrix move things around. So, what'd I interrupt? You two seemed pretty intense."

Ivory gave me a quick, sideways glance. "Travis's lawyer thought Maggie might be able to help. Find some things out. Turn over a few of those high-society rocks the cops couldn't get to. I was just making my last-ditch mother-to-mother appeal to her."

"So, what's the verdict?" asked Gus. He seemed suddenly serious, done joking around.

Ivory came around the bar and sat down next to me again.

"Are you in or are you out?"

I looked at Ivory and I saw she'd pulled rank on me. No longer just a piano player, a bar-owner, a woman who'd been disappointed in love. She was a mother. And she was in the kind of trouble I couldn't even begin to imagine. Isabella was sure he was innocent—and for no good reason on earth, I believed her. If one of my boys...I stopped that train of thought cold in its tracks by opening my mouth.

"I'm in."

CHAPTER 7

Tuesday mornings were all-hands editorial meetings at *Small Town.* Like most monthly magazines, we worked on three issues at once. We had one in final production, one in development—writing and layout—and one in planning.

Hoyt Lee, the managing editor we'd hired to take Glen's place, ran the meeting. A graduate of the University of Mississippi (Ole Miss), he sounded as if he'd been raised on a gentleman's diet of fast horses, good bourbon, and lazy afternoons on a veranda. He never lost his temper or his fine manners, and was unfailingly polite to everyone from me (who regularly offended him whenever I let a swear word slip) to our youngest, greenest interns. The truth of the matter was that he was a first-generation college graduate, son of hardscrabble soybean farmers, but he'd learned how to behave like a gentleman and found it was better armor and ammunition than the money and land his more privileged, nitwit fraternity brothers brought to the party.

It took nearly a year before he'd call me "Maggie," and he still insisted on calling my assistant, Gertie, "Miz Davis," out of deference to her age.

"For heaven's sake, Maggie," she complained, "he makes me feel like someone's mother."

"You are someone's mother," I pointed out. "You've got those two handsome, grownup sons. Indulge Hoyt," I added. "He needs to think somebody around here is a lady."

Despite his courtly manner, Hoyt ran a tight meeting. We worked off agendas and flow charts, checking in on last-minute production issues for the current issue, progress and snags on the issue under development, identified opportunities for the online content, and then subjected the current issue's plans to rigorous scrutiny.

"Remember our readers," Hoyt always admonished. "Will they find this interesting?" So, when we came to the future issue-planning chart, Hoyt gave me a chance to pitch a few angles on the Limousine Lothario story.

I sketched out the death-penalty appeal background, gave a summary of Travis Gifford's arrest, trial, and conviction, mentioned The Devil's Interval, and waited. Puck Morris, our infamous music critic, known in band circles for his vicious reviews (with fair warning given by advance distribution to the unfortunate and untalented of "Pucked by Morris" T-shirts), laughed.

"I know that spot, Maggie. It's for oldsters. San Francisco used to be a great jazz town. Now it sucks. That place of Ivory's feels like a museum."

Hoyt cleared his throat. "Say a little more, Puck."

Puck glared at him. "Holy shit, Hoyt. That's what shrinks say." He deepened his voice and affected a German accent, "Say a little more about vhy you find drowning kittens and masturbating to Strauss waltzes so pleasurable, Herr Morris."

Hoyt was not amused. "Let's remember there are ladies present, Mr. Morris," he said. "I repeat, why isn't San Francisco 'a jazz town' anymore?"

Puck sighed and shrugged off his beat-up leather jacket. "Anybody but me hot in here? That menopause stuff contagious, Gertie, or what?"

Gertie regarded him with contempt. "Oh, grow up, Puck."

"Why isn't San Francisco a jazz town? Couple reasons," said Puck. "First, we're small potatoes. You need a critical mass of appreciators to keep a club open. There just aren't enough people who listen to jazz anymore. And the people who still do are getting old. They like to sit at home and caress their vintage Monk and Bird LPs on the comfort of their own sofa. And drink their own booze while they listen. Clubs are a young person's scene."

"What about the new SFJazz Center?" I protested.

Puck shook his head. "We'll see. It's hot, it's new. But sooner or later, it will be out there trolling for old people, too."

"Jazz was just a sidebar," I said. "To provide a little color. I think the main story could be about death-penalty appeals—who does what and how long it takes and the whole Innocence Project thing."

Silence in the room. "Maggie," prodded Hoyt, "we already did a story on your Gasworks Gang ladies. More death-penalty appeal coverage hardly seems like a story our readers would find compelling."

"Okay, what would our readers find compelling?" I protested.

Puck began shredding his empty coffee cup. "They'd find the murdered broad interesting," he offered. "She was a player on the social scene, wasn't she?"

"That's good," I said. "Death of a Socialite."

Hoyt began to nod, "That's got possibilities, Maggie. Although it seems a little odd to do it two years after her murder."

I had an answer. "Now it's news again, because her alleged murderer is on Death Row and his attorneys are filing appeals. Let's go back and see if we can do a story that tells our readers how Grace Plummer went from glamorous socialite to dead body in the back of a limousine."

"Cool beans," volunteered Linda Quoc, *Small Town*'s art director. "We can do a black-and-white photo essay—from the Black & White Ball to the back seat of a black limo. Very graphic." I thought about the photos again and swallowed. Too graphic, maybe.

"It sounds a little too investigative journalism for us," said Hoyt, "but I like the concept."

"Well, let's see if we've got the chops to do it," I said. I remembered something one of the Gasworks Gang said to me.

"We've got entree to the world Grace Plummer moved in. If anybody could do the story, we could."

Hoyt caught me in the hall after the meeting. "I feel bamboozled, Maggie," he said. "We were going to do that story, come heck or high water."

"Oh, for heaven's sake, Hoyt," I said. "It's hell or high water. Who are you going to give it to?"

"Besides you?" asked Hoyt. "I know you'll be riding shotgun on this piece, invited or not."

"Hey," I said, "I'm the media mogul, I'm the one who can get next to the rich and famous."

He sighed. "I wouldn't be overestimatin' my clout if I were you," he said. "I'm putting Andrea on it. She's got the pedigree." Starchy Storch, who did both features and film reviews for *Small Town,* brought her daddy's signet ring, and a kind of rock-ribbed Northeast breeding to the magazine. Recently, she and *Small Town's* favorite arty freelance photographer, Calvin Bright, had become a romantic item. Just two crazy preppy kids in love, one of whom happened to be African-American. "If Calvin ran the United Negro College Fund," Michael once mused, "their motto would be 'A Burberry is a terrible thing to waste.'"

"Perfect," I said. I walked back to my office and picked up the phone. "Isabella," I said. "It's Maggie Fiori. I went to see Ivory Gifford."

I heard her sharp intake of breath. "Okay," she said. "Tell me."

"You win. Well, you and Ivory win. We're doing a piece."

"*Dios mio*," she said softly. "Thank you, Maggie."

"Now would be a good time to tell me why you and Eleanor gave each other a peculiar look in Eleanor's living room the other day."

"Ivory," she said. "I've always thought we didn't have the whole story on Ivory. That is one tight mother-son relationship, and it weirds me out a little."

I thought about my own boys, about how I kept a permanent, long-running tape in my head about every moment of their lives.

In an instant, I could recall the way Zach burrowed into the crook of my arm when he nursed, as if he were embedding himself back into my body. Or how, when Josh was three, every summer night he'd want to lie outside on the front lawn with Michael, and try to find Orion, which he pronounced Orizon, and how I loved that he saw a "horizon" in the sky—all the meaning I poured into that one boy and his use of that one word.

"What do you mean *tight*?" I said, trying to keep the defensiveness out of my voice. "Her son's on Death Row, of course she's obsessing about him."

Isabella was silent. "Maggie, I'm a mother, too. I know what it means to be protective. I'm not talking about why she's fighting for Travis now. I just keep wondering if she decided she didn't like Grace for any number of reasons..."

"And killed her?" I said. "You've got to be kidding."

"I know, it seems unlikely. But, you asked me what the look was about—and I've got to be straight with you. There's always been something about that relationship that bothers me. Can you imagine trying to get between Travis and his mother?"

I didn't answer. "No," I said reluctantly. "I can't."

"And that stroke," said Isabella. "I know it was real. You can't fake a cerebral event. But it sure didn't advance anybody's cause that Ivory can't remember much about a critical time in the case."

"She had an alibi," I said. "That's what it said in the file. She was at a late movie with a friend until nearly midnight. They must have had stubs or something."

"Better than stubs," said Isabella. "An off-duty cop from the homicide squad saw them at the movies. He noticed Ivory because he thought she was, and I quote, 'a silver fox.'"

"So, she seems like a dead end."

"I know, I know," said Isabella. "But still."

"Isabella," I said, "you're convinced Travis Gifford is innocent, right? No doubts?"

"Hey," she said, "I'm in the business of doubt, and shadows thereof."

"Answer the question, please."

"I am convinced," she said. "I've been doing this work a while; I started when I was still in law school. These Death Row appeals are my tofu and drink, and I am convinced."

"And not because of some hinky hunch you've got about Ivory?"

"No, that's just something I still wonder about. It's those vehicles at Grace's. I believe nosy, old half-blind Mrs. Lomax. I believe there were two other cars there that evening. Or maybe just one, if she was seeing double."

"You're not falling under the Limo Lothario's spell, are you?" I asked.

"Not my type," said Isabella. "Not even close. And it's not that I don't believe he's capable of killing someone. I think we all are. But from what I know about Travis, it makes no sense to me. None at all. What makes sense is that if he did kill someone, he'd be smart enough not to leave the body in his car. In his garage. From the very beginning, I knew that was off."

"Hope you're right," I said. "I share your opinion and I have very little idea why. Frankly, right now, I feel as if I'm working for Ivory, and that's good enough for me."

CHAPTER 8

Travis remembered what one of his mother's boyfriends had said to him when he was a sullen teenager: "Be nice to your mom. She's a class act." He thought about the inmates he'd see in the exercise yard, bulked-up guys with Mom *tattooed on a bicep, surrounded by rippling hearts and roses. Travis thought about Ivory as something much tougher than a rose. A diamond, maybe. Beauty with a flinty edge, something sparkly and valuable pulled from throwaway coal. Gave him some confidence she'd end her latest romance. At any rate, he didn't think Maggie Fiori would say no to Ivory. His mom's the one who taught him how to be still. Just listen. When women start talking, they're always checking to see if you're really listening. Grace believed he was listening. That's why she told him all that crazy stuff about her own mother. Weird that it was his mother he channeled to make it okay for Grace to tell him her stories.*

"Secret weapon, Mom," he whispered. "Always."

CHAPTER 9

Free for lunch?" I asked when Michael answered his phone at work. "I'm in the neighborhood."

"Sure," he said, "but I'm crammed. Can you grab something and bring it here? We can eat in my office."

I arrived at the law firm's minimalist white-on-gray lobby with a brown paper sack, holding turkey-on-rye for me and pastrami-on-rye for Michael. The latest in a series of pretty, young receptionists sitting behind a polished gray stone counter waved me toward Michael's office.

She gestured at the bag, "You're leaking a little."

"Sorry," I called, as I headed down the hall, holding my hand underneath the bag to capture the drips. "Remind Michael he's got a meeting in the conference room at 1," she called back.

Michael's door was closed. I knocked, called "Michael, it's me" and walked in.

He was behind the desk, listening to a guy on the other end of the speakerphone, and impatiently made a "trying to wrap it up" gesture to me. I sat at the table, and swiped at my fingers with a few napkins. He waved me over and patted his lap. Licking the last drips of mustard and mayo off my fingers, I walked behind his desk. The vertical shades were closed, and I reached for the cords to pull them open. Michael leaned backward, and in one swift motion, slapped my hand, and pulled me onto his lap.

"Uh-huh," he said, with his hand on the back of my neck,

inclined just slightly to the speakerphone.

"Well, listen," he said, "I think we have a plan. Let's get the international folks to look at the unitrust situation, and I'll get back to you. Oh, wait!"

"Wait? For what?" asked the voice coming out of the speakerphone.

"Oh," said Michael, a little breathlessly, as I found something to do with my still-mayo-sticky fingers. "Sorry, I was distracted. I've got somebody in here—uh, looking at the heating system."

We never unwrapped those sandwiches.

Later that afternoon, back in my office, Michael called.

"Hi, honey," I said. "How's the heating system holding up?"

"Just fine," he said. "I think it's performing very well, thank you. So, even without any bondage, rank the surprise factor for me."

"Oh, you boys are so competitive," I said. "But I'd give you a perfect ten—though it was a little nerve-racking since we never got around to locking the door."

"And yet another opportunity for a surprise," said Michael. "Give me a ten-plus."

"Okay," I said. "It was fun. But we never got to the postcoital bliss in which I wanted to discuss something with you."

"Why do I feel that bliss slipping away?"

"So, here's the thing. I want to be on the up-and-up with you."

"How refreshing," he said.

I described my visit to The Devil's Interval, and the story we talked about for *Small Town*. "Death of a Socialite?" he asked. "Boy, does that sound cheesy."

"To you, maybe. Our readers will lap it up," I said. "And it accomplishes several goals—we may turn up something useful for Isabella, we'll get a good story, I'll have done something for Ivory, who honest-to-God, if you met her, Michael, you'd do the same thing. She broke my heart."

Silence.

"Imagine if it were one of our sons on Death Row," I said.

"I can't," he said.

"I made myself go there," I said. "I mean, I know they're not going to murder anybody."

"Except each other," he said.

"I can't even joke about this. But I'm telling you, when I can't sleep, that's what I picture. Some weird set of circumstances where one of them mistakenly ends up in some terrible place. And I would do anything, confront anyone, recruit anyone to fix what's wrong."

"Maggie, I worry this is some projection you've got going on with that guy's mother. You don't need to lie awake obsessing about what if it were Zach or Josh."

"I'm not *choosing* to lie awake," I said grimly. "It's just what happens. And right now, there's a small thing I can do to help. And I want to do it."

"Who's working the story?" asked Michael.

"Whoever Hoyt assigns," I said. "Probably Andrea." I felt a twinge of guilt. "I'll just be helping."

"And you'll keep me posted?"

"Every step of the way," I promised. "Scout's honor."

"You were never a Girl Scout, *cara,*" he said.

"Look who's talking," I countered. "Mr. Not So Clean in thought, word, or deed."

"This is a perfect discussion to continue with Dr. McQuist," said Michael. "I can't wait to hear what she thinks."

"I don't believe she thinks independently," I said. "She's supposed to help us think."

"I thought she was growing on you," said Michael.

"Oh, you were just impressed because she could translate the Italian," I said.

"And you weren't?" asked Michael. "You're not always the smartest girl in the room, you know."

"I am, too," I said. "Knowing the most commonly quoted line from Dante doesn't make somebody smart. Or even educated."

"Yeah, well, if you think it's that common, try wandering the halls of that elitist little magazine of yours and doing a survey," said Michael.

"I've got to go," I said. "Very busy. Very, very busy."

"But relaxed," he said.

"Surprisingly relaxed."

I hung up on his self-satisfied little chuckle.

CHAPTER 10

"Tell me," I said to Travis, "about the moment when your relationship with Grace Plummer changed."

He shrugged. "I told the trial lawyer. I've told Isabella. I've told the cops."

"Uh-huh," I said, "but you haven't told me." We stared each other down.

"Or, don't…" I said. "Just as easy for me to get back to my day job." Travis had seemed pleased, but not surprised, when Isabella told him I would try to help.

I flipped the pad shut, and started to tuck it in my purse. We were sitting in the visitors' center again, and this time, because it was a weekend, the place was filled with people. Kids, mothers, exhausted-looking, but making an effort—lipstick on, earrings in place.

With Hoyt's reluctant blessing, Andrea was taking on the story. Since I had access to Travis, I was working that angle. "You are so transparent," Andrea said. "You're assuming that my cosseted Connecticut debutante self will be soiled by a trip to San Quentin. I'll have you know I've been there already. Twice, in fact. On stories, before I came to this lifestyles-of-the rich-and-famous glossy you're running. How starchy does that make me?"

"Andrea, my friend," I said, "the fact that you used the word cosseted and debutante in a single conversation makes you plenty starchy. But we love that starch! It's like going undercover on a vice squad, but you don't have to dress up like a hooker. You just have to look like your own sweet WASPy self. We all have our gifts and our connections and yours enable us to get inside Grace Plummer's social scene. You're our hidden asset in the City's A-list."

Starchy Storch had seen right through me. But she was warming to the story and got busy interviewing the rich, thin, medicated, and moisturized crowd in Pacific Heights, and the people who served them—caterers, florists, valet-parkers, and mani-pedi experts. Now, with Isabella's help, I was back at the Q, trying to understand Travis's relationship with Grace, and getting impatient with his reluctance to talk.

Travis reached over and put his hand on the pad.

"Sorry, Maggie, I'm just tired of reliving, retelling, remembering, re-everything."

I nodded. "Can't help if I don't know," I said.

"Okay, so…first, it wasn't exactly a moment. It was more a whole string of moments. Right from the start, we'd talk while I was driving her around."

"About?"

"Hell, everything. She'd give me the gossip on all those skinny, rich broads she hung out with at charity events. Books, movies, restaurants, the Minnesota Twins..."

"Twins? Baseball? She was a baseball fan?"

"I don't know how much of a fan she was, but much of her family was originally from the Midwest. Her grandparents had taken her to watch the Twins play the As when she was a kid, on trips back to Minnesota and when the Twins came to play Oakland."

"Not her parents?"

Travis looked away. "I don't know; she didn't talk much about them. Just her grandparents. Her grandmother called her Amazing Gracie, which was pretty strange, because…" he stopped.

"Because…"

"Because the night our relationship went to a different place is the night I realized other people called her Amazing Gracie."

"Other people? Like her friends?" I pushed.

"Not exactly."

"Travis," I said, "I've got limited time here, as you know. So, before they ring the bell and send us all home, I'd like to make some progress. Can you just talk to me, so I don't have to wring every last syllable out of you?"

"Christ, Maggie," he said, "wait 'til those kids of yours are teenagers. You're going to have to polish up your interrogation techniques."

"Good to know," I said. "So, *what* other people called her Amazing Gracie?"

"The people at the Crimson."

I flipped through the file lying in front of me, the summary of notes Travis's habeas attorney had given me.

"Crimson? The club on Tehama?"

All around the city, private clubs had made a resurgence. But instead of the chlorine-smelling, faux-bath environments that had flourished in the pre-AIDS days, these were primarily straight, elegant and likely to attract the moneyed and restless. I knew about them, first from one of Michael's more adventuresome partners, and then the newspaper started covering them as a trend—which probably meant they would be so-six-weeks-ago very soon.

Travis grinned, "That's the one. You hang out there, Maggie?"

"Oh, right," I said, "me and all the other soccer moms. We climb into our little black dresses and drive the SUVs with the spilled Cheerios in the backseat right down Tehama."

"Actually, the Crimson Club involves more climbing out of little black dresses," said Travis, "but I like the picture."

"Talk," I said, glancing at my wristwatch.

And he did. About driving Grace and Frederick together to nights out at the Crimson and other clubs. About how he'd wait in the car, reading, listening to music, until 3 or 4 in the morning, when they'd emerge. Usually Grace and Frederick together. Once in a while, another couple would come. The Brands, Frederick's business partner and his wife. Or sometimes, just the partner's wife.

"Ginger's her name. Anyway, I thought Frederick and Grace had one of those open marriage arrangements," he said, "but they always seemed very lovey-dovey when they got in the car, even if they'd both been kinda cool with each other when I dropped them off.

"Grace once asked me," he hesitated. "She asked if I thought it was a peculiar thing for a couple to do, hang out in a place like that."

"What'd you tell her?"

"That I'd never been married and I had no idea what it is that makes people feel good about each other, about the person they're with. And if this was it, for them, then more power to 'em." A quick picture of the lunchtime escapade with Michael flashed in my head.

"What'd she say?"

"She laughed. Told me she had no idea how progressive I was."

I felt a little prickle, just as Travis said that. Somehow I thought I'd hear those words again, and it wasn't going to be in a context that promised wholesome living.

"So, did you ever go *in* to the Crimson Club?" I asked. "As opposed to just sitting outside waiting around?"

He straightened up, as if called to attention by something—some memory, some authority.

"Oh, yeah, I went in…" he said. "That's the night I was telling you about. The night everything changed with Grace and me."

CHAPTER 11

Travis experimented with different reading lights. As time went by, he realized that most of a driver's life consists of sitting in a car and waiting outside Saks, restaurants, the airport, offices. And that suited him just fine. He'd always been a reader, and sometimes it seemed as if the best part of this job was sitting around and getting paid to read.

But the map lights were crummy, especially late at night, when his eyes would be a little tired already. So, he'd bought one of those clip-on reading lights. The "book buddies," the kind that are supposed to enable you to read into the wee-small hours of the morning, and not disturb your bedmate. Of course, when he had somebody in bed with him, there wasn't a helluva lot of reading going on. Sometimes he thought, that would be nice, to have the kind of relationship where you actually slept next to each other every night, got cracker crumbs in the sheets, read novels and worried about keeping the other person awake. But he'd never gotten around to that kind of thing.

Instead, he looked around for a better reading light to keep him and his book company, alone in the dark car while he waited for Grace or Frederick or both to finish whatever they were up to. Once, his mom had even bought him one of those miner's-light gizmos, a strap that went around his head and shone a light directly on the page. The light wasn't bad, but Grace laughed every time she saw him in it, and told him he looked like a bit player in a Marx Brothers comedy. She told him he needed to dose up with euphrasia officinalis. *"English, please," he'd said to her. Turns out it's the Latin name for "eyebright," some little plant the gypsies use to treat tired eyes. One day, she gave him a box from The Sharper Image, and inside he found a light that clipped perfectly to the top of the steering wheel and threw a warm, clear light on the page.*

One bitter November evening, he was sitting in the Tehama alley, reading You Can't Go Home Again, *and so absorbed, he didn't even see Grace approach. She rapped on the window and he jumped. Despite the cold, she didn't have her coat on. Her cheeks were flushed, and her throat and chest, down to the tops of her breasts, where the lacy black dress began, looked warm, and damp with perspiration.*

Travis opened the door. "Mrs. Plummer, get in the car. It's freezing out here. Where's your coat?"

She laughed and extended her hand. "It's inside. I came out to get you. It's a great night at the Crimson." She clasped his hand and tugged.

Travis tried to release his hand, but she tightened her grip. "No, thanks, don't think that would be my scene."

"Oh, come on," she said. "You'll have fun. My treat. I've already paid your cover."

Travis considered. It's not as if he wasn't curious. Besides, she seemed a little manic to be wandering around in there—whatever "in there" was, all by herself.

"I don't know..." he began.

She'd already turned to head back in.

"If you hate it, we'll leave. Just check it out with me. But get your jacket, it's coat and tie for men."

What the hell, thought Travis. He grabbed his jacket, shrugged into it, and clicked the doors locked. Grace turned to him, tightened the knot he'd loosened on his tie, and patted his cheek. "You look fine," she said. "Just one of the regular handsome bon vivants at the Crimson."

"Thanks," said Travis, and realized that his heart was beating just a little faster. She tucked her arm into his, and they headed for the unmarked door that served as the entrance to the Crimson Club for those in the know.

Travis didn't know what he expected—loud music, ninth circle of hell, with sweaty people embracing in every available corner.

Instead, he found a double set of glass doors, and heavy red velvet curtains inside. He parted the curtains and let Grace precede him. She was greeted immediately by a Ken-and-Barbie-like pair of welcomers, both in evening clothes, both beautiful and remarkably blank-faced.

"John, Elizabeth, this is my friend, Travis."

John gave a slight bow, a kind of maître d' acknowledgment. Elizabeth leaned forward and kissed Travis on each cheek. "Welcome, Travis. Any friend of Amazing Gracie is welcome here."

Travis shot a look at Grace. "I'm glad to know what her friends call her," he said.

She laughed, and tugged at his arm. "Come on, let's get you a drink."

And down the rabbit hole they went, through another set of crimson velvet drapes, into a dimly lit room circled all around with love seats, chaises, sofas. In the middle of the room, a dance floor, with deafening, Brazilian-sounding club-mix music that poured out of every crevice in the wall. On the dance floor, couples, singles, and here and there a trio, moved to the music. In the center of the dance floor, on a tall pedestal, stood a tall silver cylinder filled with red roses, from buds to full-blown. While the dancers moved, the floor's vibration shook the pedestal, and as Travis watched, red rose petals drifted to the floor. Travis didn't know what he'd expected, but it looked like a club, just like any other, except that several of the women were dancing in various states of … deshabille. *Travis rolled the word around in his head a few times, just to get the sound of it right. He knew that if he said it aloud, Grace would like it.* Deshabille. *Okay, these women were topless, a few of them.*

Grace laced her fingers through Travis's hand, pulled him closer, and put her lips next to his ear. "Want a drink?" Her breath was warm, fruity.

He nodded yes.

She tugged on him, and they threaded their way around the dance floor, past the upholstered seats, where Travis could just barely make out shapes, entwined. On the other side of the room, Grace parted yet one more set of red drapes, and through they went. He put his mouth close to her ear, and said, "Mr. Toad's Wild Ride," thinking of the Disneyland ride that had terrified him as a child, one set of doors opening to yet another set of doors and still another, and dark surprises behind each one. He'd buried his head in Ivory's lap the first—and last—time she took him on that ride.

In the next room, red, but with mercifully subdued background jazz, Grace led him up to a long, white bar. Two beautiful girls in black, strapless dresses presided, one feeding pineapple chunks into a blender, the other wiping down the bar. Grace motioned him over to the couch. "Find us a seat and I'll get you a drink. Beer? A Scotch? Champagne?"

"Corona, no glass, no little piece of lime, that's it." While Travis waited on one of the love seats, he looked around. There were half a dozen people scattered around the room. All dressed elegantly, as if they were at some kind of chic supper club, all talking animatedly. Then, Grace was back, with a long-necked beer, and a flute of champagne, and settled next to him on the love seat.

"Here are the rules," she said, "just in case you want to play."

Travis took a swig of the beer. It tasted cold and clean and blessedly familiar. It was a comfort, in a weird sort of way. "Rule No. 1," she said, "only a woman can make the first approach."

"For anything?" asked Travis. She nodded.

"Rule No. 2," she continued, "if you get turned down, you have to take it gracefully. And Rule No. 3, no gentleman-on-gentleman. Ladies with ladies, ladies with gentlemen, or any threesome combination thereof, or four or five or as you please."

"Sounds like homophobia to me," said Travis.

Grace smiled and sipped her champagne. "I know, it does, doesn't it? But there are plenty of clubs all over the city for the gay scene, so I guess it's supply and demand."

"But girl-on-girl is fine, huh?" asked Travis. And as if cued, one of the women in a group across the room, a fortysomething redhead with a short, spiky haircut, leaned over and began fiddling with the

precariously tied, black silk halter worn by a young Asian woman. As Travis watched, the halter fell to her waist. The redhead stood close behind her, and began tracing circles around her breasts. "What do you think?" whispered Grace.

"I think they should just get a room," said Travis.

"And deprive the rest of us of all the fun?" she protested a little breathlessly. "Come on, Travis, don't you enjoy watching two beautiful women just a little bit?"

"Sure, who wouldn't?" he asked, and noticed that he, too, needed to control his breathing.

"But I prefer my fun in private."

"You can have that too," said Grace. She waved her champagne glass at another door. "Right through there, plenty of private—or at least, semiprivate—spaces. Couches, curtains, and afterward, showers downstairs. You'll see, later. If you want. But watch out for the redhead. She bites, and she doesn't always play by the rules."

Travis considered Grace. She seemed giddy, but not drunk; provocative, but not really coming on to him. At least, he didn't think so.

"You and Mr. Plummer usually come here together," he began.

"That's right, but he often comes without me, and once in a while I come by myself or with my friend Ginger."

"What's it do for you and Mr. Plummer?" he asked.

Grace shrugged. "I don't know. It's exciting, it's dangerous, but not very. It's flattering. I think Frederick likes to see other people—men and women—interested in me. Sometimes we just dance, and flirt, and go home."

Travis took another swig of the beer. Either he was getting warm, or the beer was, it didn't taste nearly as cold or clean as it had a few minutes ago.

"Want the rest of the grand tour?" asked Grace.

"Maybe, in a while," said Travis. "It's nice just to sit here for a few minutes."

"With me?" pressed Grace.

"Yes," confessed Travis. "With you."

Travis hadn't known that, until he said it. Hadn't acknowledged, to himself at least, how much he looked forward to seeing Grace, how much he enjoyed watching in the rearview mirror as she looked up from a book or magazine, and said a new word aloud, delighted with the sound of it. "Illumine," she'd said one day. "I had no idea you could use it as a verb. Illumine, illumine." And back she went to her book. Travis didn't want to acknowledge how contemptuous he had become of Frederick Plummer and his careless treatment of his wife, she of the elegant body and even-more-elegant mind.

Ivory might have known. She'd asked him about Grace in a way she'd never asked about a client before. "You seem awfully cheery for a Monday morning," she'd observed when he stopped by for an early cup of coffee. "You must be going to drive Mrs. Plummer."

What would Ivory think about the Crimson Club? In fact, thought Travis, she'd be amused, a little intrigued, and completely self-possessed. And why, he wondered, should a grown man care about what his mother thought? He couldn't help smiling about it.

"What's the joke?" asked Grace.

"No joke," said Travis, "believe it or not, I was thinking about my mother."

Grace laughed out loud. "Okay, that's either the best—or the most neurotic—line I've ever heard in here. And I've heard plenty. Come on, let's go."

"We can't just sit here for a while?" said Travis, strangely reluctant to go further into Mr. Toad's Wild Ride.

"A ship in a harbor is safe," said Grace, "but that is not what ships are for."

"Pardon?"

"Just something my grandfather used to tell me. He was a Norwegian sailor, and that's what he'd say to me when I was afraid to try something new."

"Well, I can't be outdone by your grandfather," said Travis. "Let's go."

As Travis and Grace stood, the redhead left her prey and stalked over to them. "Grace," she said, "introduce me to your chum."

"Travis, Annabelle. Annabelle, Travis."

Annabelle presented her thin, white hand. Travis took it, vaguely unsettled and a little excited by what he'd last seen those fingers do. He hesitated, then brought her hand to his lips.

And then he, Annabelle, and Grace explored the pleasures of a private room.

CHAPTER 12

"Oh, my!" said Andrea. "What happened in that room?" She shook her head and covered her ears. "Never mind. I think I prefer not to know."

"Really?" I said. "What kind of reporter are you?"

"Prudish," she said. "It's my cross to bear."

"Doesn't matter," I said. "Not many more details to tell," I said. "Travis went all oddly chivalric on me, 'no kissing and telling' after that last little revelation. Plus, we were running out of time."

"What did you say to Travis when he finished telling you the story?"

We had walked across the street for coffee to have a little check-in on the story. "Check-in?" Andrea sniffed, when I proposed a latte break. "More like a checkup. You're checking up on me."

"Maybe I am," I admitted. "Hey, (a) I'm the boss and I get to do that and (b) when have you ever turned down a free latte?"

"Yankees are frugal," she said. "You know that."

Once we were settled at the microscopic table at Peet's, I recounted Travis's tale about the Crimson Club.

"Come on, Maggie," prodded Andrea. "I'd really like to know what you said."

"Oh, I just rattled on about where the custom came from."

"The custom?" asked Andrea. "The custom of what—spoiled, rich people misbehaving in a pretentious club?"

"No, not that custom. The one of a man kissing a woman's

hand upon introduction. It's a bit murky, but in the Bible, the hand-kiss—Kings and Job for the citations, if you're interested—was a way to pay homage."

Andrea stared at me. "Oh, dear. How on earth does Michael live with you?" she said.

"I have no idea," I said. "Okay, let's get to it. Did you bring the clips?"

When writers start major features, one of the interns generally pulls clippings on the subject as background. In the pre-web days, it meant trips to libraries and newspaper morgues and lots of copying. Nowadays, it's mostly Google and a download away.

Andrea hauled a folder out of her battered leather briefcase.

"You know," I suggested, "you ought to get one of those cool Kate Spade knockoff portfolios to carry your stuff in."

Andrea looked as if I'd suggested putting her work in a brown paper grocery bag. "First, I don't purchase knockoffs. They're illegal and probably immoral. Second, this was my father's briefcase in law school thirty-two years ago, and it's still perfectly serviceable."

"Okay, okay," I said. "Don't get all preppy on me. Let's see what you've got."

"I've organized them by Grace, Grace and Frederick, and organizations that Grace seemed to be involved with."

"Which were?"

"Social stuff. She was on the planning committee of the Black & White Ball, and she was on the board of a couple of garden-related places. Now, this one seemed a little odd, A Mom's Place—a group that served young, single mothers." She put a printout of a web page about A Mom's Place in front of me.

"Why's that seem odd?"

"Oh, I don't know—she didn't have any kids, so there didn't seem to be some natural draw. Plus, it's certainly not an A-list charity on the social circuit."

"What else?"

"That's about it for the organizations. She modeled occasionally for Junior League fashion shows, but there's nothing surprising about that. Wealth and beauty open a lot of doors."

"What about Frederick?"

"Business, money, business, money. Most of the clips are about his deals. Seems as if his venture fund didn't take as big a hit as lots of others during the tech-bust. They appeared to have gone to ground, preserved cash, and they're in the thick of it now that tech is back. He had one altruistic cause, a philanthropic venture fund that collected money from VCs and made grants with it. I believe he began the fund."

"Oh, yes," I said, frowning. "I know about that enterprise. Michael's firm is involved in some way." I picked up a pile of clips from "Swells", the *Chronicle*'s social notes column, the *Nob Hill Gazette,* and *7 X 7.*

"That's the Frederick-and-Grace-out-on-the-town-stack," said Andrea.

"All the usual places—symphony, ballet, opera galas."

On the top lay a photo of Frederick and Grace with another couple. All in evening clothes, beautiful women, handsome men. The other woman was shorter and curvier than Grace, poured into a strapless dress, with chandelier earrings nearly grazing her shoulders. Grace wore a tiny evening hat, with a froth of feathers making an elegant comma down to her cheek.

"Maggie, I see you yearning for that hat," said Andrea. "It's prudent to remember that the owner ended up dead in the back seat of a car."

"So true. But I'd like to know what happened to that hat."

Andrea looked horrified.

"Kidding, I'm kidding."

"Now, this other couple they're with," she said, mollified. "They could be interesting to talk with."

"Who are they?"

"Ginger and William Brand. He's Frederick's business partner at the venture fund, and Ginger was Grace's best friend. When you look through all the social clips," she fanned the stack on the tiny table, "you'll see the two of them together in lots of places."

"And one place you could see them together, but not in the papers," I said, "The Crimson. Travis said they went together sometimes. I'm sure the police talked to Mrs. Brand. In fact, I think she might have testified at the trial. I'll have to go look at the transcripts again."

"Maybe so," said Andrea. "But don't you think she'd be a little more open with us?"

"Could be," I said. "Though when Gertie tried to make an appointment for me to talk to Frederick, he was pretty brusque. I'm not sure why we'd have better luck with the Brands."

"We're going to put you in the natural habitat of our prey," said Andrea. She dug in her briefcase again.

"Voila!" She pushed a heavy, cream-colored envelope in front of me. An engraved drawing of a pale-green vine wound around the envelope.

"What's this?"

"It's an invitation to the dedication of the new Cloud-Forest Garden at the San Francisco Botanical Gardens. It came to the office, and Gertie passed it on to me because she knows I like to garden. But you should go, because Frederick Plummer will be there. This was one of Grace's causes, and take a little glance at this."

She pointed one impeccably manicured, natural-polish index finger at the invitation. I'd never seen Andrea with colored polish. Too vulgar, I was sure.

I read aloud: "Join us as we honor the memory of Grace Plummer with the dedication of a fountain named for her."

"You're right," I said. "I'll go. I'll tell Gertie to R.S.V.P. for me."

"I knew you'd warm to this idea," Andrea said. "It's a splendid outing for you. You can wear a hat."

"Goody," I said. "I've got a great, broad-brimmed pink number. Very Audrey Hepburn in her *Funny Face* era."

"Uh-huh," said Andrea. "Sorry I won't be there to witness it. But when you're not admiring yourself in the mirror, chat up the grieving widower, why don't you?"

"I will," I promised. "Plus, I bet Grace's best friend, Ginger, will be there. And I can interrogate her, too."

Andrea finished her coffee, took out a monogrammed compact, and inspected her lipstick. "It's difficult to think of someone in a flying-saucer hat conducting a serious interrogation," she said. "Don't let the investigating go to your head. I believe Hoyt assigned you to be *my* researcher on *my* story."

"Hey, why doesn't anyone ever treat me like a boss?" I protested.

"That's a question you ought to ask yourself," said Andrea.

"Beautiful compact," I said.

"It was my great-aunt Amelia's," she said. "We have the same initials, AFS. 'Use, reuse,' that's the New England motto, you know."

Interval No. 3 with Dr. Mephisto

It was May Day and in honor of spring, Dr. Mephisto had on even more color than usual. If that was possible. Turquoise everywhere—silk sweater, teardrop earrings, several bracelets. When she met me at the door, I couldn't help myself. "Is turquoise the new black this season?"

She allowed herself a smile. "The new black?" Sometimes I thought she always countered my question with a question because that's what shrinks learn in Therapy 101, and sometimes I thought she did it just to annoy me. I was leaning toward the annoyance option.

"You know, like last season pink was the new black? Or," I hesitated. "I guess you don't read *Vogue.*"

"It's teal, not turquoise," she said. "And yes, I did read that teal is the new black. At least in my closet." She gestured up the stairs to her office. "Shall we go up? Michael's already here."

Michael, the inveterate espresso drinker had either been

replaced by an alien or brainwashed. He sat on the couch, contentedly sipping a mug of tea.

"How are things?" asked Dr. Mephisto, once I had declined the tea and was seated primly on the sofa. I knew what was coming. I could feel the little-boy braggadocio radiating from Michael, sending out waves of testosterone.

"Good, I think," he said eagerly. And prepared to spill the beans about our lunchtime interlude.

Dr. Mephisto's eyes went from Michael's face to mine, back and forth during the telling.

"Sounds like you had fun," she said to Michael.

"I did," he said, and reached over to put a hand, possessively, on my knee.

"And I think Maggie did, too."

"Perhaps she'll tell us herself," said Dr. Mephisto.

I sighed. "I did. It *was* fun. Very."

Michael looked at me, "But what, *cara*?"

I shrugged. "I thought it was private. Between us. Now I feel—" I hesitated.

"As if Michael's reporting back to teacher?" asked Dr. Mephisto.

"Exactly," I said.

"Oh, for Christ's sake, Maggie," said Michael, removing his hand, "lighten up."

We both sat silent. I sensed a pout coming from Michael's end of the couch. I had spoiled his fun. I felt grouchy and petty.

"Okay, enough steamy sex," said Dr. Mephisto, completely deadpan. "Let's talk about something else. Maggie, the story you both mentioned to me, about the murdered socialite. Is that raising any issues for the two of you?"

I gave a brief report, pausing to point out that I was keeping Michael informed. "Every step of the way," I said. This time, I reached over and put my hand on his knee. So this was therapy—you simply show up and take turns patting your partner's knee. I felt I was getting the hang of it, though I was perfectly willing to play kneesies at home. For free. With a glass of wine instead of mungy herbal tea. And without voyeuristic Dr. Mephisto sitting around and watching.

"Is that how you feel, Michael? Well-informed?" asked Dr. Mephisto.

He looked at me and raised an eyebrow. "Yes. I guess so. Plenty of bulletins from the front."

"That sounds a little removed," said Dr. Mephisto. "As if Maggie were off fighting a battle and writing home to you."

"Well, she's got a life and a job," said Michael. "I do, too. We can't be involved in every single moment of each other's lives."

"Actually," I said, as a brilliant idea washed over me, "I'd like Michael to be more involved in this, this story or investigation or whatever it is."

"How so?" asked Dr. Mephisto.

"He's a lawyer," I said. "I'd love for him to read the transcript from the trial and help me understand it. Look for stuff that doesn't make sense. What do you think?" I asked, and this time, my hand on his knee felt legitimate.

"You don't need me," Michael said. "You've got all those criminal-defense chicks working on this."

"I do, or at least Isabella does. But they're reading it with criminal-defense eyes. I just want another lawyerly, analytic set of eyes on the transcript, someone who might notice something that the regular criminal bar types wouldn't notice. Plus, Grace's husband is a financial type. You can put those hot, number-savvy brain cells on the case."

"Is this some make-work, WPA project?" asked Michael. "Because I have more than enough to keep me busy at my day job."

"Absolutely not," I said. "I wish I'd thought of it sooner. You'd be doing me a big favor, and plus, you'll know as much as I do, and we can talk about the case."

Michael raised an eyebrow again. "You mean…talk about the story, right?"

"Yes, exactly!"

"What do you think, Doc?" asked Michael, turning to Dr.

Mephisto. “Is this some manipulative way to prevent me from objecting to Maggie’s involvement?”

“What I think isn’t so important,” said Dr. Mephisto. “But what you think is. I did hear Maggie say she’s asking you a favor. That seems pretty straightforward.”

CHAPTER 13

I was a vision in my wide-brimmed, flying-saucer-shaped black hat, with the Elsa Schiaperelli shocking-pink lining, at the Botanical Gardens dedication ceremony. The social ladies-who-lunch had turned out in force for the fountain dedication. I assessed the crowd. On one side, the traditional botanical garden supporters—well-heeled, St. John-suited, pearls-and-pumps ladies of a certain age. Surrounding Frederick, though, was a covey of Grace's contemporaries—dressed with a little attitude from San Francisco's newest, slightly edgy young designers like Colleen Quen and eco-happy Kelly B.

Frederick Plummer looked even better in person than he did in the clips with Grace: late forties, slightly receding hairline, hair cropped close enough to look like a vaguely decadent European film director, tall enough to carry off the double-breasted navy blazer and pleated fawn trousers. He either visited his money in some offshore Caribbean bank or frequented a tanning salon. He was the color George Hamilton used to be, before we all got freaked about sun damage and skin cancer.

"Mr. Plummer." I touched his arm.

He turned, smiled automatically, and extended his hand. "Hello, how nice of you to come."

"I'm Maggie Fiori from *Small Town.*"

The smile disappeared. "Ah, yes, Ms. Fiori. Your assistant called the other day."

"I'm here today because our magazine supports the Botanical Gardens," I said. "I'm not trying to chase you down." Well, that was a lie.

"Comforting to hear," he said. "Let me introduce you to Grace's close friend, Ginger Brand." He put his arm around the woman standing next to him—I recognized the hourglass-figure brunette from the photo.

"Ginger," said Plummer, with just an undertone of warning in his voice, "this is Ms. Fiori, from *Small Town*. She tells me she's joining us today because the magazine supports the Gardens."

"In fact," I said, telling at least part of the truth, "we publish a special insert for your Garden Ball every year. I think we're one of your media sponsors."

"That's right," said Ginger, "and we're grateful for your support. Today is a wonderful occasion for all of us who loved Grace." Her eyes filled. "I'm sorry," she said to Frederick. "I'm not trying to make things harder for you."

She dug in her Kate Spade bag—real, not knockoff—for a tissue.

"I picked up a program at the gate," I said. "It's wonderful you're dedicating a fountain in your wife's memory."

Frederick tightened his hold on Ginger, "All Ginger's doing," he said. "I don't know a lobelia from a libel suit, but Ginger and Grace, they could rattle all day long about this stuff. And Ginger was insistent that we do something in the Cloud-Forest Garden."

"It's a beautiful space," I said. "Where does the name come from?"

"Am I wearing mascara all down my face, Freddy?"

He took her hand and pulled her close to inspect her perfect face. "Not one drop." He released her. "I'll let you ladies chat about flowers," he said. "I need to check in with the Garden director—I think we're waiting for the mayor to arrive, so we can get things under way." He headed toward the podium set up near the new fountain.

Ginger watched him walk away, then turned back to me. She

seemed distracted. "Sorry, you were asking?"

"The name of the garden—Cloud-Forest. What does it mean?"

"Cloud-forests are high-mountain places, very tropical, very wet and often cloudy, even during dry seasons. They're interesting because such a variety of plants can grow there."

"I get it," I said. "That's why the plants around us are so abundant-looking—but San Francisco isn't a cloud-forest, is it?"

"Not exactly," said Ginger, warming to her topic. "But it has some of the same characteristics, especially on the wet, Sunset side of the park. It's one of the things that Grace loved about the Botanical Gardens. Her grandmother had always tried to re-create Midwest gardens that looked a certain way at a certain time of the year. But Grace just reveled in the fact that Bay Area weather is so mild, so many things can grow all year long." I looked across at Grace's fountain. Passion vines, tree dahlias, lush rhododendrons surrounded the stone basin. "So, even though we're not at high altitude, the way cloud-forests generally are, our climate lets us have two different kinds of cloud-forest gardens. Plus," she hesitated, "all of us who loved Grace thought of her as a kind of cloud. Beautiful, changeable, a little elusive."

"Did Grace know that's how her friends thought of her?"

Ginger laughed. "Absolutely. You know that old Carly Simon song, I can't even remember the name of it, but there's a line—'clouds in my coffee?' She told me she used to sing it to Frederick."

Over the din of voices we heard the tap, tap, tap on the mike.

"Hello? Testing?"

"Oh, oops, they're starting," said Ginger. "I've got to go."

She worked her way to the dais, and I watched Frederick Plummer reach a hand down and help her up to stand beside him. He lowered the podium microphone, so that it was at Ginger's height, and then stood back.

"Hello, everyone," said Ginger. "Ladies and gentlemen. Gardeners and would-be gardeners, welcome! Thank you all for gathering on this spring morning for such a special occasion. My name is Ginger Brand, and I had the honor of chairing the campaign to design and install this beautiful fountain."

She stopped and gestured at the fountain, an abstract, bronze shape built in three levels. "Today, we're dedicating the fountain in memory of our friend, Grace Plummer. I look around the garden today, and I realize that thanks to Grace, I know the names of most of these beautiful plants. Before Grace, I knew roses—you know, the flowers your husband brings you when he's done something wrong—and the kinds of orchids we used to wear as corsages to proms. Now..." she gestured again, this time at the garden, "I look around and I see old friends—a *Vireya* rhododendron there, a lipstick plant or *aeschynanthus* as Grace taught me to call it—over there. That was one of Grace's gifts to me. She fell in love with this garden and wanted everyone she cared about to love it as well. She knew the language of gardening, and she taught me every Latin plant name I know." Her voice was breaking. Frederick stepped close to her and put his hand on her shoulder. He whispered in her ear.

"Sorry, I knew this was going to be an emotional day," she said. "Now, it's my pleasure to invite Frederick Plummer, Grace's husband, to dedicate the fountain. Frederick..." Frederick stepped to the fountain, plucked the rose from his blazer buttonhole, and tossed it into the top section of the fountain. Magically, the water began to bubble and cascade from the top bowl into the next basin down. A little ripple of satisfied "ooohs," went through the crowd, and polite applause. "Thank you, Frederick," said Ginger. "And thank all of you for enhancing the beauty of this garden in Grace's memory. Now, refreshments are ready inside, and any of you who feel an urge to be even more generous to help us endow the Cloud-Forest Garden," she made a plucking motion with her right hand, "I'll be around to finish picking your pocket."

"Charming, just charming," said a low voice next to me. I turned to see Augustus Reeves III, arms folded, leaning against a garden wall. He was dressed a little better than when I'd first seen him in Ivory's bar, but still sporting a Giants cap. "Mr. Reeves, isn't it?" I asked.

"Gus," he said. "Or Uncle Gus." He touched his hand to the cap brim in a salute.

"What a coincidence to see you here."

"Not really," he said. "My daughter strong-armed me to come."

"Your daughter?" I asked, confused, looking around.

He cocked his hand like a kid's toy gun and pointed at Ginger. "Right there. That's my perfect little Ginger."

"Oh," I said, stunned into silence. I was having trouble connecting the elegant young woman with Uncle Gus, who looked like a longshoreman who'd stumbled into the wrong party.

"Can't match us up, huh?" He laughed.

"Well..." I faltered, "not exactly."

"I'm very proud of her," he said. "She could have been a spoiled little twit like...some of her friends. That's how her grandparents raised her."

"Her grandparents?"

"Yeah. When her mother and I split up, Ginger was just a tyke. The grandparents—my wife's folks and mine, agreed to take her in 'til we figured out what we were going to do. So, old Gus II—that was my father—and my mom had her half the year, and my wife's folks had her the rest of the time. They all indulged the heck out of her—fancy schools, riding lessons, a coming-out party, and I don't mean out of the closet. Smith College, the whole WASPY shooting match. And look at her now." We both watched Ginger greeting people near the podium, exchanging hugs and warm handshakes with people. She looked like an elegant young aunt of the bride, minus twenty years and yards of bad chiffon.

"I can see why you're proud of her," I said.

"Not proud of much in my life," he said. "But that girl turned out damn fine. She asks me to show up, I show up. Besides, I like to know the company she keeps. Rich people aren't always upstanding citizens, know what I mean?"

I didn't really, but I nodded. We were silent for a moment. "So, may I ask a personal question?"

"Shoot," he said, "isn't that what reporters do?"

"They do," I said, "though I'm not much of a reporter. I was just wondering about your relationship to Ivory. She's your ... niece?"

"Now, that's a little creepy," he said. "I live for the occasions when I can get that woman in the sack."

Another surprise. Didn't see that one coming. "But she referred to you as Uncle Gus," I persisted.

"Oh, that," he said. "I'm so used to people calling me Uncle Gus that I never think about how peculiar it must sound to outsiders."

"So, what's the deal?"

"Kinda long story. But the short version is that when I was in college, I lived with two other guys, both by the name of Gus."

I raised an eyebrow. "That seems statistically improbable."

"Sure does. But it happened. I was Gus for Augustus, just like my old man. There was a Swede from North Dakota named Gustav, Gus for short. And then there was this preppy guy from the Cape, name of George. You know the type, loafers with no socks and monogrammed shirts and shit. But none of that famous New England reserve. In fact, he talked so much, his nickname was Gusty, and so everyone called him..."

"Gus," I chimed in.

"Right. So anyway, Gus the yapper and Gus the Swede were both big boozers and potheads, and I was always having to fish one or the other of 'em out of trouble. So, everyone took to calling me Uncle Gus, because I was the responsible one. Even worked as a volunteer fireman for our college town. Which is pretty ironic, when you think about it."

"Enlighten me," I said. "Why ironic?"

He shrugged, "Let's say that I got out of the responsibility habit pretty soon after college. Went to Vietnam, became an MP, which gave me an incurable case of disliking, distrusting, and disregarding any kind of institution and most people. Came home, got married, and Ginger was born. Turns out I couldn't even be a responsible, card-carrying parent. That's why her grandparents had to raise her."

"Where was her mom?"

"Gone, took a powder. Actually she got into a whole bunch of powder." He sniffed and touched the side of his flattened nose. "Nose candy."

As if on cue, his eyes filled and he dug in his pocket, pulled out a handkerchief and honked into it.

"Where is she now?"

"Ginger's mom? Dead. Too much crap in her system. Kidney failure or something. She looked like hell the last time I saw her, and that was when Ginger was six."

"Tough situation," I said.

"Yeah, tough all around," he said. "So, since the grandparents had Ginger, I lit out myself. Did construction work in L.A., because you can work all year round, save up some bucks, then bum around 'til it runs out. I got pretty muscled up, so I used to get a fair amount of movie work, too. One rung up from an extra, enough lines every once in a while, so I got my SAG card. Mr. Man of a Thousand Faces, that was me. Right clothes, right wig, right attitude, I could be anything—a gladiator, a cowboy, a gangster. And when I came back to the Bay Area, I'd crash in Ivory's spare room, in her flat over the club."

"And how'd you know Ivory?"

"She's George—Gusty's sister. And since everyone else called me Uncle Gus, that's what she called me, too."

"And how long did you stay with Ivory?"

"Forever. I'm still there." He looked at me and grinned. "Surprised again, huh? You don't think I'm her type."

"I've given up predicting anybody's type," I countered.

"Yeah, well, I'm in love with that woman. Always have been; always will be. She just tolerates having me around, but I've come in handy over the years. After her stroke, I took care of her, and she's going through a rough patch with all this crap around Travis and that spoiled broad he probably offed, so I think she's glad to have me around. Even if Travis and I were never best buddies. Guess he thinks I'm not good enough for his mom. And he's probably right. But there I am, hard to get rid of. Plus, Travis knows Ivory can use a little extra folding green right now."

So, more surprises. Uncle Gus as nursemaid *and* Daddy Warbucks.

"And now," said Gus, "you're wondering where the money comes from."

"Okay, a little."

"I screwed around a lot in life, but I've got one of those peculiar magnetic brains. Once something goes in, it sticks. Know what I mean?"

"Oh, I know exactly what you mean," I said. "You're talking to the girl who knows what *tête-à-bêche* means."

"Head-to-ass. It's a thing in stamps, right?" he said promptly.

"I believe philatelists call it 'head-to-tail,' but you're absolutely right."

"Yeah, well, I usually am," he said. "It's my only claim to fame, besides holding cards in SAG and the carpenter's union. Just like Harrison Ford, only better looking."

"And modest," I observed.

Gus continued, as if I'd never said a word. "So one of my L.A. pals dared me to go on *Jeopardy* one day."

"And you did."

"I did and I won a pile of money. Big pile of money. And Gusty, Ivory's brother, who gave up hash and went to business school and became some Wall Street smartass, invested it for me. I'm not stinking rich, but I've got way more than enough to live on. And to help pay Ivory's mortgage. And aid and abet that precious little club of hers." He shook his head. "I know she's just tending those fires so Mr. Wonderful Travis has something to come home to." He fell silent and gave me a sly look. "You must be good at this reporting shit you say you don't do. I just spilled my whole damn life story to a perfect stranger. And we're not even drinking."

"We could be," I said. "They're serving Lemon Drops inside."

"Figures," he said. "But Ginger told me they'd have a beer

tucked away for me. Too early for those fruity drinks."

"That's thoughtful of her."

Gus shook his head. "She takes better care of her old man than I ever took of her."

"And that's why you're so vigilant now?"

"You bet your ass," he said.

I caught up with Ginger over the baked brie. "Lovely speech," I said. "Very moving."

She surveyed me suspiciously. "Is that what you really thought?"

"It is," I said, realizing I needed to take Ginger more seriously.

"It's not just the usual fundraising bullshit," she said, taking a serious gulp of her Lemon Drop, and for a moment, sounding a good deal like her father. "This place really meant something to Grace, and she dragged me here, and I ended up being a big fan as well."

"Will you stay involved?" I asked. "Now that the fountain is dedicated?"

"Yes," she said. "I was telling the truth up at the mike. Grace got me hooked on this place, and on gardening. She always said that gardens kept you humble. You learn things, you study, you pay attention to plants, and sometimes they reward you, and sometimes they don't."

"Just like kids," I said.

"I wouldn't know," said Ginger. "Bill and I are another one of those self-indulgent, childless-by-choice couples. Too busy having fun to have kids."

The phrase sounded like she was quoting someone, and I wondered whose choice it was to be childless. I also wondered if Ginger would be as willing as her father to spill her story—whatever it was—to a near-perfect stranger. Too early to tell. I returned to safer ground.

"Do you have a garden at home?"

"Teeny-tiny," she said. "We live in the City, so we have a brick patio with pots. Thanks to Grace, I only kill a fraction of what I used to. And, I've fired our gardener and do the work myself."

"Good for you," I said. "I was chatting with your father after your remarks," I added. "It sounds as if you and Grace had more in common than gardening."

"Besides the fact that we're both spoiled little socialites?" she asked, arching one perfectly waxed and feathered brow.

"Your father mentioned to me that you were raised by your grandparents, and I know Grace was raised by hers as well."

"You and Uncle Gus got right down to all the family secrets, didn't you? I guess that's why you're a good reporter."

"Editor," I corrected her. "But, I'd actually met your father before."

She held out her glass to the bartender for a refill.

"Really? Where?"

"At The Devil's Interval."

Ginger reclaimed her glass, took a sip, and looked around the room.

"Do you know the place?"

"I do," she said. "It's owned by Travis Gifford's mother, the man who murdered Grace. So, you'll understand if it's not one of my regular hangouts. Even if Ivory Gifford is also my father's—let's see, what shall we call her?"

"Your father's landlady?" I inquired.

"Yes," she said. "Correct. She is that."

"This seems like an amazing set of coincidences," I said.

"Isn't it?" said Ginger. "Downright Dickensian. But then, as you know San Francisco is..."

"A small town," I finished. "So, you know Ivory as well?"

"Barely," she said. "Despite what my father thinks, he doesn't supervise my every little move, and I certainly don't supervise his," she said. "I can't help who my father chooses as his friends."

Suddenly, Frederick Plummer was at her side. "Ginger, I'm sorry to interrupt, but there are some people we should go thank together." He gestured across the room. "You'll forgive us, Ms. Fiori."

I opened my mouth to say "Of course," but they were both gone. Ginger had her arm linked through Frederick's, and was smiling up at him with what athletes call a "game face." Freddy, huh? Wonder how many people got to call him by that name? Wonder if the best friend and the widower were consoling each other in particularly intimate ways? And with that, I took my flying-saucer hat and suspicious mind right back to the office.

It wasn't until late that night that I realized what had been bothering me about Ginger's remark that Grace would sing the line "clouds in my coffee" to Frederick.

I went to the stereo cabinet to flip through our old CDs, looking for the Carly Simon album that had the song in it. Michael looked over my shoulder. "Hey, there's *Brenda and the Tabulations*. What's it doing next to the sound track from *The Rugrats*?"

"I don't know, honey," I said. "Feel free to alphabetize these any old time you want."

"I did," he said. "I do periodically. And then you and the boys just throw things back willy-nilly."

"You must be very secure in your masculinity," I said, flipping through the discs, "to use a phrase like willy-nilly in public."

"Not in public," said Michael. "I believe we're at home, *en famille.* What are you looking for?"

"Make yourself useful," I said. "I want the lyrics to that Carly Simon song where she talks about 'clouds in my coffee.'"

"*You're So Vain*," said Michael smugly.

"That's right! It was supposed to be about Warren Beatty or some other big-deal movie-star boyfriend she had. Sing some of it for me."

And in a nicely in-tune baritone, Michael obliged.

"You had me several years ago
When I was still quite naive
Well, you said that we made such a pretty pair
And that you would never leave
But you gave away the things you loved
And one of them was me

I had some dreams they were clouds in my coffee
Clouds in my coffee…"

He stopped. "I don't remember the rest of it."

"Okay, so what's the song about?"

"It's about some egomaniacal, careless guy who..."

"Careless, like how?"

"Like giving away the things he loves."

"So, if a wife sang that song to her husband, what would that mean?"

"That she liked Carly Simon?"

"Come on, put that fine, legal analytical mind to work for me for a minute."

Michael shrugged. "I guess the obvious reason would be that the husband's a jerk, like the guy in the song. That he's careless with the stuff—or the people—he loves."

"And what are the clouds in the coffee?"

"Beats me. Impurities? Cream gone bad? Who knows?" Michael leaned past me. "Hey, there's my Shirelles' *Greatest Hits*." He fished it out of the pile. "This is so cool, I'm going to put it on the hall table so I remember to take it for the car tomorrow."

"Yet another thing you ought to be embarrassed about," I called after him. "Listening to old, moldy 'girl groups.' On a CD. Which is such an outmoded music-sharing technology."

"You're just jealous," he retorted. "Because you're not from Passaic, New Jersey, like The Shirelles and me. And how can a romantic not love a song like *Dedicated to the One I Love*?"

I didn't answer. I was thinking about how adding something like cream does obscure the purity of the coffee. How it changes color, taste, everything. But why would Grace sing that to Frederick? Was he the cream? The coffee? The clouds?

CHAPTER 14

Michael called me mid-morning the next day. "*Cara*, do we have any mystery social engagements I know nothing about this weekend?"

"That's a Zen-like question," I countered. "If you don't know anything about them, how could they exist?"

He snorted, "Cut me a break. You're always booking stuff and just telling me I have to show up. And wear a tie. And talk to people I don't know."

"It's good for you," I said. "Lubricates those social interaction muscles. But the answer to this particular question is just the usual—Saturday soccer for both boys, birthday party for Josh's little wannabe-Madonna friend, Esme. Why?"

"I'm inviting a couple of students over for Sunday afternoon. Pizza, beer, conversation."

"Anyone I know?"

"It's the two stars on my moot court team. The one I'm coaching for the competition at Hastings this year. Your little pal Isabella had the reporter's transcripts sent over from Gifford's trial. My office is now a wasteland of banker's boxes. I'm couriering them home."

"And your moot court team is going to argue about them?"

"Maybe. You ever seen what a special circumstances trial transcript looks like?"

"No. But I'm going to if those boxes are coming to live in our family room."

"They're coming to take over our family room. This is 20,000 pages of transcript."

"Geez," I said, taxing my brain to remember how long *War and Peace* was. "That's like more than twenty volumes of some really big, dense Russian novel."

"Uh-huh," said Michael, "and without the cool plot twists. Though actually, that's what we're going to be looking for. Plot twists. My students are each going to look for different things, try to identify anything that needs more exploration or offers some possibilities for alternatives to the 'Travis Gifford did it' scenario."

"And these are criminal-defense lawyers-in-training?"

"Nope, not either one of them," said Michael. "You've got plenty of those types with Isabella and her cronies. I'm just building on your idea about fresh—by which I know you meant, ignorant—eyes. I've got a bunch of tax and corporate geeks on my team. But, the two I'm asking to take this on are very analytic, and besides, they'll do anything for pizza and beer. They're all starving students. Sunday, our house, I'll order the pizza; you make sure we've got plenty of beer."

"Done. Michael, thank you. This is a very, very big favor."

"Oh, I know that, *cara.* I just hope you do when it comes time to calculate those partner points. I'm thinking I'll get a hall pass out of going to Seder at your Aunt Goldie's for the next ten years. Or at least until somebody else volunteers to make the matzo balls. Or she stops asking me if I really believe the Jews murdered Jesus."

On Sunday, Michael invited me to drop into the family room and kick off his meeting with a briefing about the case. I was happy to do so. "Seth, Krissy—my wife and our client, Maggie Fiori." They both scrambled to their feet and shook hands. They looked young and smart and happy to see the pizza and beer. And maybe me.

I gave them a quick overview of the case, Travis Gifford, and how I'd become involved. Two young lawyers in training, a guy and a gal, both in variations of the jeans-and-T-shirt uniform, listened intently. Seth was wiry, intense, and seemed to take down every word I said on his laptop. The front of his T-shirt read: "First, kill all the lawyers." Krissy's jeans-and-T-shirt ensemble included a form-fitting, scoop-necked camisole. She was luminous, from the top of her extra-curly gelled blond head to the end of her Rockette-worthy long, long legs. And while she and Seth watched me as I talked, I couldn't help but notice that Michael watched Krissy. When I finished my ramble, Michael stood up. "Thanks, Maggie—I appreciate you stopping in. I'll let you get back to the boys, now. We've got plenty to get started."

"I'll bring homemade brownies in a little later," I said. "I appreciate everything you two are doing."

"Wow," I heard Seth say. "That is so nice of you, Mrs. Fiori."

"Oh, I'm just the delivery girl," I corrected him. "Michael baked them."

Four hours, two extra-large pizzas, a platter of brownies, and more than a six-pack later, Michael called Josh and Zach to help schlep the boxes out to the curb. Josh looked starstruck, just being in Krissy's presence; Zach was completely bewitched by the motorcycle Seth was riding and watched him snug a surprising number of boxes in the hard cases on either side of the bike. When Seth hoisted him onto the seat, put his helmet on Zach's head, and shot a photo with his cell phone he promised to e-mail, I thought Zach was going to swoon with pleasure.

"Would you look at the two of them?" I said to Michael. "I thought we were raising our sons as feminist models of un-stereotypical behavior. You put them in front of hot wheels and long legs, and they revert to type."

Michael put his arm around me. "Get over yourself, Susan B. Anthony. You couldn't even make a go of your crummy little one-dollar coin. You think you're going to fight biology? Cars and babes and the NFL draft, and when they're old enough, cold beer. That's it. That's what occupies guy gray matter."

"And to think," I said, watching Josh practically trip over himself to help Krissy load bankers' boxes in her trunk, "I always tell the boys what a model feminist dude you are. Oh, well. So, how'd you think it went tonight?"

"Good," said Michael. "This is a piece of genius, if I do say so myself. Free, exploitable labor. They're both sick of poring over tax codes, and ready for blood, sex, and sensationalism."

The boys were finished "helping," so Michael escorted them back into the house after they watched Seth put on his helmet, wave, and zoom off on his bike. Krissy slammed the trunk and came back to say goodbye to me.

"I really appreciate you taking this on," I said. "I know how busy every minute of every day is when you're in law school."

She shook her head. "I just came back to say thanks to you, Mrs. Fiori."

"Maggie, please. Otherwise I'm worried someone will get me confused with my mother-in-law. And why on earth would you thank me?"

"This will be interesting to work on and it's about something that matters," she said. "Plus...now I know what I want my life to look like."

"You want to do criminal law?" I asked.

"No. I mean I want the life you and Professor Fiori have. A beautiful house that looks like real people live there. Two great kids. And the two of you…" she faltered. "The two of you seem as if you have fun together."

Oh, my, I thought. How simple things could look on the surface. She turned around and gestured at the house. "What do you call this kind of home?" she asked.

"I call it messy and in constant need of repair," I said. "But I think it's meant to be Mediterranean in style. Probably shows our longing to be in some beautiful Tuscan town, I guess. We both love old houses, so we're willing to live with all the problems they come with."

"Mediterranean," she said. "I'll remember that. Just look how beautiful your house is right now, lit up from inside." For a moment, I did see it through her eyes: floor-to-ceiling windows that ran the length of the dining room and faced out onto the street. A heavy, dark-oak front door, teak planter boxes overflowing with early jonquils and tulips. Not to mention two skateboards and a bocce set on the front porch. "I know it's just your house to you," she said. "But it looks like a whole world to me."

Impulsively, I pulled her close for a hug. "You can make exactly the life you want, honey," I said. "It's just that you have to be willing to reinvent it every single day."

And then she was off, climbing into the world's oldest Honda and heading down the hill and back to the city.

CHAPTER 15

"You're something else, Gifford," the guard had said when he took Travis's lunch tray away. "Even in this dump, you get attention from the ladies." Travis had heard the guards commenting on the visit from Isabella and Maggie. He found what they said distasteful, disrespectful, but you've got to go along to get along in this miserable place. "Yeah," he retorted, "but it's all talk and no action." He amused himself by imagining Maggie and Isabella and their lives on the outside. He thought Isabella was single, somehow. She wouldn't tell him, but he just got that vibe from her. And Maggie, very married. But then, what did that really mean? He thought about a photo he'd seen once of his mother and father on their wedding day. None of that white gown charade for Ivory. She was in a hippie-dippie flowered miniskirt, standing in front of the Amherst City Hall, and his dad had his arm around her. Dad, thought Travis. Damn sentimental name for somebody who wasn't much more than a sperm donor. At least they got married. Maybe if Grace's parents had been married…he censored himself. Thinking about Grace's childhood made him feel sick. But she had entrusted him with her stories, so he was honor-bound—not to speak, but to remember. And what did he know about raising kids or marriage anyway? At least there was no chance Ivory would ever marry that bullshit artist Gus, and give him an even bigger loser as a stepfather. His mom and Gus. What a crime.

CHAPTER 16

Okay," said Calvin. "This is my idea of heaven. One guy with a really long lens and three hot babes, out on the town. Hoyt, nice of you to come along to pick up the check. I know it's just part of the Southern gentlemen reparations for all that oppressive slavery stuff your folks perpetrated on my folks."

Calvin, Andrea, Hoyt, Linda, and I were perched on barstools at the champagne bar at Neiman-Marcus. As part of the *Small Town* story on Death of a Socialite, Calvin and Linda were planning a shoot of Grace's haunts around the city.

"You are a wonder, Mr. Bright," said Hoyt. "You manage to insult these lovely ladies and me in the same breath."

"You're insulted to be called a fine Southern gentleman?" asked Calvin, while he signaled the bartender for another round.

"As the great-great-grandson of a sharecropper, indeed I am," countered Hoyt.

Linda and Andrea were ignoring the exchange, flipping through pages of notes and oversize computer printouts of a rough layout.

"Okay," said Linda. "Let's go over the shot list and see what we've got—and what we're missing."

She distributed a summary of photo locations to all of us and shuffled a set of digital printouts like a deck of cards. "I've got digital scouting shots of all potential locations from one of the photo interns, so we can see what's worth pursuing and how Mr.

Long Lens here is going to shoot these places."

She placed two photos on the bar, slightly overlapping. The first, a small, wood-frame house with a tidy front garden; the second, a Moorish-styled, generously proportioned house with arched windows facing the street and a courtyard fountain in the front.

"Grace's grandparents' house in Oakland," said Linda. "The place she was raised. And, the house where she and Frederick lived in St. Francis Woods."

"Upward mobility. Just one short trip across the bay and marrying a few million bucks got her there," I said.

Linda quickly shuffled a handful of other photos onto the bar, capturing Grace's piece of social San Francisco: first, a head-on shot of the white-tented entrance to the Black & White Ball, the City's signature charity event; the second, the front door to the Crimson Club.

"The older ladies-who-lunch are trying to give a more contemporary feel to the big social events," said Andrea. "Grace was well-liked, fearless about fundraising, and involved lots of Frederick's venture capital colleagues and their wives in bringing some younger energy to the event, and in contrast…" she pointed to the Crimson Club front door.

"And we all know about the Crimson," said Linda. "Though my guess is some of us here at the bar know more than others."

"Hoyt, you devil," said Calvin.

Hoyt looked uncomfortable. "The appeal of those places eludes me, I'm afraid."

"I know what you mean," said Calvin. "Gorgeous women, no inhibitions, really good call brands at the bar, no-tell policies, really, what's to like?"

Linda glanced at her watch, "Gang, I've got to get home to my boring little underage darlings soon and get dinner on the table."

"Oh, man," said Calvin. "I can just picture an art-directed dinner at your house. One perfect piece of sushi on a white plate."

"Put a plug in it," said Linda. "It's mac-and-cheese on

Fiestaware. If I'm lucky, I'll sneak a couple of carrots or tangerines by them, too. They'll eat anything orange."

She quickly spread four more shots in front of us. "Ocean View Day Spa, the place that kept Grace beautiful; San Francisco Botanical Gardens, where she worked as a volunteer; St. Francis Yacht Club, where she and Frederick kept their sailboat; and, here's the wild card," she finished, tapping a finger on a nondescript row house, with a tricycle and two collapsed strollers on the front porch. "A Mom's Place. It's like a halfway house for single mothers."

"The plot thickens," said Calvin. "Maybe Grace had some little bastard somewhere along the way and left it in a basket on the front door of the joint."

"It's not an orphanage," said Andrea. "And according to Grace's medical records, she'd never been pregnant. Grace worked at A Mom's Place as a volunteer. It's a residential program for single moms in recovery and their kids. Anywhere from four to six moms and their children live there at any one time. Grace designed and put in a vegetable garden in the backyard. They've kept it going, and according to the intern who scouted, it's quite wonderful. The director says that one of the moms who Grace got really involved in the garden still comes over to tend it, even though she's got a job, husband, another child, the whole shebang. And, the director also says the garden is so productive, it makes a significant contribution to their weekly food budget."

"It might be interesting to talk with the mom who's still involved," I said.

Andrea gave me an exasperated look. "Gee, Maggie, that never would have occurred to me."

"Sorry," I said, meekly.

Linda moved the photos around on the bar, rearranging them into groups of two and three, "I've got to run," she said. "I'm giving Calvin a final shot list next week, so you guys need to think about anything else we want to add. And, I'm assuming Andrea will go with Calvin on most of the shoots, but Maggie, since you're taking such an interest in this piece, maybe you'd like to tag along on a couple of them."

"I don't want to intrude," I began, until everyone but Hoyt burst into laughter.

Hoyt held up his hand. "Ladies and gentleman, a schedule check, if y'all don't mind. I've got this story on the docket for the July issue. That means lockdown in late May—art and copy. Does that work?"

Calvin said, "Works for me." Everyone else nodded around the table.

"We're short on evergreens, Andrea," Hoyt pointed out. Evergreens are magazine safety nets, backup stories that aren't time-sensitive that can be dropped in at the last minute in case a story blows up, a writer flakes on deadline, or worst of all, the magazine's lawyers start to back-pedal.

"Shouldn't be a problem, Hoyt. Unless…" she hesitated.

"Unless?"

"Unless the unassigned writer who's riding shotgun on this piece throws me a curve." All eyes on me.

I shook my head. "It's your story, Andrea," I said. "That's the only way this works."

Linda gathered the layouts and started packing up her briefcase. "Calvin, you cool on the look of these shots? I really want that moody, black-and-white noir feel to the whole thing."

"Got it," he said. "You'll think Lana Turner has come back to life in these shots."

CHAPTER 17

A week later, Andrea and I were standing in the family room of A Mom's Place. At least it looked like a family room. Two beat-up couches, a wall of built-in shelves overflowing with games, puzzles, and open bins of Legos. A kid-scale table and colorful chairs were tucked in the corner. A girl who looked no more than fifteen had answered the door, with a baby in a shoulder-tied sling on her hip and a toddler clinging to her jeans. We'd asked for Purity Meadows, the director, and the child-mom and her entourage disappeared to get her.

Now Purity stood before us, five-feet-nothing, probably 105 pounds dripping wet, but ten of those pounds had to be breasts. First Krissy, now Purity. Lawyers, do-gooders, apparently everyone had boobs but me. Purity's were encased in a snug T-shirt that read, "Bountiful Baskets." The type was picked out in rhinestones. It was hard not to stare, or giggle. But with superhuman effort, I managed to keep my eyes firmly placed north of Purity's chest. Watching Andrea, decked out in her usual New England prep gear—black cashmere twinset, gray linen trousers—shake hands with Purity was like observing visitors from different planets, maybe even different solar systems, have a close encounter.

"Welcome to A Mom's Place," said Purity formally, shaking hands with me.

"I apologize for being a few minutes later than we said we'd be," I said.

"No need for apologies," said Purity. "Everything happens in Jesus's own time." An unbidden image of the classical image of Jesus—shoulder-length gold curls, blue eyes, white robes, updated with a digital watch—floated into my brain.

"Your photographer friend is already here," said Purity, gesturing in back of her. "He's outside taking pictures of the backyard garden. It's still pretty early for the vegetables to be doing much, but we've got snow peas and lettuces up." She shook her head, "Calvin, that's his name? He said something funny."

"Did he?" Andrea and I asked together, exchanging a glance. The thought of Calvin's reaction to all that bust packed into the rhinestone-labeled T-shirt sent off warning bells for both of us.

"He's always making jokes," I said hastily. "I hope he didn't offend you."

Tiny lines appeared between her eyebrows. "Offend me? He wasn't joking; he just told me he was taking black-and-white pictures. Isn't that an odd way to photograph a garden? Nothing much is going to show up."

"Oh, our art director has a photojournalistic vision for this story," I explained. It didn't seem like the right time to go into a lot of detail about noir films and an homage to Lana Turner. Although, as a fellow "sweater girl," they might have seen eye to eye, or at least nipple to nipple.

"Well, we're happy for the publicity," said Purity. "The more people know about what we do here, the better. And I'm so pleased to do something that will honor Grace Plummer. We called her Amazing Gracie; she did so much for our girls."

I remembered the last time I'd heard that sobriquet applied to Grace: Travis had told me that the people at the Crimson Club had called Grace Plummer by that same name.

"I've made fresh coffee," said Purity. "Why don't we sit down and talk in the kitchen? Unless you need to supervise what your photographer is doing?"

"You two get started," I suggested. "I'll just go say hello to Calvin out in the backyard, and catch up with you in a few minutes."

I slid open the glass door from the family room, and descended two stone steps into the backyard. It was an ordinary, Mission District, pocket-size backyard, but every available inch was under cultivation. Four diamond-shaped raised beds occupied the flattest part of the yard, divided by neatly raked gravel paths. Calvin was kneeling in front of one raised bed holding a light meter near a row of staked snow peas. Even from a distance, I could see the slender peapods with their curly hats, dangling off the stalks. The outside borders of the yard were edged with low rock-wall borders, planted with purple, pink, and white sage. Low lavenders and white verbenas spilled artfully over the rocks. A sturdy picnic table with benches, and a scattering of brightly painted Adirondack chairs were tucked into the few empty corners. The effect was an artful combination of French *potager* and unpretentious mountain vacation home.

"Calvin," I called. "How's it looking?"

He unfolded himself, brushed gravel off his knees. "Good. A little wholesome, though."

"What do you mean?"

"It's a vegetable garden, Mags. Hard to make that look very noir."

"Oh, you'll manage," I said.

"Do I get to put Ms. Overflowing Baskets in one of the shots?" he asked.

I looked over my shoulder. "Calvin, for heaven's sake. That's exactly what I came outside to talk to you about."

Calvin looked delighted and unchastened. "Come on, Maggie. Is she an irony-free chick or what? Absolutely no self-awareness. Just too tempting to poke a little fun." I must have looked alarmed. "Don't worry, I won't misbehave in front of anyone. Did she tell you where she got the T-shirt?"

"That topic has not yet come up in conversation," I said. "I'm too busy trying not to react to the Jesus talk."

"Too bad. I admired it and she was just happy, happy, happy to tell me that it's the name of a food-gleaning operation. The volunteers go to growers and restaurants and collect extra, usable food and A Mom's Place is one of the beneficiaries. Anyway, she's such a fan of the operation that the girls who live here had the T-shirt made for her with the name spelled out in rhinestones."

"That's a relief," I said. "I couldn't quite see a food-gleaning operation issuing rhinestone cowgirl, double entendre T-shirts."

Calvin reached over and pecked me on the check. "Come on, Mags, lighten up. This whole story is weirding you out."

"It is weird," I said. "And it just seems to get stranger and a little more puzzling at every turn. How could somebody hang out here and at the Crimson Club—and have the same nickname at both locations?"

"Amazing Gracie?" asked Calvin. "That's what they called her at the Crimson Club, too, huh? Ms. Big Baskets already told me that's what they called her here."

He gestured around the yard. "It is amazing what she accomplished here. Purity showed me the 'before' pictures of the yard—lots of dirt and weeds and a couple of broken-down metal porch chairs."

"It is beautiful," I agreed. "And productive. So, what's your thought on the photos?"

"I don't know, I'm going to do some medium shots and get the whole place, and then I thought I'd try some tight shots. Maybe compose something." He pointed to a canvas bag on the ground. "Purity got that out of the garage for me. It's still got Grace's gardening gloves and trowel in it, and one of those aprons with pockets you put stuff in—seeds, I guess, plus those goofy gardener shoes."

"Clogs?"

"Yeah, I guess that's what you call 'em. You know, they look like what Hans Brinker would have worn when he took off the silver skates. Anyway, I think I'll do a still-life close-up—you know, dead broad's garden paraphernalia in the shadow of the baby peapods."

"Sounds good. I'm going to look around a bit, and then go talk to Purity."

"Hey, Maggie," called Calvin, as I began walking around the perimeter of the yard. "See if the girls in the house can get one of those T-shirts for you."

"Calvin," I hissed. "Just shut up and shoot."

"Oh, I'm sorry," he added, sighting through the viewfinder, "I guess your baskets aren't so bountiful, huh?"

I wandered around the yard, admiring the elegance with which Grace had designed the space, giving the people who lived there—the ones she knew, and the ones yet to come—a place of both beauty and function.

"It's our own little Garden of Eden," said a voice near my shoulder. I jumped a bit, and looked down to see Purity, two mugs of coffee in hand, looking out over the yard. She handed me a mug.

"Grace designed this, right?" I asked.

"Designed, organized the volunteers to build the raised beds, paid for the rock edging, and got everyone in the house to help her with the planting. We even had a meeting to discuss what vegetables we wanted in the garden." She sighed. "She was a gift from God, taken from us too soon."

I took a sip of coffee, so I didn't have to respond. Being around big-C Christians always makes me nervous. I'm just waiting for them to start trying to convert me or introduce the notion that most of the things I believe in—from a woman's right to choose to drinking really good Merlot with dinner—are at the least indulgences and probably full-fledged sins. But, it was hard to be very annoyed at Purity, given how she was spending every day of her life.

"How'd you get involved in this place?" I asked. "And how'd Grace get involved?"

"I started A Mom's Place," said Purity. "I came out of seminary on the East Coast and my first assignment in the Bay Area was at a short-term shelter for runaway kids in the Tenderloin. After a while I realized that preaching at them was kinda counterproductive. These kids needed socks and something to eat, and a reason to try to stay clean. Plus, we kept getting these young moms in there. I mean really young."

"Like the girl who answered the door?" I asked.

"That young and younger. And even though they were really screwed-up and hungry, and most of them had been turning tricks, they loved their kids. And they wanted to keep Child Protective Services from taking the children away. Turns out, no matter how wrecked these girls were, they love their kids, in their own broken-down, self-destructive way."

I thought about how most of my mom-pals spent much of every day obsessing about filmmaking camp or tennis clinics for their kids, and snapped at their husbands when they forgot and cut Little Madison's sandwich into rectangles, after having been issued strict instructions to cut it on the diagonal. I thought about my own willingness to carefully bite the nuts out of Josh's chocolate chip cookie at a birthday party, because he loved the cookie, hated the nuts. Now, when I mentioned that story, he'd sigh audibly and say, "Is this about me being a picky eater or about you being a great mom, little buddy?"

"Yeah, I know what you mean," I said. "Moms are like that."

"Anyway, the seminary trustees back home sent me some money to start this place, because I knew if I could get the moms on their own, away from people who weren't nearly as motivated to clean up their act, everybody would do better—the moms, the kids, everybody."

"And here we are," I said.

"Day to day, here we are," she said. "Every morning I worry about how we're going to pay for groceries, but God always provides. That's how Grace got to us, I know."

"How?"

"God sent her."

"Okay, I get that part," I said, a little impatiently. "But did God actually deliver her to your front porch, in a reed basket or something?"

Purity smiled, for the first time. "Almost."

I waited. She gestured at her T-shirt. I tried to keep my eyes on her face, and not on what the T-shirt packaged. "Bountiful Baskets, the food-gleaners, used to pick up food from those gardens out in Golden Gate Park."

"San Francisco Botanical Gardens?"

"That's the place. Mostly I think they grow ornamental stuff, but they've got fruit trees and nut trees, and the extra goes to places like us, and St. Anthony's Kitchen. Anyway, one day, Grace dropped off a couple baskets. I guess it was on her way home, and the Bountiful Baskets truck hadn't arrived, and she didn't want the fruit to go to waste."

"So she just knocked on the door?"

"Yes. And at first, I thought she was a new volunteer for Bountiful Baskets. She was coming from her work at the Gardens, so she had on jeans with muddy knees, and a big smear of dirt on her cheek and a beat-up baseball cap. Minnesota Twins. That was five years ago, the Friday before Labor Day. She had two big baskets, one of lemons and limes, and one of almonds in the shell."

I thought about Travis's story about Grace at the Crimson Club, and thought: not only does God move in mysterious ways, but she sends her angels out to far-flung neighborhoods, too. Maybe I should rethink my knee-jerk negative reaction to big-C Christians.

"Okay, so she dropped off the baskets," I persisted.

"I took the baskets, and asked her if she wanted to come in. She apologized for how she looked, and I told her she looked just like the rest of us." She took a deep breath.

"Can we sit down for a minute?" I asked. "Where's Andrea, by the way?"

"I asked one of our moms to show her around the house. Let's sit over there." Purity led me to a bench under an apple tree, white with blossoms.

As we sat down, a breeze shook the branches and a little shower of pink and white blossoms rode the spring air down to our bench. Out of a window above our heads, I heard a woman singing, a sweet soprano. I strained to hear the words, "Over my head/I hear music in the air/there must be a God somewhere." Calvin turned at the sound of the music, and pointed his camera at the upper window.

I felt my antireligious guard start some serious dissolving. "This place is magical," I said.

Purity smiled. "It is, isn't it? That first time Grace came in, she caught sight of the backyard and said, 'We need a little Eden out here.' So that's what she created."

"What did you think about her getting involved?"

Purity looked puzzled. "What did I think? I was grateful. I didn't know anything about her, except that she had an idea what she wanted to do in the backyard and it made a lot of sense. I'd grown up with a big vegetable garden in Kansas and knew you can feed a lot of people out of not much ground. But I never had the time or the money or help to put it in. Grace made all that happen."

"Did you know who she was?"

"You mean, did I know she was a rich society lady?" asked Purity, and continued without waiting for me to answer. "Not the first day I met her, and not for a long time afterward. But I figured out she had money pretty early on. Every time we needed something for the garden, she'd bring it. And she organized a lot of volunteers from the San Francisco Botanical Gardens to come help us. It's not like I spent my day reading the society pages, but one of the moms who was here at the time read everything in the paper, front to back, and one day she gave this little yell and said, 'Hey, there's Amazing Grace. In a really, really fancy dress.' All the other girls who were home came to look. And there was Grace, not in jeans, like we saw her here, working outside, but in this glittery, strapless dress. And the mayor had his arm around her."

"Did that make you treat her differently?"

Purity shrugged. "It didn't matter to me, I don't take the Bible so literally that I think angels have to dress in wings and robes all the time. If God wanted to send us an angel in an evening gown or in muddy jeans, smelling of chicken manure, what did I care?

By then, Grace had the backyard in pretty good shape, and she'd brought us a brand-new barbecue, and we were having cookouts. One of our moms said, 'Just like we're a real family on television.'"

I breathed in the fragrance from the apple tree and watched Calvin wandering around in the late afternoon light, shooting the yard. Somehow the idea of making this little piece of paradise look "noir" seemed vaguely disrespectful. Irreverent. Ungodly. I shook myself. A few more visits here, and this little Jew would be confessing Jesus Christ as her personal savior.

I turned back to Purity. "So how much did you get to know about the rest of Grace's life?"

"Not much. Every once in a while, she'd stop by to drop something off, not to work in the yard, and she'd be dressed up. I think she felt self-conscious about coming here looking like that. But the girls loved seeing her. Plus, one of our moms was finishing regular high school. She was a really good student, and very pretty, and this very nice college boy who was tutoring at the high school invited her to his fraternity formal dance, and she was so excited. But, of course, we couldn't afford to buy her a fancy dress. So, Grace brought a whole bunch of beautiful dresses over here, from her closet, and probably from some of her friends. And the girls all had a fashion show, and helped Carol Ann, that was the mom with the date, pick out a dress to wear. Plus, it was Carol Ann who had found her in the society pages, and she started a scrapbook of Grace all dressed up at her parties. She'd scour the paper, and clip everything she saw that had Grace's name or photo in it."

"Did Grace know?"

Purity shook her head. "I don't think so. Carol Ann was a little shy about how closely she followed Grace's life."

"Where's Carol Ann now?"

Purity sat up a little straighter. "She's one of our miracles. You know, she married that boy who invited her to the fraternity dance. He adopted her daughter, and now they both work, and she's finishing college, and he's in law school. They had another little girl, not long after Grace died. Actually, Grace helped her get her job. She started out as a manicurist at this fancy spa, Ocean View, and now she's the assistant manager. She's really busy, with the job and college and two kids and all, but she stops by here sometimes and works in Grace's Garden. That's what we call it." She shook her head. "Carol Ann was so upset after Grace was killed, I thought we were going to lose her."

"Lose her? Meaning..."

"She'd go back on the street, start using."

"But she didn't?"

"No, I think Grace gave her a vision of herself. She took her to get a manicure the day of the fraternity house formal, and stayed around to help her get dressed and meet her date. I can still see Grace, holding Carol Ann's daughter, Jenny, in her arms, waving goodbye from our front window. Every time Carol Ann comes over, and she's tired from juggling school and Jenny, and now, her younger daughter and work, I remind her that Grace is watching her."

Not one irreverent smart-mouthed comment floated through my brain. I just sat there with Purity and watched the apple blossoms drift through the spring air. The voice floating out from the upstairs window had moved from gospel music to the itsy-bitsy spider, and I could hear a child's voice giggling at the end of each line.

"Who's that singing?"

"One of our moms. Doesn't it sound pretty?"

"Angelic," I said. And meant it.

CHAPTER 18

Sunday evening, kids in bed, Anya out with the latest in a string of yet another so-so romantic choices, Michael and I comparing iPhones.

"Monday night, nothing, Tuesday night, Dr. Mephisto for both of us, Wednesday night is the soccer dinner for Josh's team, Thursday night, nothing." I sat back. "Those are my hot dates, what about yours?"

"Monday night, partners' dinner, no spouses this time."

"Thank you, Jesus," I said.

"I'm not sure Jesus arranged that for you," said Michael.

"You never know," I said, thinking of Grace's Garden. "I think I know where he hangs out these days."

Michael continued, "Tuesday and Wednesday nights, same as you. Thursday, though, we've both got something."

"Really, what? I was looking forward to dinner at home that night."

"Haven't you been trying to get to Frederick Plummer, the grieving widower, for a real conversation?"

"I have. Gertie's been working on his assistant to schedule an appointment for us to meet, but he keeps ducking me. And he was too preoccupied at the Botanical Gardens thing to spend any time with me."

"Perhaps you've forgotten what an amazing, thoughtful, and enterprising husband you're married to," said Michael. "The Give-

Back Venture Fund is honoring Plummer at this event, and guess who's introducing him?"

"Who?"

"Your brilliant husband. The guy who's chief legal counsel to them is out of town, and the managing partner asked for a volunteer to pinch-hit. I raised my hand. Which means that we get to sit at the head table, and I've asked the woman who's coordinating arrangements for the event if you could be Plummer's dinner partner. She said 'no worries,' as long as you were attractive. Apparently Mr. Plummer is pretty picky about his dinner companions. I told her you were one hot babe, at least in my opinion."

"Michael!" I leapt up and draped myself in his lap. "You know, between those students you put to work on my behalf and this little coup, I'm really enjoying having you as a codetective."

Thursday was a packed day at work, so I'd schlepped my lowest-cut, tomato-red evening getup to work to make a quick change there. Andrea perched on the worn-out easy chair in the ladies room and watched me put on fresh makeup.

"Far be it from me to complain," she said, "but precisely why do we have an easy chair in the ladies' room?"

"I think at one point we didn't have just a bunch of dried-up crones like me and unspoiled young things like you working here. There must have been some nursing mother in the mix at some point in time. Do I have too much blush on? I can't tell with this light."

"Look at me," said Andrea.

I turned from the mirror. "Well, I'd say you simply look flushed with good health. But I'd stop now," she said. "On the other hand, you can load on a little more eye shadow. That's all the look." She stood up. "Here give me the eye goo. I'll give it a try."

I stood obediently still, with my eyes closed, while Andrea brushed on something called Mauve Twilight.

"This is kinda fun," I said. "Like getting ready for the prom with a girlfriend."

"Don't talk," said Andrea. "It makes your face move. And I'm hardly the right person to do this. My mother still thinks that only vulgar women wear anything but pale-pink lipstick. There we are. Take a look."

I turned to the mirror and blinked. My green eyes looked smoky and intense, or maybe I'd just read those exact words in the last issue of *Vogue.* Even in the bathroom's unflattering light, I looked pretty damn good. "Cool. Thanks, and as long as you're here, you can help me zip up the side of this slutty sausage casing I'm wearing." I took the dress out from under the plastic, shrugged out of my bra and tossed it over the empty hanger, and wriggled into the dress. Then, I raised my arms and said, "Just pull the zipper very slowly. If you catch my tender skin in this you'll hear a whole lot of screaming."

Andrea held the top of the dress together with one hand and slowly tugged on the zipper. "This is a marvel of engineering," she said.

"It is," I said. "You'll see in a minute, when I'm in place. All that boning and built-in infrastructure gives me the illusion of cleavage. Which is good, because I hear that our Frederick enjoys sitting near sexy-looking broads."

Andrea frowned. "Maggie, don't you worry…" she trailed off.

"Worry what?" I asked, screwing the backs into the small diamond-stud earrings Michael had given me for our tenth anniversary.

Andrea was silent. I caught her eye in the mirror. She looked preoccupied and distracted. "Oh, it's probably nothing," she said. "But nobody knows who did kill Grace, after all. Just be careful."

I stepped into my backless, red brocade heels and began throwing essentials—lipstick, mints, keys—into my evening bag. "I'm careful," I said. "But even if we don't know anything else, we know that Frederick couldn't have killed Grace. Remember he had a rock-solid alibi that night: he was having dinner with some of his venture capital pups, and they vouched for him, as did the entire waitstaff of the restaurant. Plus, Michael will be sitting right nearby, and I hardly think Frederick is going to make an attempt on my life in front of an entire ballroom of people. And he can't exactly follow me to the ladies room. Okay, this is it—as good as it gets. Will I do?"

"You look great," said Andrea. "Very unmatronly."

"Don't you wish Brooks Brothers made strapless tweed evening gowns in red, so you could go right out and buy one?" I said.

Andrea shook her head. "That is neither kind nor accurate, Maggie," she said. "You can sound mean, you know."

"I'm sorry," I said hastily. "I shoot my mouth off without thinking."

She regarded me closely. "Watch yourself, Maggie," she cautioned.

"I will, I will," I said, gathering my cast-off work clothes and tossing them in a handled shopping bag.

"By the way, O Mighty Detective, exactly what do we want to find out from Frederick this evening?" Andrea asked.

"I don't know exactly," I confessed. "But lots of things could be interesting to get his perspective on—like, why did he think Grace got so involved at A Mom's Place? Did he know about Grace and Travis? Why did they first start going to the Crimson Club, and whose idea was it to keep going—his or Grace's? And I'm just wondering if he's absolutely sure Travis killed her? And just how close is he to Ginger Brand?"

"And you'll be uncovering all this information before dessert?"

"I'll be lucky if I discover anything at all," I said. "But at least I'll get a chance to talk to him. And see what he's all about."

"Have fun tonight," said Andrea. "You do look like a million bucks, cleavage and all."

"Or, as your peeps would say, like a very well-endowed trust fund."

"My 'people' would never say anything remotely like that," Andrea called as I headed out the door. "And they only know 'peeps' as those disgusting little yellow things you eat at Easter."

Michael was already chatting up folks near the bar when I arrived at the St. Francis Hotel. In the old days, before the hotel's face-lift and the upscale Michael Mina restaurant moved into the lobby, like generations of San Franciscans before us, we'd rendezvoused "under the clock." The grand clock had been the traditional place shipping-out soldiers and sailors had promised to meet their sweethearts when they returned from war. My own grandparents had kissed goodbye under that clock. But, alas, in the hotel's sleek new remodel, the clock had been banished to an upstairs corner, far from the lobby.

I waved to Michael and made my way through the buzzing, black-tied crowd to his side. It was still a thrill to see his eyes widen. I leaned in for the perfunctory spousal kiss greeting, and he whispered in my ear, "Who are you? And what have you done with that soccer mom I'm married to?"

"She sent me tonight," I whispered back. "And maybe you'll get lucky, and I'll go home with you."

Michael let go, and turned me to meet the couple he'd been talking with. "Maggie, this is…"

"Hello, Ginger," I said. "Maggie Fiori, we met at the Botanical Gardens the other day."

Ginger took my outstretched hand and looked momentarily puzzled. "Oh, yes, the magazine editor. I remember your hat."

"Better than not being remembered at all," I said cheerily. I turned to the man she was with, "Hi, Maggie Fiori. Good to meet you."

The man looked like a whippet, sleek, thin beyond belief, with slicked-back graying hair. "Bill Brand," he said. "A pleasure."

"Bill and Ginger are friends of Frederick Plummer's," Michael explained.

"Yes," I said. "I had the opportunity to meet Ginger with Mr. Plummer the other day."

For the tiniest second, I saw Bill shoot a quizzical look at Ginger.

She put her hand on his arm, "You remember, Billy, I told you

Frederick and I were on the program to dedicate the fountain in Grace's memory at the San Francisco Botanical Gardens."

"Of course," he said, and took a slug of his champagne. I watched him carefully, certain I'd be able to watch the progress of liquid go down his reedy throat.

Ginger began surveying the room, looking for more interesting—or more important—people. "Billy," she said, "I really need to go say 'hey' to some people. Will you come with me?"

"Your wish is my command, my pet," he said, with absolutely no affect. It was impossible to tell if that was a send-up of a Stepford husband or completely straightforward.

He nodded to Michael, and touched his hand to his forehead in a mock salute to me. "Mrs. Fiori, an honor. I'll look forward to talking with you again."

Michael and I watched them walk off, her hand slipped in his, halfway across the room.

"I think we just got dumped for more important people, *cara*," said Michael.

"Or they both just wanted to get away from us," I said.

"From you, maybe," said Michael. "Who could possibly want to escape the pleasure of my company?"

"Who, indeed?"

"So, how was your day? Did you talk to the boys?"

"Day was fine. Talked to the boys, haven't seen them. Zach squealed on Josh, that he's allegedly texting Esme and writing on her Facebook wall when he's supposed to be doing his homework. Isn't he a little young? Isn't he still supposed to hate girls?"

"I don't ever remember going through that phase," said Michael. "He's just a chip off the old block. Precocious in matters of the great feminine mystique. You just don't like being replaced as the most important woman in his life."

"I will never be replaced," I said. "I'm studying your mother's every controlling, clingy move."

I continued with the litany of the day. "Anyway, Anya was on pickup and dinner duty. I just changed into this getup in the ladies room at the office."

"And a fine getup it is," said Michael. "How come you never look like this for dinner at home?"

"I do," I said. "You just never notice, right down to the backless 'fuck-me' shoes."

I placed a hand lightly on Michael's shoulder, and lifted my foot to dangle the shoe off my toe for his admiration.

"I can't wait 'til you explain to the boys why that's what you call those kind of shoes," said Michael.

"Don't hold your breath. You're the dad, you've got to have those father-to-son talks with them."

"I love how you throw off those feminist principles and turn traditional every time something awkward or difficult comes up."

"Me, too," I said. "Okay, brief me on this shindig a little more. So I can make small talk with Mr. Philanthropist at the head table."

"There's a program at your seat," said Michael. "But here's the executive summary. The Give-Back Venture Fund was established about twenty years ago, when the dot-com heyday was in early sizzle. And it was Plummer's idea—the deal was that every time one of the start-ups that a venture capital outfit had funded went public, the venture firm would put a portion of their IPO money into a charitable fund. It was a no-risk way of deflecting some of the negative press about the obscene profits these firms were realizing. They'd look like good guys after an IPO made them even richer, and they'd shelter some of the profits at the same time. Anyway, Plummer cooked up the idea, and rounded up half a dozen other VC funds to join him as charter members. And it just grew from there. Today, there's virtually no local VC firm that doesn't participate in the fund. And we are, very happily, their legal counsel."

"So, what's tonight about?"

"Big milestone. The fund hit $100 million this year. Plummer isn't as involved any more. There's a small staff that runs the administrative side of the fund, accepts applications, and makes grants from the endowment. Lots of Frederick's buddies made extra, personal gifts to the fund in Grace's memory over the past few years, so the slow-down in IPOs hasn't really hurt the growth of the corpus."

I shuddered. "Cold?" asked Michael.

"No. There's something creepy in hearing the word corpus associated with money, when there's an actual corpse involved."

"Maggie, corpus means the 'body' of the fund, as opposed to the growth it generates."

"I know what it means. I'm just saying it sounds a little peculiar in this context." I sipped my champagne and looked around the room. "So, these folks are all rich, rich, rich from VC money?"

"More or less."

"I always feel like an imposter at these things," I said. "I'm not rich or social."

"No, but you look the part," said Michael. "You and I are nothing but staff to these folks. I keep them out of trouble and you cover their world."

I laughed. "We don't live in the big house."

"Pardon?"

"Oh, a fundraiser friend of mine always says that. When you hang out with rich people—like she does, because she's always raising money for one cause or another—you start to know these folks, and they know you. But she says it's always good to remember that we don't live in the 'big house.' We're just glorified servants."

"My point exactly," said Michael. "Now go mingle with the big house types; I've got to check in with the event chair and see when my five minutes of fame come up and I'm at the podium to introduce your pal, Frederick."

Half an hour of drifting in and out of conversations followed. I did know a fair number of people—from Michael's firm, from various organizations we'd covered one way or another in *Small Town,* even a college chum or two who'd either married well or was in a mover-and-shaker job.

Just when I was wondering how much longer I could teeter around on the red heels, a beautiful Asian woman in a lime-green *cheongsam* tapped on the mike. She was one of the apparently limitless supply of ethnically diverse, well-dressed, well-spoken news anchors who showed up to emcee every charity event in town.

"Ladies and gentlemen, please take your seats," she called with a polished voice-over authority.

"I'm Pearl Soo, and it's my pleasure to welcome you this evening. Please enjoy your dinner and the opportunity to visit with your friends. We'll be starting our program to honor one of our own, sometime between the organically grown lamb and the flourless chocolate cake."

Michael and I made our way to the head table, and found our place cards. True to his word, I was seated next to Frederick Plummer. He was standing by his chair, and Ginger Brand was at his side. He had inclined his head downward; she was on tiptoes, apparently whispering in his ear. They moved apart as Michael and I approached. Ginger gave us both a pasted-on smile and disappeared.

"Mrs. Fiori," said Plummer, "I'm delighted to see we're dinner partners."

He didn't look delighted, but I was willing to take him at his word. He held the chair for me, and Michael beat a retreat to the other side of the podium, where the rest of the head table waited.

A carefully composed salad, the kind Julia Child used to say made her think someone had had their fingers all over her food, waited in front of each place. Splayed Belgian endive, a tiny heap of exotic mushrooms, a puddle of what appeared to be hothouse raspberries, and a nut-crusted, baked goat cheese.

"No iceberg here," I observed.

"Mmmm," said Plummer, noncommittally. Though the din of people talking, forks gently raking on china, and glasses clinking continued to rise around us, the table suddenly felt very quiet. The man on the other side of me, another lawyer from Michael's office, was deep in discussion with the glamorous Pearl Soo. There was nothing but a podium on Plummer's other side, so for better or worse, the guy was stuck talking to me.

"This is such a remarkable milestone," I offered. "The fund you started, hitting $100 million. You must feel a great sense of accomplishment."

"Many people were involved," said Plummer. "This is hardly a one-man show."

"Still," I persisted. "I know you started the fund. And," I said, nibbling on one of the unidentifiable mushrooms, "it must be so meaningful to you that so many people have added to the fund in your late wife's name."

Plummer put his fork down. He put a pleasant smile on his face and leaned close to me. "Mrs. Fiori, why don't you put your cards on the table? I know that your assistant has been trying to get an appointment for you to see me. And, in all candor, I find it disingenuous of you to suggest that this evening's seating is a coincidence."

"Okay," I said, putting on my oh-so-gracious smile from the head table, right back at him. "You're right. I have been trying to see you. We're doing a story on your wife's life and death in *Small Town,* and I wanted a chance to talk with you."

"I have no obligation to talk with you about some sleazy, tabloid piece you're trumping up."

"I'm sorry," I said. "I'm sure all of this must be painful to you. But the reality is, your wife's murder was big news in our small town. And, since you've been candid with me, I'm going to be candid with you."

He looked stony, picked up his wineglass, and took a long drink of Merlot. I glanced out at the audience and saw a couple at the table just below the dais giving us curious looks. Probably didn't understand how head-table small talk could evince such intense reactions. I fixed the nosy pair with my best, noncommittal "caught you looking" smile.

Frederick broke his silence. "Imagine how much I'm looking forward to your candor," he said.

"We started working on this story because we were interested in the fate of Travis Gifford, the man who..."

"Murdered my wife. Brutally."

"The man who was convicted of murdering your wife," I continued. "There's a contingent of people..."

"Hysterical, besotted women criminal attorneys who have misguidedly fallen for Gifford's charms," he interrupted.

"A contingent of people," I persisted, raising my voice just a bit, "who believe that the actual murderer is still at large. Still not brought to justice." Now, I saw that Pearl Soo and her dinner companion were giving us curious, sideways glances.

"I find that nearly impossible to believe," he said.

"As I started to say," I pressed on, "I'll confess to you, I was persuaded to look into the story because there are people who believe, deeply believe, that Travis Gifford is innocent."

"But you've changed your mind?" he asked.

I picked up my wineglass. "I haven't made up my mind about Gifford, one way or another," I said. "Frankly, I'm not sure what I think about him anymore. But I became very interested in your wife's life, as well as her death."

He shook his head. "Death of a shallow, beautiful socialite? Is that where you're going with this?"

I was startled. How did he know what we were planning to call the story—minus the shallow, of course.

"Not exactly. I admit that's where we started. But the more I learn about Grace, the more I admire her—and the more puzzled I feel."

"What do you mean?"

I took a deep breath. Now or never. "She seemed paradoxical," I said. I held up one hand, and began to tick off what we'd learned. "A beautiful woman, who marries very well indeed, and becomes a beautiful, *wealthy* woman." One finger goes down. "To use your own word, yes, a socialite, one who seems to revel in the spotlight—the photographers captured your wife at every high-profile event, in every beautiful evening gown, all over town." Another finger goes down. "But then..." I hesitated.

"You're counting on your fingers," said Plummer. "Go on."

"Okay. Then, there are all the pieces that don't fit together."

"Such as?"

"Her involvement at the Botanical Gardens. She didn't just show up for parties, she got dirty—in the nursery, out in the beds." Another finger down. "Then, there's her involvement at A Mom's Place."

"What about it?"

"I don't know. Why don't you tell me? You don't think it was an odd place for Grace to get involved?"

"Because it wasn't 'social'?" asked Plummer, his voice tired and bitter. "You think that Grace was only interested in the kinds of things that get you in the *Nob Hill Gazette* or the "Swells" page in the *Chronicle*." He shook his head. "I wish you'd known her. You wouldn't make such...such blind and narrow assumptions." Glancing to my left, I realized that the lawyer and Pearl Soo had fallen completely silent. They were both eavesdropping with frank interest. I cheated to my right a little more, effectively giving them a fine view of my not-so-covered back, and giving Plummer and me a little privacy.

"Okay," I said softly, "I didn't know her. Why don't you tell me what you wish I knew?"

Plummer sank back into his chair. "I don't even know how to start. Grace was so full of life, so full of ideas and energy. Yes, she had fun with the social scene. She was a beautiful, beautiful woman, and she loved to walk into a room and enjoy the effect she had on people. She loved the cameras, and as you could see in every photo, the cameras loved her right back," he said. "But most of all, she loved to work."

"To work?" I asked, puzzled. "At what?"

"At whatever she picked up," he said. "She came home in filthy jeans with broken nails from the gardens. She used to scrub the bathtubs at A Mom's Place—for fun. She had the sensibility of that Norwegian grandmother of hers. No matter what was bothering her, she would cheer up if she could make something clean. I don't think I ever saw her with a sponge or cleanser at home, but that's what she'd do at A Mom's Place." He sighed. "It made her happy to make things clean and beautiful."

"And why was she drawn to those girls?"

He shrugged. "Who knows?"

"Really?" I pressed. "You didn't ever talk about it?"

"If you'd known Grace, you'd understand. She did what she wanted to do. And you didn't want to get in her way."

"So, did you disagree about her involvement in A Mom's Place?" I asked.

"There would have been no point," he said. "And if you're hinting around, wondering if Grace had been, at some time in her life, an unwed mother or a junkie, the answer is no. Now, how about if I ask you some questions?"

I smiled my sweetest. "Seems only fair."

"Why are you doing this story? Grace is..." He picked up his wineglass and took a healthy sip. "Grace is dead. And Gifford's been tried, found guilty, and sentenced." He waved his hand in the air. "I know, I know, there are appeals pending, but unless there's evidence no one has seen, it seems highly unlikely that Gifford won't pay for what he did."

I put my hand on his. "Forgive me. This must seem very insensitive to you."

He withdrew his hand. "Insensitive, but more than that. Intrusive. And frankly, deeply distasteful."

"Distasteful?"

He shook his head. "You're looking for dirt, I think."

"We're looking for whatever we find," I said.

"I wonder," he said, stabbing a mushroom.

We both fell silent. "Why don't you finish what you started?" asked Plummer. The waiter appeared over our shoulder and whisked the plates away. "You want to ask about going to the Crimson Club. About why Grace got involved with my driver?" I glanced over my shoulder. The eavesdroppers seemed to have given up and re-engaged each other in conversation. A little chemistry seemed to be developing; maybe if they started steaming things up, they'd lose complete interest in our conversation.

"I've read the trial transcripts," I said. "I know what you said in your testimony."

"Of course," said Plummer quietly. "Of course, you and your criminal bar friends would have combed through every dark moment of my life."

"Just out of curiosity," I asked, "were they really all dark moments?"

He looked at me bleakly. "Are you really this insensitive?" he asked. "Or just insane?"

"Look," I said, "here's what I mean. I can't even imagine how awful this must be—losing your wife in that terrible way. But, my impression was—that at least your activities, your involvement at the Crimson Club was something you enjoyed together."

Plummer regarded me curiously. "Mrs. Fiori, how long have you been married?"

I took a sip of wine. It was dark and fruity and almost washed away the vaguely bitter taste in my mouth. "Fifteen years," I said.

"Long enough to know that every relationship has its," he said, making a flat plane in the air and tilting it up and down, "turbulence and rocky landings." The couple at the table just below ours had given up all pretense of non-nosiness, openly watching us.

I nodded to Plummer. "Couldn't agree more."

"Grace and I loved each other, but we were very different people. And I was consumed with my work. Still am. It's exhilarating and frightening and overwhelming, all at once. I know that must sound silly—after all, we're just pushing money and paper around. But it's a fine art, and I'm a very good practitioner of that art."

"I'm sure you are," I said.

"I had a very difficult time relaxing, a very difficult time getting away from what preoccupied me virtually 24/7. And Grace was a woman who liked a certain amount of attention. She's the one who first took me to the Crimson—it was playful and intoxicating, and like my work, it seemed a bit dangerous. But it was something we could enjoy as a couple. And no matter what happened, we always went home together."

"But sometimes...," I faltered.

"Sometimes?"

"Sometimes Grace went alone, or with her friend, Ginger."

He shrugged. "So?"

"That wasn't threatening to your marriage?" I said, asking a question I'd asked myself at 3 in the morning on sleepless nights.

"We didn't have that kind of marriage," said Plummer. "You know how there are things inside a relationship that only those two people know? Grace and I didn't have what people like you and your husband have—kids, soccer games, getting costumes together for Halloween." He raised an eyebrow at me. "See? Your life is as strange to me as mine must seem to you."

"So, instead of trick or treat, you had...the Crimson Club?" I persisted.

"In a way. For us, it was harmless, silly, amusing, and something we shared."

The waiter was back, putting an overdressed, highly-decorated plate of baby lamb chops on the requisite bed of sustainably grown wild rice in front of each of us.

"Two last questions," I ventured.

He sighed. "Perhaps."

"First, this seems very silly, but I keep thinking about it. Someone told me that Grace used to sing the 'clouds in my coffee' line to you from the old Carly Simon song, "You're So Vain.""

He stared at me. "Why on earth could that possibly matter to you?"

"It just seemed puzzling, like it was some kind of inside joke."

He shook his head. "It wasn't about either one of us being vain," he said. "It was something Grace would say whenever I asked her about her childhood. She'd say, 'Oh, that's just clouds in my coffee.' And if I pressed her, she'd laugh and just sing the line to me." He fell silent for a moment. I didn't know any more than when I asked the question.

He threw his napkin on the table and crossed his arms. "Okay,

Mrs. Fiori. Last question."

"I was just wondering why you decided to talk with me tonight?"

He glanced over my head, toward Michael.

"I don't know. Sitting up here," he gestured at the head table, "feels like being on an airplane. You know how people talk to perfect strangers on airplanes? It feels oddly safe, almost anonymous. Although I would guess that's simply evidence of how poor my judgment is, to think of talking to someone from the Fourth Estate as safe."

"It's okay," I said. "No one seems to take me very seriously as a journalist. I started out as a kind of Kelly Girl temp in the job, and every day, it feels like an accident that I still get paid to do it."

Frederick looked back at Michael again. "There's something else," he said. "I've known about your husband's work with foundations for a long time. And once we began our foundation and needed tax counsel, many people recommended his firm. And, as I asked around, I heard about..."

I put my fork down. "You heard about our troubles last year," I said flatly.

"I did," he said. "Frankly, it made me think better of you both. That you seemed to have weathered those storms. And tonight, it made me believe I might as well talk with you because you might be less judgmental than many about the life Grace and I shared."

I couldn't tell if my head was feeling a little buzzy from the predinner cocktails or the unexpected twist the conversation had taken.

"Are you offended?" asked Frederick.

I shook my head. "No. I think I must have some small glimpse of how you feel, though. Well, how anyone feels who finds that their private life has moved into the public domain. Though, it does make me wonder..."

"Yes?" Frederick said, patting his coat pocket. "Excuse me, I think it's almost time for the speechifying. I need to find my notes."

"It makes me wonder why you ducked me when Gertie was

trying to schedule time to talk."

"Can you blame me?" asked Frederick. "I'm hardly enthusiastic about either seeing my life with Grace used as fodder for some magazine piece or encouraging someone who thinks that Gifford is innocent."

"You don't think there's even a chance of that?" I asked, as Frederick drew a stack of oversize index cards out of his inside breast pocket.

He sighed. "Not much of one," he said. "I found the evidence very compelling. And if it's not Gifford, who else could it have been?"

"Who else?" I murmured to myself, as I watched Michael walk to the podium. It's always a slightly strange, parallel universe kind of experience to watch your spouse take on a public persona. When Michael has had a high-profile podium opp—lecturing at his alma mater, hosting a benefit for his law school scholarship fund—I've gone to watch. It's the odd combination of the very familiar—the last-minute check to make sure he hasn't forgotten a smidge of shaving cream on his neck, the tie knot centered, no stray hockey cuts that need tending—and the wonder that the man I've seen change messy diapers, weep at movies, roar down the ice in pursuit of a puck with frightening intensity, and do a serviceable imitation of Dame Edna is standing, poised and handsome, looking downright distinguished and relaxed in front of a hall full of people.

Michael was all that and more this evening—charming, articulate, respectful of the fund and Frederick's energy and entrepreneurship in creating it. Frederick watched, with a persuasively self-effacing smile, and chuckled at Michael's jokes. Then, just as he stood up, I put my hand on his arm, and mouthed "good luck."

He leaned down and whispered in my ear, "Remember what I said. Who else? If you find out, you tell me."

Then, in half a dozen paces, he was standing at Michael's side at the podium, waving to the audience. It suddenly struck me that I was making a career out of watching Frederick give speeches.

This one, like his talk at the Botanical Gardens, focused on the idea of giving back to the community that had showered him and his wife with such prosperity.

"Once upon a time," he said, "people in my business would occasionally get their hands dirty." He paused. "But then, copiers came along, carbon paper disappeared, and now, there's virtually no way a man can get a little honest dirt on his hands in my business. I thought about that," he said, turning the first card face down, "when I came here this evening, because my late wife, Grace, was actually a big fan of getting her hands dirty. She volunteered at the Botanical Gardens, and she also gardened at a transitional home for young women in recovery and their children. It was not unusual to find Grace at the end of the day scrubbing dirt from under her fingernails. I think her manicurist despaired of Grace as a client." Manicurist, I thought to myself, Ocean View Day Spa. We still need to check that out.

Frederick continued briefly in this vein, tying it together with a thank you to his partners and fellow venture capitalists in the Bay Area for their gifts to a fund that would enable social change.

"Grace always told me we should all be gardeners," he said. "I thought she meant that in the literal sense, because she found the work so satisfying. Now that she's gone, I realize that what she meant was that we should all be involved in helping things grow, whether or not we actually get our hands dirty. This evening, I want to thank you for helping our fund grow, and through that fund, helping countless Bay Area nonprofit organizations grow and continue to meet real needs. Good evening."

Warm applause. Pearl Soo joined him at the podium to say thank you and invite the guests to linger over coffee and dessert. I had some hopes for another conversation with Frederick, but he was immediately swarmed with friends and colleagues. Michael edged his way around the crowd and came to sit in Frederick's chair.

I reached over and gave him a kiss on the cheek. "You were brilliant," I said. "Also handsome and distinguished. And even a little witty."

He looked pleased. "It's just the tux," he said.

"Well, it is slightly more flattering than your average hockey uniform," I said.

"You and Frederick were attracting some attention," he said. "Looked like anything but head-table social chatter from where I sat."

"Later," I said.

In the car on the way home, we deconstructed the evening. I have friends who claim their husbands are unwilling to do this, too distracted or aloof or important or something to notice the food, the misbehaving guests, the undercurrents—whatever they might be. I find Michael's keen eye and shameless willingness to accidentally-on-purpose overhear one of his more engaging attributes.

We postmortemed the dinner and were in agreement: The salad was delicious, though a little foo-foo, entree forgettable, dessert chocolate so it didn't matter how good it was. "Okay, I said, "worst dress."

"Easy," he shot back. "The pink, feathery thing our new audit associate had on."

"Hmmm," I temporized. "Not sure I agree. She's a little wisp herself, so she can carry those feathers off."

Michael disagreed. "You're wrong. She looked like an underfed piglet in a boa. Kinda like if Porky Pig's daughter was anorexic. Go ahead, make your call."

"Also easy," I said. "Our big-boned Court of Appeals justice in the silver lamé. That must have been about three rolls of aluminum foil she had going on there."

"You are so catty," Michael retorted.

"Look who's talking. And speaking of talking, thanks again for getting me a seat next to Frederick Plummer."

"You two looked as if you were telling each other the secrets of your lives," he said. "I'm serious, *cara*, people were watching you."

I shrugged. "Oh, well. Let 'em talk," I said.

"Find out anything?"

"Actually, he was surprisingly open," I said.

"You sound bothered about that." I eased my shoes off and wiggled my toes to get some feeling back in them. Who invented high heels anyway?

"Not bothered. It's just...well, two peculiar things. First, I actually *like* the guy."

"And you didn't expect to?"

"Not really. From what I'd read, he seemed like the kind of careless rich guy who ignores his wife, and then gets outraged when she goes looking for companionship somewhere else. Plus, I have to admit, even though I realize how disgustingly bourgeois this sounds, that I was bothered by them hanging out at the Crimson Club."

"We probably are disgustingly bourgeois," said Michael. "Even if you do secretly look forward to getting spanked occasionally."

"Am I ever going to hear the end of that?"

"You bet your cute little ass you're not," said Michael. "See, here's the thing, Maggie. Even our life can sound pretty sordid if you just report on the events."

"You mean, spoiled housewife betrays upright husband, who turns out to be a stereotypically hot-tempered Italian who may or may not take out his aggressions with a hockey stick?"

"Something like that," said Michael.

"Yeah, well, that's the other strange thing. Plummer apparently knows all about our troubles and that's partly what made him willing to talk with me."

"Fellow sinner, huh? Well, don't let him entice you to the Crimson Club to cement your newfound friendship," said Michael.

"Does everybody know everything?" I asked.

"As you should know better than anyone else. It's a 'small town.' You were involved in a high-profile murder, and the personal motivations that got you involved in it weren't much of a secret by the time the whole thing was resolved."

"Doesn't that bother you?" I asked.

"I try not to think about it," said Michael. "I think everybody's got some pile of bones in a closet or under the bed. Most people aren't tactless enough to bring up other people's messes."

"It wasn't as if he was being tactless," I protested. "It almost seemed kind. Letting me know that he understands what it's like to go through some public scandal."

"Well, his ended a lot more publicly and tragically than ours," said Michael. "Although someone will get murdered if it ever happens again in our household."

"I had really, really, really hoped he'd be a suspect." I sighed.

"Well, he's not," said Michael. "And you knew that going in—he had an alibi and validating witnesses out the door."

"I know," I protested, "but he's rich. He could have hired somebody to do it."

"So did you learn anything useful?" asked Michael,

"I did," I said. "I don't know what exactly, but I think that I did. Made me want to track down a few more loose ends."

"Oh," said Michael, turning up the hill to our house, "why doesn't that fill my heart with gladness?"

"You do," I said, turning to him as we pulled into the garage. I unlocked my seatbelt and leaned over to whisper in his ear. "You fill my heart with gladness."

Even in the dark, I could see his dark eyes grow bright, reflecting light back at me. "Why, Mrs. Fiori," he said. "Are you trying to seduce me?"

I moved my hand to just below his cummerbund. "How energetically," I asked, "do I have to try?"

CHAPTER 19

Sometimes in the endless nights, when sleep was something to fear rather than seek, Travis found himself thinking about Frederick Plummer. It's not as if he knew the guy; Grace would hardly speak about him. Some Girl Scout code of honor or something—not talking to your sweetheart about your spouse. But sometimes Travis thought: You and me, Frederick, old buddy, now we've got stuff in common. And he would wonder what Frederick missed the most about Grace. He knew what he missed, and it had nothing to do with the sex, although that had been pretty damn good. He missed her saying a new word aloud to him, trying it out. "How would you pronounce c-h-i-m-e-r-a?" Sometimes he'd know; sometimes he wouldn't. But it didn't matter, because he'd taken to carrying a paperback Webster's in the glove box. He'd reach over and hand it back to Grace, and that day, they'd both learn something new. He teased her once about being such a perpetual student. "I bet you were a grade-grubber in school," he'd said. She hadn't answered. He still remembered how the silence grew in the car. "Gracie? I'm just giving you a hard time," he said. "I'm just remaking myself," she said. "I've been doing it a long, long time."

His thoughts went back to Frederick. Oh well, thought Travis, it's not as if Frederick and I were exactly blood brothers, even if we had Grace in common. It's not like I can move on to someone else, but Frederick can. Maybe that little firecracker, Ginger. Not my type, he thought, but that is one powerful armful of girl. He felt a smile sneak across his face. "Go get her, Fred," he said aloud. "Anyone would be better for her than that ice-cold prick, Bill Brand."

CHAPTER 20

Michael's moot court duo had nicknamed themselves "Death & Taxes" for the purposes of their temporary assignments as investigators. When I walked in the door after picking Josh up at soccer practice and Zach at Cub Scouts, the boys let out a shout, and began chanting, "Pizza, pizza, pizza!"

We followed the aromas to the den, and saw that it had been transformed into a war room. Seth and Krissy on the couch, tapping furiously on their laptops. Projected on the TV screen was a series of color blocks with times assigned to each one. Isabella, in black jeans and a lacy, red boat-necked top, was settled in our old rocker. Andrea, in her leisure hours adaptation of prep, was sitting cross-legged on the rug in loafers, pegged jeans, and a cable-knit sweater. "Holy Cow," I said. "Is this what the situation room looks like at the White House?"

"Hi, *cara*," said Michael. "Hey, guys—come get some…"

But before the words were out of his mouth, Josh and Zach had dropped to the floor next to the coffee table and were wolfing down pizza.

"Hi, Mrs. Fiori," said Krissy of the golden curls, which were, I saw to my relief and Josh's disappointment, demurely tucked into a bun on the top of her head.

"Sorry we're cluttering up your entire den."

I dropped my briefcase, and stepped out of my shoes. "No problem," I said, "as long as there's a beer around here somewhere with my name on it."

"Hey, Maggie," said Isabella. "Michael invited Andrea and me to join you guys this evening. And you just missed the little speech I made to the entire room."

"Give me the highlights," I said.

"Just one big highlight," said Isabella. "That even though we're sitting around drinking beer and eating pizza, and even though Seth and Krissy are working for free, everything we do and say is protected by attorney-client privilege."

"We agreed," said Seth. "For us, it's kind of exciting to be in an attorney-client relationship."

"It gets less exciting," said Michael, "when you're just talking taxes."

"So, does this apply to Andrea and me, too?" I asked.

Isabella considered. "Probably not, you're here as journalists." She thought a minute and frowned. "Let's see how things go. I may ask you and Andrea to vamoose if I think we're getting on dangerous ground." She glanced at Josh and Zach, then back at me. I raised my eyebrows in inquiry. Isabella shrugged and mouthed, "Okay for now."

Half an hour later, Death & Taxes were in the midst of making their presentations to Michael, Isabella, Andrea, and me. Zach, stuffed full of pizza, was sitting on my lap, his head nodding, while he struggled to stay awake. Josh had begged to stay in the room and listen while he did his homework. "It's just dumb math problems, Mom," he said. "I can practically do these in my sleep, and this way, I'll learn something at the same time. About law. And stuff. And attorney-client privilege," carefully repeating the words he'd heard. His face had that careful, bland innocent look I knew my own held when I was trying to get away with something. Who could say no to someone who had learned techniques so skillfully at his mother's knee?

Seth quickly sketched out their work plan—he had taken legal issues and people, researching anything that could help Isabella; he had assembled a cast of characters, listing principals in Grace and Frederick's life, with stars next to those who had testified in the trial, and developed a timeline. Krissy had delved into financial information on Frederick's company, the ownership of the Crimson, A Mom's Place.

"I'd never have thought of that," I confessed. "That's great." Krissy's cheeks flushed. "You get a bunch of fledgling tax lawyers helping out," she said. "We always want to follow the money." She had also looked at everyone else's work and highlighted what she called AWE factors. "What does that mean?" I asked.

"It's an acronym we made up," she explained, "Anomalies, weirdnesses and exigencies."

" 'Scuse me," said Josh, "What's an exigency?" He gave me a "See, Mom, I'm learning a new word" triumphant look he knew I'd be a sucker for.

"Oh," said Krissy, "it's something we should investigate, urgently—because it doesn't make sense."

"Thank you very much," he said solemnly.

"You're so welcome," said Krissy. "It's nice to see someone who's hungry to learn. Your parents must be very proud of you."

Michael caught my eye and controlled a smile.

"Okay, AWE me," I said.

Seth cleared his throat. "We have a PowerPoint to run through on each of them," he said, "but I'm not sure all the slides are appropriate for our..."

"Entire audience," finished Michael.

"Okay, guys," I said, gently rousing Zach. "Run and see Anya. I'll come help with your bath in a few minutes, Zach. Josh, you can finish your homework in your room or at the kitchen table."

Grumbling, they both wandered across the floor and out the door. "Good night," called Krissy.

Josh stuck his head back in the room. "Good night. Thanks for the vocabulary help," he said.

Once they were gone, Michael dimmed the lights, and Krissy fired up her PowerPoint. The first slide read: *"Who else knew about Grace and Travis's taste in S&M?"* Yes, I thought, probably not the best question to put in front of my boys.

"We think this is an important point," said Krissy. "Whoever murdered Grace had to know about the nature of the sexual relationship between her and Travis Gifford. Otherwise, they wouldn't have been able to stage the scene in the car and essentially set up a frame for Travis."

Half an hour later, the room was in complete shambles—smelling faintly of pizza and beer, with cartons scattered everywhere, as the Death & Taxes duo dug through boxes to back up one point or another.

"So," Seth said. "Want to review the five points quickly, and see if you or Isabella can answer any of them? And assign one of us to follow up on the others? Or, in some cases, we think you or Isabella may be the only ones who can follow up."

He clicked the first slide on again. *"Who else knew about Grace and Travis's taste in S&M?"*

"Ginger knew," said Michael and Isabella in chorus.

Added Isabella, "It's in the trial transcript. Ginger said Grace told her about the kind of sex play she and Travis had liked, and that Grace had found herself increasingly compelled by it. And by extension, it seems as if Bill Brand might have known, too, if Ginger had told him. It seems like the kind of thing a wife would tell her husband. A little too juicy to keep to yourself."

Krissy typed Ginger's name on the screen, and added Bill Brand's name with a question mark.

"Who else?" asked Michael.

"Not Ivory," I said. "I asked her directly. She said it didn't surprise her, but she didn't know specifically."

"Should we assume Frederick didn't know? Unless Grace got a real taste for the rough stuff and introduced it into their marriage?"

"Or," mused Seth, "if some of that came up in their adventures at the Crimson?"

Krissy added Frederick to the screen with another question mark.

"Who else?" asked Michael.

"Could be anybody," I offered. "Another one of her friends, a therapist, her Brazilian wax specialist. Ginger's father."

"Her father?" chorused the entire room.

"Gus. Ivory's friend and, well, sometime lover, I think. Although not exactly the kind of information you'd share with your father, no matter how unconventional he was."

"Did we know Ivory's live-in is Ginger's father?" asked Michael.

"I did," I said.

"Me, too," said Isabella, "although it hardly seems important. He and Ivory alibied each other. They were both at some obscure art-house film in the Mission that night."

"I thought Ivory had a stroke," said Andrea. "That's why her memory is shaky about events around the time of the murder."

"She did," said Isabella. "Right after Travis was arrested. But she was fine the night of the murder, and the cops vetted both of them after Travis became a suspect. They both had pretty complete recall about this quite eccentric one-night-only showing of some independent flick about a West African musician who comes to New York and gets a gig playing in a klezmer band and ends up converting to Judaism."

"Not something you could catch another night at the multiplex," observed Michael.

Isabella shrugged. "Well, good enough excuse to start an alibi for both of them. And then, that mutual alibi got corroborated by some off-duty cop who happened to be at the movie that night and happened to notice Ivory and Gus, because he didn't think they looked as if they belonged together. So, the short answer is—we don't know if Ginger confided in dear old dad about her willingness to play Miss Scarlett at the Crimson, along with her best pal."

"I can't imagine she would," I said, "given how protective Gus is."

"Okay, so back to who knew about Grace's taste in the rough stuff," Seth reminded the group.

"Someone *else* at the Crimson?" offered Isabella.

We all fell silent.

"Field trip," said Seth, a little too eagerly. "I think we need to check out the Crimson first hand. Who's in?"

"Hold on," said Michael. "Absolutely not. I'm probably on thin ice even asking you guys to look at these issues. I don't want to think about the ethical implications of sending you to a sex club." He set his beer bottle down, a little forcefully. "Forget it. Plus, you couldn't afford the cover charge. And I'm sure as hell not paying for you to go."

Seth looked crestfallen.

"Okay," said Krissy, "next up." She clicked the mouse and the next AWE question appeared. *"Who had a key to the Plummers' house?"*

"This is important," said Krissy, "in order to check out the possibility that Travis was telling the truth, that he had, in fact, delivered Grace home, and that someone else had been waiting for her there."

"Or," interjected Andrea, "it could have been someone Grace let in. Someone she knew."

"Maybe," said Isabella, "but I think you're asking the right question. According to Travis, Grace was exhausted when they got back to her house, plus she'd had a fair amount to drink, so she told him she was going right to bed, that she was locking the door and turning the phone off."

"So, do we know who else had a key?" I asked.

"Frederick, of course," said Krissy.

"But the timetable still rules him out," said Seth.

"Could he have given his key to someone else?" asked Krissy.

"Oh, like—what's that movie? *Dial M for Murder*?" I interjected. "When that loathsome Ray Milland leaves the key for the burglar he's hired, when he's plotting to kill his wife."

"I love that movie," said Isabella, "except for Bob Cummings. What a weakling! How could Grace Kelly fall for him? Why would any woman get tempted into adultery by that *baboso*?"

"And we're off-topic," said Michael.

"Wouldn't Ginger have a key?" I asked. "They were best friends."

"During the trial," said Isabella, "the key thing came up. But Frederick testified that only their housekeeper had a key, because the security code was complicated, and the housekeeper was there full-time, so she could let tradespeople in. So, there didn't seem to be a need to have keys spread around the neighborhood, or among friends."

"But did anyone *ask* Ginger and Bill if they had a key?" I persisted.

Isabella shook her head. "No, they didn't. At least not while she was testifying."

"So, that's something to follow up," said Krissy, entering the words on the screen: *Did Ginger and Bill have a key?*

"Okay, here's the next AWE point," she said, and the screen read, "*Whose gun?*"

Isabella sighed. "We've been down that path. It wasn't Travis's weapon, or at least, not the one he was registered to carry. In fact, he says his gun was upstairs with him that night in the apartment, and there's no evidence he was lying. Besides, his gun was a different caliber from the one that was used to kill Grace. It was like one of those wise guy movies, the serial numbers had been filed off."

"So what did the police conclude?" I asked.

"They didn't conclude much, and they didn't need to," said Michael. "There was so much physical evidence linking Travis to the murder, that they just assumed he'd managed to get his hands on another, 'identity-less' gun, and that he wouldn't be dumb enough to use his own gun to kill Grace."

"Oh, but he would be dumb enough to stash her in his parking place, overnight? In an unlocked car?" I asked.

"Those were always the 64-million-dollar questions," said Isabella. "But the state insisted it wasn't that big a risk. Why would anyone look inside the limo? They were used to seeing it there. And, they theorized, he was overwrought after the killing and just needed a few hours to get his head together and figure out what to do with the body."

"Who else in our little collection of folks owned guns?"

asked Seth, clicking back to the list of names and timetables he'd assembled. He scrolled quickly through them: Travis, Frederick, Ginger and Bill Brand, Purity Meadows, Ivory.

Quickly we agreed to follow up on the likeliest suspects—Ivory, as a bar-owner, and Purity, since A Mom's Place sheltered women from their former lives on the street. Travis had been licensed to carry a gun, but his had inconveniently disappeared.

I turned over the thought of Purity having a gun in the house, with all those kids around. It seemed very unlikely to me. "I don't think so," I said, "but I'm willing to check it out."

"Though I don't see much of a motive for Purity," said Andrea. "Grace was her guardian angel. No reason to kill the golden goose."

"Although," said Michael, "take a look at what Krissy's turned up on the money front."

"That's the last AWE issue," said Seth, as he clicked the last question onto the screen. *"If we follow the money, what do we find?"*

"I'm all ears. What do you find?"

"A few interesting things," said Krissy. "First, even though Frederick was the major beneficiary as surviving spouse, Grace had recently redone her will and had created an irrevocable trust for A Mom's Place, along with generous bequests to several of her other causes, including the San Francisco Botanical Gardens."

"Why didn't that come up in the trial?" I asked.

Isabella said, "The terms of the will came up briefly, but it was hard to make much of them. Those other gifts are pretty minor compared to how Frederick would benefit from Grace's death. Some of their assets were jointly held. In addition, Grace had her own life insurance, and Frederick was the big winner of that jackpot. So, all these other relatively small bequests seem to pale in comparison to the way Frederick would benefit. And, we knew he had an alibi for the time of the murder."

I thought about Purity's day-to-day struggle to make ends meet. Could she have been desperate enough to murder Grace to get some security for those young women? It just didn't compute. Grace had already been generous to Purity's program; she was likely to become even more generous. Why limit that possibility?

"Anything else on the money front?" I asked. "Were Bill and Frederick fifty-fifty partners, by the way?"

"Not exactly," said Krissy. "Frederick brought more of the founding capital to the business, but Bill apparently attracted a lot of the new, young start-up geniuses. Plus, at this point, they've got ten partners in the firm. Frederick and Bill each hold twenty-five-percent ownership positions; the balance is divided among the other eight partners, about six percent each."

"So they're equal partners, though?" asked Andrea.

"Right," said Krissy, "as far as we can tell."

"That's funny," said Andrea. "Somehow the way news gets reported about that firm, it always seems as if Frederick is Mr. Big, and Bill is his able lieutenant. Wonder if that riles Bill?"

"And if it did," said Krissy, "why would that be a reason to kill Frederick's wife?"

She entered another question on the screen: *Any financial tension between Frederick and Bill? Any tension between the two of them and any other partners?*

"One other thing," Seth said, "before we finish. I wondered who might have been in trouble with the law at some time in the past. Anyone who had a little something buried in the personal-history department."

Isabella said, "We looked briefly at that on the principals, of course. During discovery we had asked for everything—health records, service records, criminal records, all that stuff. And there wasn't much there. Ivory had been arrested in college for some sit-in protesting the war. Bill Brand and Frederick Plummer both had a DUI apiece. But we couldn't look through every single sheet of paper on all those records, and we pretty much ruled out the people who had alibis—including Plummer and Ivory. So, what's the deal? Did you find anything?"

"Probably nothing significant," said Seth. "But a couple other interesting things with the peripheral characters." He consulted his notes. "Purity, the woman who runs A Mom's Place, was arrested for assault. And Gus, Ivory's friend, and some sketchy friend of his in the military had both gotten in trouble with the locals in Ho Chi Minh City during the war, for harassing some teenage girl."

"Gus had an alibi," I said. "The same as Ivory's, but what's the deal with Purity? Hard to imagine her assaulting someone."

"Maybe so," said Seth. "But apparently she got mad at some abusive ex of one of her residents who showed up on the doorstep making threats." He glanced down at his notes again. "Went after him with a baseball bat she kept by the door. He was knocked out and had to have his forehead stitched up." He handed me a paper-clipped bunch of papers. "I made a copy for you of both of these little run-ins."

Isabella rubbed her eyes. "Okay, gang, this has been a very instructive evening. But I've got an early court date tomorrow, so I'm going to pack it in." She picked up her briefcase. "You all are doing terrific work."

"Especially for a bunch of tax weenies, huh?" said Krissy.

Isabella laughed. "And now," she said, "you're fired."

A chorus of protests greeted her pronouncements. "We're just getting started," said Krissy.

Isabella shook her head. "Michael agrees with me."

"Sorry, guys," said Michael. "I do agree."

"You've raised some issues we need to follow up, and I'm grateful for that. But I can't have the bunch of you running around playing private detective any more. We'd be taking way too many risks of botching some piece of evidence—and frankly, I don't want to see you guys taking any personal risks either."

Seth groused, "That sucks."

Michael spoke up. "It does. But here's the thing—you're already coloring way outside the lines of the moot court topic. And I'll be liable if something goes wrong, or God forbid, if something should happen to one of you. Besides, we're getting close to showtime for moot court, and you guys have got to be ready. Or you make me look bad, and hey, what could be worse than that?"

Suddenly I realized just how young Michael's students were.

The slightly pouty, sullen looks that settled on their faces reminded me of the way my boys looked when they were on restriction for some transgression.

"Before you go," I said, "Seth, can you put that list of players up there one more time?" Seth obliged. We all looked at the list. Something was nagging at me. "Add Carol Ann to that list, would you?"

"Who?" came back to me in another chorus.

"She's a young mom Grace befriended at A Mom's Place. She's not there any more. In fact, according to Purity, she's really gotten her life together. She's married, going to college, working nearly full-time, and her husband's in law school."

"Sounds like a success story to me," said Michael "Not a suspect."

"I don't think she's a suspect," I said, "but I'd sure like to talk to her. Besides, guess where she works? At Ocean View Day Spa, where Grace got her a job, and she's moved up the ranks to a management job. And it's where Grace used to hang out. I'm willing to bet Ginger goes there too."

"Okay," said Andrea. "I'm on it."

Krissy said, "There's one more deader-than-dead end we couldn't figure out—so, we didn't highlight it as an AWE factor."

"Two cars that the nosy neighbor spotted at Grace's," said Seth. "Could be imaginary, could be real. But no corroboration anywhere, and the neighbor's dead, so it's literally a dead end."

"The late, sadly nearsighted Mrs. Herbert Orson Lomax," I said. "We all wish she'd lived a little longer."

"Still you've given us plenty to think about," said Isabella. "Thanks everybody, and Michael, thanks for the pizza and beer."

Seth and Krissy began packing up, as we sorted out who should follow up on the remaining unresolved AWE items.

Krissy lingered on the steps, as Michael waved to Seth as he roared off. I said, "Krissy, I know you and Seth are really disappointed about not finishing what you started."

"I am," she said. "But I guess I understand. I just hope…"

"Michael will keep you posted about how things go," I said.

"That would be great. But I hope I get to see you again," she faltered.

"Of course," I said. "Good to have an older pal or two."

"Oh, thank you," she said. She grinned. "Now that I know who I want to be when I grow up."

"Yes, well, good to know that no one is perfect," I said. "Although I hope you won't share that information with my boys."

She made a zipper gesture across her lips.

We had a girl hug, and off she went down the steps to the ancient little Honda.

After she was gone, Michael cleared up the mess, while I went to check in on baths, homework, and bedtime. Zach was already out of the tub, tucked into bed, warm, fragrant, and drowsy. "One story, Mom, please," he roused himself to say.

I perched on the side of his bed and complied, reading half a chapter in *The Phantom Tollbooth*, until I heard the little puffs of air that meant he was out of the tollbooth and on the road to Nod. I imagined him dreaming about rolling through that tollbooth on a motorcycle like Seth's, and I reached over to pull the covers more snugly around his neck. "Wear your helmet," I whispered. "Even in your dreams." I wondered what things Ivory had whispered to Travis when he was a boy.

I knocked on Josh's door. He was hunched over his math book and a notebook, and had his socks and shoes off, and his bare feet buried in Raider's fur.

"How's it going, honey?" I asked.

He looked up. "I'm just about done," he said. He looked sheepish. "I thought I'd get most of it finished while I was listening to Dad's team," he said. "But I got way too interested in what they were saying."

I moved his shin guards to the floor, so I could sit on the edge of his bed. "What did you find most interesting?" I asked.

He regarded me suspiciously. "You're interviewing me, Mom," he said.

Busted! "Okay, maybe I am," I said. "You're a pretty interesting subject to me."

He put his pencil down. "I thought it was cool how they weren't competitive. Like, they help each other out, and they're into paying attention to each other. I know it's hard work, what they're doing. Dad said so. But it looked like they were having fun. And nobody's telling them to work that hard. It's not like it's a class or something."

"You're right," I said. "That's when work gets really fun. When nobody tells you what you have to do, when you have to do it, and how—you just have a job to do and you figure it out. That's one way work is way better than school."

"Geez, I hope so," said Josh. "School sure seems dumb a lot of the time. Read this; answer these questions; do a topic sentence; blah, blah, blah."

"It gets better," I said. "Trust me on that. Soon you'll have choices about what you work on. High school is different. College is way different. College is like a reward for all the stupid stuff you have to do in school."

"And if you go to law school, you get to hang out with girls like Krissy," he said with a sly smile.

I stood up. "Let's remember our feminist principles, young man. Krissy is a beautiful young woman, but she's also talented and hardworking, and more than worthy of your respect."

"I know, Mom. You don't have to get all PC on me. You let Dad call women 'hot babes' sometimes."

Note to self: Continue to clean up Michael's language. "Uh-huh," I said to my young, politically incorrect son. "Your father has earned a certain latitude through years of being a good citizen-feminist in the real world—changing diapers, doing laundry, voting for women candidates. So, now you've got to earn the right to be a smart-mouth."

"Can I tell Dad you called him a 'smart-mouth'?"

Adolescence had arrived, and apparently I wasn't ready. "I would never censor what you discuss with your father. Now, finish up your math and hop into bed. You can take a shower in the morning." He turned back to his math. "And no more texting Esme at 11 o'clock at night," I said.

"Come on, she's just letting me know who's coming to her birthday party."

"Sleep tight, Romeo," I said, and shut the door.

CHAPTER 21

Gertie was stationed by my office door when I walked in the next morning, holding a stack of folders.

"Good morning," she said with distressing energy.

"Oh, Gertie, I hate it when you start the day all chirpy. It means you've got lists of awful things for me to do."

"Buck up," she said. "I do have lists and lists and lists. But only half the things are awful, and after all, you're the one who accepted this job."

"Yeah, but who knew I'd have Little Mary Sunshine as my constant companion?" I complained. "Okay, sit down. Let's get going."

While I sipped my latte, Gertie walked me through her color-coded folders—things to sign, invoices to approve, lists of requests for media sponsorship from worthy nonprofits.

"Oh, here's a fun one," she said. "Want to be the prime media sponsor for the Miss Tranny competition?"

"Absolutely not," I said, thinking about the sweet young thing on Michael's moot court team. "It's irritating enough to hang around women who look so much better than I do when they're in jeans and a T-shirt. Why should I subject myself to transvestites and transgendered people who get all dressed up and put me to shame as well?"

Gertie looked at me over her readers. "Get over it," she said. "Soon you'll be my age and you'll have to hope you're loved for how you think and feel, instead of how you look."

"I love you for how you look," I protested. "You make L.L. Bean look chic."

Gertie gave me a disgusted look. "I'm from Chicago," she said, "not East Frostbite, Maine. I wouldn't touch L.L. Bean with a ski pole."

"Okay, okay," I said. "Where were we?"

Gertie handed me the schedule for the rest of the day. "Staff meeting this morning, lunch with some J-school seniors at Cal. They're coming here. I've ordered in Middle Eastern. Hoyt said to remind you your Editor's Note was due today, and Calvin said he'll pick you up this afternoon for a shoot in the East Bay. Oh, and here are your messages," and with that, she dropped a handful of pink slips on my desk. I shuffled through them: Alf Abbott, our dipsomaniac publisher, wanted me to rethink the editorial budget for the rest of the fiscal year and was trying to decipher my message about the Death of a Socialite story and the link to Michael's firm. Alf was never enthusiastic about making a call to the magazine's counsel. No matter what, it would cost something. A job-seeker fresh out of journalism school at Missouri. Lulu Brown, the annoyingly perfect head team mother, who wondered how I was doing on gathering auction items for this year's youth soccer benefit. And Michael, reminding me we had Dr. Mephisto late this afternoon. "Oh, goody," I said.

"One more thing," said Gertie, pushing an envelope over to me. "Who said 'the social ramble ain't restful'?"

"Satchel Paige," I said. "And it sure ain't, considering how much work it was to pour myself into that red number for that Give-Back Venture Fund dinner." I pulled the card out of the envelope. *It's an old-fashioned rent party,* the card read on the cover. I opened it. *Benefit for Ivory Gifford & The Devil's Interval.*

Come for the jazz, the drinks, the friends, for Ivory.

Oh, just come for the hell of it.

The date was two weeks from Friday, at The Devil's Interval. I didn't want to miss it.

"What's it all about?" asked Gertie, reading over my shoulder. "What's a rent party?"

"Old idea," I said. "In the Depression, jazz musicians used to get together and play music, eat and drink, and throw some money in the pot to cover rent for whoever was in the worst shape."

I looked at the names listed on the bottom of the card: Alex Acuna on drums, Frank Martin on piano, Sheldon Brown on reeds, Karen Blixt on vocals. "Look at that," I said. "They've got some good names lined up for this. R.S.V.P. yes for me, would you? Let's buy two tickets; if Michael doesn't want to go, I'll take Andrea or Calvin."

The rest of the day went by in a blur, and at 1:30, as I left the conference room after falafels and career chat with the Cal students, I ran into Calvin.

"Let's go," he said. "I'm in a towaway zone, the engine's running, and I've burned through my traffic luck for the month."

I grabbed my hat, coat, and purse and ran after him.

"Don't you want to know where we're going?" he asked.

"Not particularly," I said. "I was ready to get out of there, and I've got to meet Michael at Dr. Mephisto's at four o'clock, so I'll be on the right side of the Bay and you can drop me."

"And once again," said Calvin, "the world arranges itself for Maggie Fiori's personal convenience."

"I know," I said. "Isn't it grand?" I punched a few buttons on Calvin's stereo system, until he slapped my hands.

"Will you stop that? Last time you fooled with my system, and I had some continuous loop of 'Raindrops Keep Falling on My Head' for a week." He hit one button, and the car filled with the sound of the Dixie Hummingbirds.

"Calvin," I said. "I love gospel music. But isn't this way too ethnic for you to listen to?"

"I'm trying to be more open-minded," he said. "My mom keeps sending me gospel classics and she asks every week if I've listened to them. Dixie Hummingbirds, Blind Boys of Alabama, Soul Stirrers, Mighty Clouds of Joy—I've got the greatest hits of all of them. What do you think?"

"Loves Me Like a Rock" was pouring out of Calvin's speakers. "It's great," I said. "I grew up on this stuff. My mom worshipped Mahalia Jackson."

"Yeah, well, it's not Green Day," said Calvin, "but it's pretty listenable."

I shot back, "When Green Day is dead, buried, and biodegraded into the ground, people will still be listening to The Byrds," I said. "Okay, now I'm ready to know—where are we going?" We were heading across the Bay Bridge, and since it was early afternoon, there was mercifully little traffic. The view from the bottom deck looked south back to the City, and the never-ending construction retrofitting the Bay Bridge, and northeast to Oakland's port, bristling with containerships, cranes, and huge containers suspended in thin air. Once San Francisco's port had been important for shipping—now it was home to touristy faux-amusement parks like Pier 39, chi-chi restaurants, and one great idea, the old Ferry Plaza building reconfigured into the world's most delicious stroll-and-nibble venue. Organic vegetables, a champagne-and-caviar bar, high-end chocolates of every kind, places for tea, sushi, Vietnamese haute cuisine at The Slanted Door, flowers, wines—it was a delicious destination.

I turned my attention back to Calvin. "So, we're going where?"

"Back to the place it all began for Grace Plummer," he said. "Her grandparents' house in Oakland."

We pulled off the bridge, out into the sunlight, and took the 580 split to Oakland. Within five minutes, we were parked on a side street near Holy Names College. The houses were older, not particularly large, and well-kept, and the trees had plenty of years on them. Some were showing spring color.

I pulled my ever-growing Death of a Socialite folder out of my briefcase and riffled through the latest batch of info Andrea had compiled. "So, according to the property tax rolls, Grace's grandparents died within a year of each other, nearly fifteen years ago. And Grace sold the house, to a family named..." I turned over a page. "Hothan. Mr. and Mrs., Harold and Joyce."

"Wholesome white people," said Calvin. "The 'burbs are way too full of them."

"Look who's talking," I said. "Mr. Prep himself." I flicked his Burberry scarf. "Honest to God, you went to Stanford, not Yale. Do you have to look so preppy all the time?"

Calvin grinned. "Not preppy. Classic. Drives the women wild. Besides, I've got the world's preppiest girlfriend now. I think of Burberry as our family-crest-in-the-making."

"Uh-huh," I said. "I'd just love to hear what Andrea thinks of you discussing family crests. You've got a long row to hoe with that girl before you start talking about family anything."

"I don't know," he said. "Andrea's modeling in the Junior League fashion show this year, and her mother is coming out from Connecticut to cheer her on. And guess who's invited to escort Mumsie to the show?"

"Mr. Guess Who's Coming to Dinner himself?"

"Exactly. I'll be in killer-charm mode. She won't be able to resist me."

"That I'd like to see."

"*Small Town*'s got a table at the show," said Calvin. "The magazine is always a sponsor. I assumed you were coming."

I rummaged in my purse for my Blackberry.

"When is it?"

"Like next week or something," he said. "Hey, you should come. You know who else is modeling? Grace's best buddy, Cinnamon or Fennel or Nutmeg...whatever that chick's name is, the one who sounds like a Spice Girl."

"Ginger," I said. "And of course she's modeling."

There it was, on my calendar, high noon at the Design Center. The beautiful people would be out in force.

"You're right, I'm in," I said. "Boy, I'd love to get a chance to talk to Ginger's beloved, Mr. William Brand, too. Not to mention," I looked over at Calvin, "being witness to your lovefest with Andrea's mother. May I suggest you practice calling her Mrs.

Storch, so 'Mumsie' doesn't slip out by accident?"

Calvin ignored me, pulling into a place right in front of the Hothans' home. "Hey," he said. "Actually, I think these are highly integrated 'burbs. Maybe the Hothans are cooler than we think. I'm willing to bet money they're not white folks."

"Why do you say that?"

"Front door," he said. I looked at the front door. It was a distinctive color of green-tinged blue.

"*Haint* blue," said Calvin, "the color that keeps bad spirits away. Somebody in this house is from the Carolinas."

I unsnapped my seatbelt. "Let's go find out."

In fact, the Hothans were not white, and were delighted to tell us that Calvin was correct, they were from the Low Country, and had painted their front door to honor Mr. Hothan's Gullah grandmother. They were, as Mr. Hothan explained to us, both retired schoolteachers. He had to shout a little to be heard over the tango music playing in the background. Mrs. Hothan peered over his shoulder. She seemed to be wearing a rather slinky black dress and very high heels for the middle of the afternoon.

"Honey, go turn that down a minute," her husband told her. "We're practicing for our tango class," he explained. "Competition coming up."

Although the Hothans wanted to be helpful, especially when Calvin revealed that his great-grandmother was from Savannah, it turned out they had very little information to offer. "Oh, we read about the death of that woman in the paper when it happened," said Mrs. Hothan. "Remember, honey? It was so sad. She seemed like a nice person. Doing charity things and what have you."

"But you never met the grandparents?" I asked.

Mr. Hothan shook his head. "It was a probate sale. The Anderstatters were long gone."

"Excuse me," said Calvin. "Anybody on the block who's lived here a long time? Someone who might have known Mrs. Plummer's grandparents?"

"The Hawks, three doors down, this side of the street," offered

Mrs. Hothan. "They've lived in that house since they were married, right after World War II. Of course, it's just Mrs. Hawk now. Mr. Hawk died several years ago. But they might have known Mrs. Plummer's people."

"Think she'll talk to us?" asked Calvin.

"I'll call ahead," said Mrs. Hothan, "tell her you're not Jehovah's Witnesses or serial killers." She looked us up and down. "You're not, are you?"

We both tried to look innocent and upstanding, and I spoke quickly before Calvin could make a wisecrack and botch our chances.

"We're happy to show you identification," I said. I dug in my briefcase and pulled out an issue of *Small Town.* I riffled the first few pages and opened it to the Editors' Note. A blissfully un-soccer-mom photo of me graced the page.

"See, there I am," I said.

"And she looks that good because I took the shot," said Calvin. "Turn it sideways, you'll see my credit next to the photo."

Mrs. Hothan laughed, "Okay, okay, I believe you. Give me a few minutes and I'll call Mrs. Hawk right now."

With the power of neighborhood watch on our side, we were soon sitting on Mrs. Hawk's chintz sofa and chatting, sipping cups of cherry-licorice tea.

"My own blend, dear," she said to Calvin. "It will keep you regular." She had to be close to eighty, but sat ramrod straight and regarded us with mild curiosity.

"This seems very late to be doing an obituary on that poor woman. She died two years ago," she said.

"We're not doing an obituary," I said. "The man who was accused of murdering her was convicted and is now on Death Row. So, since his case is on appeal, we're doing a story in the magazine on who she really was."

Mrs. Hawk narrowed her eyes. "I don't believe in speaking ill of the dead."

"In all candor," I said, "we're turning up much more evidence of what a good person Grace was."

"I thought she was murdered by her paramour. That's the man you were talking about, the one on Death Row, isn't it?" asked Mrs. Hawk.

Hard to believe that con artists went after the elderly, I thought. Not if they were all as alert and skeptical as Mrs. Hawk.

"Yes, that's Travis Gifford," I said. "And it turns out there's some question about whether he did—or didn't—commit the murder. For our story on Grace, though, we're mostly trying to flesh out who she was. As a human being, not just a murder victim."

"I didn't know her very well after she was grown," said Mrs. Hawk, relaxing slightly. A picture of Mrs. Hawk walking around a room somewhere with a book on her head flashed in my brain. Maybe that's where her great posture came from. "But she was a lovely little girl and young woman," she continued. "Her grandparents adored her, without indulging her, if you know what I mean. And she had been so shy and frightened when she came to live with them. Horrible, horrible start to that child's life."

Both Calvin and I sat up a little straighter ourselves. "What do you mean?"

"Oh, her father died in a motorcycle accident when she was young, and her mother..." She shook her head. "Just awful."

I could feel Calvin fidgeting, wanting to ask questions.

"Calvin," I said. "Why don't you shoot some photos of the neighborhood, while the light is so good?" Calvin started to protest, and I gave him a wan smile, packed with as much apology and pleading as I could manage.

Mrs. Hawk leaned forward, and picked up her teacup.

"She's right, dear," she said to Calvin. "We need a moment of girl talk."

I sat quietly as Calvin shouldered his bag, and huffed his way outside. I knew I'd have to grovel once we were in the car, but I could feel Mrs. Hawk wanting to tell her story, and somehow not wanting to tell it to two of us.

She put her cup down, folded her hands in her lap, and

began. "I still remember the day Grace came to live with the Anderstatters. It was the Saturday before Easter, and I was putting out spring annuals in the front border, and Jakob and Petra drove up in their old station wagon. Petra had to coax Grace out of the backseat. I stood up to go say hello. I'd met the little girl before. Her mother often left her with Jakob and Petra. But this time, she burst into tears when she saw me, and buried her face in Petra's skirt. Everyone seemed very upset, so I just made some excuse and went back to my garden."

I waited. "Later that day, Petra came to see me and apologized for the little girl's behavior. She sat down at my kitchen table, and her entire body was shivering, even though it was a beautiful, warm spring day. So, I made her some tea, and then she told me this terrible, terrible story." She took a deep breath. "I have no idea why I'm telling you, but it's haunted me, ever since I read that Grace had been murdered."

"I'm grateful to you for confiding in me," I offered gently.

She reached out and clutched my arm. "This is not a story for your magazine," she said. "You have to give me your word of honor."

I reached over and covered her hand with mine. "You have that," I said, once again conscious I had not one single get-the-story-at-whatever-price instinct I thought a real reporter needed.

On that Saturday, when their invitations to come for Easter dinner had gone unanswered for several days, Petra and Jakob had gone to the studio apartment where Grace and her mother lived. When they got there, no one answered the door, though they could hear faint sounds of the television coming from inside the apartment. The manager said she had not seen Grace's mother for a few days. "What the manager really said was that he had not seen 'that whore' for several days," Mrs. Hawk corrected herself. "You have to understand that Petra and Jakob were devout Lutherans. Their entire world revolved around the church, their Norwegian folk dance club, and Jakob's friends at Sons of Norway. It caused Petra physical pain, I could see it, to say that word." She repeated it, "*Whore.* To hear that word describe your daughter. Well, you can imagine."

I could not imagine. But I gave the tiniest of nods, just to keep her talking.

"The manager let her into the apartment, and that's where they found the little girl. Tied to a heavy table in the room, by a dog leash. There was a box of cereal on the floor, but it was empty. She was asleep, lying in her own..."

"Oh, my God," I whispered.

"Petra cleaned the little girl up, took her to their doctor who said she was in remarkably good shape, just terribly dehydrated. As far as they were able to piece the story together, when they ran out of money—and drugs—her mother would leave Grace—not to do the secretarial job she told her parents she had, but to sell herself."

"And her parents didn't know?"

Mrs. Hawk gave a short laugh, "I know I must look very unworldly to you, my dear, a silly old widow drinking tea on the sofa. But I was a sophisticate, compared to Petra and Jakob. They knew very little beyond their circle of hardworking, Norwegian immigrants and churchgoers. Grace's mother was able to tell them any story she wanted to—and they believed her."

"Or wanted to believe her," I said. "And what happened to her? To Grace's mother."

"She died," said Mrs. Hawk. "The police found her a few weeks later. She'd been beaten and discarded, like some heap of trash, in an alley in West Oakland. She died there."

I was silent for a moment. "How did Petra and Jakob ever recover from that?" I finally asked.

She shrugged. "They had no choice. They were awarded custody of Grace, and in the beginning, she was so damaged, she took all their time and attention."

"She eventually recovered?"

"I think so. She turned into a funny, happy little girl, to all intents and purposes. Very bright in school. Went to Mills College. But I don't think those experiences ever left her. She had night terrors for years. And she would..." Mrs. Hawk broke off, hesitating.

"She would?" I prompted her gently.

"She would occasionally tie herself to something. She'd take a piece of ribbon from a gift, or a jump rope, and she'd tie it around her wrist and tie the other end around the leg of a table or chair."

"How awful!"

"That's what I thought, and of course, it would upset Jakob and Petra terribly. But the doctor told them it might give her some comfort. She'd often curl up on the floor and go to sleep. Eventually she grew out of it."

Suddenly visions of the police photos of the murder scene flooded over me. Was it some terrible irony that Grace ended her life tied up? I had assumed the bondage was some kind of sex play Travis had suggested. But perhaps it had been Grace.

"Are you all right, dear?" asked Mrs. Hawk. "You're very flushed."

"I'm all right," I said. "Just thinking about lots of things."

She tightened her lips. "I shouldn't have told you that story," she said. "But I've thought about it so often. Petra and Jakob did all they could for that girl, and I thought she was going to grow up and have a wonderful, happy life. She certainly deserved that. And then, to read about her murder! I'm only glad that her grandparents were already gone, and didn't have to know. They had been so proud of her."

There was a sharp rap on the door and we both jumped a bit.

Calvin stuck his head in the entryway. "If you ladies are done with your girl talk," he said, "I've finished shooting. And Maggie, don't I need to drop you off somewhere?"

I shook myself back into the present, away from the vivid pictures Mrs. Hawk had painted. "Just one more thing," I said. "Did you ever tell any of this story to the police?"

"No," she said. "I would have called if it had seemed relevant in any way. But the police seemed to have found her killer, and I couldn't imagine how something that happened all those years ago would have to do with her death."

She stood to walk me to the door. She took Calvin's hand in both of hers, and I could see his hurt feelings start to dissolve. "You must forgive me, young man," she said. "I felt too uncomfortable to tell my story in front of both of you. But your colleague is free to share what I've told her, as long as you honor the same promise she made me, not to use any of this in your publication."

Calvin glanced at me. "Scout's honor," he said. "If Maggie's agreed, I'll agree."

Back in the car, as we headed up to Berkeley to Dr. Mephisto's office, I filled Calvin in. "Oh, Christ," he said when I'd finished. "What a fucking tragedy."

"My sentiments, exactly," I said.

"No wonder Grace wanted to help those women at A Mom's Place," said Calvin. "She knew what kind of hell it could be if mothers got desperate to feed their kids—and their drug habits." He shook his head, "And boy, that tying-up story was pretty freaky, huh? Think it had anything to do with how old Grace and Trav liked to get it on?"

"I don't know," I said, "but the thought crossed my mind—and makes me think it came from Grace, not Travis."

"Hey, ask your shrink about it," suggested Calvin. "You're already paying for that fifty-minute hour anyway, and haven't you and Mikey worked out all those kinks by now? I mean, either he forgives you or he doesn't. How complicated can it be?"

"Gee, Calvin," I countered. "So great to get marital advice from someone with your depth of expertise. Turn here, by the way, it's the fourth driveway from the corner."

"My pleasure," he said, swinging into the driveway. He peered up at the lime-green cupola. "Looks like whoever art-directed "It's a Small World" at Disneyland worked on this place, too. Hey, is it kinda like Therapy Disneyland? Are there rides and things?"

"Oh, there are wild rides, all right," I said. "Just not the kind you're thinking about."

Interval No. 4 with Dr. Mephisto

Dr. Mephisto was a vision in lemon-yellow and orange, down to her adorable, flower-trimmed, kitten-heeled shoes. I willed her to slip them off so I could peek inside and see if they were—as they appeared to be—whimsical Jimmy Choos. What did it say about my therapist if she could afford shoes I couldn't, I mused. Probably that she was more successful as a therapist than I was as an editor. Or didn't have kids. Or had a rich spouse? Does everyone do this, I wondered, speculate about their therapist's personal life? Search head to kitten-heel for clues?

"You're quiet, Maggie," observed Dr. Mephisto.

"Just thinking about footwear," I said. I gestured with my mug at her shoes. "Cool shoes."

"Thanks," she said shortly, giving me an "I know what you're wondering, and you have no chance in hell of finding out" look.

Michael sighed, "Okay, *cara*, you are way too preoccupied to be thinking about shoes. What's up?"

I remembered Calvin's counsel, and decided it was not a bad idea to go for the free—well, already paid-for—advice.

"I just had a very upsetting conversation about the story I'm working on, the one," I added hastily, "Michael's helping me with."

"How's that going?" asked Dr. Mephisto.

"Good," I said, "at least from my point of view. Michael involved some of his students and they've been very helpful."

"How about for you, Michael?" asked Dr. Mephisto.

Michael leaned back on the couch, and stretched his arm along the back, his most relaxed, least-defended pose. "Pretty good," he said. "My students got into the assignment, and I do think they've turned out some decent data, and frankly, it felt good to be more involved."

"That's great," said the therapist, putting her feet up on the ottoman, all the better for me to admire those expensive shoes. I could tell she was taking credit for this idea, but I couldn't think of a graceful way to remind both of them that it had been my inspiration to ask for Michael's help. I gritted my teeth and smiled back at both of them.

"So, do you want to talk about what upset you this afternoon?" asked Mephisto.

"I do," I said. "In fact, I'm hoping you can help me understand a little more about it."

I sketched out the conversation I'd had with Mrs. Hawk, what I'd learned about Grace's childhood, and what Calvin and I had started to wonder about Grace's sexual adventures with Travis Gifford.

"Boy," said Michael, "for a woman who rates having sex right around the level of laundry-folding, you're sure spending a lot of time speculating about walks on the wild side."

"Michael, that is *not* what I said," I protested.

"In all fairness, I do think," said Dr. Mephisto, "you're misquoting Maggie."

"But here's why I was excited we were seeing you this afternoon," I continued. "I want a therapist's point of view. Is it likely that someone who was abused in that way as a kid, tied up,and, in the last case, virtually abandoned—or at least that's how it must have seemed to her, how is it possible that she'd like getting tied up for sex play?"

"I'm not an expert in abused kids," said Dr. Mephisto, "but it's actually quite common to see people re-creating some sense of the trauma they've experienced. Since you've already described the fact that Grace would sometimes revisit the 'tying-up' as a kind of comfort gesture when she was a child, it does make some sense she'd experience that kind of practice as some kind of emotional clue."

"But wait," said Michael. "Lots of people get into bondage or some playful S&M, no matter what happened in their childhood, right?"

"That's true," said Dr. Mephisto. "And again, I'm only speculating. But what Maggie describes is a very specific activity, and assuming it was consensual between Mrs. Plummer and her partner, it might have enabled her to regain some sense of control over her childhood memories. In other words, as a child, being tied up was something terrible that happened to her. As an adult, she found a way to desensitize—and, in fact, to eroticize—the act of being restrained."

Michael shook his head, "I don't know. Seems pretty speculative to me. And in the end, does it matter? Travis readily owned up to their particular brand of sex play; he never said Grace coerced him into it. And what if she had? Hardly seems grounds for murder."

"No," I said slowly, just thinking back to the AWE factors Michael's students had raised. "But remember, one of the things your students suggested we figure out is who else knew about the bondage. Whoever murdered Grace, assuming it wasn't Travis, had to know about it in order to stage the murder scene in the back of Travis's limo."

"So who could have known?" asked Michael. "Did Travis's mother, Ivory, know? Did Ginger know? Those seem like the logical suspects."

"Do you happen to know..." began Dr. Mephisto.

"What?" I prompted her.

She laughed, "I think we've moved way behind the reason for our work together today. You've managed to get me caught up in your mystery."

"So you're saying we need to get back on topic?" said Michael.

"We do," she said.

"Okay, okay," I countered, "but go ahead and finish what you were going to ask. Do we happen to know what?"

"Well, I have to wonder if Grace had also involved her husband in this kind of sex play. In other words, if this is something she'd initiated because of all the reasons we were discussing, she might have engaged in this kind of activity with her husband as well."

"She might," I said, "but it hardly matters. He has an ironclad, cast-in-cement alibi for that evening."

"Perhaps he has," said Michael slowly. "But if he and Grace

were into 'tie-me-up,' might he have mentioned that to one of his buddies?"

"You mean Bill Brand, Ginger's husband, don't you?" I said, getting excited.

Dr. Mephisto raised her hand, "Time-out, folks. First, I'm lost with all these names. Second, you're paying me to work with you on your relationship, not be the third Harvey Girl."

"Hardy," I muttered. "And they were boys. Harvey Girls were in that movie Judy Garland did. Okay, okay."

Michael nudged me with his foot. "Say thank you, Maggie. It was helpful for Dr. McQuist to talk about this stuff, wasn't it?"

"It was," I said, somewhat grudgingly. "Thank you."

"You're welcome," she responded politely. "And now, back to work." And more yada yada yada about the questions of trust, intimacy, and how and why we managed to turn unloading the dishwasher into a power struggle.

CHAPTER 22

At 3 a.m., I sat upright in bed, my heart doing that too much caffeine, just averting a midintersection collision kind of race. I swung my legs over the bed, slipped into my squirrel slippers (a hideous, furry birthday present from the boys, but I couldn't part with them), threw on my robe, and crept downstairs. The bluish light from the stove made the kitchen eerie and unfamiliar. I turned on all the overhead lights, even though the sudden brightness made my eyes hurt. I filled the kettle and turned the burner to high, fished out a Sleepytime chamomile tea bag, and waited for the kettle to whistle. "Sleepytime," I said in disgust, as my heart began to slow down. "You are such an old lady."

While I waited for the kettle, I flipped through the latest issue of *Bon Appétit,* stacked on top of yesterday's newspapers on the kitchen table. "Great American Breakfasts," was the cover story. Lemon pancakes. I could mix up a batch, surprise everyone when they got up. I yawned. Or not. The kettle began hissing and rocking, preparatory to one big whistle. I turned it off, poured the hot water into the cup, gave the teabag a perfunctory dunk or two, and took a sip. My heart was back to normal. At the edge of my consciousness, I felt the dream that had awakened me nibbling away. Like the "mousey on the housey" in *Hansel and Gretel.* The kids' book? Or the opera? We had taken the boys to see the San Francisco Opera production last season, thinking the color and drama and, of course, the magic of an all-candy house would enchant them. But it was a noirish production, and the children's poverty and hunger heartbreaking. And everything looked gray, even the candy house seemed foggy and depressing. And the witch was truly frightening. Had I dreamed about a different witch? I coaxed the memory, struggled, and let go. Took a sip of tea, and suddenly the image from my dream was clear. I saw Ginger standing in the San Francisco Botanical Gardens, as I had seen her that day when she and Frederick dedicated Grace's fountain. But there was no one else there, in my dream. Just *Little Shop of Horror* plants, growing and grasping, but nothing was the right color. Like that disappointing production of *Hansel and Gretel,* everything looked gray. But the plants were growing all over Ginger, choking her, and in my dream, she was calling for someone to help. Not Bill. Was it her father? Was it Travis? Grace?

I remembered reading that creative people dream in color; the rest of us in black and white. Raider padded into the kitchen and put his nose on my lap.

"I'm not even creative enough to dream in black and white, buddy," I said aloud. "Just gray." Raider lost interest. He didn't care for middle-of-the-night conversation; he just wanted a treat. He collapsed on the floor, and took up his preferred semivigilant position, half on, half off my feet. I spied my briefcase, stationed next to the window seat, and brought it back to the table. Once upon a time I had thought being an editor was glamorous, fantasies of Anna Wintour, front seats at the Fashion Week runways, all that. Ha. Instead, my life was a computer and a briefcase. I rummaged inside the briefcase. Two files of work awaited me—first drafts of this month's standing features and columns. Hoyt had whipped the deadline-ignoring troops into order, which meant I got their work in plenty of time to review. But not now. The other folder was filled with office detritus—correspondence Gertie thought I should review, invoices to approve, especially vicious Letters to the Editor for past transgressions. Yuck. Tomorrow. I glanced at the kitchen clock, 3:30. It was tomorrow. Well, later today. Instead, I took out the list of AWE questions Michael's young overachievers had posed.

"Who else knew about Grace and Travis's taste in S&M?"

Underneath the question, I had written: Ginger, yes; Bill, maybe; Frederick, who knows? Ivory, no, not til after the murder. Or so she said.

"Who else is a player?" I said aloud. Raider didn't even stir.

I scribbled: Purity, Carol Ann, Carol Ann's husband? Who else am I forgetting? Gus? Why would he or wouldn't he know? If Ginger knew, would she have told her father? Too kinky. Anyone else at A Mom's Place or the Botanical Gardens?

I circled Carol Ann's name. Hard to know why Grace would have told her—according to Purity, Carol Ann hero-worshipped Grace. That made it seem unlikely that Grace would have let her young protégé see a darker side. Stapled to the AWE sheet was a three-year-old clip from *Small Town*'s Glam Around Town feature the researcher had pulled for me. Grace and Frederick, the beautiful couple, at yet another swank party, she in form-fitting black, with a white rose pinned in her hair; he in black-tie. They were both mugging for the camera, arms around each other. No one could link up this self-confident, seemingly untroubled young woman with a little girl leashed, dirty, and neglected in a cheap apartment. "Oh, Gracie," I whispered. "I am so sorry this happened to you."

I felt a hand on my shoulder, and jumped. "Maggie," said Michael gently, "it's the middle of the night. You're down here talking to yourself."

"Not myself," I said, swiping at my eyes, suddenly wet and prickling with tears. I pointed at the picture. "I'm talking to Grace. I woke up at the witching hour, 3 a.m. exactly, and I was thinking about that witch in *Hansel and Gretel.*"

"I've always wondered where that expression came from," said Michael. "Is it when witches are supposed to catch their broom ride or something?"

"Jesus was born at 3 o'clock in the afternoon, according to Christian lore," I said. "So, the exact opposite moment at night is the witching hour. *Amityville Horror*, when stuff starts going crazy in the house—remember that? It happened at three o'clock in the morning every time."

Michael rubbed the back of my neck. "Here's the thing, *cara*, being married to you is never boring. Sometimes even instructive." He sat down next to me and took the picture from my hand. "This thing is making you crazy," he said.

"It wasn't," I said, "until this afternoon." I rubbed my finger across her face in the photograph. "It was interesting, it was provocative, it was a cool story. Even though I'm fascinated by Travis, even though I really like his mother, and I was—oh, I don't know—flattered that Isabella wanted my help, it was still kind of a lark."

"Lark, Maggie? The guy's on Death Row, the woman was murdered."

"Bad word," I said, digging in my bathrobe pocket. I dug out a cocktail napkin with dancing olives, arranged Rockette-style along the edge. "Where did this come from?" I asked.

Michael shrugged. "I never know where those weirdo little napkins come from. You buy them every place we go."

"It's my small rebellion against my mother," I said. "She thinks it's a crime to use paper napkins for anything." I mopped my nose with the dancing olives. "Anyway, not a lark, I didn't really mean that. I know this is serious. But I could think of it as..."

"Some kind of adventure?" asked Michael.

"Yeah, I guess," I confessed. "But this afternoon, sitting in Mrs. Hawk's living room and listening to that story, I've got Grace under my skin. I keep thinking how far that sad, ruined little girl must have come to turn into Grace Plummer, elegant, generous woman about town. And then," I snapped my finger, "she's gone. Brutally, horribly, degradingly gone."

Michael put his arm around me. "You've gotten yourself into something pretty ugly, *cara*."

"What happened was ugly, but that's what I'm trying to say. Grace wasn't ugly. She could have been narcissistic or selfish or shallow—or all those things I sometimes think when I see society photographs like this." I picked up the photo and shook it. "But she wasn't any of those things—she turned into somebody kind and hardworking. I keep wishing I'd known her—and known her grandparents, what good people they must have been. They dealt with the tragedy of losing their daughter and raised their granddaughter."

"A *mitzvah,* your mother would say," Michael observed. He took the photo from my hand again, and put it in the file. "Come to bed, Maggie. You're going to be wrecked in the morning."

I resisted. "I was looking at the AWE issues. I don't know if I'm going to be able to sleep."

He clasped my hand and raised me to my feet. "I'll wear you out," he said. "You'll drift off."

He did. And I did.

CHAPTER 23

Occasionally Travis would think, "I should tell Isabella about Grace. I should tell her it was Grace's idea, no, her request, that I tie her up." But why? It wouldn't change anything, and it wouldn't be—what was that word? Gallant. Who would it help? No one. He'd actually told Ivory the truth about it, how odd it seemed that Grace wanted it so much, that she visibly relaxed once he'd tied the knots. His mother had frowned, not in disapproval, but more puzzlement. But that was before the stroke. Now Ivory seemed to have forgotten they'd ever talked about it. It was just something else unpleasant she'd read in the paper about the murder. Yeah, there was plenty dark stuff in Grace's childhood, before she went to live with her grandparents. But those were secrets she told him. And what did it matter now? "You can trust me, Gracie," he whispered. "Even now."

CHAPTER 24

Isabella and I were sitting in Joe Kotter's office, drinking surprisingly good Italian pear spritzers, presented with a flourish after Kotter opened the most microrefrigerator I'd ever seen. Kotter, who had been Travis's trial attorney, worked from digs tucked into a corner of Pier 9, upstairs from some architects, and featuring two floor-to-ceiling windows with million-dollar views of the bay.

"Must be distracting," I said, mesmerized by the scenes unfolding outside the window, ferry boats docking, and from one angle, a straight shot at the tiny float-boats that bobbed outside AT&T Park, filled with mitt-wearing fans, just hoping for a home run to head out of the park and toward the water.

He laughed. "It should be. It used to be. Now, it's like wallpaper. Unless I'm staring out the window trying to solve a problem, I hardly notice it any more."

On the way over to Kotter's office, with my sheaf of AWE questions stashed beside me in an increasingly tattered folder, Isabella gave me a little more background on Kotter. "Worked in one of the big firms, finagled a half pro bono commitment from the firm to handle Travis's case—partly because it was a high-profile trial, and the managing partner thought it wouldn't be bad to shine a little light on their criminal-defense work, and partly because that same partner loved jazz and was a fan of The Devil's Interval."

"Where'd the other half of the fee come from?" I asked.

"That rough trade boyfriend of Ivory's," said Isabella. "Gus Reeves." She shook her head. "Boy, I don't see that as couple-of-the-year material, but I gather that guy would do anything for the woman he loves. Of course Travis doesn't think he's good enough for Ivory, but even he admits Gus has been a stand-up guy. Which kinda makes me think well of old Gus. Rich guy who stays loyal to a beautiful, but definitely middle-aged-plus woman."

"Lifelong love affair," I said. "At least that's how he described it to me. Not exactly reciprocal, but that doesn't seem to deter him. And he seems very loyal and supportive of his daughter. Definitely a guy who admires women."

"Just like Travis," said Isabella.

"Maybe," I said. "But you should have seen Gus watching Ginger giving her little talk in the garden."

"Makes me think better of little Ginger," said Andrea, "that she invites her dad to events like that. I mean, he's hardly Father Knows Best material."

"Love, love, love," I said. "Go figure."

"Anyway," Isabella said, "getting back to our guy, Kotter. After the trial, he didn't make partner, so he decided to hang out his own little shingle and left the big offices in the Embarcadero Center and moved out here. He subleases from some architect buddies, old friends from college, I think."

Isabella whipped her car into the cavernous hangarlike entrance to Pier 9. "Watch for number six on the parking spots," she said. "Joe snagged the guest parking slot for us today."

Kotter put his feet up on the table and patiently listened as we went through the AWE factors. "Michael's students did a pretty good job," he said, "but I don't think there's any smoking gun they've turned up." He gave a wry smile. "You could always go for the incompetent representation, Isabella," he said.

"I would if I could," she said. "But, I think you did a pretty good job."

"And does that mean you'll go out with me?" he said.

Isabella shook her head. "I'm a single mom with a toddler. Trust me, I'm not the girl of your dreams."

"You have no idea what I dream about," said Kotter.

"No idea, and not much interest," said Isabella.

I listened to the banter and felt as if my romantic radar was tuned to frequency zero.zero. Was Isabella *really* not interested? Or just playing keepaway? Was Kotter flirting out of reflex, or was he in pursuit? All too tough to figure out. Note to self: You and Michael need to make this marriage work; you'd never survive out in the brutal reality show known as dating.

"So, Maggie asked me an intriguing question the other day," Isabella was saying. "She wondered if there was something that really bothered you about the trial, now that it's over and done and you've had time to think about it."

"Sure," said Kotter, "it bothered the hell out of me that we lost. And not just because I hate losing, but because I happen to think Travis is a pretty good guy—and I honestly don't think he did it."

"But something else," I persisted. "Something that never sat right with you."

"A bunch of stuff," he said. "Maybe that old lady across the street was right, and there was another car—or two there that evening. We just couldn't find anything to back that up. But the real ball-breaker was all the complexity in this crime. If somebody wanted to kill Grace, fine—go do it. Drop some poison in her drink at one of those dozens of parties she went to. Break into her house and kill her and leave her there. But why murder her and then frame Travis? And then why do it in such a risky way?" He shook his head. "It made no sense. Whoever killed Grace took one chance after another. They're moving a body, maybe across town, wrestling it in and out of some vehicle, and then into Travis's limo. I know she didn't weigh much, but wrangling any adult body isn't light work."

"But people who murder don't have to make sense, do they?" I asked. "They get mad or scared or greedy or they're protecting something or someone or getting revenge, and they just do it."

"And that's why most people get caught," said Kotter. "They're doing something stupid and impetuous and they leave tracks all over the place. But again, that's what was so weird about this murder. The killer wasn't stupid—he or she used an untraceable gun, either to distract or confuse the cops about the broken neck, and left no calling cards we've been able to uncover. But this is what kept me up at night: Why would somebody that smart then make as dumb and risky a move as transporting the body just to frame somebody else?"

"Because," I said slowly, "it had to be somebody who didn't just want to get rid of Grace. They wanted to get rid of Travis, too. One murder, two victims."

"See?" said Isabella. "That's why Frederick was so tempting a suspect. First of all, you always look to the spouse in a murder. And second, Grace had certainly given Frederick ample reason to be jealous."

"Great theory," I said, "except for Frederick's ironclad alibi. And I suppose you did enough work to rule out the murder-for-hire theory?'"

"Maggie loves that theory," said Isabella.

"I did love it," I admitted, "but there's something about Frederick that doesn't fit with that theory. He just seemed sad about Grace's affair with Travis, not angry, and maybe even a little understanding. Plus, he strikes me as the kind of guy who only knows how to do what he knows how to do—run a company, make money, make deals. I think he'd be baffled enough by finding a hired killer, that he'd screw it up or leave a trail or something."

"Doesn't matter," said Kotter. "We burned through a fair amount of PI resources tracking that avenue. Turned up zilch. In fact, antizilch. Just before Grace was killed, Frederick had helped establish a charitable remainder trust for A Mom's Place, which meant that if something happened to her, Frederick would get less, not more, of her assets. So, he didn't have any kind of a financial incentive to set a little fire under the jealousy motive."

We all sat in silence. Kotter had been fiddling with the bottlecaps he'd popped off the pear spritzer. He picked one up, took aim at the trash can several feet away, and with a practiced shot, banked it off the side of the can and neatly into the bottom. He picked up the second, and then the third, and did the same thing.

"Good shots," I said.

"Practice," Kotter replied. Isabella walked over to the window and looked out at the water. I could feel the energy draining out of all of us.

"Okay," I said. "Not to obsess about this, but you both know these transcripts up, down, and sideways. Anything else that struck you?"

"I could never figure out why it was so difficult to trace Grace's tracks that evening," said Kotter. "I mean, Travis said he brought her back to her house. It was pretty late. And I don't know about you girls, but after I get laid, I'm pretty whacked. I'm ready to catch some Zs." He picked up a paper clip, and sent it ricocheting into the trash can. "But if Travis is telling the truth, she went home, she probably took a shower, so Frederick doesn't come home and—let's not be indelicate—get a whiff of some other dog who's been sniffing around his kennel, right?"

"That's delicate?" asked Isabella. "I'm moving the odds that I'll ever go out with you from one thousand to one, to one million to nothing."

"Sorry," he said. "But you get my point. She's home, she's either taken a shower and in the pj's and robe, or about to get into the shower. So, why in the hell did she go out again? And where did she go? And who the hell with?"

"No chance she was murdered at her house and then moved to the limo?" I asked.

Kotter shook his head. "Forensics says no. Gunshots make a big mess, and even if the killer had spread plastic bags down and put Grace on top of 'em and then did her, there'd have been something. A little blood spray. Or, just the tracks pulling that plastic with her on it would have made on the floor. The place was pretty clean, because these rich folks have good housekeepers, but there's still a little everyday life debris on the floor, and nothing had been disturbed. Anywhere."

"Plus," added Isabella, "if she had to go out unexpectedly, since it was so late, wouldn't she have left Frederick a note, so he wouldn't worry?"

"Wouldn't he just assume she was with Travis?"

"According to Frederick's testimony, she didn't lie when she was seeing Travis, but she often said she was 'having dinner with a friend,' and he didn't pry."

"But he got worried," said Kotter, "because she didn't make their Cinderella deadline."

"Come again?"

"Oh, apparently they had an agreement that they'd both be home by midnight, if they weren't together, or they'd leave a note or message on each other's cell."

"Because," Kotter picked up the end of the story, "Grace would occasionally go very late to the Crimson."

We fell into silence. "The rich are different," said Isabella.

"So, what do any of these loose ends tell us?" I asked.

Kotter shook his head. "Not one damn thing."

"We need to figure out *why* Grace went out and who she went with. Or who she met," I said.

"Good luck with that," said Isabella.

CHAPTER 25

"Do you know what the witching hour is?" I asked Andrea a few days later.

"I know what the triple witching hour is," she replied promptly. "It's some confluence-of-timing phenomenon in the stock market."

"It is?"

"Third Friday of the month four times a year, when contracts on options and futures expire at the same time."

"How is that witchy?"

"I think all that activity at once makes the stocks act weird, go up and down—fluctuate, you know."

"How do you know that?"

"My father, my brothers, my uncles, my cousins, my grandfathers—all guys on Wall Street."

"It's all about witches," I said. "I woke up at 3 a.m. a few days ago, with some improbable *Hansel and Gretel* witch left over from my dream, and I haven't been able to shake it."

"Maybe you're thinking of Grace as some kind of witch. An enchantress," she said.

I shook my head. "I'm just growing sadder and sadder about Grace, the more I learn about her. She was no witch."

"I know what you mean," said Andrea. "I'm starting to feel like we're in some remake of *Laura.* The movie where the detective falls in love with the dead woman. Who was that detective, anyway?"

"Dana Andrews, and Vincent Price played that really creepy guy who hid the gun in the grandfather clock. But you're exactly right. We're getting to know this dead woman, and we're getting enchanted by her."

"Well," said Andrea, "unlike *Laura*, I think there's virtually no chance our dead woman is going to walk in the door."

"Before you go," I said. "What's up with Carol Ann? Did you get a chance to talk with her?"

"I did," said Andrea, "and I'll e-mail you my notes." She fingered her pearls. "Another sad story. She really believed she's come as far as she has in her life because of Grace."

"She finished school, right?" I asked

Andrea nodded. "Finished high school, is just a few credits away from her undergraduate degree, married a nice young man who's in law school. Oh, and two adorable little girls. I went with her to pick them up at day care after she finished work at the Ocean View Day Spa, so we could keep talking."

Andrea's eyes welled with tears. She swiped at them impatiently. "Her second daughter was born just six months after Grace died. They named the baby Grace."

"How sad that the grown-up Grace never knew," I said.

"She didn't even know Carol Ann was pregnant," said Andrea.

"Funny," I said. "You'd think she'd share that kind of good news right away with Grace."

Andrea shrugged. "I guess she didn't get a chance. She said she was going to tell Grace the night she died."

"That night? That very night?" I asked, sitting up straight and catching Andrea by the arm.

"Calm down, Maggie," said Andrea. "That's what she said. I know it's sad, but I don't know what you're getting so worked up about."

"Because if she was going to tell her that evening, maybe she tried to call Grace that night. Or went over there and saw something."

Andrea looked skeptical. "She didn't say anything like that, and I'm sure the police questioned her and it would have come up. In fact, I know the police questioned her; she told me. She said it was very upsetting for her husband."

I looked at my hands. "Will you just look at these raggedy nails?" I said.

Andrea raised an eyebrow. "You have no nails at all, Maggie. You cut them off to play the piano."

I ignored her. "I think a mani-pedi is the perfect indulgence, don't you?"

"I knew you wouldn't be satisfied with whatever I found out," said Andrea. "Just do me the kindness of looking at my notes so I feel that it was worth my while to go through the charade of talking with Carol Ann myself."

"Not a charade," I said, trying to sound chastened. "You turned up an interesting piece of information—that Carol Ann was about to tell Grace she was pregnant just before she died. I just want to have a chance to talk with her myself.

"Besides," I added, "I need a little grooming tune-up. I'm going to be at the Junior League fashion show, watching you strut your stuff and making your mother feel welcome at the *Small Town* table."

Andrea paused, and turned around. She narrowed her eyes at me. "I'd hoped you'd forgotten we had a table at the show," she said. "And don't try to pull a fast one on me. You are not going to be there to watch me. You're not even interested in seeing anything on the runway."

"How do you know?" I protested.

"Because you're going to be there watching Calvin and my mother together. Or, you've got some nefarious detecting planned."

"Or both," I said. "That's a possibility. We women are multitaskers, you know."

When I walked into Ocean View Day Spa later that afternoon, I actually started to believe the indulge-oneself philosophy women's magazines spout. The hectic hours between coffee with Andrea and stepping into the taupe, cream, and brown understatement that was Ocean View Day Spa seemed to disappear. Apologizing to a theater company about wrong information and a vicious review—gone; explaining six ways to Sunday why we were paying a kill fee instead of accepting a lame-brained feature on some wacky, herbal alternative to Botox—gone; gobbling a carton of yogurt and a KitKat while sitting through an excruciating budget meeting, with time out to field a call from Josh's teacher about the increasingly risqué jokes he seemed to be telling on the playground—gone. Well, the last item wasn't gone, but it seemed less urgent when I realized that I could make an excellent case for Michael dealing with the problem.

Little matter, I thought, as I sank into the sueded easy chair, with my feet up on an ottoman, sipping unexpectedly delicious herb tea, while I waited for my mani-pedi adventure. From the waiting room, a series of picture windows opened onto dramatic ocean views—ocean, not bay, with the rocky coastline just below, and the afternoon sun starting to edge toward the western horizon. Gulls wheeled outside the windows. Best of all, instead of the predictable spa soundtrack—goopy New Age harp music—I could hear the late Beethoven string quartets softly pouring from the speakers. It was so blissful just sitting there, I was somewhat startled when Carol Ann came out of her office to greet me and apologized profusely for the "aesthetician," who was running just a little behind.

"I'm early," I said. "This is heaven in a teacup just to sit here for a few minutes. And you're so nice to come say hello."

"Purity told me you were doing a story on Grace," she said. "And I talked to the writer who's working on the story the other day. I just want you to know how happy I am that you'll be saying nice things about Grace in the article."

I was silent.

"You are, aren't you?" she asked. "Saying good things?"

"Well," I hedged, "it's a magazine article, not a eulogy."

She looked troubled. "I don't want to talk to you if it's not a positive story." Trouble, on Carol Ann's creamy-skinned, perfect-featured young face, simply dimmed a little of the incandescence.

I raised my hand. "Carol Ann, I want to tell you something." I took a deep breath. "When we began this story, I didn't know what I thought about Grace Plummer. And when I first saw the background on her, I have to admit I jumped to a pretty stereotypical set of conclusions—some spoiled socialite with more time and money than the rest of us."

Carol Ann started to bridle. "But then," I continued, "I began to get to know who Grace really was. I visited A Mom's Place, I talked to people like Purity and the folks at the San Francisco Botanical Gardens. And a completely different picture of Grace started to emerge."

Her face brightened. "Thank you for telling me that. You know," she colored a little, "I'm taking a journalism class to finish out my writing requirements at San Francisco State. I'm almost done with my degree," she added shyly.

"Andrea, the writer who talked with you, told me," I said. "Congratulations."

"Thank you. I have to say I feel proud of myself, and I think that Grace would be proud of me as well. But anyway, in this class, as we're reading news stories, I've started to see how—well, wrong so many stories are in the media. Not just print," she said hastily, "television and radio and online, too. I mean, sometimes you can recognize the truth in a story, but it's as if no one has the time to get things really right. They may get some of the facts, but..." she faltered.

"I know just what you mean," I said. "Fortunately, we're a magazine, so we get to take a little longer when we're working on a story than daily newspapers do, but it's still never enough to get things exactly right. But, I'll tell you this, we're doing our best on this story, and we keep turning up new and interesting information."

"Information on Grace?" she asked.

"On Grace and other people as well," I said.

I looked at Carol Ann and made a decision. "You know," I said, "I want to tell you a story about Grace's childhood that may help explain why she was drawn to A Mom's Place."

It was a judgment call, but I knew we couldn't use the information in the story that ran in *Small Town*, and somehow it seemed as if Carol Ann should hear the story anyway. So I told Carol Ann—about Grace's childhood, about her mother, about being raised by her grandparents.

She went from puzzled to wide-eyed to stricken in just a few minutes.

"She never told me," said Carol Ann.

"Nothing about this story?" I pressed her.

She shook her head. "No, but it explains so much. She always told me that I could invent my own life. That whatever I wanted, I could just decide, and go after it and make it a real thing."

"What did she mean by that, do you think?"

"It wasn't just about material things," said Carol Ann, "though I know she wanted me to be able to earn a good living. She wanted me to get an education and feel happy. She said she knew it was possible to just—what was her phrase—'gut through' the bad stuff and create a whole new life." Carol Ann laughed. "Once when we planted a winter garden at A Mom's Place, broccoli and things, we woke up one morning, and all the outer leaves were gone. Some neighborhood kid's pet bunnies had gotten into the yard and nibbled everything in the raised beds down to nothing. We were so upset, but Grace just laughed. She said gardening taught her to be humble and persistent. That someone else might try to wreck what you were doing, but you always have another planting season to try again."

A young woman in a taupe smock leaned over my chair. "Mrs. Fiori, I'm ready for you."

Carol Ann stood up. "You know what, Charlene? I'll take care of Mrs. Fiori myself." Charlene looked startled, and a little offended.

"It's all right," Carol Ann said, putting her arm around the young woman's shoulder. "I'm crediting this to your account. It's just that Mrs. Fiori and I..." she paused.

"We're friends," I said hastily. "This gives us a chance to catch up."

"Go get yourself a coffee," said Carol Ann. "Put your feet up for a few minutes. Think of it as an unexpected vacation."

The young woman's face brightened. She hugged Carol Ann, "Thank you. I was up all night with the baby, and I'd love to sit down for a few minutes." And in an instant, she disappeared back through the billowing, chiffon curtains.

Soon, Carol Ann had me settled at a manicure table, positioned so that whoever sat on the client side of the table could look out on the view. There were oversize arrangements of exotic white flowers everywhere—and the room was filled with fragrance I dimly remembered from a long-ago trip to Hawaii. "This feels wonderful," I said, almost whispering, though no one could hear us. "It reminds me of staying up late with a girlfriend and doing each other's nails and discussing important issues like did we think Bobby Gage was cute or not?"

"Soak," said Carol Ann, gently guiding my hands into a bath of warm, sandalwood-scented water. "Well, then, you'll have to do my manicure next."

"Sure," I said.

She shook her head. "I'm just being silly. This is fun for me, too. Mostly I do paperwork in the office these days, juggling work schedules, ordering supplies, things like that."

I sat in silence and watched her work.

"Purity told me a story about Grace taking you for a manicure the night of your high school prom," I said.

"She did so many things for me," said Carol Ann. "I always wanted to do something for her."

"Is that why you named your daughter after her?" I asked.

Carol Ann patted my hands dry, one at a time.

"I just wish she'd known."

"You didn't have a chance to tell her?"

She looked down at my right hand, busily pushing the cuticle back.

"No, I wanted to tell her, just as soon as I knew I was pregnant. But Steven, my husband, thought we should wait 'til I was past the first three months before we told anyone."

"In case something happened?"

"Yes," she said. "But that was so hard for me. Hard to keep something like that from Grace."

I was quiet for a moment, watching Carol work. I'd heard something in her voice that seemed not quite right.

"Carol Ann," I said. "Did you really keep that news from Grace?"

She looked up, startled. "What do you mean? I told you I didn't have a chance to tell her."

I looked at her carefully. She broke eye contact and picked up my other hand.

"I think you couldn't stand keeping that kind of secret," I said.

She kept her head down, but I could see the curve of her cheek turning pink.

"I assure you," she said, still not looking up, "Grace died without knowing I was expecting another baby." She put my hand down, looked up and met my eyes straightforwardly. "And I don't think it's very nice of you to come here and accuse me of telling a lie."

Good going, Maggie, I thought. Nothing like insulting a lovely young woman who's had troubles you never dreamed about. I put my damp hand on Carol Ann's. Her eyes were blazing at me now.

"I'm so sorry," I said.

She blinked quickly, and I realized she was about to cry.

"Carol Ann," I began again. "I didn't mean to upset you. I just..." I trailed off, as tears began to run soundlessly down her cheeks.

"Why are you asking me about this?" she said. "Oh, never mind. I want to tell someone. But..." she snatched tissues from the box next to the manicure table, and blew her nose. "How did you know I told her? Well, actually I didn't tell her. But I almost did."

And then the words came tumbling out. How her husband,

Steven, was studying at the library late one night. And her toddler was fussy, so she'd packed her in the car and gone for a ride.

"I didn't mean to go to Grace's," she said, "but we ended up on her street. Jenny had fallen asleep, so I was just sitting outside Grace's house. I could see lights on upstairs, and her husband's car was gone, so I thought I'd wait 'til Jenny woke up, and surprise Grace by ringing her doorbell."

I could feel my heart speeding up. The water was cooling, and feeling a little slimy, but I was afraid to move my hand out; afraid that if I made a move, I'd spook Carol Ann and she'd stop talking.

Carol Ann looked over her shoulder. "I can't believe I'm opening my mouth and all this is coming out," she said.

"I'm listening."

She gulped, the way kids do when they've been crying, and are ready to get control of themselves again. She sat back in the chair.

"I was going to call Grace from my cell, and tell her we were outside, but..."

I caught my breath. Mrs. Lomax had been right. The mystery car belonged to Carol Ann.

"But?"

She shrugged. "You know how you get some picture in your head sometimes? I just had this picture of waiting on Grace's doorstep, and as soon as she opened the door, saying something like 'guess what? There's going to be another baby—and if it's a girl, we're naming her Grace.' So, I wanted to surprise her. I couldn't wait to see her face!"

"You didn't get a chance to do that, did you?"

She shook her head. "No. Jenny was just starting to stir, so I'd climbed into the back, to get her out of her car seat, in case she needed changing, before we went up to Grace's doorstep. The diaper bag was on the floor of the backseat, so I was bent down, rummaging in it, and when I sat back up, I saw someone standing on Grace's front porch. And then Grace was opening the door for him."

"Him? You could see him?"

She shook her head. "No, I couldn't see anything really. It was dark, and he had his back to me, but I could tell it was a man."

"Didn't you get out of the car?"

She shook her head. "No, it was weird. The man had clearly said something that upset Grace—she disappeared back into the house, came back with a coat, and literally ran across the lawn with this guy. She was moving so fast, I didn't even have time to call out to her. I remember," she stopped and swallowed. "There was a scarf hanging out of her coat pocket, and she was running so it looked like a kite tail, floating out in back of her. I couldn't be sure because it was pretty dark." She hesitated. "But it looked like a flowery scarf I had given her for her birthday." She stopped. I hoped Carol Ann would never see the grim police photo I had seen, the one with Grace's hands bound in back of her—by a flowery scarf.

"Then what?"

"There was a van parked in the driveway, and they both got in it and zoomed away."

Right again, Mrs. Lomax, I thought. There *were* two vehicles.

"What time was that? Do you remember?"

"Around ten, I think."

"You didn't notice the license plate?"

"No, Jenny was awake, and had started to fuss, so I was dealing with her, and besides—it all happened so fast."

"You never told the police any of this?" I asked.

She flushed. "I didn't. Wasn't that dumb? But Steven said they might think I had something to do with the murder. Since I was kind of lurking around her house. Plus, Grace's body was found in that guy's limo, and this was a van, so I didn't see how they could be connected."

She was silent for a moment. "At least, I couldn't see how it would have anything to do with the murder. So, I really haven't let myself think about that night since then." She hesitated. "And then, there was one other thing. It's odd but, as the van was pulling away, I thought, 'Oh, that's funny, I think there's someone in the backseat.'"

"You mean you saw someone?" I asked.

She shook her head. "Not exactly. It's just that, as the van was driving away, I had this vague impression there was someone..." She paused to think. "A short someone, who must have been lying down on the seat, or something, because I had this impression of some figure cautiously sitting up. I assumed it was a woman, because the person was short. But, I guess it could have been a young person or a short man. I remember thinking, 'Ah, somebody besides Jenny had a nap,' " she finished. She looked at me. "What do you think?"

"I think you have to tell the police what you told me," I said. "Or maybe the lawyer who's handling Travis's appeal. I don't really know. But somebody needs to know this."

Carol Ann nodded. "I know," she said miserably. "It just didn't seem to have anything to do with the murder," she repeated. "I mean, I assumed she'd run out that night on an errand or something, and then somehow, ended up with Travis Gifford later that night. I knew." She hesitated.

"Knew what?"

"That sometimes, when Frederick wasn't home, Travis would come by and take Grace out. Just for a drive. Or..." she faltered.

"Or for a late date," I suggested.

She looked uncomfortable. "Yes, I guess so."

"Did Grace tell you about...those dates?" I asked. "Or you just concluded that?"

Carol Ann hesitated. "It's not like we had some big talk about her relationship with Travis. It's just that she didn't make it much of a secret. I guess," she hesitated again. "I guess I didn't think it was a secret from Frederick, either. From Mr. Plummer," she corrected herself. "I thought maybe they had some kind of agreement."

"Did that bother you?"

She shrugged. "I loved Grace, and so whatever she did was okay with me. I don't mean I think it's great to be unfaithful or anything," she amended hastily. "But I don't know much about the kind of lives people like the Plummers have. It's like a book Grace gave me, *The Great Gatsby*."

"The rich are different from you and me?" I asked.

"That's right," said Carol Ann. "Or at least that's how I explained it to myself. But anyway, none of it seemed important—it didn't interfere with what a good person Grace was."

"Except maybe it got her killed," I mused.

"Maybe," said Carol Ann, "but maybe not. Maybe Travis didn't even do it, is that what you're suggesting?"

"I didn't make the original suggestion," I said grimly. "But people I respect are saying just that, and I have a feeling they're going to be glad to hear from you."

CHAPTER 26

I had Michael on the phone before I was out of the parking lot at the Ocean View spa. All those mellow feelings, all that relaxation, all those unknotted muscles—vanished. I rattled out my report to Michael, dodging slow-moving Pacific Heights Lexuses, Baby Benzes, and enormous SUVs, so critical to navigating the off-road retail opportunities along Union Street.

"So what do I do now?" I demanded of Michael, sitting on the horn in hopes of persuading a double-parked gaggle outside of Stuart Hall School for noblesse oblige–to–be Boys to move on.

"Maggie," said Michael. "Slow down. Stop driving like a NASCAR nutcase and calm down."

"I'm calm," I said, a little too loudly. "And I'm just trying to get through this after-school traffic mess. Geez, can't any of these kids walk home?"

"Oh," said Michael, "you mean like our little princes? As opposed to having you, me, or Anya pick them up?"

"That's different," I said. "It's not elitist if you're doing the schlepping in Oakland, instead of Pacific Heights."

"Uh-huh," said Michael.

"Okay, don't you think this is an exciting development?" I demanded. "I think I turned up something no one else had uncovered. There *were* two vehicles at Grace's that night."

"You turned it up probably because you hectored the poor girl to death," said Michael. "But yes, in fact, this could be very important. And it's too damn bad she hadn't reported this to anyone else."

"She didn't know it was important. She wasn't at the trial. She didn't hear Mrs. Lomax's testimony. Okay, so what do I do first?"

"Nothing. You drive home, and we'll talk about it tonight. You're already scaring me to death, this full of adrenaline and probably a couple of double espressos, talking on the phone and threatening the locals in Pacific Heights behind the wheel. I'll call Isabella—that's who you owe the information to first. She needs to talk to the trial attorney, and together, they can talk to the cops."

"I think I should call Isabella," I protested.

"Don't worry, you can give her word-for-word, play-by-play tonight," said Michael. "I'm not stealing your Nancy Drew thunder, but let's get her going on things, and you just get yourself home."

By the time I'd crossed the Bay Bridge, picked up the boys at school, and made my way home, Michael was in the kitchen, a bottle of Pacifico nearby, agitating something on the stove, with chopped peppers heaped on the cutting block. The kitchen was filled with the fragrance of cumin, chili, and onions.

"Tostadas!" yelled Josh, dropping his books, backpack and hockey stick in the entryway, and creating an obstacle course for his little brother. Zach dealt, as he always did, by nimbly leaping over each and every item. They thundered through the kitchen, swiped chunks of cheese off the counter, raced upstairs.

"Hey, guys," shouted Michael. "Get your homework done and we can watch a movie tonight." Vague calls of compliance and excitement drifted back down the stairs.

I stashed my briefcase under the kitchen table, greeted Raider, and made my way to Michael for a kiss. "Yum, smells great," I said. "Thanks for getting things going."

"And here's the most amazing part," said Michael, "not only does Wonder Husband manage to get dinner well in hand, but he simultaneously acts as his wife's dedicated legal staff and supervises late-breaking bulletins from the 'cold case' front."

I dug a companion Pacifico out of the fridge, sat at the kitchen table and eased off my pumps.

"Okay, Wonder Dude, I'll wash up and help in just a minute," I said, "but bring me up to date so I don't have to interrogate you."

Michael raised his eyebrows, "Will tying up be involved in the interrogation?"

Between stirring the sizzling chicken, peppers, and onions in the pan and taking swigs of beer, Michael gave me the news bulletins. He'd reached Isabella, she'd reached the trial attorney, they were meeting this evening, talking to the cops tomorrow, and would keep us informed.

"Keep us informed?" I demanded. "What kind of deal is that? I'm the one out gathering intelligence."

"And aren't you proud of yourself?" asked Michael.

I grinned. "You bet I am," I confessed. "I mean, everyone at work is always giving me such grief because I'm not a 'real reporter.' I didn't come up through newspapers or anything serious, so it's pretty cool when I feel as if I really can get people to talk to me." I swigged. "Like a real reporter."

"You are so transparent," said Michael, "and just a little full of it. You mean, 'like a real detective,' don't you?"

"Oh, maybe. Doesn't really matter how the information gets uncovered, does it? After all, it was a journalism class at Northwestern that broke that death row story, and proved that guy innocent. Detective, journalist, we're all after the truth."

"And let's not forget justice and the American Way," said Michael.

"Come on, Michael, cut me a break," I protested. "If this turns out to be useful to the case, if there is something here that helps Isabella with Travis's case, this really is important."

He turned the flame down under the pan, picked up his beer, and folded himself into the chair next to me. "I know, *cara*," he said. "I don't mean to belittle this. In fact, you may have turned up something useful—or maybe not. We don't know enough yet, and probably won't until the police look into this. I'm afraid," he hesitated, "this could turn into something pretty sticky for Carol Ann."

"Really?" I asked. "She didn't do anything wrong."

"Technically she did. She had information, she had been in a conversation with the police, and she made a decision not to share everything she knew."

"Damn," I said. "She's such a good egg, and she's had such a tough time in life, I don't want this to get ugly for her. Plus, her husband is the one who discouraged her from reporting what she saw."

"Doesn't bode well for him, either. Especially not for a guy in law school," said Michael.

I looked at the wall phone. "Don't even think about it, Maggie," said Michael. "You're at least playing by some semblance of the rules now. Isabella's got the info, she's talking to—what's his name? The trial attorney?"

"Joe Kotter," I said, tearing my eyes away from the phone.

"Okay, you're right." I stood up, collected my shoes, and headed for the stairs. "I'm going to wash up, change, and come help. Where's Anya?"

"Out," said Michael. "With Dr. Bollywood. That's the good news." Off and on, between her not-so-smart romantic choices, Anya had gone back to dating Dr. Reza Singh, the young Indian doctor who'd treated me at the ER the night my last detecting adventure turned dangerous. It had been love—or lust—at first sight, and despite Anya's spectacularly checkered romantic past, the infatuation was turning into a real relationship. And we more than approved—charming, well-educated, and so achingly movie-star dishy that the staff at the ER, women and men alike, referred to him as Dr. Bollywood. Plus when he came to dinner, he brought an endless supply of delicious chutneys his aunts made for him. And such a relief from her track record of bounders, slackers, and deliberately underemployed beaux.

In fact, the phone rang less than usual that night—the disingenuous little strumpets for Josh, with their alleged requests for homework clarification; a hockey buddy wanting to carpool to Saturday practice with Michael; and Michael's mother, wondering if we were going to show up for some distant cousin's first communion Sunday after next. Michael caught my eye, and I made a beseeching face in response, "Ma, we'll have to get back to you on that. Maggie's got to check her schedule."

He settled next to me on the couch, and hit play, bringing the 400th showing of *Rudy* to life on our screen. The boys sprawled on cushions on the floor, prepared to repeat every line of dialogue by heart.

"And yet," I whispered into his ear, "another reason we should have had a daughter."

"What's that?"

"Chick flicks, occasionally, instead of *Rudy* or *Hoosiers* for family movie night, and the only cool things about being Catholic are those white dresses little girls get to wear for first communion. I'd have loved to have shopped for one of those."

"Still time," Michael whispered back to me.

I looked over the den, littered with boy clutter. "I don't think so," I said.

"Well, don't worry," said Michael. "You're going to have more than enough girls around the joint pretty soon. Every time I pick up Josh, there's some little cupcake with a bare midriff hanging around, talking to him."

"Oh, goody," I said. "I can hardly wait."

"Hey," shouted Zach, "you guys are making too much noise. We can't hear the movie."

CHAPTER 27

I needn't have worried about Isabella letting grass grow under those red-hot heels of hers. By the time I emerged from the BART station the next morning, Gertie intercepted me on my cell phone. "Big doings, huh?" she said.

"What, Gertie?" I asked, juggling phone and wallet, as I tried to dig out three bucks and change for my overpriced double-double latte.

"You'll see," she said cryptically. "You've already got quite the dynamic duo waiting for you in the office."

And that was fair warning. The elevator opened directly in the waiting room, and I saw Isabella and Joe Kotter perched on the edge of our reception chairs. Both looked highly caffeinated and ready to pounce.

"Maggie," Isabella called, leaping to her feet. "I called home, but you'd already left, so we decided to meet you here instead."

"I see that," I said, taking a sip of my latte. "Hi, Joe," I said, nodding at him. He, too, was on his feet and about to start pacing, I could tell.

"Come on in. Let me get out of my coat and check in with Gertie and I'll be right with you." I waved at the visitor chairs in my office, hung up my coat and headed back out into the hallway. Isabella followed me, her quick breath and faint clouds of Arpege warm on my neck.

"Maggie, I'm sorry to descend on you," she said, "but we've

got to get a little strategy shaped up, and I wanted to hear your report first."

"And why's Joe here?" I asked.

"We've got to decide how we're going to handle how and why this info you pried out of the little mother-to-be didn't come out before. Who screwed up? The cops? The DA? Joe?"

"Does it matter?" I asked.

Isabella gave me an incredulous look. "Are you sure you're married to an attorney, *chica*?" she asked. "Of course it matters. It's all about who screwed up and who we can saddle with the blame. That's our vehicle to getting things reopened."

We had reached Gertie's office, and she stood to greet us. "Oh, good," she said with an innocent smile, "I see you found your visitors."

"Uh-huh," I said. "Anything I need to deal with right away on my day job?"

Gertie shook her head. "Heavens no, nothing that can't wait. This seems awfully important."

"Thanks," I said, "I'm sure we won't be long."

"Oh, just one thing," called Gertie. I turned. She waved a little pink message slip at me, "An old friend called this morning. John Moon. Lt. John Moon. From Homicide."

I winced, "Any message?"

"I'll read it to you," said Gertie."Ask Mrs. Fiori what in the hell is going on over there?"

I walked back to Gertie, snatched the pink message slip from her fingers, and led Isabella back to the office.

"John Moon?" she asked. "I didn't know you two knew each other."

"Oh, we know each other," I said tartly. "He and Michael play ice hockey on the same team."

"Isn't that handy?" said Isabella. "One of his guys investigated this case."

Back in my office, silence fell as I complied with Isabella's request to recount the conversation with Carol Ann, as completely as I could.

"Syllable by syllable," she said. "Don't leave anything out."

"That's it?" demanded Kotter, when I was finished.

"That's it," I said.

"And she was pretty sure it was 10 o'clock or so?" asked Kotter

"Pretty sure," I said. Which confirms Mrs. Lomax's story about seeing two cars."

"And gives plenty of time for whoever the mystery people were to take Grace somewhere, murder her, and then stash her body in Travis's limo," said Kotter.

"But we still don't know anything about who or why though," I pointed out.

"Not as critical right now," said Isabella. "This demonstrates that someone else was with Grace just before she was murdered. Maggie, you haven't had any further conversations with Carol Ann?"

I shook my head. "Nothing. Although, I'm worried about her. I think she just didn't realize that her information was important, and then..."

"Her husband discouraged her," Kotter completed my sentence.

"So, what happens now?" I asked.

"This is definitely extra-transcript information," said Kotter. "But until we learn more, we don't know how important it is. Although, the fact that there may have been another person involved, the mystery guy or broad in the backseat, opens up still more interesting possibilities."

"And why's Lt. John Moon, SFPD, Homicide calling?" I asked.

"I put in a call to the DA and the police last night," said Isabella. "That's our obligation."

"And now," said Kotter, "let the games begin."

Kotter and Isabella spent a few more minutes talking about next steps, filing documents to get the case reopened immediately, speeding up the habeas appeal process, ordering me not to talk to Carol Ann again, and doubled-timed it out the door.

Gertie was hovering in the hallway, clutching another batch of pink message slips.

"Well, Ollie, it's a fine mess you've gotten us into, isn't it?" she said.

I sighed. "I hope not. I hope there's something here that's a way out of this fine mess."

"Here's the good news," said Gertie. "That handsome Lt. Moon wants to take you to lunch."

I groaned. "Not today," I said.

"Oh, I don't think it was an invitation," said Gertie. "I think it was a command performance."

CHAPTER 28

At precisely high noon, John Moon and I were seated at the Burger Bistro. He perused the menu, while I jiggled my knee. He closed the menu, reached under the table, and put his hand on my knee.

"Why, Lt. Moon," I said. "I never!"

He removed his hand. "Calm down and stop jiggling, Maggie," he said. "You're going to overturn the table. This is lunch, not an interrogation room."

The waitress came by—messy, avocado and grilled onion-bedecked classic patty for me, rare; veggie burger for John, on a whole wheat roll. "No fries," he said.

"I'll eat yours," I said.

He nodded at the waitress.

"Don't you ever do anything wicked?" I teased.

"If I did, I certainly wouldn't tell you," he said.

"Okay, so what's this lunch about?" I countered. "Get to it."

"No," he said, "that's my line. Why don't you get to it? Tell me what you've been up to. Michael mentioned..." he paused, "at practice the other day, that he was helping you with a story. Like a fool, I thought, 'How nice.' Michael seemed pretty pleased with himself, and all I could think was that it's good to know you two got past that bump in the road."

"We did," I volunteered. "We're seeing some weird, color-nut therapist in Berkeley, and Michael really seems to like her."

"Dr. McQuist?" he asked.

"You, too?"

Lunch arrived. John carefully righted the lettuce and tomato on his wholesome choice. I splashed mustard and pickle relish on my burger, and squished the avocado into an even layer on the bun.

"Don't wrinkle your nose at me, John," I said. "Isn't it nice in this era of eating disorders to watch a girl dive right into her lunch?"

"Very nice," he agreed promptly, "though you might want to swipe at the corner of your mouth, because all that yellow mustard dripping down is making you look a little jaundiced. And, in answer to your question, no, my wife and I are not seeing McQuist, but I know lots of people who are. Or have. She's supposed to be very effective."

"Yeah, well, she may be like sex on the beach," I grumped. "Highly overrated."

"Sex on the beach, the drink? Or actual sex on the beach?" he inquired mildly. "Come on, Maggie, just tell me what's going on. Two young hotshots from the DA's office were crawling all over the Homicide bureau today, looking at interview transcripts."

"And why do you think I'm involved?"

"Tell me now," he said, "and I buy lunch. Or, don't tell me, and you pick up the check, and I'll find a reason to haul you down to my office and wreck your entire afternoon." He took a tidy, satisfied bite out of his not-very-appetizing-looking veggie burger. "Your choice."

So I told. A very workmanlike, crisp summary, if I do say so myself.

"That's it?" asked Moon, pushing his plate aside, and pulling his mug of tea in front of him. "You're doing a story?"

"That's about it," I said cheerfully.

He pulled a notebook from his breast pocket. "And the story is what took you to San Quentin with Ms. Fuentes?"

I sighed. "Okay, why are you asking me to tell you all this if you already know everything?"

A small smile lifted the corners of his mouth. I thought of the nickname Moon's wife had for him, "Lt. SmugBuns." He folded his arms, and leaned back on the wooden bench. "Maybe I just wanted to see how forthcoming you'd be. And, of course, I'm wondering how forthcoming you've been with Michael."

"You'd be surprised. There's a whole new Maggie in town. Michael's very involved in the whole thing. I'm sure that's why he mentioned it to you," I observed, all the while wondering why Michael felt so obliged to blab about the story to Moon at practice. "Michael happens to know—just for your information—everything I know."

Moon narrowed his eyes. "Uh-huh. Sure he does."

"He does," I protested. "Now, it's your turn. What was going on at the office today? Guys from the DA, huh? What interview transcripts were they looking at?"

"And she's back, ladies and gentlemen," observed Moon to the room at large. "Ms. Nosy Fiori, girl detective, woman of a million questions. Not cured, not retired, merely resting for a while."

"Hey, I just spilled every little shred of info I've got," I said. "Turnabout is fair play."

"In a relationship of equals, it is," said Moon.

"Okay," I said, "how's about if I tell you what I think and you can confirm or not."

"You're free to speculate," said Moon. "And I'm free to do absolutely nothing. You need to know that Travis Gifford is already a trophy on our wall at SFPD. Case solved; case closed. No one's going to be anxious to reopen anything."

I nodded, impatiently. "So, I think that all those baby ADAs were looking at the interview transcripts of Carol Ann Masters, trying to see where they'd screwed up, missing some critical piece of information."

"It's possible that's the transcript they were reviewing," said Moon.

"Plus, I bet they wanted to see the transcripts of the interview with Purity at A Mom's Place." I sat back, satisfied. "I think this is great. One little Q&A session with Maggie Fiori, the master interrogator, and the wheels of justice are back in motion."

"Did anyone ever tell you that it's more attractive to let other people find and praise your good qualities?" asked Moon.

"That is practically a direct lift from Miss Manners," I countered.

"What's your interest in this case, Maggie? Beyond the trumped-up story angle?"

I stopped to consider. In fact, the excitement I felt about the conversation with Carol Ann seemed out of proportion to what the information might actually mean. It's not as if it cleared Travis, and we might never know who the guy was or if there was someone else in the backseat or what they were doing with Grace. "I don't know," I confessed. "Michael probably told you that some of the Women Defenders got me involved."

"I know Isabella Fuentes," he said. "She's a good person and a terrific lawyer. I'm not sure she needs your help."

"Hey," I said, "I didn't go looking for this experience. The Women Defenders came and found me. Plus..." I hesitated.

"Plus?" he prompted me.

"Plus, Isabella took me up to San Quentin, and it's an experience you don't forget." I wrapped my hands around the coffee mug.

"So you've met Travis Gifford?"

"Oh, yes," I said. "I've met him and his mother."

Moon shook his head, "That's a sad story. I knew Ivory Gifford from The Devil's Interval. We used to go to their Sunday afternoon jams, because they'd let kids in during the day. I can't imagine what kind of hell she's gone through with all of this."

"Me, either," I said. "That's really why I got involved, I think. Travis asked me to go meet his mother, and I thought—well, you can guess what I thought."

"Suppose that was my son?"

I nodded.

Moon frowned. "The world's full of tough-luck stories, Maggie. Hardly seems like fodder for *Small Town*."

"It's not," I said. "I had to sell our managing editor on the story. But it's turned out to be full of surprises. For our readers, Grace Plummer is really the compelling story. Glamorous social butterfly, living the high life, married to Mr. VC."

"Hanging out at the Crimson Club," added Moon.

"Yes, well, there's that," I said. "But Grace turned out to be a far more interesting and substantive person than I ever imagined. You know, you read the social notes and you think—spoiled, rich, idle, useless."

"More complex than that," said Moon, catching the waitress's eye and signaling for the check. "Most people are."

"I know," I said, "but Grace was really someone special."

"You mean her 'good works' stuff?" asked Moon, easing a twenty out of his elegant, snakeskin wallet. "I think that's what lots of those social butterflies do. But I know what you mean. From the files, it looks as if Grace Plummer actually broke a sweat, as opposed to just sitting on boards and booking tables for charity events."

"Wow," I said, reaching over to touch the wallet. "Do the PETA folks know that a committed vegetarian like you carries his dough around in something like this?"

"Faux," he said. "My wife, the Hong Kong superstar shopper, got it for me."

Moon shrugged into his jacket and helped me into mine. Ever the gentleman. We headed out into the street. Almost overnight, real spring had arrived in San Francisco. Boots and tights and tweed skirts had given way to bare legs and floral skirts. That was the good news, but real spring meant summer was just ahead, and the habeas clock was ticking away. Moon walked me to the corner of Montgomery and Post, where the financial district met the start of serious retail. North up Montgomery, the do-it-yourself investors hung out in the lobby of Charles Schwab, watching the ticker, kibitzing, and giving one another unsolicited advice. West up Post, the windows of Armani beckoned, bright with silky, well-cut fabrics, hanging on the kind of bodies Grace and her pals put in long hours at the gym to achieve. Maybe if I got some advice from the geezers in Schwab's lobby, I could afford to shop at Armani.

"Doesn't it seem like an awful lot of weird coincidences in this case, John?"

"Like what?"

"You know Ginger, Grace Plummer's best friend, is the daughter of Ivory's sweetheart, on and on it goes. Some cop noticed Ivory and Gus in an art-house theater the night of the murder."

He shrugged. "Anybody who likes jazz in this town knows Ivory. And police officers, for your information, don't just like shoot 'em up movies. In fact, they generally think they're silly. So, no, I don't think it's farfetched that a cop was in the theater that evening, and that he'd notice Ivory. She's a striking woman. When the case came in, and we did a briefing for the whole homicide squad, this guy spoke up and said, 'Now, that's weird. I've just seen that woman and the big guy with her.' As for the rest of it, it's a small town. Isn't that what your chic little magazine is all about?"

"I guess," I said. "In fact, that's an excellent reason for me to get involved, isn't it?"

"It may be a legitimate reason for you to do a story on Grace Plummer, but that's a far stretch from playing girl detective again."

"Thanks for lunch, John," I said, reaching up to give him a peck on the cheek. "Since the girl detective told all, does this mean I get to go back to work, instead of off to the hoosegow?"

"The hoosegow?" he asked. "Where do you come up with these ridiculous words?" He put up his hand. "Never mind, I know you're going to tell me the derivation of the word, and I just can't accommodate one more useless bit of Fiori trivia in my brain today."

"It's a *gringo* version of *juzgao*, variant of *juzgado*, meaning jail, of course."

"Of course," said Moon. "Thank you. And since I warned you I couldn't absorb anymore know-it-allisms from you, I'll have forgotten what you told me by the time I get to the BART station in three hundred yards. Just as," he turned me to face him, "I know you forget everything I ever tell you."

"Oh, not everything," I said. "Let's just keep each other in the loop, shall we?" And with that, I headed up Post. As I walked, breathing in the sweet, spring fragrance that seemed to clean even diesel bus fuel from the air, I wondered when my picture of Grace had changed so completely. And I thought back to sitting under the early apple blossoms with Purity, looking out on the tidy raised beds Grace had created. And I realized that in that moment, some shell had cracked open for me, some hard nut of judgment about who mattered in the world, and who didn't, the terrible life lists we keep—as Ken Kesey used to say, of "who's on the bus, who's off the bus" in our regard and good opinion. I had seen Grace not for who she was, because I would never know that, but for whom others thought she was, and how she was loved.

I stopped in front of the Armani windows and looked in, just enjoying the custard-yellow silk sundress with the draped neck. All wrong for me, even if I could afford it, but so beautiful. Inadvertently, I found myself reaching toward the window, as if I could put my hand through and touch that gossamer fabric. Through the windows, through the long-limbed mannequins, I could see the store and watched as an older, beautiful, slender woman, trying on the first cousin to the silk dress, in plum, instead of yellow, stood in front of a mirror. A stocky man stood very close to her, leaning forward, almost as if he were trying to soak her in, through his skin. She turned, with a smile, and I stepped back from the window, short of breath. It was Ivory, and the man admiring her was Gus. He put his hand on the back of her neck, and pulled her a little closer, and kissed her forehead. She rested her head on his chest, briefly, then pulled away and disappeared, back toward the dressing rooms, I imagined. I looked over my shoulder, embarrassed I might find someone catching me, intruding like a voyeur on such a private moment. Still, I wondered about what I had witnessed. Was this how I envisioned the mother of a Death

Row inmate watching the habeas clock run down?

"And the judgments are back," I muttered to myself. "In plum and yellow, available at a boutique near you."

I stood a minute more, and on an impulse, went to the front of the store and pushed the heavy glass door open. A saleswoman, elegant and thin in a soft gray sweater and tailored slacks greeted me.

"I'm just browsing," I said. "Actually, I thought I saw a friend in here."

She watched me look around. "She might be in the dressing rooms," suggested the saleswoman, gesturing to the back of the store. I thanked her and wandered back in the direction she'd pointed.

As I drew near the dressing room, I heard breathy noises coming from one of the rooms. I stood, startled, listening for a moment. And then I understood. Ivory Gifford was crying.

I felt trapped. Listening to her was agonizing, and made me feel like the worst kind of snoop.

I crept closer, looking over my shoulder again, expecting Gus to come looking for her any minute. "Excuse me," I called softly. No response. "Excuse me," I raised my voice. "Are you okay?"

The noises stopped. "I'm fine," she called from the dressing room. "I didn't know anyone was out there. I'm sorry."

So, was it kinder to leave? Or to speak up? Maggie Fiori, woman of action and generally awful judgment, spoke up. "Ivory." I hesitated. "It's Maggie Fiori." The dressing room behind the elegant curtain grew very quiet. I heard her blowing her nose.

The curtain parted, and Ivory was completely dressed in her own clothes, except for her shoes. Standing there in her socks, the silky plum number on a hook behind her, she looked terribly young and completely vulnerable.

She looked puzzled, "Ms. Fiori? What are you doing here?"

For a moment, I considered a small equivocation like, 'Oh, just shopping,' but that seemed to compound intrusion with a dumb lie.

"I was looking in the window," I said lamely, "admiring a

dress, and I saw you through the window. You were trying on the dress I was looking at." She stared at me, swiping at her eyes with a crumpled tissue.

"In a different color," I added, with meaningless detail. "The one I was looking at. Kind of buttercup."

The elegant sales associate rounded the corner. "Oh, your friend found you," she said. She looked more closely at the two of us, taking in Ivory's tear-stained face. "What do you think about the dress?" she asked briskly. "Your...companion says he'd like to buy it for you, if you're happy with it."

Ivory looked confused, as if she couldn't quite figure out where she was, what she was doing, and why on earth I was standing there with her.

Then, she stood a little straighter, turned and went back into the dressing room, lifted the dress off the hook, and put it gently into the saleswoman's hands. "It's perfect," she said flatly. "I'd love it. Tell him thank you."

She turned away from me, slipped on her shoes and threw her handbag over her shoulder.

"Last week, when I was visiting Travis, he asked me why I wore black so much. He said," her voice began to break again, "are you mourning me already, Mom?"

"Oh," I said.

"Gus and I were running errands, and I was telling him the story, and that I wanted to wear anything but black this week." She paused. "And suddenly, he stopped in front of this window and just pointed at this dress and said, 'Let's go in. You try it on.' I joked and said yellow wasn't my color. I'm lots of things, but never a coward, so I couldn't wear yellow." She paused, and swallowed hard. "He said, 'Maybe they've got it in another color. When you get to the Q, you'll class up the joint.'"

I nodded. "You will," I said. "Absolutely, you will."

"Plus, Gus said," she stopped, took a breath, "I should wear something pretty for the rent party. Keeps me from looking desperate."

"Are you?" I asked.

She nodded, "I'm desperate about Travis. About The Devil's Interval, I don't care so much anymore. But a bunch of our friends convinced me it's important to Travis that we keep it going. And I just can't do it without help from Gus every month, and that's..." she paused. "Not right," she said firmly. "It's just not right, not for the long haul."

Gus was waiting by the sleek, stone counter in the center of the store when Ivory and I emerged. He looked puzzled when he caught sight of me.

"Gus," said Ivory, "you remember Maggie Fiori. She's working with Isabella."

"Well, not exactly," I protested, in exactly the same moment that Gus said, "Yeah, sure. I remember."

"Excuse me," I said. "I just happened to be walking by and saw Ivory in the store." Gus didn't say anything. "She looks beautiful in the dress," I offered.

Gus said gruffly, "She looks beautiful in any damn thing she puts on."

I heard Ivory give a little sigh. She glanced at her watch, "I've got to get back to The Interval," she said. "Things to do before we open."

"Nice to see you both," I said, in some vain attempt at figuring out what Miss Manners would do in this circumstance. What *is* the proper way to say goodbye to someone whose life is shredding before her, after an encounter in a chic store, while her unlikely sugar daddy beau stands by?

CHAPTER 29

It was nearly two o'clock when I got back to my office. Gertie raised her eyebrows and handed me yet another batch of message slips. "Phone calls from people who say you haven't answered their e-mails or texts." I was shedding my jacket by the time I pushed open my office door. Puck Morris, our music critic, was behind the desk; Calvin was in the visitor's chair. They were arm-wrestling and barely looked up when I walked in the room.

"Oh, give me a break," I said, hanging up my coat. "Can you two boytoys work out your competitive stuff by comparing equipment in the men's room? Or playing pool or something? You've got to do this right now, in my office?"

Puck had already turned bright red. With a whoop, Calvin slammed his arm on the desk.

Puck scowled. "How about two out of three?"

"That was two out of three, my man," said Calvin. "Get over it."

"Both of you, get over it, and get out of here," I said. "And Calvin, you should be ashamed. You're bigger and younger than Puck."

"And blacker," offered Calvin.

"You are not," snapped Puck. "You're the whitest black guy I've ever known. You're not even an Oreo."

"Hey, you ought to feel twice as bad then," said Calvin, unfolding himself from the guest chair, and ambling to the couch in the corner of the office. He redraped himself in the corner.

"Sit down, Maggie," said Puck, his face slowly fading to pink.

"You're sure I shouldn't call 911?" I asked.

Puck put his feet up on the desk, "I'm the picture of vitality," he said. "I'm just trying to give the kid a sense of false confidence. Then one day, wham, blam, slam it on the desk."

Calvin shook his head. "Bravado, my friend."

I looked at both of them. "Don't we all have work to do?"

"Don't you want to tell us about your lunch with Lt. Moon?" countered Calvin.

"No," I said. Silence fell. Calvin and Puck exchanged glances.

"Okay," I said, "What's going on?"

"Here's the deal, Maggie," began Puck.

I waited.

"See, this opportunity came up to help you with your detective work."

"What detective work?" I asked.

"Chill," Calvin said. "We all know what's up with this story. How dumb do you think we are?"

"Depends on what day it is," I muttered.

"Let me handle this," said Puck to Calvin. "As I started to explain to you, we have an opportunity to kinda, sorta—well, double-date somewhere interesting."

"Double-date?" I asked, with as much incredulity as I could muster. "Are we in study hall or what? And who's double-dating with whom? Last time I looked, I was married, Calvin's chasing Andrea, and you haven't been able to get somebody to go to the malt shop with you, much less out on a real date, for several months."

Puck adjusted his feet and leaned back even farther in the chair. I winced, waiting for the crash. "You know, Mags," he said. "You are one ungrateful, uncooperative—what's the word I'm looking for here, Oreo-man? Help me out."

"Well, she's your boss, so you can't call her a bitch," said Calvin. "Shall we just settle for a 'mean girl'?"

"All right," I said, trying not to glance at my watch again. "I'm sorry, guys. I'm a little zonked, preoccupied, behind in work, and what else?"

"PMSish," offered Puck, helpfully.

I narrowed my eyes at him. "Okay, just spill it."

"The Crimson Club, Friday night, you and me, Calvin and Andrea. Dig out something you wouldn't wear to the PTfuckinA."

That caught my attention. "Could be some double date," I said. "Tell me more."

"We could probably get an extra ticket for old Mikey, too, if you think he'd be into the scene," offered Puck. "But the deal is that I got sent four comp tickets for Friday night, because they're actually having some kind of real band, instead of that trancey, club-mix crap they usually pipe in as background to all the steamy sex."

"I didn't realize it was a performance venue," I said, raising my hands. "And skip the performance jokes."

"I think they're trying to attract a slightly more mainstream crowd," said Puck. "So, they've sent out a media advisory and comp tickets and the whole deal. Maybe they'll hand out party favors, too—flavored K-Y jelly or French ticklers or something."

"Setting aside just for the moment how I'd position this adventure to Michael," I said, "how would this be helpful to me?"

"Maggie," Calvin said patiently, "don't be a nitwit. You know that your murdered lady hung out at the Crimson, with or without her husband and paramour. Aren't you curious to see the inside of the place?"

"Not particularly," I lied. Of course, I was curious. I'd wondered about it from the first moment Travis had described it to me. I kept picturing some impenetrable, smoky red-and-black nest, hosted by some guy in a long red cape, and maybe some boots to hide his cloven feet.

"Chicken," said Puck, at exactly the same moment Calvin said, "Liar."

"Okay, you're right," I admitted. "Plus, it would be useful background for the story. For Andrea," I added hastily. "And me, as her editor. Geez, what's she going to wear?"

"As little as possible, I hope," said Calvin.

Interval No. 5 with Dr. Mephisto

I had to hand it to Dr. Mephisto: She seemed to be able to take one look—or sniff or something—and tell when there was something new in the air between us. We were settled in our self-assigned places, watching her pretzel herself into one of her tantric positions, sipping at her peppermint-chamomile-borage-blossom-milkweed or whatever brew it was in that mug of hers.

"What's up?" she asked.

We both sat silent. I glanced at Michael. He was extraordinary at waiting me out. I knew he could sit there in complete, self-satisfied silence until I couldn't stand it a minute longer and spoke up. When my friends went on and on about how Michael was too perfect for words, I would say: "You can't imagine how exhausting it is living with someone who's *always* right.

He waited. I broke. "I'm going on a little field trip, I think." I added hastily, "That is, unless Michael really objects. In which case I would want to reconsider."

"I have no objection," said Michael with a bland smile.

Dr. Mephisto looked from one of us to the other.

"A business trip?" she inquired.

Michael cleared his throat.

"Not exactly," I said.

I had presented the Crimson Club opportunity to Michael after dinner the night before. The kids were in bed, Anya smooching on the back deck with Dr. Bollywood.

We both had our feet up, me on the couch, Michael on the ottoman. He was reading *The Leopard*, in his quest to deconstruct what it meant to be an Italian man. He had politely—if a little impatiently—put his book face down on the arm of his chair once I cleared my throat and started talking. Raider was curled up, crammed into the space between the ottoman and the easy chair, content just to be breathing the same air as Michael.

"So, that's the story," I said. "What do you think?"

He swirled the brandy in his glass, and looked at it.

"I think I should start drinking *grappa*," he said. "More in keeping with my heritage."

"I meant," I said, "what do you think about going to the Crimson Club?"

"With Puck and Calvin and Andrea?" he said. "I think you should go."

"You do?" I asked, somewhat astonished.

He took another swig. "Sure. You'll find stuff out, and tell me about it. And how much trouble can you get in, if Calvin and Andrea are along? Besides, maybe you'll find out you're a PWP and invite me along."

"PW what?" I asked.

"'Poly wanna potluck'" he responded. "It's when polyamorists get together for dining and more."

I sat up a little straighter. "Polyamorists? I don't even know what you're talking about."

"Oh, really?" he asked. "Not familiar with the expression? Polyamorists are people who have multiple sexual relationships at the same time."

"Oh." We sat in silence for another minute. "How'd you know that?"

"You're not the only one who collects arcane pieces of information, *cara*."

Michael picked up his book and began reading again. His right foot slipped off the ottoman and rested on Raider's fur. Raider let out a huge sigh of contentment. The master's touch—oh, divine!

Try as I might, I couldn't get him to say another word on the topic the rest of the evening. He wasn't unfriendly, or even deliberately distant, just not engaged.

After an unrestful night, with Raider snuggled between us, virtually preventing any serious contact, I found myself actually looking forward to the conversation with Dr. Mephisto. I don't know what I'd expected, but I had some hope she'd coax a little more information out of Michael.

"Okay, I'm not a mind reader," said Mephisto. "One of you might explain to me. Maggie, since it's your field trip, why don't you start?"

So I did. Briefly. I felt, rather than saw, Michael's lazy smile emerge next to me. It's his "Oh, this should be good," look, and it usually accompanies his conviction that he's given someone just enough rope to hang him—or her—self. As I talked, I began to feel very much like the guest of honor at the necktie party.

Dr. Mephisto took a gulp out of her witch's brew.

"I got the picture," she says. "Michael, you told Maggie you had no objections to her going?"

He nodded. "Right."

"So, then," she turned to me. "Sounds like you're good to go."

This was not evolving as I'd hoped. I rearranged myself so I was facing Michael. "And you don't want to talk about this?"

"Not particularly," he said.

"Do you have any interest in going *with* Maggie?" interjected Dr. Mephisto. "Just out of curiosity?"

"She didn't invite me," he said.

"Puck only had four tickets," I said. "It wasn't my place to issue an invitation. I just got invited as a fourth."

Neither Michael nor Mephisto responded. Oh, great, now they've both taken up some vow of silence. Of course, I had to start babbling. "Well, I mean, maybe I could get an extra ticket," I said. "I mean, if you're interested in coming." I added lamely, "The tickets Puck has are comped. So, an extra ticket would be a little pricey."

"How pricey?" asked Mephisto. "Again, just out of curiosity."

I wondered if that was emerging as her mantra. "About what it costs to spend an hour with you," I snapped.

"Well," she offered, "I don't provide music. Or refreshments. The evening sounds like a reasonable value to me. But Michael, you need to respond to Maggie's question: Are you interested?"

"Am I interested in accompanying my wife to a sex club?" said Michael mildly. "I might be, assuming I wouldn't be cramping her style."

On the way home, I cleared my throat in the car several times, waiting for Michael to look over. Nothing. "Okay," I said, "I give up. Why didn't you come right out and say you'd be interested when I brought up the Crimson Club the other night?"

"What's your theory about why I didn't bring it up?" he countered.

"Oh, for heaven's sake," I snapped. "How should I know? You were mad. You're shy about going to weird places like that. Which, for the record, I *am* shy about places like that."

"How do you know?" asked Michael, mildly. "Have you ever been to a place like that?"

"Well, no, but I've been in analogous situations."

Michael laughed. "I'd enjoy hearing what those analogous situations were."

"Yeah, well, I'm sure you would," I said. "But I did have a life before you, you know."

"Not much of one," he said. "You were an innocent little sorority sister when I met you."

"Turn in here," I said, gesturing at the Whole Foods driveway. "We need milk and yogurt and peanut butter."

Michael grumbled, "Getting milk and yogurt at Whole Paycheck is like buying a lug wrench at Tiffany's."

"No wonder I can't tell you about my 'analogous situations,'" I countered. "You can't even do a decent analogy. You should say—it's like getting a pop-bead necklace or something at Tiffany's. They wouldn't have any kind of a lug wrench at Tiffany's."

"You know," said Michael, narrowly missing a sideswipe with a Land Rover loaded with kids and dogs, "you are in a dangerous drift from amusing to pedantic. And not fun."

"I'm helping you exercise those analogy muscles," I said innocently.

CHAPTER 30

It was 11 p.m. on Friday night by the time we pulled up to the Crimson Club door. Apparently, as Puck explained, only the non-*cognoscenti* would dream of showing up before 10 o'clock. San Francisco's maniac valet service, the Parallel Universe Parkers, were on hand for this evening, complete with roadie jackets that read PUPs on the back. We had done a story on them in *Small Town* some years ago, in a roundup on essential services for the rich and famous. Their owner had patiently explained to me that since there are *no* parking places in San Francisco, they take the cars to a "parallel universe" to find spots.

Although the Crimson Club patrons usually had to fend for themselves in parking adventures, management had decided that the nonregulars would need some help navigating the SOMA alleys. Either that, or a bunch of guys from the local methadone maintenance clinic had just scored some PUP jackets and were going to whisk the cars away. Forever. To the parallel universe. Oh, well, good luck fencing the aged Volvo.

Michael handed me out of the car—part gallantry, part necessity, since I'd managed to borrow a painted-on black number from my neighbor's twentysomething daughter, and I could hardly walk, let alone hop out of the station wagon.

"If I see something I'm interested in," said Michael into my ear as we walked toward the door, "should I give you the high-sign so you can catch a ride home with someone else?"

I looped my arm into his and pulled him closer to me. "I assume you're talking about refreshments when you say 'something you like,'" I said fiercely. "And just FYI, a little reminder that only women can make the approaches."

Michael smiled serenely. "Okay," he said. "All the better."

"Well, aren't you the self-confident Italian stallion?" I said.

Calvin, Andrea, and Puck were waiting at the front door. Andrea and I gave each other the once-over. She had on white leather pants and an off-the-shoulder, white cashmere sweater. And unless my eyes deceived me, there was not even a suggestion of a bra underneath.

"Nice threads," I said.

"You, too," she replied.

Calvin draped his arm possessively around her shoulder, his fingers coming to rest right above her right breast. "Isn't she a vision in white?" he asked the group at large. "If she ever proposes to me, I'm going to insist she walk down the aisle in this getup."

Andrea rolled her eyes.

"Or maybe 'sex up' that prissy Junior League fashion show in a few days. Show Mommy Storch some moves."

"Calvin," said Andrea sweetly. "Shut up or you'll never see another move from me of any kind."

"Okay," said Puck. "We're going in. Check your weapons at the door, boys and girls, and let's party."

I had a visual landscape from Travis's description of the place, but nothing prepared me for the feel inside. The music was uber-trancey, repetitive, and seemingly without melody, the red walls appeared to glow, and I could feel the floor vibrating under my stilettos. Since the ceiling was red as well, and the floor was polished black, and there were no windows anywhere, I felt as if I was in a large, red candy box, or more accurately, like a slutted-up doll abandoned inside a giant music box.

All around us, people were moving to the music. Even though I could see the dance floor ahead, packed with people, it was as if the whole place was a giant anthill moving together, trying to get somewhere and not particularly caring where. “There’s a reason they use the verb ‘throb’ in all those softcore porn novels,” I yelled into Michael’s ear. “This place is one large, throbbing organ.”

“Oh, baby,” he said. “Is that how you talk about me to your friends?” During our pregame chat about the evening, we’d agreed to split up. I pointed toward a doorway, where I could see strobe-style flickering lights ahead. I put my mouth next to Michael’s ear again. “I’m going in, coach,” I said. “If I don’t come back...”

Michael shrugged and pointed to the bar, “If you don’t come back,” he said, “there’s a delicious-looking Ornamental behind the bar.”

“Racist, sexist...” I began

He covered his ears. “Can’t hear you,” he pantomimed to me.

I headed into the next room and stood for a moment, just getting my bearings. A drink would help, I thought. At the bar, a Nordic-looking sleek blond, with the eyes of a raptor swooping down on prey, asked what I wanted. “Merlot,” I said. She reached under the bar, poured a glass, and presented it with a flourish. I looked around the bar for a tip jar. She raised an eyebrow. “Looking for something?” she asked.

“No, nothing,” I said.

“Never been here before, have you?” she asked.

I shook my head. “What should I know?”

She shrugged, “Nothing. Relax. Have fun. That’s why we’re here.” Well, that wasn’t exactly why I was here, but I thought it better not to diagram the “we” in that sentence.

“Go ask someone to dance,” she said.

“I will, in a minute,” I countered. “A friend told me about this place. Maybe you know her—Grace Plummer.”

“Never heard of her.” She hesitated. “And just a piece of advice: Our clientele doesn’t go in for last names very much.”

With that, she turned dismissively, and lavished a brilliant smile on a linebacker-size guy dressed in silk, from unconstructed jacket to loose trousers. I wandered away from the bar. Get going or get out, Maggie, I muttered.

There was, precisely as Travis had described, an uplit tall vase filled with red roses in the middle of the floor, and as the dancers moved around it, the vibration kept sending petals to the floor. I squinted through the dim room to the vase. The stems stopped me. They were white, and almost seemed to glow. I began working my way toward the vase to get a closer look.

A man's voice in back of me said, "Glow-in-the-dark stems. Couldn't possibly occur in nature." I turned around and almost stepped on his toe. He put his arms out to steady me. "Whoa there, little lady. You're going to end up on the floor." He let go of my arms, but not before he lightly ran his fingers the length of them. He was in his late fifties, not quite my height, well taken care of, and wore a bolo tie with a snakehead at his collar.

"I was looking at the stems," I said. "I've never seen that kind of rose used as a cutflower. And usually the stems don't turn white til after the flowers drop." He stared at me. "They're ghost brambles," I finished, helpfully.

"Are you here from the garden page or something?" he asked, raising his voice. The room suddenly got quiet for a split second, as the piped-in music disappeared. Over the system came a disembodied voice, "Ladies and gentlemen, thank you for joining us for the Crimson Club's first live concert. It gives me great pleasure to introduce the Spring Ramp Coalition, performing in our Carmine Room."

From the next room, I could hear a few aggressive guitar riffs, followed by a moment of silence, and then—well, undistinguished weirdly mellow metal. "Whaddya think?" asked my garden conversation partner.

"Ramones-meet-Enya," I said. "Not to jump to conclusions after just a few bars of music," I added hastily. "Maybe they're pals of yours?"

He laughed. "No, but I'm mighty interested in their name. Do you think it's about freeway onramps?"

"Couldn't say," I murmured. "Maybe it's all about early onions."

He looked puzzled. “Come again?”

“Ramps are like onions. Or maybe they are onions, or at least a member of the family. And they come up early.” I gestured with my glass. “Hence, Spring Ramps. And maybe they’re a coalition because they’re fighting the good fight against, I don’t know—green garlic or something.”

“You sure know a lot about gardenin’,” Mr. Bolo said suspiciously.

“I know a little bit about a lot of stuff,” I said. “None of it’s very useful.”

“My name’s Doc,” he said.

“Pardon? I’m sorry, I didn’t quite hear you—Doc like a doctor or Doug?”

“Doc,” he said. “Delta Oscar Charlie,” using the military alphabet. I wondered if he was really a vet, or was just doing a little macho swagger.

“Maggie,” I said and shook his hand. He didn’t quite let go, until I let mine go limp in his hand.

We stood for a moment, and I watched him let his eyes wander with undisguised frankness over the little black dress and what was contained therein.

“You haven’t been here before, have you?” he asked.

“No, I haven’t,” batting two for two. I’d talked with two people and they’d both made me as a newbie in a flash. Turnip right off the truck.

“Let me clue you in on something,” he said. “You’ve got to ask me.”

“Ask you?” I said, confused. And then, I suddenly remembered our little coaching session.

“You mean, I have to ask you to dance?” I said.

“That’s a start,” he said.

Not just a start, I thought to myself, as we headed to the dance floor, it’s the middle and end, as well, Delta Oscar Charlie.

The music changed to some Latin salsa–style number as soon as we shoehorned ourselves onto the floor, and Doc snaked an arm around my waist and pulled me close. For a guy who came across as a bit player from a cheesy Western, he could move. It took a minute, and a little readjustment on the stilettos, for balance, but soon I was following his moves just fine.

"What brought you here, Miss Maggie?" he breathed into my ear. "Looking for some adventure?" He smelled of Scotch and breath mints, not the worst combination.

"A friend told me about the place," I said. "He came here once with his..." I hesitated. "His girlfriend. I think she was a regular."

"Lots of couples come here together," he said, giving me a little twirl, and then bringing me back quick and pulling me even closer.

"Gets the juices running again."

"I can imagine," I said brightly. Suddenly, I spotted Michael on the dance floor. A redhead in a hot pink halter and skirt was molded onto his body, chest to groin. As they moved by, I only had time to notice the extraordinary muscle definition in her legs, which were on very fine display, since her shocking-pink dress was slit up both sides.

"Do you think redheads should wear pink?" I asked Doc.

"Beg pardon?" he asked.

"Oh, never mind. Just making conversation," I said, resolutely turning away from the sight of some other woman in my husband's arms. Suddenly, I began to see the point of couples coming to a place like this. Michael was looking sexier and sexier by the minute to me, and I felt a little flutter of impatience, until I could get him home, out of the station wagon, upstairs, and have my way with him. Or vice versa.

The music stopped, and the lead guitarist, who I could just make out at the edge of the slightly raised stage, leaned into the microphone. He was a vision in black leather and rivulets of sweat. "Hey, folks," he breathed into the mike, "we're going to take five or ten. Have fun. See you in a few."

Doc began steering me toward the couches at the edge of the dance floor. A couch didn't seem like such a good idea, even if I did have the power to do the asking. So, I began out-maneuvering him toward the bar. "Aren't you thirsty?" I asked. "All that dancing. Let me buy you a drink."

He followed, "Never say no to a pretty girl who asks me anything," he said. Oh, brother, work on those lines, would you?

I got another glass of Merlot, Doc got another something on the rocks, never heard exactly what, and we turned around, each planted an elbow on the bar and surveyed the room.

"So, about my friend's girlfriend..." I began, "who was a regular here, I think. I wonder if you knew her. Since..." I glanced sideways, "you have a taste for pretty girls."

He regarded me curiously. "Are you into girls?" he asked. "That's just damn fine with me, but I like to know going in."

Oh, buster, you're not going into anything, I thought. "No, not that kind of friend," I said hastily. "Or maybe she was, I don't really know. It's just that she told me about this place, and I thought you might have met her."

He shrugged. "Lots of girls in and out of here. What made your friend so memorable?"

I took a sip of my wine. "I hear that people called her Amazing Gracie," I said.

He put his glass down on the bar with a thud. I jumped a little.

"I don't know what kind of game you're playing, girlie," he said. "Grace is dead. She was murdered. I didn't even know her last name until I saw it in the paper, and recognized her photo. It was all over the news a couple years ago. And this place nearly shut down, because there were cops crawling all over the joint." He picked up his glass again. "I'll see you around. Thanks for the dance."

I put my arm on his sleeve. "Wait, I'm not playing a game. I know she was murdered. I'm sorry, I should have been more straightforward. Just talk to me for a minute, would you?"

He regarded me suspiciously. "Why? What do you want to know?"

"Here's the thing," I began, wishing I had thought this through a little more carefully. "I didn't know Grace, but the magazine I work for is doing a story about her. The man who was convicted of her murder is on Death Row."

"Where he belongs, if you ask me," said Doc.

"Well, maybe," I said. "If he really did it."

"So, what are you—out playing Nancy Drew or something?"

"Not exactly," I said, wondering if I should cross my fingers. "We're just trying to get a picture of her life."

"Must be some magazine if you're going to publish stuff about the Crimson Club in there," he said.

"So," I persisted, ignoring his observation, "you did know Grace?"

"Sure, I knew her. She was sort of a regular. Sometimes with a guy, her husband, I guess from looking at the pictures in the paper, and once in a while with somebody else, sometimes alone."

"What was she like? While she was here?"

"What happens if I tell you?"

"Nothing much. Helps me understand her more while we're doing our story. Maybe there's something more to the story. She didn't..." I hesitated. "Didn't exactly seem like the type to hang out here."

"Oh, yeah," he said, "what type would that be, Miss Priss?"

"Sorry," I said. "I don't have any idea what I'm talking about."

He gave me a hard look. "No, you don't. Grace wasn't a special pal of mine, but I liked her. She was fun. A little wild, and sometimes things got stirred up some around her."

"What do you mean?"

"Whatever you think, this is a pretty classy joint. There aren't bar fights or anything here. But one night Grace was here with a girlfriend, and some tall guy came in and yelled at Grace and grabbed the other girl's arm and pretty much dragged her out the door."

"Really?" I asked, feeling like a very alert hunting dog, every instinct on call.

"Really."

"What did this guy look like?" I pressed him.

He shrugged, "I don't know. Big. Had on a cap, which was

strange. Usually you have to leave your hat at the door."

"What about Grace's girlfriend?" I persisted. "What'd she look like?"

He frowned, "I don't remember. Pretty. Little. Nice boobs. Nothing special overall."

Carol Ann, I thought. Maybe her husband came after her. But, would Grace have brought her here? Seemed too weird. Or Ginger? Maybe Frederick got pissed that they had a girls' night out. Or Bill, Ginger's husband.

"Anybody else know about this?" I asked.

"A few people," he said. "I'm sure somebody ran his mouth about it to the cops." He looked at me as he rattled the ice cubes in his glass. Was that code for wanting another?

"Another drink?" I asked.

"You're not here to do anything but ask questions, are you, little lady?"

I felt my breakthrough interrogation slipping away.

"I'm afraid not," I confessed.

"Well, I don't want another drink then," he said. He put his glass down on the bar. "Thanks for the small talk," he said.

He straightened his bolo with one hand, and put the other firmly in the small of my back, as if we were going to dance again, and pulled me closer. "Just watch yourself, asking all these nosy questions, missy. Not everyone's going to be as friendly as me."

He held me to him another minute and scanned the room. "You'll excuse me," he said. "The night's still young." I saw his eyes narrow, and then brighten a moment. He released me, and sidled off across the room, just another snake with prey clearly in his sites.

I leaned back on the bar and scanned the room. This detecting stuff was getting easier. Tomorrow, I'd call Lt. Moon and find out what he knew about this little dustup with Mr. Mystery. I was so lost in my private, self-congratulatory reverie that I jumped when I felt a hand on my shoulder.

I turned to see Puck, lounging against the bar, and watching me.

"You look like you're unraveling string theory," he said.

"Oh, like you know what that is," I sniffed.

"I do, as a matter of fact," he said. "Most musicians are math-nerds in their hearts. I think the string theory is all bullshit. But guitar players like it because maybe the universe does go 'twang' like a bunch of guitar strings resonating in space."

"I believe the strings are virtual, not real, Mr. Morris. And they have to be Planck length. Planck, as in Max, not as in walk the plank."

Puck shook his head. "It's a wonder you ever got laid, Maggie. Talking physics theory is not a reliable turn-on."

"Speak for yourself, little man," I said. "As a matter of fact, I'm just celebrating the fact that I've turned up an interesting bit of information." I filled him in, as he signaled one of the Nordic princesses behind the bar for another beer. When it arrived, he took a swig, and shook his head.

"Not bad, Mags. Turns out it's kinda useful to be such a nosy parker, huh?"

I frowned. "Okay, you're the second person in five minutes who's called me nosy."

Puck used his pilsner glass to indicate the whole room. "Let's take a poll, Maggie. I bet we can get a dozen people to call you nosy in under ten minutes."

"Yeah, well, what'd you turn up, Mr. Detective?"

Puck made a circle with his hand. "Goose egg."

I scrutinized him. "So, why do you look so satisfied with yourself?"

He drained the last of the beer. And set the glass down on the bar. He was practically preening. "Oh, no reason in particular," he said. "Except..."

"Except what?" I asked, impatiently, starting to scan the room for Michael. Seemed like a good idea to at least have a vague notion where he was.

He cocked his finger like a gun and shot it at a tall brunette across the room. "She's just a little bit smitten," he said, slyly.

I narrowed my eyes to bring the brunette, dancing in a little circle all by herself, into focus. "Geez, Puck, she's got to have a foot or so on you."

He bridled, "So what? She's not auditioning me to play forward on her basketball team."

"She's got a basketball team?"

"Maybe. She's got a Lakers logo tattooed on her right breast."

"Really? That must have been quite a dance if you were able to check that out."

"I just saw the top of it," he said. "Kinda peeking out. But later, who knows?"

Who did know? Later arrived in fairly short order, as our little group reconvened, out on the sidewalk, waiting for the PUP squad to bring our cars around. It was 2 a.m., and we were drooping. And I was feeling oddly cranky. No one could find Michael when it was time to go, so Puck and I had formed a search-and-rescue posse and toured the nooks and crannies of the Crimson Club. When we got to the last room, we'd found Michael dancing with the redhead. Or, rather, just swaying to the music. Pelvis to pelvis, with Michael holding her around the waist. She'd draped her arms around his neck, and although there were other couples on the dance floor, and one highly enmeshed trio of two women and a man, all I saw was Michael and the redhead. Puck started toward them, and I put a hand on his arm to stop him. For a moment, I just stood and watched. My face grew warm, my heart sped up as if I'd downed three cups of coffee and run up two flights of stairs. I felt Puck reach over and gently unclench my fingers on his arm.

"Come on, Maggie," he said. "It's time to go." I stood silent. He leaned close and whispered in my ear, "Whatever you're doing, this is not a cool idea, babe."

He walked onto the dance floor and tapped Michael on the shoulder. Michael turned, startled, and let go of the redhead. She kept one arm draped around his neck, slowly shook her head, as if she was just coming awake. Michael listened to Puck, glanced over at me, and completed disentangling himself from the redhead. He offered her his hand and she brought it to her mouth, and put her lips on his palm. Oh, for heaven's sake. What a softcore porn cliché that was! Michael and I walked briskly to the front door, nobody touching; Puck elected to stick around a bit longer. In a few minutes, Michael and I were back out on the street.

We compared notes with Calvin and Andrea. Turned out my little discovery about the confrontation between Grace and the mystery man was fairly common knowledge at the Crimson Club. Michael had heard about it from his hot-pink redhead, and Calvin had talked to a guy in the men's room who knew someone who knew someone who was there that night. I was crestfallen.

"So, that's it?" I said. "All we get for our night of debauchery."

"Maybe all *we* get," said Michael. "Since Puck's still in there, maybe he'll turn up some other intelligence."

Andrea laughed, "Oh, yeah, I know that's just what he's trying to turn up in there...intelligence. I think he's looking for something else entirely."

"A little slap and tickle with the basketball-playing brunette," Calvin offered.

"All that height," mused Michael, "won't you just bet she's able to contort herself into some interesting positions?"

Andrea and I exchanged glances, equal mixtures of exasperation and pity. "Hope springs eternal," she said. She tucked her hand into Calvin's arm. "Honey, don't you wish I had a few extra inches on you?"

"Oh, you're perfect," he said reassuringly. "And I think with a few remedial gymnastics classes, you'll be able to twist yourself six ways to Sunday."

Andrea rolled her eyes, and waved to the valet who had just pulled up in Calvin's Jetta. "Here we are," she said. "You can drop me at the twenty-four-hour gym on the way home and I'll check out the action..." She paused for dramatic effect. "On the pommel horse?"

We all exchanged goodnight hugs, and I watched Calvin roar down Tehama. "Remedial," muttered Michael. "That was a mistake."

Our Volvo appeared a few minutes later, and I wiggled in, backside first, then cantilevered my legs in afterward. I reached forward and cranked the heat up in the car. Though I was wrapped in my coat, I felt chilled and shaky.

"Mags," said Michael, "it's like an oven in here. Can't we turn the heat down?"

He looked over at me. "My teeth are chattering," I said.

He reached over and put his hand on my cheek. "You're burning up. Are you getting sick?"

I shook my head, feeling miserable. We drove the rest of the way home in silence. The house was dark and quiet. I took off my high heels and crept up the stairs, and went into the kids' bathroom and locked the door. I ripped off the black dress, and climbed into a scalding hot shower, hoping to warm up. When I got out of the shower, I could hear Michael knocking on the door.

"Are you sick, Maggie? What's going on?"

I put the lid down on the toilet, and sat down. Wrapped in a big towel, I was still shivering.

"I'm okay," I called in a hoarse whisper. "Go to bed. I'll be there in a little while."

And then the nausea hit me. I leapt up, flung open the toilet and lost everything. When I finished, I rinsed my mouth, washed my face, wrapped up in another towel, and crept silently down the hall. I could hear Michael's breathing coming from our room. I stood in the doorway a moment, watching my husband sleep, and shivered again. I stood beside the long gallery of goofy family photos hung on the hallway wall. Right next to me was one of Michael, covered in mud, with his arms around both equally muddy boys. The photo had been taken one rainy Thanksgiving at my cousins' house, and all the kids had ended up playing kickball out on the rain-drenched back lawn. Michael had gone out to investigate and never came back. When I went out a half hour later, he was in the midst of the kids, running, yelling, and also covered with mud. My cousin had snapped a photo just before we shooed everyone inside for showers.

I put my hand on the photo, covering the three of them with my palm. I stared into Michael's face—had I just seen him with his arms around some strange woman, transported to some other place by the way she looked and felt and smelled in his embrace? I shivered again as another thought settled over me like a sudden snowfall. Was this how Michael felt when he looked at me and thought about my betrayal with Quentin? Once you've pictured your beloved in an intimate way with another person, do you ever shake the image?

I felt confused and exhausted, and completely unable to crawl into bed with Michael. I tiptoed down the hall to the TV room, picked up the hideous aqua and brown afghan Michael's *nonna* had made us for a wedding present, wrapped myself in it, curled up on the couch, and just before I fell asleep, I could hear her voice, saying "For the *letto matrimoniale*," and wished I hadn't brought dishonor to that bed.

CHAPTER 31

Michael was out the door early the next morning, taking the boys to Saturday morning soccer. He stuck his head in the TV room, looking as fresh and rested as I felt sticky and exhausted.

"Sleep in, *cara*, I've got the morning games covered."

Zach was right next to him, looking puzzled.

"Are you sick, Mom? How come you're sleeping in the TV room? Did you stay up late and watch a movie? I'd have kept you company."

Michael put his hand on Zach's head. "Slow down, buddy. Mom just needs a little more sleep."

I struggled to focus. "It's our turn for snack," I offered feebly.

"Got it," he said. "Oranges already cut up and in the cooler."

With that, he disappeared, with Zach trailing behind him, giving me one last curious look. "And there they go," I mumbled disconsolately. "Saint Michael and the sons who'll grow up to hate me." I pulled the afghan over my head and sighed. Maybe Michael was rendezvousing with the redhead. At the soccer game. Oh, I felt my stomach roil again. I roused myself, stumbled into the bathroom and stood under a hot, hot shower again until I'd turned bright pink.

Coffee seemed an unthinkable addition to my fragile digestive system, so I made tea, and collapsed at the kitchen table to contemplate my sins. Why couldn't I think of a single girlfriend to call to talk about all this? None of them would understand. They all thought Michael really was a saint, and I had a life-size version of explaining to them how I'd reacted at the Crimson Club. "Good riddance," they'd say, every disloyal one of them. The doorbell rang so loudly and unexpectedly, I tried to put my hands to my ears and managed to slosh hot tea all over my robe and the table.

"Can't even suffer in privacy," I grumbled and walked to the door, expecting my neighbor or the early-morning brigade of Girl Scouts out peddling their little chocolate-coated thin-mint fat pills.

I opened the door to John Moon.

"Holy shit," I said. "It's a miracle. You're absolutely the only person I want to see this morning. And here you are!" I opened the screen door, grabbed his arm, and pulled him inside. Suddenly, I felt myself coming back to life.

"Maggie, what's wrong?" he said. "You look..."

"Ravishing." I said. "I know. Nothing like a combo plate of too much alcohol, guilt, and insane jealousy to make a girl look her very best. Come on in. I'll give you coffee and you'll..." I gestured to a chair, "sit down and give me advice."

He sat down gingerly on the edge of his chair. "Where's Michael?"

"Out being Father of the Year, where else? Leading his admirable, sainted, patient, kind, generous, self-righteous life," I said. I think I was shouting. I shook the thermos. It was full. "Coffee, and it's hot? Or, do you want tea?"

He waved his hand. "Whatever you're drinking, I guess." He hesitated. "You seem like you're on a roller coaster between manic and depressive, with a hangover holding the whole thing together."

"Right you are," I said grimly.

And the manic me sat down and ran through the whole story—going to the Crimson Club, finding out about the night Grace was there and the ensuing kerfuffle.

"You could have just asked me about that, Maggie," Moon said when I took a breath. "It's all in the case file. We questioned several people who were at the club that night."

"And?" I asked, taking a last gulp of tea. It was only lukewarm and had no taste whatsoever. Oddly, just talking to Moon had settled my insides. My stomach now felt secure enough to think about coffee. I stood up and grabbed a new mug, and splashed dark brew from the thermos inside. It smelled divine.

Moon shrugged. "And, not much. No one had seen the guy who caused the commotion before. He'd paid the cover charge in cash, so there was no record we could trace. And he'd disappeared with Grace's friend. And," he held up his hand, "no, we don't know who that friend was."

"Ginger? Carol Ann?" I asked.

"Ginger said no. And we didn't think about Carol Ann 'til recently, but I asked her if she'd ever been to the Crimson Club as part of our follow-up. And she'd never even heard of it."

"Or so she says," I suggested.

"Maggie," said Moon, with a sigh. "How dumb do you think the police are? We've now shown photos of both women to the people who work at the Crimson Club—and who were there a couple years ago as well—and no one's recognized either of them as the woman who was dragged out that evening."

I felt my headache coming back. I put my head down on the table.

"What are you so miserable about? You'd put all your investigative eggs in this basket?"

"I have no investigative eggs," I said miserably. "I'm just a mediocre editor of a silly, shallow city magazine."

"That's useful to know," said Moon, crisply. "I imagine there are many people in town who'd be happy to relieve you of your silly, shallow job."

"Oh, just shut up."

"I will," said Moon, "in fact, I'll leave you to your misery. It's a beautiful Saturday and I've got a million or so errands to run. Tell Michael to call me, would you? Our hockey team has a chance to play in an invitational in Wisconsin."

I sat up. "Don't go," I begged. "I'm just in a horrible, terrible mood."

"Is this the aftermath of a festive night out at the Crimson Club? I thought people went there to have naughty fun, fun, fun."

"Well, *I* didn't have any fun," I said.

Moon regarded me thoughtfully, and sat down again. "And from that statement, may I conclude that someone else had fun?"

I nodded. "I think so."

"And might that someone be Michael?"

So, I told him, the whole wretched story, from the moment I'd first seen Michael and the redhead, and felt just a little titillated and newly hot for my husband, to finding the two of them together, at the end of the evening, and feeling desperate and depressed.

"You've never been jealous before?" asked Moon.

I thought about it. "I don't think so," I said. "Michael's such a straight arrow. I mean, I've seen other women—even men—be attracted to him, but he always seems so oblivious."

"Last night was different?"

"I guess so. I mean, that's the whole point of being in a place like the Crimson Club—exploring other options. And I just felt overcome by the whole thing. And," I sat up straighter, "I had to go find him. He never came to find me."

Moon was silent for a moment. "I think you two were playing with fire," he said. "And I can't say I think it's a very good idea."

"Hey," I said, "it was Michael's idea to come along."

Moon narrowed his eyes. "You were going to go alone?"

"Well, with Puck, and Calvin and Andrea."

"An intriguing foursome," observed Moon.

"Okay, so now what? Give me some advice," I demanded. "You usually have some ideas."

Moon shook his head. "I think this has stirred up some complicated stuff for you, Maggie. And that's what therapists get paid to unsort. You and Michael are still seeing McQuist, aren't you?"

I sighed. "Yes, but I never feel as if she's on my side."

"That's a fine thing, isn't it? Isn't she supposed to be neutral?

Or on the side of the two of you, not each of you as individuals?"

"Oh who the hell knows?" I snapped. "You're right, I'm sure this will come up. I just..." I faltered. "I just wanted advice from someone I trusted. Someone who's been married longer. Who's a friend."

"Sorry to disappoint you," said Moon, standing up. He carried his mug over to the sink and rinsed it out. "You're way out of my league. I can't even imagine venturing out to the Crimson Club with my wife." He laughed. "She'd worry too much about what to wear."

"As little as possible," I said. "And something that's easy to slip out of."

Moon stopped and put a hand on my shoulder. "Talk to your therapist," he said.

CHAPTER 32

I showed up early at the Junior League fashion show, for the sponsors' meet-and-greet cocktail party, and to drop by the backstage dressing room and wish Andrea luck. Navigating through the ballroom's sea of tables, dressed within an inch of their crème caramel and white-organza-draped selves, and awash in hotel silver, white orchids, caramel and black-ribbon-wrapped goodie bags, and programs, I thought, "Oh, excess." That was followed shortly by a moment of jubilation when I realized that there would be really, really good dessert to make up for the predictable ladies' lunch salad main course. Desserts, always motivational.

The dressing room was actually another near-ballroom size hall. As soon as I opened the door, the noise assaulted me—thirty-five Junior League models, squadrons of dressers, makeup and hair artistes, photographers, and hangers-on. Discussing, exclaiming, laughing, all at larger-than-life sound levels. An emaciated woman with glasses dangling off a cord and bouncing on her nonexistent chest took my hand and pulled me through the door. She was dressed in a leopard-print jumpsuit and wide, black belt, which showcased two hipbones so prominent and sharp they looked like woolly mammoth tusks.

I started to introduce myself, and she interrupted, "You are *so* shockingly late. All the other girls are just getting final touch-ups." My heart leapt for a moment when I realized she had mistaken me for a model, but it was a momentary thrill. She grabbed her glasses, jammed them on her face, and consulted the clipboard she was clutching. "Name, name?" She looked up, and her face relaxed. "Sorry," she said brusquely. "I thought you were a model, but obviously you're not."

"Obviously," I said, just hoping she wouldn't expand on the how and why of that statement.

"I'm Maggie Fiori," I said. "Editor at *Small Town.* We're sponsors, and one of our writers, Andrea Storch, is a model. I just came by to say hello."

She shook her head. "We don't like to disturb the girls so soon before R-time."

"Our time?"

"R, R, R! For runway, runway liftoff," she said impatiently. "There's a sponsor's lounge right through there," she pointed at a billowy curtain. "You can have a drink, but I have to ask you *not* to disturb the models right now."

"Of course," I said meekly. "I'll just cut through here and go right to the lounge."

She started to protest, but a tiny man, dressed all in surgical greens, was standing at her elbow, talking urgently about a tattoo emergency. "It shows, Alexandra, it shows! We didn't know she had a fucking unicorn tattooed just above her ass. The designer is going to have a fit when he sees it."

I watched Alexandra and Dr. Tattoo take off across the room. I stood for a moment, scanning the room full of beautiful, privileged women dressed in expensive clothes. I knew that each one had a story—an errant spouse, a child with a frightening disease, an alcoholic parent, Conservatory training reduced to giving music lessons to the untalented and ungrateful, but for just that moment, they looked absolutely golden. Luminous, lit up from within. It was like being trapped inside a sorority for God's fortunate—and not getting a bid. Or an invite, or whatever they call those things.

I caught sight of Andrea, who was perched on a high stool, with people fussing around her. Looking over my shoulder to make sure that the leopard-skin gatekeeper and her pal weren't watching,

I wound my way to Andrea and her fluffers.

Starchy Storch, of the tweeds and twinsets, and one string of pearls, had been transformed into someone else entirely. I couldn't see what she was wearing on top, because she was swathed in a protective cape, while a tall guy with ropy arms, head-to-toe in black, leaned carefully in with a comb so tiny it could have been used to groom the cilia on paramecia. He gently tended to each eyelash.

Underneath the cape, I caught sight of black leather pants, laced up the side with what appeared to be buckskin strings. The highest, spikiest, pointiest high heels I'd ever seen dangled from her toes. The eyelash groomer cast a quick look over his shoulder at me. "I don't know who you are," he hissed, "but do not speak to the model. She cannot move right now. Not one centimeter."

I nodded, intimidated by his intensity, and by the wicked-looking tools he wore in a handyman's apron around his waist. A young woman, who was standing on a stepstool, slicking Andrea's hair away from her face and cupped around the back of her head, rolled her eyes at me. "Don't worry," she said. "Victor gets jumpy just before liftoff. You can talk. Andrea just can't open her eyes or talk back to you."

"Okay," I whispered. I watched for a moment, fascinated by the tools, the concentration, the products arrayed around the table. "What's she got on top?" I asked.

The young woman, who wore a bowling shirt with the name Emerald embroidered on the pocket, giggled, "More—and less—than you think," she said. At the same moment, she and Victor ceased their ministrations. They stepped back, looking exactly like the television ER teams when somebody shouts "Clear" and they put the paddles down.

"Can I move?" whispered Andrea.

"Open your eyes, honey," said Victor, and whipped a mirror out so Andrea could look at herself.

"Oh, my heavens," she said. She stared into the mirror, and I stared at her.

"What's the look you're going for?" I asked, surveying Andrea's black-rimmed eyes, shadowed in three shades of purple, and lips lined with what appeared to be the burnt-umber crayon in the sixty-four pack of Crayolas.

"We needed to slut her up," said Victor, "so she could carry off the leather-and-lace look."

"Mission accomplished," I murmured. Victor was tucking tools back into his belt. Somehow it didn't seem like the kind of thing a guy could buy at Ace Hardware, but what did I know?

"Another triumph," said Victor, looking Andrea over with satisfaction. He reached out a hand to her. "Stand up, honey, we need to get the full effect, and we don't want you falling on your ass in those shoes."

Andrea took his hand, and stepped down. Victor touched his Bluetooth. "Yes? What? I'm here." He listened for a moment. "Okay, on my way. The little magazine writer is all tramped up and ready to go."

"Got to run," he said, "emergency in Dolce & Gabbana evening wear."

Andrea looked stunned. "Okay. I guess, I'm fine."

Victor laughed, "Baby, you're superfine."

As Andrea stood there, still a little teetery on the spikes, the young woman carefully undraped the smock covering her from neck to waist.

I was anxious to see what was underneath, but my eyes were drawn to Andrea's lips. "Hey," I said, "did you get your lips shot up with something? They look swollen."

The young woman piped up, "We put Lip Venom on 'em, and they temporarily plump up."

"Oh, thanks," I said feebly.

She looked at me over her shoulder. "It's a commercial product. You can buy it."

I touched my fingers to my lips. "Do I need it?"

"Everybody needs it," she replied. She turned Andrea to face me, and I gave a little gasp. Topping those lace-up leather pants was a glittery, black sweater, cut in a vee so deep and wide, that only the very tips, okay, well, the nipples, on Andrea's breasts weren't showing.

"Oh, my God," I breathed. "Did they put venom on your boobs, too?"

Andrea grimaced. "How bad do I look?" She looked down.

"You don't look bad at all," I said. "You look sexy, and stacked." I came a little closer. "Not to be nosy, but how did you do that?" I asked the makeup girl.

"Lots of tape," she said. She made a round-and-round gesture. "We taped her breasts closer together to create more cleavage, and then we used double-stick tape and body cement to make sure the sweater doesn't fall off. Last thing we do is shadow the cleavage with bronzer and some blush."

"Well," I said, "I can't wait to hear what Calvin thinks and what your mother says. We'll be together at the table, and I can't remember looking forward to anything with quite this much anticipation." Andrea narrowed her eyes at me. "Just a happy spectator, that's me," I said blandly.

Andrea groaned. "This is a mistake, it's a terrible mistake."

I reached out to touch her arm reassuringly, but Emerald snapped, "Don't touch. Don't touch her anywhere."

I nodded, chastened. "Hey," I said. "Besides cheering you on, I really came back here for the sponsors' party. I wanted to put in an appearance."

Emerald waved at some curtains in back of rolling racks of clothes. "Through there."

I gave Andrea one last encouraging smile and a thumbs-up. "I can't believe Gertie talked me into this," she muttered, rocking gingerly back and forth on the heels. "Oh, Maggie, wait." She gestured me to come closer, then leaned in to whisper in my ear. "Before I forget—at the models' orientation, Ginger mentioned that her husband would be here for the show. Why don't you cruise around the reception and bump into him? Find out about if the best friends *did* exchange house keys or whether or not he knew about Grace and Trav's fondness for S&M."

"Perfect small talk subjects," I said. "I'll do my best."

I headed through the champagne-colored curtains, and emerged into an entirely different world. A small combo played Brazilian-style jazz in a corner, and a long bar, snakelike in shape, wrapped around the wall. I greeted a few people I knew from other media organizations and worked my way toward a bartender.

"What can I get you?" he asked. "Champagne cocktail, chocolate-infused vodka, or a Scorpion?"

"I'd recommend the Scorpion, Ms. Fiori," a voice advised me, just to my right. And there he was, the object of my not-yet-begun search, delivered right into my hands. Bill Brand, sleek and gelled as ever, stood relaxed, ranking and rating the crowd as if he were assessing the strengths and vulnerabilities of a start-up's management team. He held a martini glass filled with an amber liquid in his hand. He raised it to me in a mock toast. "To beauty, in all its forms."

"Tomato juice, no ice, lemon twist, please," I said to the bartender.

I smiled at Brand. "You must be here to cheer on your bride."

"I am," he said, "and to admire the fine collection of femininity the Junior League has assembled on behalf of good works and overpriced fashion." He took a sip. "Our firm's a sponsor, and I'm hosting our table."

My tomato juice arrived, and I raised my glass to return his toast. "To fashion and good works," I said.

The crowd was starting to move away from the bar and swarm together, in the proscribed social ritual—exclaiming, air-kissing, exercising the face-to-face greet, while peering over shoulders to see if someone more interesting was lurking behind pillar or post.

Brand and I leaned against the bar in companionable silence. Key or S&M, where should I go first?

"You didn't want to model?" he asked.

"One of our writers is a member of Junior League," I said. "As was her mother in Connecticut, and I think her grandmother before her. In fact, were there Junior Leaguers on the Mayflower?

I'm sure some Storch ancestor was there, probably organizing an onboard fashion show." I paused. "So, Andrea was the best choice. In fact, her mother is here today from the East Coast to support her." I waited a moment. "Ginger is in the show, isn't she?"

Brand nodded. "Absolutely. Fifth year running. She's a veteran. Well, actually, she skipped the year that Grace died. Too hard to revisit something the girls had done together, I guess."

"I can imagine." I said. "What's she wearing?"

He shrugged. "She doesn't tell me much."

"In general?" I asked. "Or just about this event?"

Brand looked annoyed. "Are you conducting a survey, Ms. Fiori?"

"Perhaps," I said. "Communication practices of the privileged and powerful."

"Ah," he said, "that would make you part of the study group, yes? Media people have the power of the pen."

"I think what matters these days is the power of the YouTube," I said.

"Evasive, I see." He rattled the ice cubes in his glass. "Do you and your husband exchange every little secret?"

"We do now," I said, tersely.

"Pity," he said. "Spoils the mystery and intrigue a bit, I would think." He gave me a sidelong smile.

"I guess that's what BFFs are for," I said.

"Pardon?"

"You know, how kids say 'best friends forever'? Isn't that what Grace and Ginger were?"

He shrugged. "A little sophomoric for two sophisticated, grown women, I'd say. But yes, definitely the best of friends."

"I can't even imagine what it must have been like for Ginger," I said. "Losing Grace like that—the person you confide in, who has your house key and can check on things when you're gone. The one you call in the middle of the night if you're lying awake worrying about something."

"They were close," said Brand, "but I don't think there were any midnight calls to exchange girlish confidences. And I would be very surprised to learn Ginger and Grace had exchanged keys. We both have housekeepers and security systems; nobody needs to be handing around keys. You're describing some nostalgic view of friendship from fifty years ago."

I was about to protest that my next-door neighbor and I have keys to each other's houses, but I thought it would just prove Brand's point about how quaint and retro our lives are.

I scanned the room, wondering if Gus was somewhere. This hardly seemed like his kind of hangout, but then, Gus had shown up at the garden party and watched Ginger with particular enthusiasm. "Is Ginger's father coming?" I asked.

"You mean Gus?" drawled Brand, elongating the name into something that sounded like it was best treated with multiple doses of strong antibiotics.

"Yes," I said. "He seems so proud of everything she does."

"I don't have the faintest idea. I don't even know if Ginger invited him. I just know," he paused, and took a healthy sip of his Scorpion, "he's not a guest at *my* table."

I was silent for a moment, then mused aloud, "Too bad for Ginger, I guess. Not having all her guys in the same cheering section."

Brand's face resettled into its bland, pleasant, revealing-nothing expression. "Well, where are you seated, Ms. Fiori?" he asked, refusing to rise to my not-so-subtle bait. "We do have one seat open at our table, and I'd be delighted to have you join us."

I smiled politely. "So kind of you, but *Small Town* is actually a media sponsor, so I'm hosting a table as well."

He drained his glass, and turned around to put it on the bar. He caught the bartender's eye and tapped the glass. The bartender immediately whisked the glass away and began making swift pours into a shaker.

Brand turned back to me. "Need a little liquid sustenance to sit through these things in the middle of the day," he said.

I scanned the room, nodding, and then I caught sight of a

familiar face. "Look," I said, "Gus *is* here." Ginger's father was moving through the crowd like a broken-field runner, coming our way. I gave a little wave. He caught my eye and smiled.

Brand picked up his fresh drink with a snap of the wrist, touched his index finger to his forehead, in an encore of the way he'd made his escape from Michael and me at the event honoring Plummer, and said, "Enjoy the program." It was fascinating to watch him. Even with a substantial amount of alcohol in his system, he looked unruffled, precise in every word and move.

I caught his arm. "Don't you want to say hello to Gus?" I asked directly.

He shook free of my arm. "Try not to be obtuse, Ms. Fiori. Does it appear that I want to greet that charmless old man?"

"So sorry," I said, holding his eyes.

"No, you're not," he retorted, and headed purposefully away just as Gus drew near.

Gus greeted me enthusiastically and knocked on the bar. "Bloody Mary," he said, "and hold the celery and all that other crunchy, vegetable crap." He raised his eyebrows at me and smiled. "Did I see you shooting the shit with my stick-up-his-ass son-in-law?"

"You did," I said. "I gather you're not best pals, hanging out watching the Friday Night fights and playing poker."

"Man wouldn't know a good poker hand if it fell out of the sky and arranged itself in his manicured little girly-paw," said Gus. "Plus, he doesn't need to play poker. Makes plenty of money doing all that hocus-pocus with other people's money."

"You mean his partnership with Frederick Plummer?" I asked. "I don't think it's hocus-pocus. It's just what VCs do."

Gus tossed a five on the bar as a tip to the bartender, who pushed his "vegetable-free" Bloody Mary to him.

"Yeah, well, any work that doesn't involve a little honest sweat seems like bullshit to me," he growled.

"Oh, really?" I said. "Were you sweating when you won all that money on *Jeopardy*?" I asked.

Gus laughed. "You bet I was, sweetie," he said. "Those were hot lights. Hey, if you don't believe me, you can rent a compilation of those old shows—I'm on one of the 'best of the big winner' DVDs. Sweating like a pig."

"I believe you," I said. "So, where are you sitting? Since I gather you're not sharing your son-in-law's table?"

Gus shrugged. "I get too restless to sit at these shindigs. I just want a good vantage spot to watch Ginger steal the show. I'll have a couple of drinks, and watch from the sidelines. She'll know I'm here. Then, I've got to make a quick getaway. I'm doing some repairs on my cabin in the Sierra foothills. Getting it ready for summer." He sighed. "I've never talked Ivory into going up there with me. Maybe this will be the year."

"She doesn't like the woods?"

"Who knows? Too much time in the car with me, probably. And it's pretty middle-of-nowhere. Once you're there, you're not going anywhere. Nope. Take that back. You can hike to a bait shop that also sells the best mountain trout po'boys you'll ever taste."

"Stout's Trout?" I asked.

He looked amazed. "That's the place. How'd you know?"

"I used to fish up there with my dad when I was a kid. Hiking to Stout's for lunch was the culinary highlight of my childhood."

He shook his head. "Amazing. Most people can't even find the place." He took another swig of his Bloody Mary.

"How'd you get into this reception? Don't you need to be a sponsor or something?"

He grinned, and pulled a crumpled card out of his pants pocket and waved it at me. "My little Ginger gave me a ticket. She looks out for her old man, even if she's always worried I'll embarrass her."

He raised his glass to me. "Here's how."

"So, Gus," I began, "I was wondering."

He shook his head. "You ask a lot of questions. Don't you remember what killed the cat?"

"Nothing," I said grimly. "My kids have two of them, and they seem to have nine thousand lives. The cats, not the kids. But, I was just wondering what all the tension is between you and Ginger's husband?"

"No tension," he said. "He thinks I'm a carbuncle on Ginger's perfect little life. And I think he doesn't treat my daughter right."

This was getting interesting. "What do you mean?"

With that, Gus launched a small litany of wrongs he felt Bill perpetuated on Ginger from not taking her arm to cross the street to not having children, etc. etc.

"Whoa!" I said. "Maybe Ginger doesn't want children?"

He frowned. "She'd be a great mother. She's terrific at everything she does."

"You really know he never takes her arm when they cross the street?" I asked.

Gus put down his glass and curled his hands into two circles and brought them up to his eyes, mock binoculars at the ready. "I miss nothing," he said flatly, "when it comes to the people I love." He glanced at me. "You've got kids, right?" I nodded.

"Thought so. Then you know, it's your job to protect them. I wasted a lot of years not looking out for Ginger. I won't make that mistake again."

"How about kids looking out for their parents?" I asked.

"I can take care of myself," he said gruffly.

"I didn't mean you." I said, "I meant Travis looking out for his mother."

Gus shook the ice cubes in his glass and polished off the rest. "You mean, Travis *protecting* Ivory from an unclassy guy like me, don't you?"

"I don't know exactly what I'm asking," I said. "But Travis seems very proprietary about his mother, even from prison. Seems like a hard club to get into."

"Damn near impossible," said Gus. "I've tried. The Prince of the manor will always be first in her heart, and Ivory tells me to chill because Travis hasn't approved of any of her boyfriends. And believe me, I know I'm not the first."

A horn fanfare sounded in the next room. "Ladies and gentlemen," called an amplified voice. "Please find your seats in the dining room. Luncheon is served."

I reached out my hand to give Gus a farewell handshake, and he ignored my hand, pulling me close for a hug. "I like you, little lady," he said, directly into my ear. "Even if you ask too damn many questions."

He released me, and made a general swat in the direction of my backside. I sidestepped, waggled my fingers goodbye, and hurried off into the dining room.

Small Town was definitely a "second-tier" sponsor, so it took a few minutes to navigate halfway back and to the side to our table. I spotted Andrea's mother and Calvin first. Mrs. Storch was simply a slightly faded version of Andrea—her skin a little paler, her hair a slightly washed-out blond, her cashmere twinset a softer gray than Andrea usually wore. Regulation pearls, in place, but unlike Andrea's standard single strand, Mrs. Storch featured a double-strand.

But, here was the surprise. Even from several tables away, I heard her let loose with a delighted shout of laughter. Her head was close to Calvin's, and as I watched, she dug in her handbag, and pulled a handkerchief out to dab her eyes.

The rest of the table—advertisers we had invited as our guests, the columnist who covered the social scene, and Gertie—were all chatting amiably, but sneaking surreptitious glances at Calvin and Mrs. Storch, wishing they were part of their conversation. Calvin stood as I came to the table, and gestured to the empty chair next to Mrs. Storch.

I slipped into the seat and shook hands with Andrea's mother. "So lovely to have you here," I said. "I know it means a good deal to Andrea."

"I'm delighted to be here. And Mr. Bright promises me that Andrea is wearing neither tweed nor Burberry. This is a bit of a thrill!"

Thrill, huh? Hold that thought, Mrs. S.

A few speeches, a multiscreen presentation on the Junior League's projects, a breeze through the artfully arranged seafood salad, and it was time for the show. The lights went down again, and then came up on the elevated catwalk, edged on either side with larger-than-life white orchids.

It was about what you'd expect—a local anchorman plus a *SF Chronicle* fashion reporter providing commentary, an onstage combo that changed tempo and tune every time the clothes changed theme—casual wear, mom-about-town wear, sports clothes, elegant work clothes. Mrs. Storch leaned over to me, "I told Calvin I thought they'd put Andrea in one of those handsome tennis outfits," she said. "She's such a tennis addict, you know."

"Guess not," I said, blandly. "I think the sports part of the show is over."

"He did tell me that he thinks she's dressed for indoor sports."

"Really?" I whispered noncommittally, not anxious to hear Calvin's speculations on Andrea's participation in indoor sports.

The lights on the runway dimmed once more, and came up with a little silver sparkle edge to them.

"And now," intoned the fashion reporter, talking directly into the mike in a hoarse, sexy voice, about an octave lower than she'd been speaking. "Here's a little segment we're calling Fashion on the Edge."

"Oh, goody," I said aloud, realizing that this segment had to feature our own leather-and-lace prepster.

The musicians laid down a disco beat, and the notes of "I Will Survive" began rocking the room.

Andrea was the first model out. Gone was the hesitancy and apprehension I'd seen as she'd slid off the high makeup chair. Instead, she strode out on the catwalk as if she were taking possession. The impeccable Starchy Storch posture was there, shoulders back, chest out—and oh, my, what a chest it was. But in addition to that classic New England field-hockey/tennis-playing stance, she'd clearly had some model-coaching as well. She led with her hips, seemed completely secure on the spike heels, and had a look on her face that suggested decadent-European-film-star-as-dominatrix. Charlotte Rampling in *The Night Porter.* I could hardly bear to look away, but I had to watch Mrs. Storch. She leaned forward, back no longer touching the chair, her hands folded in her lap. She blinked a few times. And then leaned over to Calvin and whispered something. He listened intently, shook his head, and pointed to me. "What?" I asked.

"Shh," said Mrs. Storch, "we have a question. We'll ask you after Andrea is offstage."

The anchorman was speaking: "Lovely in leather and lace from Ella True," he said, "a local designer who's all about the bad girls. Welcome our first-time model, Andrea Storch." A ripple of applause and a few whistles pierced the clatter of cutlery in the dining room. "Andrea's a film critic from *Small Town,* one of this year's media sponsors," he added. "And her friends tell me that her nickname is..." He looked down at the card in his hand, "Starchy Storch." Laughter washed across the room. Andrea had reached the end of the catwalk, posed, one hip thrust at an angle. Her mouth twitched, and then she broke into a wide grin.

The anchorman waited 'til the laughter died down. "I'd say Miss Storch needs a new nickname—and fast."

The smile disappeared; Andrea was all business again. She turned smartly on her spikes, and strode back down the runway and disappeared.

The rest of the segment featured other models in edgier fashion—shredded shirts, miniskirts with seams on the outside, a shocking-pink, faux-fur tankini, and the closer, a spiky-haired mom in black hot pants and a fringed, black leather jacket over a red lace bustier pushing a twin-stroller with towheaded kids, also dressed in black. All very homage to Vivienne Westwood.

The big finale segment, as always, was evening wear. Ginger was the last model out in that segment, before the traditional bridezilla closer. Dressed top to bottom in Ralph Lauren British racing-green, beaded silk, with a knockout heavy emerald-green necklace topping the strapless bodice. "My word," said Mrs.

Storch. "Those emeralds must weigh more than the model." When Ginger paused to strike her pose, a yodel-like "Yahoo" pierced the air, punctuating the applause. Gus, I felt sure, was expressing his fatherly approval. And then, the music changed once again, and lush strings played poor old, worn-out Pachelbel's *Canon in D* to signal the parade of brides. Since it was the San Francisco Junior League, in addition to the elegant Vera Wang zillion-dollar white slip dresses, there were models in traditional red Chinese wedding gowns and an Indian bride wearing a gold-embroidered red sari.

A final round of applause, the lights came up, and at last—dessert on the table. Mini chocolate éclairs. Mrs. Storch took a ladylike sip of her wine and dug into the éclairs with gusto.

"Isn't this fun?" she asked. "Éclairs! In the middle of the day. It's like being on holiday. All we ever have for dessert is fruit. Melon balls in the summer, apples and cheese in the winter. But chocolate—this is an immense improvement."

"So," I leaned toward Mrs. Storch and Calvin, "what did you think about the show? And what were you trying to ask me?"

"I thought Andrea looked very sexy," said Mrs. Storch. She turned to Calvin, "What did you think, dear?"

"Hot," said Calvin. "Hot, hot, hot." I raised an eyebrow at Calvin. He added hastily, "But in a wholesome way."

He watched Mrs. Storch polish off her éclairs, and gently pushed his untouched plate toward her.

"Aren't you eating yours, dear?" she asked.

"All yours," said Calvin, gallantly.

"Oh, tell Mrs. Fiori what we were trying to remember," she prompted Calvin.

"You always have all this ridiculous trivia in your head," said Calvin. "Mrs. Storch thought Andrea looked like Marlene Dietrich when she was vamping that old professor in *The Blue Angel.* But we couldn't remember her character's name."

"Naughty Lola," I said promptly. "And the professor was played by Emil Jannings. This isn't trivia at all. This is important information any movie buff knows." I polished off my éclairs;

I wasn't trying to butter up Mrs. Storch, I had no intention of handing mine over. "And, you may be right. That slicked-back hair—very Marlene in her cross-dressing days."

Gertie caught my eye across the table, and tapped her wristwatch. I looked at mine. "Yikes," I said.

"Meetings this afternoon. So sorry I have to run." I shook hands all around and took off out of the dining room. As I hurried out, I couldn't help but acknowledge a tiny, wicked disappointment that Mrs. Storch had not seemed more discomfited, less enthusiastic, about Andrea's appearance. But then, oh, well, that's what comes from jumping to narrow, judgmental conclusions. Why *couldn't* a pearl-wearing, New England mother muse about her daughter's resemblance to Marlene Dietrich at her most debauched? And polish off four small éclairs in the process?

Interval No. 6 with Dr. Mephisto

Dr. Mephisto was in black, head to toe. What was that about? Had the *Vogue* police come by to confiscate her wardrobe? Had she taken vows in a religious order?

Once again, she caught me giving her the once-over. She delivered one of her unreadable smiles, which I imagined translated directly into "I know what you're thinking and just remember how incredibly shallow it is to judge people by what they're wearing."

"Going to a funeral, Dr. McQuist?" I inquired mildly.

She gave me a placid smile. "No. But it's funny that you ask, because I'm sensing some real sadness in you. Are *you* going to a funeral?"

Michael looked back and forth, at both of us.

"Am I missing something?" he asked.

"No," I said at the same moment Dr. Mephisto said, "Yes, I think so."

We all sat in silence.

"We had an interesting time at the Crimson Club a few nights ago," Michael volunteered.

"Tell me about it," she said.

Michael summarized, as if he were highlighting facts in a deposition. Or that's what I imagined. I'd never actually seen a deposition. Except in the movies. He focused on what happened when, what we discovered, when we left, all delivered without much affect or embroidery. He could have been describing a trip to Home Depot with the boys.

Dr. Mephisto sat quietly, listening. Michael fell silent.

"And," she prompted gently.

"And that's it," said Michael, a little impatiently.

"Maggie?" She'd turned her attention to me.

Oh, no, I thought. She's trying to turn this into one of those *Rashomon* things, where people who experience the same thing have entirely different takes on it. I expressed that view. Michael sighed.

Dr. Mephisto observed, "Is there something wrong with that? Don't we all have our own experience of the same moment?"

I felt a little headache beginning at the back of my eyes.

"Okay," I said. "That's not all. Or at least, that's not the whole story."

Michael raised his eyebrows.

"So, tell us the whole story," said Mephisto. "Or at least, your whole story."

I took a deep breath. "What Michael said is correct, or at least, I think so. We found out some information about a scene that happened at the Club, and that may prove useful. Or not." I glanced at Michael. "Lt. Moon says they knew all about it."

"You called him?" he asked.

"I was going to," I said, "but he stopped over, the morning after, while you were out with the boys at soccer. I'm sorry. I forgot to tell you. He wanted to talk to you about playing in Wisconsin or Minnesota or somewhere cold. I don't remember exactly where."

"And you get mad at the kids for not remembering messages," he said.

"Promise me we're not going to have another dishwasher-unloading conversation today," protested Dr. Mephisto.

"No, no, okay," I said, feeling short of breath. "What I wanted to say was this: I got really sick after we got home that night."

Michael regarded me curiously. "Is that why you were sleeping in the TV room?"

I nodded. "It was," I searched for the right word. "It was very upsetting to see you at the Club. Dancing with that woman."

Michael didn't say anything.

"It made you jealous?" prompted Mephisto.

"Not at first. At first, it was exciting. I was watching you with that redhead, and it was kind of thrilling. Like watching someone in a movie. You looked so sexy, and so—different. Not like a dad, you know?"

Michael nodded. "I didn't feel like a dad, for just a few minutes."

"Anyway, I kept thinking—I couldn't wait 'til we got home. It was like thinking about going home with a stranger. Only someone familiar, someone I already knew. I was having very entertaining fantasies."

I stopped talking, so desperate to have something to do with my hands. I reached out and picked up Michael's mug of horrid green tea, and took a gulp.

Mephisto watched me.

"But then..." I closed my eyes, and I could see Michael again, at the end, dancing with the redhead, with her hot-pink dress cupping that perfect butt, and her hands wrapped around his neck. "But then, we couldn't find you when it was time to go. And Puck and I went looking for you, and there you were and it was just awful. I thought—how could you touch someone else so intimately? And be so distracted that you didn't even know I was there?" I stopped again. "And you know that thing Fran Lebowitz says. That there's no conversation in life—there's just these standard remarks everyone makes. Like—I just have this one thing, can I go ahead of you in line. And..."

"'Good. Now you know how it feels,'" finished Michael.

"Right," I said. I sat back on the couch. "Pretty dumb revelation, huh? Pretty obvious?"

"A reminder, Mrs. Fiori," said Michael coldly. "I believe you're the one who said you wouldn't mind a few surprises in our love life. You might have anticipated that an evening at the Crimson Club wouldn't be as predictable as..." He paused, and pretended to pluck something from his memory. "Ah, yes, 'folding laundry.'"

My own glib words hung in the air. No one said anything. "I didn't mean that kind of surprise," I protested weakly.

"Here's the thing with surprises, Maggie," observed Michael. "You can't control what they are. Or then, they won't be surprises, will they?"

"So, anyway," I finished briskly. "It was awful, and after we got home, I didn't want to have sex anymore. I just wanted to die, because I couldn't figure out who the hell this person was, this person I knew so well, who could look like that, and touch someone else like that. And be so remote from me."

"And that made you feel sick?" asked Mephisto.

I shook my head. "I didn't *feel* sick. I was sick. I threw up, and I couldn't stop shivering, and I thought I was dying from some awful flu. But instead," and I felt the tears well up, "I was dying from knowing all over again what a terrible person I was. I am. And now I have some small glimmer of how you must have felt." I scrabbled in my handbag for a Kleenex. Dr. Mephisto pushed the box on the table closer to me, but I ignored her. I wanted *my* tissue from *my* purse; somehow it made me feel less pathetic. Michael watched me. He leaned forward a little, and I thought for one moment, he was going to put his arms around me. Then, he leaned back again, and crossed his ankle over his leg.

"Michael?" prodded Mephisto. "Do you want to say something?"

"I don't know," he said. "I just don't know."

"I'm so sorry," I said.

He waved his hand at me, a little dismissively. "I know you are,

Maggie. You've said so. I believe it. This is not new information."

"But I think there is something new here," said Mephisto. "At least, for Maggie."

"What's new?" asked Michael impatiently. "She screwed up. She knows she did. She's apologized. She's not going to do it again. Or at least, that's what she tells me."

"Here's what I think is new," said Mephisto. "I don't doubt Maggie's sincerity in her remorse. I don't doubt that she's sorry. But, what's different from my point of view, at least as Maggie's reporting it, is that she had just a glimmer of how it might have felt to be you."

Michael shook his head. "Not one single clue," he said. "She has not one fucking clue. The Crimson Club was...silly. Harmless. What Maggie did was lethal."

The ride home was completely silent. I kept glancing over at Michael, looking for something. Nothing. The stillness in the car felt like an uninvited hitchhiker. Finally, I reached over and hit the radio. National Public Radio filled the car, earnest, intense reporting on another, slightly inexplicable move by the Fed. I listened intently. I figured that if this was the end of our marriage, I might as well learn something about monetary policy.

"Maggie," Michael ventured.

"Yes?" I responded eagerly. Whatever he had to say, I'd listen. I'd pay attention.

"Do you mind switching it to the ball game? Oakland's at Boston."

"Oh, sure," I said, and hit the button, so that sound of "swing and a miss," would fill the immeasurable space between us.

CHAPTER 33

Travis sat erect in the hard plastic chair. All around us families were having Sunday supper experiences. Instead of roast beef or fried chicken at the dining-room table at home, they were sitting at beat-up aluminum tables, dining on the contents of the vending machines, but the spirit was the same. Lots of noise, people kidding one another, kids racing around the room, while mothers called for them to "come on, sit down, stop that running around right now." Mostly they ignored their mothers, as children do. And, as the adults finished eating, the anachronistically elegant promenade started up around the room.

Travis, Isabella, and I sat in a triangle, facing each other. Isabella, as restless as the kids, was tapping one of her trademark red pencils on the table. Travis reached out and put his hand on the pencil. "Isabella, please," he said.

She'd brought him up to date on our developments, and his face brightened at the report of Carol Ann's information.

"Don't get too excited," said Isabella. "We don't know what it means yet, but at least we've got an eyewitness who saw someone with Grace the night of the murder."

Travis allowed himself a smile. "See Maggie, I knew you'd turn something up."

"It's a start," I said. "And there's something more," I added. "A group of us went to the Crimson Club the other night."

"Really?" said Travis. "I wish I'd been there to see that."

"Yep," I continued. "We drove up in the Volvo stationwagon and everything. If the valet hadn't been ripped out of his mind, I'm sure he would have commented on our choice of ride."

I briefed Travis on our evening, including the information about the altercation.

"So, any theories about the tall guy? Or the woman he dragged out of there?"

Travis shook his head. "Not really. You know the cops had already asked around about that scene. And the trial attorney didn't think there was anything there for us to follow up. I mean, theoretically there was somebody who seemed angry at Grace, but we don't know why."

"Grace never mentioned it to you?"

"Nope."

We sat in silence for a few minutes. Isabella started tapping her pencil again, and then launched into an update on the appeals process, and the progress on the habeas brief.

"Tick-tock," said Travis.

"I know, I know," said Isabella. "Try not to worry."

"I'm going to see your mother again," I offered.

Travis looked interested. "Oh, yeah? You two hitting it off?"

I thought about the scene in the dressing room at the boutique.

"Maybe," I said. "But I'm seeing her because I was invited to the rent party at The Devil's Interval next week."

"Oh, yeah. The rent party. I just love the idea of my mom collecting charity," he said bitterly. "Of course, charity from strangers may be better than my mom's live-in sugar daddy."

"He's kept that place going," I pointed out.

Travis frowned. "I know and I should be grateful. And I don't think he's a bad guy. Just not the kind of man I want to see my mother hang out with." He leaned back in the chair and folded his arms. "But you know something? Worse than me being here in this hellhole, I hate the thought of my mom losing The Devil's Interval. She loves that place, and we..." he broke off. "Forget it. It is what it is."

"I'm actually looking forward to the party," I offered tentatively. "It doesn't seem like charity. It seems like a creative fundraiser—and boy, I've been to my share of not-so-creative fundraisers in this town."

"Oh, it should be an interesting scene," said Travis. "And good music. You can count on that. One of my mom's 'discoveries,' Karen Blixt, is singing. She's got this sexy, throaty alto and she used to sing church music, so she's got a lot of soul that she's putting into that music. And great sidemen." He was warming to the topic. "She's such a good musician, that all the great local guys like playing with her."

"You ever play with her?" I asked.

"No, but my mom did. And maybe she will at the party. She's still playing left-handed, but my mother left-handed can play rings around the average two-handed piano man."

We spent the last minutes of our visit going over Carol Ann's recounting of the evening in minute-by-minute detail.

"I know that girl," said Travis. "Once in a while, I'd drop stuff off at A Mother's Place, and she was always the one who helped me unload. She hero-worshipped Grace. And Grace got her her first job at that fancy spa where she works."

"Ever meet her husband?" I asked.

Travis frowned. "I don't remember meeting him. Grace said she thought he was a good guy. He'd gotten himself an education, and I think he was going to law school or something."

"He's almost done," I volunteered.

"That's great," said Travis. "His life is just starting."

CHAPTER 34

The music critic from the *Chron*, Jon Noble, sat at the front door, perched on a high stool and harassing people as they walked into The Devil's Interval. "No cover," he said, "but we're looking for $50,000 tonight, and I'm not afraid to shake people down."

Puck greeted him, "My man! How they hangin'?" They went through one of those elaborate fist-touching, arm-punching rituals men engage in. Michael had sent his regrets, so Puck was my date.

"Who's the squeeze?" asked Noble, glancing my way.

"My boss," said Puck. "And she's not as cute as she looks."

"I look *cute*?" I asked in amazement. "How cool is that? You just earned a raise."

People were gathering at the door behind us. "Get on in there," said Noble. "There's chow and liquor and some damn fine music. I've got to bleed these folks dry as they come in. That's my job and I'm happy to do it."

Puck and I wandered into the bar. It was wall-to-wall people—hard to imagine where Noble was going to send anyone else he shook down at the door. A fortyish singer, in loose black silk pants and shirt, with long, sparkly earrings, was on the small raised stage, holding the mike and swinging the heck out of "My Favorite Things."

She had a good haircut, a kind of hipped-up version of a Dorothy Hamill bob, and it moved with the music. "And to think I always thought that song was the most saccharine of the whole sound track," I shout-whispered into Puck's ear.

He grinned. "I know. Karen Blixt, she's great. And you got it, babe. I always thought *The Sound of Music* made you root for the Germans, just to get the damn kids off the screen. In their friggin' window-curtain dirndls."

We listened for a moment. The singer was exactly as Travis had promised. Easy, low alto, wrapping around the notes like just-warmed caramel. And she was generous, stepping back to give her sidemen plenty of solo time. When the song finished, she beckoned to Ivory, pouring behind the bar.

"Ladies and gentlemen, Miss Ivory Gifford!" The applause started, then people began chanting, "Ivory, Ivory, Ivory." From where we stood, I could see Ivory shaking her head, laughing, waving a bar towel at the room. Suddenly, Gus loomed behind her, pulling her to his side. She stood there for a minute, then glanced up at the singer. Karen put the mike down at her side, and waved at Ivory. Gus leaned down and whispered something in her ear. Ivory straightened, shook herself free, tossed the towel on the bar, and began making her way to the tiny stage. The bass player reached down and gave her a hand up. She came to the mike stand, gave Karen a hug, and then took the mike from Karen's outstretched hand. She was wearing the plum dress, and looked like a million bucks.

"Hello, everyone," she said softly into the mike.

Across the crowded bar, people shouted back at her. "Hey, Ivory."

"I can't tell you what it means to me and," she hesitated, "to my son, to see you all here this evening." She gave a nervous laugh. "You know that song Karen just sang, the one we all hear with new ears, because of the way she delivers it? Well, this joint is just like that song. It's one of my favorite things, because it's the place Travis and I created together. It's the place that keeps me going, because I've got a job to do every day. And all of you..." she gestured around the room. "You're my favorites, too. Most of us got to know each other because we all love jazz, but along the way, we became friends as well. I know I haven't been the easiest friend to have these last few years, between the stroke and the—" She paused for a moment, and then spoke in a loud, clear voice. "The miscarriage of justice with Trav." A murmur of protest came up from the group. Ivory put up her hand. "It's okay. I think I still remember how to have fun—and that's why we're here tonight." Ivory was gathering strength as she went along, transforming herself before our eyes into a public person, a performer. "We're here to have some fun, make some music, and what else?" She put her hand on her hip, turned to the side, so the plum skirt swirled around her, cupped her ear, and leaned toward the crowd. I saw the spark of who Ivory must have been before her troubles—sexy, fun-loving, and comfortable in front of a crowd.

"Come on," she said, "tell me why we're here tonight?"

"To make some money, honey!" shouted a guy from the back of the room.

"You bet your sweet ass," she shot back. "And the fine members of the fish-wrap trade have volunteered to pick your pockets. Give us a wave, guys," she gestured to the front door. Puck's pal, Jon Noble, and his beat-up-looking colleagues stood up, looking like a rag-tag group of cheerleaders from a twelve-step program.

"Think of those guys as The Devil's Interval kissing booth," she said. "Drop some green stuff, or a big fat check in the hat, and I'm sure you'll be well-compensated."

A wave of derisory hoots and "ewwws" came up from the crowd. "Hey, Jon," called the guy from the back of the room, "I'll pay big bucks for you *not* to kiss me."

"You don't know what you're missing," Noble shouted back.

Ivory held up her hand, and leaned into the microphone.

"Okay, okay," she said. "I've got to be serious for one minute. Thanks to all of you. From me and from Travis. We've got a great attorney," she paused and scanned the room. "Where are you, Isabella?"

Isabella stood on tiptoes and waved. Ivory gave her a crooked smile. "We've got some well-placed friends helping us." Her eyes met mine briefly, and I gave her a tiny nod. "And we've got a whole roomful of the coolest, most generous folks in town." She leaned in close to the mike again and lowered her voice to a throaty, come-hither whisper. "Remember, I said...'most generous folks in town.'"

"It's a shakedown," shouted the obnoxious guy in the back.

"Oh, you are so right," said Ivory. "As the late great Otis Redding said, 'Ain't too proud to beg.'" She stepped back for a moment, wavering. "It's important to me that Travis have a place to come home to. I want the piano tuned up and ready to go, I want the beer cold and the jazz hot, and folks like you in the room, the day that Travis comes home."

Once again, the room had grown very quiet, very still. Puck leaned close to me. "That woman is banking on a miracle," he said.

"Amen, sister," called the guy with the sax, leaning against the piano.

Ivory gestured to Karen to come join her at the mike. "So, what do you say we get Karen and the guys to give us another tune?"

Karen put her arm around Ivory, and took over the mike. "How's about, 'Come on baby, let the good times roll,' with Miss Ivory Gifford at the keyboard?"

Folks began hooting and applauding. The hoots turned into a repeat chant of "Ivory, Ivory, Ivory," with some good-natured floor-pounding and rhythmic clapping. Ivory gave Karen a look of mock exasperation, and walked over to the piano.

With one graceful slide, she was on the bench, left hand on the keys, right hand in her lap. I could see her lean forward, breathe into the keyboard, precisely the same way I'd seen Glenn Gould or Horowitz, in old documentaries. I'd watched Eubie Blake, long about his eighty-fifth birthday, do the same thing, just before he ripped into "Joshua Fit the Battle of Jericho." Breathing into the keyboard, being one with the music. Playing a mean piano is playing a mean piano, didn't matter the genre.

Ivory gave the bass player a nod and then did a chord progression, up from the bass to the first note of the tune. Then the clarinet, then the bass player, and then Karen leaned into the microphone, and pretty soon there were good times rolling all over The Devil's Interval.

I felt a light hand on my shoulder, and turned around. John Moon was standing there, a bottle of Singha in hand and an unexpectedly blissful look on his face.

"Hey," I greeted him. "Pretty good tunes, huh?"

He shook his head, "Not pretty good. The best." He looked around, "Michael here?"

"No," I said. "He's in charge of the home front. I came with Puck."

He raised his eyebrows and sipped his beer. "How are things?"

I scowled at him. "Who knows? And, as you keep reminding me, that's what we have a shrink for."

Moon gave me a mild, vaguely remonstrative look. "Okay, Maggie, just asking. Being polite and concerned. You remember those fine character attributes, don't you?"

"Sorry," I said. "Come on, I'll buy you another beer."

As the evening wore on, the crowd grew louder, happier, and the music just kept getting better. When I finally retrieved Puck from his scuzzy press buddies at the door, he shouted in my ear that they'd cleared about $30,000, with pledges of another $22,000 coming in. We left at one o'clock, and the joint was still cooking.

I crept into bed, after showering off a layer of beer fumes, perspiration, and smeared makeup and checking on the boys. Michael turned over, too lost in sleep to remember he didn't like or respect his wife all that much, and threw his arm over me. I settled in, under the comforting feel of that unconscious embrace, and drifted off. When the phone rang, I woke up with a start, his arm still over me. It was dark out, and the bedside digital clock radio rolled from 4:29 to 4:30 as I answered, too groggy to properly panic.

"Maggie," I heard John Moon's voice in my ear. There was a terrible racket in the background. Sirens, people shouting, and street noise.

"John? What's going on?" I sat up and clicked on the light, not too gently moving Michael's arm off me. He moaned and put his head under the pillow.

"I'm at The Devil's Interval," said Moon. "Or what used to be." He turned away from the phone and I heard him shout. "Hold on, I'll be there in a minute."

"Got to go, Maggie. The arson squad is here."

I clutched the phone. "What are you talking about?" I said. "Wait, John, don't go, tell me."

"It's Ivory's club," he said. "A fire started about half an hour ago, and it's already three-alarm."

"Oh, my God," I said, swinging my legs over the side of the bed. "Is anybody hurt?"

"We don't think so," said Moon. "I think that big gentleman, Mr. Reeves, Ivory's friend, got her out of the building."

"I'm on my way," I said.

"Wait, Maggie," I heard him call. But I hung up the phone, and felt around for my slippers.

By now, Michael was awake and sitting up. He turned his light on.

"What's going on?"

I explained, while rummaging through the bureau, and throwing on underwear, jeans, and a sweater.

"Want me to come with you?" he asked.

I stopped, about to sling my bag over my shoulder.

"Anya's home?"

He looked exasperated. "No, she's out at some after-hours dive with Dr. Bollywood. Maggie, for Christ's sake, are you nuts? Would I even suggest going..."

I put my hand up. "Okay, I get it. I'm an idiot. I'm sorry. I'm not awake yet, and it's just so upsetting. I'm sorry, I'm sorry."

Michael was up, doing the same rummage. "I've got to throw some water on my face. Why don't you make some coffee we can take with us and leave a note for Anya? I'll be down in five minutes."

CHAPTER 35

Some terrible "if it bleeds, it leads" journalistic instincts were eroding my sense of decency. Even in the rush to get out the door, take one last look at the kids, and the dread I felt for Ivory and the place she loved, I had enough presence of mind to call Calvin as we sped down the hill, onto the approach to the Bay Bridge.

"This better be good," he answered the phone.

"Get over to The Devil's Interval," I said. "It's on fire."

"On my way."

Michael glanced at me, as we both gulped coffee and tried to shake off the middle-of-the-night funk. "You're heartless, Maggie," he said, as he listened to my side of the call to Calvin. "You just want some good shots for your story."

I felt my face go hot. "Maybe I do," I said. "But Calvin would have been furious if I hadn't called him. And I don't think it's irresponsible to think about our readers. This could be a whole other dimension to the story," I concluded self-righteously. "Plus, I already know that Ivory's okay."

Michael looked back at me, and a small grin started. "You are so full of crap," he said. "You've turned into an ambulance chaser."

I grinned back. I couldn't resist Michael's uncanny ability to see through whatever little self-deluding detour I was taking. Despite the awfulness of the circumstance, it was wonderful—and comforting—to be in the car with him. "Takes a fire," I thought, "to melt the ice."

For a few minutes, on the way over, I felt one of those disorienting flashes of joy. Sitting in the car, Michael at the wheel, up and out of the house before anyone else, the freeways almost deserted—it reminded me of our predawn trip years ago to walk across the Golden Gate Bridge, when it was closed to all but pedestrians to celebrate the span's fiftieth anniversary. Then, with a crash back to earth, I remembered why we were on this predawn quest, and what terrible consequences it was going to have for Ivory—and Travis. We could smell the smoke a mile before we got to the club, and see it curling up against the night sky, the smoke fighting with the first pink of dawn to claim the morning. The smoke was winning.

When we were within a few blocks, the sky had turned as dark and threatening as an Oklahoma thunderstorm, but the lights and engines were filling the street with clamor and so much illumination, it looked like a movie set.

The street was crowded with fire vehicles, and big, bulky-jacketed firefighters were distributed up and down the street. Despite the bright lights, I couldn't even see the front of the club through the equipment, smoke, and people in front of the place.

Michael spotted John Moon across the street from the club, talking to a small knot of people and herding them farther away as they talked. A yellow-coated firefighter and cop shared the road, both armed with big flashlights, waving cars away from the intersection where Clement and 23rd came together, and The Devil's Interval had swung high and low just a few hours earlier. Michael turned the corner and parked in the first semilegal spot. I grabbed the thermos and a couple extra mugs to bring along for whoever we ran into. We didn't have to look hard for Ivory. When we came to the first ambulance parked on 24th, there she was, sitting on an overturned paint can, wrapped in a Raiders jacket. Gus was sitting on the ground, just to the side of the can, and holding her hand. His face was streaked with black, and the watch cap on his head looked damp with perspiration. Moon was next to both of them, his hand on Ivory's shoulder and a cell phone tucked between ear and shoulder. Michael and I walked over to Ivory. I knelt in front of her and looked up into her face. It was frighteningly blank, wiped clean of any emotion. Gus was talking a slow, steady murmur. "It's all right," he kept crooning. "We'll rebuild. You and me, babe. We'll start all over again. Just us. We can do this."

"Gus," I said gently. "I don't think she can hear you."

I stood up and caught Moon's eye. "Okay, okay," he said into the phone. "I'll wrap up here."

He snapped the phone shut. His eyes were hard. He inclined his head toward the end of the street, and I followed him. From the tiny, shuttered dim sum place on the corner, we watched Michael pour coffee into a mug and put it in Ivory's hands. They'd never even been introduced, but he held his hands over hers and guided the mug to her mouth. She took a sip, choked a little, then took control of the mug and gulped at the coffee.

"This is just cruelty," said Moon. "We will find the damn bastard who did this, and he will pay." I was startled. I'd never heard a single profane word come out of Moon's mouth.

"You're sure somebody did this?" I asked. "It wasn't just an accident? The place was full of people, and there were candles burning on the tables."

He shook his head. "The arson squad will do their real work tomorrow, but I'm willing to bet significant sums of money it was arson. There had to be some kind of accelerant for the place to burn like this." He swore under his breath. "At least, it's under control now," he said. "I was worried we were going to lose half the block."

I watched Michael and Ivory. She was leaning back against him, and he was rubbing her shoulders. Gus had hauled himself to his feet, and was sipping coffee from the other mug I had brought from the car. He was dividing his attention between Ivory, still murmuring to her, almost continuously, and shooting occasional glances over to where Moon and I stood. He seemed torn, wanting to stay with Ivory, yet curious about our conversation. Moon and I watched as the firefighters began advancing closer to the smoldering building, drenching the near-skeletal structure with powerful blasts from the hose.

"What happens now?" I asked. "I mean, if it's arson, isn't the fire department in charge?"

"They're in charge of figuring out what happened," said Moon. "And with the information they provide us, we'll go after whoever did this." He shot a glance at me. "I meant 'we,' as in my police colleagues, Maggie. Not 'we,' as in you and me."

I shook my head. "I don't even know enough to try to meddle, John. Don't worry. I keep thinking about Ivory. Who decided to turn her into Job?"

Moon sighed. "This is not some random, divine action," he said. "I'll tell you that. It's not God visiting plagues on Ivory's house. At least not this latest plague. It's someone very wicked and quite human."

We walked back to Ivory, Michael, and Gus. Ivory had put her arms in the oversize jacket, and was standing. She held her right arm close to her, her left arm dangling at her side, and her fist in a near-clutch.

She handed me the coffee mug. "This is yours, I think," said Ivory. "I'm done. Thanks for the coffee." She straightened up, and subtly shook Gus's proprietary hand off her shoulder.

"I'm done here," she said. "The fire guys and cops have this under control." She turned to Michael. "I don't know your name," she said, "but thank you for your kindness. Gus," she turned to him, "Let's go..." She stopped.

He put his finger on her lips. "Home." He sighed. "I know, babe. Don't worry, home is..." He hesitated, "wherever we'll be together. I put a call in to my buddy over at the St. Francis. We've got a room already. All clean and beautiful and comfortable. We'll go over there, get a good night's sleep, and figure this out tomorrow morning." He looked at Ivory. "You'll like it there, doll. They've got bathrobes and fruit baskets and stuff."

Ivory gave him an exhausted look and looped her arm through his. "That sounds just fine, Gus. Thank you."

She turned to us. "Good night. Let me know what you find out," she said flatly.

I looked at Gus. "The St. Francis?" I confirmed. "You'll be there 'til you figure out where to stay?"

He shrugged and gave me a sheepish grin. "And that's what *Jeopardy* money is for," he said. "Give the traveler a place to lay his or her weary head."

Michael gave him a quick look. "Be careful, Gus," he said. "Look out for yourself and Ivory."

Gus nodded. "Don't worry." He patted the pocket of his jacket. "Didn't get much out. But got my Golf Uniform November."

We watched Ivory and Gus head down the street. They stopped to talk with Lt. Moon. He kept patting Ivory's arm and shoulder, awkwardly but earnestly.

"Is that guy Gus nuts or what?" asked Michael. "Golf Uniform November?"

"Gun," I said. "He said he's got a G-U-N in his pocket."

Michael shook his head. "That doesn't put my mind at ease."

I looked back up at the street. It seemed as if some of the urgency had gone out of the firefighters' work.

"Something isn't right here," I said quietly.

Michael put his arm around me. "Oh, *cara*," he said. "Nothing is right here. Absolutely nothing."

CHAPTER 36

The kids were up by the time we got home, eating cereal and playing video games, reveling in Saturday morning and a relaxation of the rules.

Josh couldn't be bothered to look up, but Zach threw himself at me in his usual still-in-love-with-Mommy greeting. I hugged him back and waved to Anya, who'd emerged from the kitchen as soon as she heard the front door. She looked puzzled and worried. I held onto Zach and watched Michael make a beeline for the kitchen. "Tell me there's more coffee, Anya," he said. "Please tell me it's already made."

"It's made," she said. "In the thermos."

Zach suddenly let go of me and pushed away. "Mommy, you smell funny." I brought my arm up to my nose and sniffed my jacket sleeve.

"Yuck. You're right, sweet pea. I smell like smoke. Dad and I got too close to a fire."

At that, Josh abandoned his game, and came to see what the excitement was all about. "Really? Anya said you guys went to a fire. I thought she meant a bonfire or something."

"Coffee, Maggie," Michael called. "It's poured."

I herded everybody into the kitchen, gratefully accepted a mug from Michael, and we all took our usual spots around the table. Both the boys and Anya were peering at us as if we were visitors from another planet.

"So, here's what happened," said Michael. "You know that story Mom's been working on? And how my students from Hastings were trying to help figure some things out about it?"

"Josh remembers Krissy," volunteered Zach. "He thought she was pretty."

Josh scowled at his brother. "Shut up, you dumbhead, you don't know what you're talking about."

"Gee," I said to no one in particular. "I must have misheard. I was sure there was a rule against saying 'shut up' in our house."

Josh muttered, "I thought she was smart, that's all." He turned to Michael, anxious to get away from the language discussion and back to the topic at hand. "But Dad, what does that have to do with where you and Mom were all night?"

Michael took a sip. "So, Mom's become friends—well, acquainted with the mother of the guy who's in prison. The guy my students were trying to help. And his mom owns a jazz club in San Francisco. And last night, something pretty bad happened. It caught fire and burned down. And the police think someone might have set the fire."

"Wow," said Josh. "This is like a movie."

"Not a movie with a very happy ending, sport," said Michael. "This guy's mother has a whole lot of troubles. Her son's in prison, her home is gone, because she lived over the club, and the way she makes her living is gone, too."

Zach looked stricken. "She can have my birthday money this year," he said. "You know, when Nonna sends it to me."

Michael shook his head. "That is really generous of you," he said. "But Ivory has a friend who helps take care of her, I think. And I'm fairly sure she has insurance, so there will be money to help her rebuild the club."

"Why do the police think someone set the fire?" asked Josh.

"I don't know exactly," I said. "Something about the way the fire burned. But they've got people investigating it, so we'll know more pretty soon."

"But why would they do it?" asked Josh. "In the movies,

people set buildings on fire for the insurance. But that's like if they're broke and need money right away." He hesitated. "Hey, maybe that's it. Maybe this lady set her own place on fire."

Michael and I exchanged glances. "I don't think so," I said. "It's hard to explain why, but she really loved that place, and wanted her son to come home to it. When he gets out of prison."

"You mean 'if,'" corrected Josh.

"That's right," said Michael. "Mom meant 'if.'"

We all sat silent around the table. Anya's eyes had welled with tears. "This is such a sad story," she said.

"It is right now," I said. "But the story isn't over yet."

Michael got up suddenly and began pulling milk and eggs out of the fridge. "You guys had anything but cereal this morning?"

"No," said Anya, "that's all they wanted when they got up."

"How's about pancake men?" he asked.

I watched in admiration as he began handing out assignments. "Josh, rinse these blueberries, would you? Zach, why don't you go set the table. Anya, want to make some more orange juice?"

"I can help," I offered.

Michael shook his head. "Go take a quick shower, *cara,* you'll feel better and smell much better." I struggled to my feet and walked over to Michael who was breaking eggs into a bowl. I slipped my arms around him and rested my head against his back.

"How do I smell?" he asked. "Same as you, I bet."

"You smell like heaven," I said. "Thank you."

"Hey," he countered. "It's just blueberry pancake men with raisin eyes. Doesn't fix much in the world."

"It does in mine," I said, and headed upstairs to the shower.

CHAPTER 37

The phone rang half a dozen times during breakfast, and I resolutely let it go to message. When I listened afterward, I jotted down the calls: Isabella, Calvin, Andrea, Hoyt, Puck.

Before I could return calls, there was a knock on the front door, and Calvin and Andrea let themselves in. Calvin had his camera bag; Andrea was lugging two enormous shopping bags.

"Come on in," I said. "There's coffee and maybe even a few pancakes left." I gestured to Andrea's bags. "What's in there?"

"Clothes for Ivory," she said. "We're more or less the same size. I'm assuming she doesn't have much of a wardrobe left. I thought I'd throw in whatever you wanted to add, and we could drop these things off at the hotel. And I went to the all-night drugstore and got some basics—toothbrushes and stuff."

"You're productive," I said.

"I got up with Calvin when you called. He wouldn't let me come with him, and I couldn't go back to sleep, so I had to do something useful," said Andrea.

We settled around the table, while the kids cleared up from breakfast. Michael returned to the stove to pour more pancakes.

Calvin was setting up his laptop on the kitchen table and inserting the memory stick from his camera. "Come over here, Maggie," he said. "Check out what I got."

"I don't know if I can stand to look," I said.

He glanced up at me. "You have absolutely no instinct for

news, do you?"

"Not much," I said. "It's not as if *Small Town* covers breaking news, anyway." I sat down next to him, and leaned over his shoulder. "How'd you get close enough to get all these photos? Weren't the firefighters keeping people away?"

Calvin gave me a smug, self-satisfied look. "I have press credentials from a couple publications I freelance for. I keep them in the glove box; you never know when they'll come in handy. Plus Moon helped me get a little closer, on the condition that I let him look at the shots. Since I wasn't really shooting on assignment..."

I bridled. "You were, too. You're shooting for us."

"Chill, Mags. You're not going to care if I let Moon see the shots. He and the arson guys are just looking for whatever they can find."

He clicked on the little camera icon, and a shot of Ivory, sitting on the overturned paint can, her usually elegant, squared-up, dancer's shoulders slumped, filled the screen. "God help us," I said. "What is going on here?"

Calvin shook his head and began clicking through the photos, stopping occasionally to zoom in, or blow the image up for clarity. Andrea leaned against the counter, talking with Michael.

On the screen, I watched images of the latest wretched chapter of Ivory's life—a shot of the bar, with overturned bar stools, and a shattered mirror in back of it; the ashy skeleton of an easy chair from what must have been her bedroom; a kitchen counter, its surface peeling in great strips like a smoke-blackened, peeled orange.

"This is so awful," I said. "It's like watching somebody's life go by." Calvin continued silently clicking, image after image. He came to a sequence of burned books and bookcases. On top of the bookcase, there was a scatter of picture frames, smashed, the photos inside the frames, soot-streaked beyond recognition.

Something caught my eye. I put my hand on Calvin's arm. "Slow down a second," I said.

He took his finger off the mouse. "I don't think any of these are usable, Mags," he said. "I was just shooting whatever I saw."

"I know," I said. "But hang on." I pointed to a corner of the image, a pile of old VHS tapes, half-melted, cardboard covers charred, in a heap on the floor. "Can you zoom in on that? Make it a little bigger?"

"Sure," he said, and the image got bigger, and blurrier. I blinked my eyes, trying to see more clearly.

"It's too fuzzy," I said.

"Hey," protested Calvin, "I told you these weren't usable."

"I don't want to *use* this image," I said. "I just want to see it." Calvin clicked a few more times, and the image resolved a little.

"Can you read that title?" I asked. "Your eyes are younger than mine." I pointed at the screen.

"Just pieces of it," said Calvin. "Something-vah in Mal?" He squinted at the screen. "Must be a place. It's capitalized. Malaysia? Malaga?"

"Mali," I said. "Isn't that in West Africa?"

Calvin nodded. "Yeah, I think so. Used to have some other name, I think." He looked at me. "Should I go on?"

"No, wait a minute," I said.

"Pancakes are ready," said Michael. "Andrea, why don't you and Calvin sit down and eat something? Maggie will get you some plates and silverware." Something was nibbling at my brain, but I stood, went to the cupboard, and pulled out plates and silverware and more napkins. I added two juice glasses to the stack and put everything on the table.

Michael delivered pancakes to the waiting plates, and I pushed the butter and syrup toward Calvin and Andrea. I pulled Calvin's laptop screen so that it was facing me. "Michael," I said, "get yourself some coffee and come sit down a minute. You've been doing all the work."

"And don't you forget it," he said, bringing his coffee mug to the table and collapsing in the chair next to me. "You're definitely on soccer duty this afternoon. Both the boys have games, but they're playing at adjoining fields. So you luck out."

"Uh-huh," I said. "Right. Look at this." I turned the screen to face him.

He peered at the screen, rubbed his eyes, and peered again. "What do you want me to see? It's just a very sad shot of a big mess."

"No," I said. "Look again. Can you make out the title of that movie?" I pointed to the blackened box on the screen.

Michael leaned closer. "Something-vah in Mal?" he said. "Maybe it's that awful candy-bar stuff the kids like, Halvah?"

"Suppose it's something-vah in Mali," I said.

"I give up. Suppose it is?"

"I really wish I could figure out what the title is," I said.

"You are obsessing about some strange stuff," said Calvin. "But, if you're so hot to figure it out, it can't be that hard."

"What do you mean?"

"Here, give me that thing," he said, pushing his plate to one side, and reaching for the laptop.

He licked the syrup off his fingers, and then cast an eye at Andrea. "Hey, honey, want to do this for me?"

She gave him her signature Starchy Storch stare.

"Okay." He grinned. "Just asking."

With the laptop in front of him, he put his fingers on the keyboard and started typing. "So, let's assume Mali is the last word," he said. "Means it's a movie set in West Africa. How many of those could there be? Well, let's just see." I peered over his shoulder. He gestured with one hand, "Maggie, go eat another pancake or something, I can't concentrate if you're breathing down my neck."

I stood up and started clearing the table. Andrea had finished her pancakes, put her head on the table, and fallen sound asleep.

It was startling to see such a self-possessed person off-guard. I began rinsing the dishes and loading the dishwasher as quietly as I could. Calvin, glancing over at Andrea, stage-whispered, "Get over here, Maggie, and check this out."

I wiped my hands, slung the dishtowel over my shoulder and

sat down. There, on the screen, I saw a short list of movies.

"I went with your assumption, that it's something set in Mali. Could be just part of the word at the end, like something in Malice or Malicious, but it looks as if there's enough unburnt cardboard at the end of the word that Mali is the whole word. So, check out the list of titles."

I scanned them quickly. "Here it is," I said. "Mitzvah in Mali."

"Fine," said Michael. "Let's say that's the title of this old VHS tape that's burned to a crisp. Who cares?"

I got up from the table and began pacing around the kitchen. Andrea had started to stir. She sat up and looked around, bewildered. "What's going on?"

"Maggie is having a completely private epiphany," said Calvin. "We don't know what she's excited about, but her little motor is racing."

"Michael," I said, ignoring Calvin, "remember your students' review of the case?"

"Sort of," said Michael. "Highlights, I guess."

"Do you remember Gus and Ivory's alibi? What they said they were doing at the time of the murder?"

"Seeing some obscure movie out in the Sunset."

"Exactly! Some obscure movie about a West African musician who comes to New York and starts playing in a klezmer band, and as a result, converts to Judaism."

"*Mitzvah in Mali*," said Andrea, opening her eyes, and trying the title out.

"And, if I remember why that alibi was so persuasive, it was because it was some independent flick that was only playing that night at one of those crummy, old, independent art houses out in the Sunset. And Ivory and Gus both recalled very specific pieces of the plot and shots and everything, according to Moon. But, nobody ever wondered if they might have seen it on videotape and known so many details for that reason. But look," I pointed at the screen. "They owned the movie! Of course, they had recall."

"Hold on, Maggie," said Andrea. "There was also a

corroborating alibi. Provided by a cop."

"Are you suggesting that Gus and Ivory lied about being at the movie?" asked Michael. "What about the police officer? What reason would he have to lie?"

"None," I said. "But maybe he was wrong. I'd like to know *how* specifically he identified them. And there's something else..."

"I think I know where you're going," said Andrea, putting her hand flat on the table. "Maybe Ivory didn't offer the alibi at all."

"That's right," I said slowly. "Gus provided the alibi. Ivory had a stroke around the time Travis was arrested. She admits her memory was vague about that period, and that's what she said during the investigation. What if..." I stopped. "Well, wait, we don't know when she was questioned. If she'd had a stroke, the cops probably would have waited to question her until after she'd recovered a little bit."

"Which would have given Gus time to plant the idea in her head," said Calvin. "And remind her about the movie. Since they'd already seen it, she'd just have to remember a little something about a film she'd already seen. But why?"

"Did Gus think Ivory knew something? Was he protecting her?" suggested Andrea.

"Hold on, my friends," said Michael. "Lots of speculation going on here. This may be simply a coincidence. Maybe they *were* at the movie that night and they loved it so much, they bought a copy to keep."

"Maybe," I said doubtfully. "But that would have meant they bought it within the last few years, and why would it be in VHS format? I think they already had it. Which means..."

"Not much," said Michael.

"It could mean," I hesitated, not liking to think about what one possibility might be, "Ivory killed Grace."

Andrea shook her head. "That seems impossible."

"Everybody's capable of murder," said Michael.

"Say she did. Say she really didn't like her precious son screwing around with a married woman," pressed Calvin. "Maybe that's what precipitated the stroke. And Gus was covering for her."

"I don't like Ivory for the murder," I said.

Michael rolled his eyes. "You don't *like* Ivory for the murder?" he mimicked me. "Who are you, little Ms. Cold Case?"

I ignored him. "Somebody needs to find out if something like committing a murder can bring on a stroke." I got up and paced around the kitchen. "We need a doctor in the house," I said. "Why doesn't Anya invite that nice Dr. Bollywood to sleep over more often?"

"Because you've told her they can't have 'sleepover' dates with the kids in the house. They have to wait 'til the kids are on a sleepover at a friend's house or we're all out of town," Michael reminded me. "Or they have to go to his house."

"Exactly," I said. "Let his parents worry about them."

"We don't need a doctor," said Calvin. "We've got WebMD. Give me a minute."

"If you insist on speculating," said Michael, "isn't Gus the other possibility?"

"But why?" I protested. "He barely knew Grace." And suddenly a little real-life movie clip flashed into my mind. "What about Gus's daughter? Ginger?"

Andrea looked puzzled. "Ginger? Grace was her best friend. I don't get that at all."

"Well, it's possible. Maybe Grace and Ginger's husband had something going on over at the Crimson Club, and Ginger got pissed. But that's not what I meant. Maybe Gus did it, because Ginger gave him a motive to get rid of Grace."

"I don't get it," said Calvin. "What motive?"

I shook my head. "I don't know. But I've watched Gus with Ginger. He dotes on that girl and he's so proud of how she turned out. Maybe he got wind of what was going on at the Crimson Club and thought Grace was corrupting his little princess."

Andrea sighed. "Seems pretty farfetched to me. Gus hardly strikes me as an overprotective father. Didn't he let someone else raise Ginger?"

"And maybe that's why he's so protective now," I argued.

"Bingo," said Calvin, turning his laptop around so we all could read about trauma-induced stroke, complete with information on how extreme emotions—sadness or anger—could cause blood vessels to narrow. "Wow, look at this," said Calvin, pointing to the screen. "Some Italians did some work on upticks in stroke, post–September 11."

Andrea yawned and put her head down again. "I know you may be having some kind of breakthrough here, Maggie," she said. "But I have to go home and get some real sleep, on an actual bed, instead of your kitchen table."

"Excellent idea," said Michael. "An excellent idea all around. We can all get some sleep, except for Maggie who's masquerading as a soccer mom this afternoon." He looked at the kitchen clock. "Better get cracking, *cara*. Slice up those oranges and gather the troops."

"Okay, okay," I said, distracted. "But what do we do next?"

"Prudent people would call John Moon," said Michael.

"Right," I said, pulling oranges onto the cutting board.

"He'll know the details of Ivory and Gus's alibi for that night." I whacked the first orange in half, then in quarters. "Like how is it that the cop actually identified them? And how specifically? The report says he was struck by what a 'silver fox' Ivory was. There are lots of women who could be described that way."

"Well, not lots," said Michael. "I see a lot of very nice silver-haired ladies when your little heathen Jewish self deigns to go to Mass with me, and there's not one I'd call 'a fox.' Besides, that's not precisely what I meant when I said to call Moon. I meant, run your theory by Moon and let him follow up. That's his day job."

Andrea let out a gentle snore. Calvin stood up, and brushed her hair off her face. "Hey, Starchy," he said, "you're already in bed with the Sandman. Let's get you home."

She moaned. "Okay, okay, just help me up."

Michael walked them to the door, and came back to watch me power through the rest of the oranges. "I'm just giving you grief,

Mags, I can take the boys if you want."

I shook my head. "I can't sleep now. I'm all wired. You go get a nap." I looked over at him. "You do look beat. And you did make breakfast."

"Twice," he said. "If you're counting." He headed upstairs. "Call Moon," he hollered back at me.

CHAPTER 38

A person simply can't think at a soccer game. First, there's the search for the parking place, the unloading of the camp chair, hauling the wheeled cooler out of the back of the car if you've got snack duty, retrieving the errant shin guard that's always left behind between the seats, juggling purse and sunglasses, and climbing the slope with all that baggage up to the fields. Coolers with wheels, now those were a great innovation. And, along the way, you're navigating the gauntlet of other soccer parents, all of whom have too much of their own stuff to offer to help carry, and are inevitably looking to recruit you for another job. Since I was carrying my sunglasses in my teeth, because they kept slipping down my nose, I couldn't talk. Which meant all I could do was nod okay to a request to organize the coach's end-of-season gift, drive between the temple and the party venue for Emily Leventhal's bat mitzvah, and sign up to bring dinner to another soccer mom and her family (breast cancer surgery, who's going to say no?) next week.

Every time I hear that the military has trouble meeting their recruiting goals, I think they ought to enlist a few of the Oakland Buccaneer team moms to hit the road as recruiters. There may be no crying in baseball, but for damn certain, there's no naysaying in soccer.

When I'd finally dumped the cooler, unfolded the camp chair strategically between the two different fields where the boys were playing, delivered the missing shin guard to Josh, smeared my face and arms with sunscreen, reperched the sunglasses on my nose, and sank into my chair, I realized I had not chosen my location wisely. Right next to me was the head soccer mom, the *ne plus ultra* of momhood, the one who put all the rest of us to shame. Lulu Brown, Yale undergrad, Wharton MBA, now volunteer CFO of every underfunded nonprofit in town and domestic goddess of her family.

"Maggie," said Lulu, "it's great to see you. I usually see Michael at these games."

"Oh, we trade off," I said. "Unless we can come together. How are you, Lulu?"

I knew how Lulu was. She was great. She was always great. She looked great—snug jeans on long elegant legs, a crisp, pinstriped pink-and-white blouse, with the collar turned up, one heavy, twisted silver bracelet on her wrist, and tiny pearl studs in her ears.

"Oh, I'm great," she said. "Don't you just love this time of year? All my snap peas are up, and Hal and I started our spring dance lessons."

Throughout our conversation, Lulu's hands were briskly knitting away, as what appeared to be a tiny blue-and-gold sweater sleeve emerged from her needles.

"Spring dance lessons?" I asked, glancing up at the field to see if I'd missed anything. Maybe I needed to station myself at the line, in case they needed someone else to call "out of bounds." Of course, that seemed risky. I could never remember what circumstances called for a corner kick. I shook my head, trying to clear the no-sleep fog.

"Yes," she said, glancing over at me, continuing in a matter-of-fact tone. "Every season Hal and I take up a new dance form." She paused to think, "Let's see. We've done the Viennese waltz and West Coast swing, and oh, the tango. That was fun." She twinkled at me. "Very sexy dance, you know. Hal just loved watching me put on those fishnet stockings."

I remembered Mr. and Mrs. Hothan on the street where

Grace had grown up, and wondered if there was some rule that guys named Hal had to do the tango. Then, I moved on, trying to figure out if there was a way to work salsa or even the occasional fox trot lesson into our schedule. It sounded like a good idea. I like hobbies that require interesting wardrobes.

"Anyway," she continued briskly, "it's a busy time of year. But you," she said, shaking her head sympathetically, "I don't know how you're orchestrating everything now that you've gone back to work. I know the kids must miss you terribly. But then, you've always had that pretty foreign girl helping out, haven't you?"

I didn't know where to begin. "Anya," I said. "Yes, she is a help." I considered for a minute. "Maybe I should send Anya to dancing lessons with Michael, since I'm so overcommitted."

Lulu glanced at me sharply. I'd forgotten how dangerous it was to wise off around her. She might seem a little Stepford-like, but she was anything but dumb.

"What are you working on?" I asked, hoping to change directions, before my smart crack got me in trouble. "Those colors are lovely."

"One of the moms in my National Charity League group is having a second baby," she said. "And they're such Cal fans. Her husband practically bleeds blue and gold." She held up the sleeve for me to admire. "So, I dyed two yarns in shades of blue and gold, and I'm weaving in the baby's name and year of birth, so it will look like a little team jacket on the back."

I wanted so very much to ask if she'd made the dye herself from homegrown, mortar-and-pestle-pounded blue forget-me-nots or something. But I restrained myself.

I watched as she slipped one of the needles out of the tiny Old Blue work-of-art-to-be and consulted a pattern secured by a rock next to her chair, and fluttering gently in the breeze.

"I saw you last night, by the way," she said.

"Where?"

"At that party in the city, for the jazz club. You know, The Devil's Interval."

I blinked. "You were there?"

She nodded. "Yes, Hal and I were there. We just popped in and out, because we had tickets to San Francisco Symphony. But we wanted to go support that poor woman who owns the place."

I kept readjusting my picture of Lulu. "So, you know The Devil's Interval?"

She looked up from the pattern, and reinserted the needle. She seemed puzzled. "Well, sure," she said. "Anyone who likes jazz knows that place. Hal and I go there from time to time. Sometimes we stop by late, after a concert or dinner or something."

Of course you do, I thought, once again wishing it were possible to *be* Lulu, instead of desperately envying everything about her.

"I didn't see Michael, though," she said, just a little pointedly.

"No, I went with another friend. Michael had kid duty last night, because Anya was out." I suddenly realized that Lulu didn't know what had happened.

I filled her in about the fire. Her blue eyes opened wide, and the knitting fell on her lap.

"How awful," she said.

"It is," I agreed. "It is absolutely awful."

We both sat in silence for a moment, glancing with glazed eyes at both fields.

In a moment, I could see Lulu straighten, and pick up her knitting again.

"What does she need, do you think?" asked Lulu. "I hate it when terrible things happen to people and everyone rushes in with help that isn't any help at all. Then, it's just one more thing they have to deal with. A friend of mine lost her husband suddenly just before Christmas last year, and all she ended up with was a freezer full of mediocre lasagna and banana bread." She shook her head. "With nuts. And one of her kids is allergic to nuts. What were her friends thinking?"

"Better to do something than nothing, I guess," I said feebly.

She looked determined. "No, it's not. She was writing thank-you notes and surreptitiously giving all that stuff away for weeks."

"Well, it sounds as if you know her better than I do," continued Lulu. "You let me know what she needs, including a place to stay. I have a cousin in the City with an empty guest house."

"I think she's fine for now," I said. "Her friend Gus seems to be taking care of her."

"Oh," said Lulu. "That not-very-well-groomed man who's always following Ivory around at the club?"

"That very one."

Lulu said nothing. We both watched the big boys' field again. Josh's team was getting trounced by the Berkeley Hobos. Zach's team played shorter periods, and the boys were already sacked out on the ground. "Sometimes when I can't sleep," said Lulu, "I make up new names for the teams. That Berkeley team really bothers me. I think it's disrespectful to both the hobos and the kids to call the team by that name."

I looked at Lulu. She seemed very serious. I couldn't actually visualize her lying sleepless in bed. I would have assumed she'd get up and mill flaxseed for homemade bread or balance the federal budget or something.

Before I could say anything, Lulu continued briskly, "I bet I know what *you're* thinking about when you can't sleep in the middle of the night," she said, stopping a moment to count stitches. I braced myself, wondering what piece of trivia, or worse yet, deep remorse Lulu thought occupied my middle-of-the-night thoughts. "I bet you're working on your case."

"My case?" I said, puzzled.

She shot a sideways glance at me, and then returned to her knitting, her eyes on the field. "You're investigating what happened in Ivory's son's case, I imagine," she said.

"Well, not exactly," I said. Lulu turned her bright blue eyes on me.

"Oh, really? I remember reading all about your last case in the paper. You figured out who murdered your boss, right? Well, it's none of my business..."

"Okay," I interrupted. "You're right. I'm not exactly investigating, but we're doing a story for the magazine on the woman who was murdered, and it's turned up lots of interesting angles."

"Goody!" she said. "I hoped you were. You're so smart, Maggie, and it seems so unbelievable to me that Ivory's son could have done such a thing."

I was astonished. Lulu, the perfect, the brilliant, the accomplished, thought *I* was smart. And more important, believed that Travis was innocent. Suddenly, it seemed like an inspired idea to tell her everything. Fresh eyes, fresh ears—powered by a formidable mind. And unlike me, she didn't appear to be sleep-deprived or wallowing in marital challenges.

"Lulu," I began, "are you really interested in this? I would love to be able to talk it through with someone."

"Sure," she said. "Is that okay? It's not breaking confidentiality or anything?"

"I don't think so," I said. "I've got a couple colleagues at work who are working on the story, and I need to call the guy over at SFPD who knows about the case. But, I don't really want to do it from here, it's just that..." I trailed off.

"What?" she prodded, her knitting now in her lap, those perfectly manicured hands still, not moving at all.

"I think we may have figured something out last night, but I'm so sleep-deprived, nothing is making sense."

"I'm listening," she said. "Tell me the whole thing, beginning to end. They used to call me the deal-breaker at the investment bank where I worked before my kids were born, because I could always find the flaws. I was hell on wheels during due diligence."

She reached into her handbag and pulled out a note pad and a mechanical pencil. "Start talking," she said. "It's going to be snack time pretty soon, and I know you're on duty."

I blinked. And in ten minutes, sketched out the highlights of the story, what we knew, what we thought we knew, what we didn't know. Lulu listened intently and jotted notes on her pad.

Just as I finished, I heard shouts from the field and watched as Josh gave me the high sign for break.

"Gotta refresh the hordes," I said, scrambling to my feet. Lulu carefully tucked her pencil and pad into her purse and rose in one elegant, effortless motion.

"I'll help," she said. "We'll get done faster. And I think better when I'm working."

Together we moved the cooler closer to the playing field, distributed water and Gatorade, and portioned out orange quarters to the sweaty, pink-cheeked boys. "Having fun, honey?" I asked Josh.

He glared at me, "Mom, are you even watching the game? We're getting killed."

"We're watching," said Lulu kindly. "Those Hobos are pretty good, but you guys work together as a team.

And that was a great block you did a few minutes ago."

I was dumbfounded. How could she knit, listen to me, and pay attention not just to her kid but mine as well?

After snack, Michael showed up to take Zach home.

Lulu and I pulled the cooler back to our post, settled in, and resumed our conversation. Lulu dug in her pink Prada and pulled out a Three Musketeers candy bar and a Swiss Army knife. She sliced it in two and handed half to me. "These are disgusting," she said, "but we need some energy." She peeled back the paper, took a bite, and consulted her notepad again.

"I think there are too many people with alibis," she said. "And that seems pretty unusual to me. I mean, except for moms, who else is always, always, always surrounded by people who know where they are every minute of every day?"

"Just a coincidence," I offered.

"I don't think so," she said. "I think somebody's lying. Maybe two somebodies."

"Who are your candidates?"

She wrinkled her nose. It was like watching a very elegant bunny consider the merits of conflicting bunches of carrots. She tapped her pen on the pad.

"Ivory, Ginger's husband (the guy who looks like an anorexic dog), Carol Ann, and Ivory's friend, Gus."

I shook my head. "You think they're all lying?"

"No," she said. "That would be improbable. Unless they're in cahoots, and that, all by itself, seems improbable. But anyone in that bunch could be telling a big, fat whopper."

"So, the task is..."

"To figure out which one of those alibis is full of holes. And, figure out who had a reason to kill Grace and blame the whole thing on Travis."

She looked thoughtful. "You told me that Gus and that woman who runs the shelter for young moms and their kids have both been accused of violent crimes?"

I frowned. "I read a little more about both of those 'crimes.' Purity went after some vicious jackass who showed up to threaten his ex-girlfriend. He was trying to push his way in, and Purity took him on with a baseball bat, before he got off the front porch. Seemed pretty idiosyncratic to me."

"Justified, too," said Lulu. "But still, we know she can be provoked to violence. What about Gus?"

"That one's harder to pin down. Apparently Gus and one of his army buddies accosted a young woman on a deserted stretch of road leading out of Ho Chi Minh City. She'd apparently rebuffed their advances in a bar, where she was just trying to wash and dry glasses. They ran into her later and supposedly kidnapped her briefly to 'teach her a lesson,' or at least that's what the charges said."

"Did they rape her?" asked Lulu in disgust.

"Not according to the report. They just restrained her for a while and let her go. Scared her senseless, of course. But no witnesses, and they covered each other, insisting it had been a practical joke."

Lulu shook her head. "Lovely joke," she said. "Wonder how Gus would like it if some creep went after his daughter like that?"

The Hallelujah Chorus went off next to my knee. I rummaged in my own, nonlabel purse, and fished out the phone. It was Michael. How was the second half of the game going? Did Josh score? Had I called Lt. Moon yet? And should he and Zach stop at the store to get stuff to barbecue for dinner?

"Game's fine. Josh doesn't seem very happy about it, though. Haven't called Moon yet. It's too noisy here. Get some fish to barbecue, the kids have been eating too much meat, meat, meat, meat," I said.

"Red meat and when they grow up, brown drinks," said Michael. "They'll be manly men."

Lulu had been making notes on her pad while I talked. She looked at what she'd written, put the pen and pad down, and picked up her knitting again. The blue and gold was emerging quickly, in between flashes of needles.

As soon as I snapped my phone shut and tossed it back in my bag, she picked up our conversation, as if we'd never been interrupted. "Who had a reason?" she persisted. "Who benefited from Grace's death?"

"We went through the usual motives," I said. "Money. There were a couple of people Grace had put in her will, for small bequests—Purity, over at A Mom's Place, and Carol Ann."

"Did they know that?" countered Lulu. "Doesn't mean much if they didn't know."

I shrugged, "I don't know."

"And then there's jealousy," said Lulu. "And, oh my, wouldn't we have a whole trailer-truck full of that stuff—Frederick's jealous of Travis and what he's up to. Ivory could be jealous of her son's beautiful, high-society sweetheart. Or maybe Bill Brand thought Grace was corrupting his sweet, innocent wife. Or Ivory thought Grace was corrupting Travis."

"You haven't met Travis," I said. "He's very, very charming, but I wouldn't put any good money on who's doing the corrupting in any relationship that he's involved in."

"That's plenty of negativity," said Lulu briskly. "If you're going to be negative, you have to have a purpose—like ruling people out. That's the principle of due diligence. So, here's my list." She ripped a sheet from her pad and handed it to me.

Gun owners? Will beneficiaries? Who knew where Travis lived?

Lulu had returned to her knitting, fingers moving swiftly, while she scanned the field.

"That little Tran boy ought to play more," she said firmly. I squinted at the kid under discussion. Skinny, fidgety, never seemed too interested in the game.

"What makes you say that?" I asked.

She shrugged. "He's awkward but he's focused and really moves the ball." She glanced over at me. "Sometimes you can't tell how someone's going to perform until you let them show you their stuff."

I looked away. "Good point," I murmured. I tucked the paper in my bag. "I don't know why I never thought about that last question," I said. "Of course, if someone framed Travis, it would have to be someone who knew where he lived."

"Unless he's listed in the phone book, that limits the field a bit," said Lulu. She rolled her knitting up into a tidy ball, and tucked it away in her bag. "I'm going to go collect my kids," she said. "Don't forget to let me know what Ivory can use. Nice hanging out with you, Maggie."

"Better than nice for me," I said. "Thanks for your help."

Lulu collapsed her sand chair, tucked it under her arm, and set off down the hill. She gave me a little backward wave as she left. And another snap judgment about a fellow being needs re-evaluating. "Boy, I hate having to change my mind," I said aloud.

CHAPTER 39

If Ivory and Gus owned the obscure movie that had provided their alibi, what did that mean? It could, as Michael pointed out, simply mean they enjoyed it so much they'd purchased a copy. Or, it could mean that was why they both had recall about the plot, whether or not they'd seen it that night. And, of course, Ivory knew where Travis lived. But why would she frame her own son?

Later that evening, after soccer debrief, after dinner, after bedtime for Zach, I got Moon on his cell phone. He sounded more exhausted than I felt.

He listened to my report on the burned-up video, the theories about who might be lying, and Lulu's observation that the killer had to know where Travis lived.

"We did actually think about that, Maggie," said Moon. "Not that your friend isn't a crackerjack detective. But once there seemed to be enough evidence to convict Travis, we stopped knocking ourselves out to look for the mysterious Mr. or Ms. X who could have planted the body. And, of course, now we know it could have been Mr. and Ms. X, or Mr. X and a small guy friend."

"Could it have been a Ms. X?" I asked. "Grace couldn't have weighed more than 110, but I don't think a woman would have been much help moving Grace's body into Travis's car."

"Good guesser," said Moon. "Grace weighed 108. We know that from the autopsy. But sure, if it's a good-size man, a reasonably fit woman could have been plenty of help moving the body. But again, we stopped looking for Mr. or Ms. X, because the DA was simply building his case around Travis."

"Bad idea," I said, "very, very bad idea."

Moon sighed. "So you say, Maggie, but that's just your idea, which could be good, bad, indifferent, or just wrong."

Before we hung up, Moon agreed to track down some answers. "We can easily find out if Purity's registered for a gun and double check Bill Brand's whereabouts once again."

"I still don't know how you do that," I said. "I couldn't possibly remember what I did a few months ago, never mind years."

"Fortunately," said Moon dryly, "people like Brand and or his assistant keep datebooks or very detailed data in some other format. Enables them to maximize their productivity and identify tax deductions."

"Lucky for us," I observed.

CHAPTER 40

Travis held a photo in his hand. It was Ivory, dressed in a deep-purple dress, sitting on the piano bench at the club. He turned it over and read the back. "Do I look like I'm in mourning?" asked the note. He turned it back to the image again. "Not mourning, Mom," he said. "Just suffering."

CHAPTER 41

Travis seemed distracted and distant when Isabella and I arrived at the Q the next day. Though Isabella chattered away, with an edge of urgency and excitement, about some new areas to follow up, Travis remained disengaged. At one point, as we were talking, he suddenly stood up, shook his head briefly, and started pacing. Isabella looked nervously around. "Travis," she said, catching his arm, "you're not paying much attention to us."

He put his hands down on the table, resting them flat, almost pressing them against the surface, as if he were willing the table to help him levitate right out of the place.

"How's my mother doing?" he asked. "She sounded dead to me on the phone."

"She was exhausted when I saw her," I began. "But that was understandable."

Travis shook his head. "I don't mean dead tired; I mean she sounded dead. Lifeless. That place meant so much to her, and I think she was motivated to hold onto it so I'd have a place to come back to."

I thought back to the "rent party" just a few nights ago. Those had been almost exactly the words Ivory had used.

"She has insurance," I said.

Travis put his hand up to stop me.

"What she has," he said carefully, "is the very frayed end of a rope. And she and I are both hanging on for dear life."

He leaned back in his chair, and gave a short, bitter bark of a laugh. "Hey, too bad they don't hang people in California these days, isn't it? That would have been a damn fine little joke."

Isabella clapped her hands. Both Travis and I looked at her, startled at the sharp crack the sound made in the room.

"Okay, Travis," she said. "Enough with the pity party. Your mom's in a terrible place, and you're in a worse one. So, let's see what we can do to get back on track. Because at the end of the day, and believe me, mister, that end will come, that's all your mother really cares about."

He shrugged. "What choice do I have?"

"Exactly," said Isabella. Impatiently, she flipped through pages in her notebook and stopped at a sheet covered with yellow highlighter.

"I know we covered this already, but think out loud with us about who knew where you lived."

"A few friends, my mom, of course, Grace."

"How about Grace's friends—Ginger?"

"Not unless Grace told her, and I don't know why she would have."

"How about her husband?" I said.

"Bill Brand?" asked Travis. "The world-class stick-up-his-ass?"

"That's the one," I said.

"Again, I don't know how he'd know where I lived unless Grace told him." He paused. "That is one weird guy."

"Talk to us," I said. "What makes you say that?"

"I don't know all that much," said Travis. "It's not like I was his regular squash partner at the club. Like I told you before, he and Ginger and Grace and Frederick used to hang out together."

"At the Crimson Club sometimes, right?"

"Right. Or sometimes just Ginger and Grace, or just Frederick and Grace."

"When you'd drive them home," I pressed him, "how'd they act?"

"A little drunk, a little silly." He paused. "Well, not Frederick, he never seemed like he had too much to drink—or if he did, he didn't show it."

"So, *how* would the rest of them act silly?" I persisted.

He thought a minute. "Well, Frederick would usually get in the front seat with me, and Bill and the ladies would get in the back. They'd giggle and kind of cuddle together back there."

"And did you get jealous?"

"What do you mean?"

"Well, if Bill was snuggling with the wives, didn't it bother you to watch him with his hands on Grace?"

Travis shook his head. "That's not how it was. It was a little, you know, fun to watch."

"What do you mean?"

"I mean, Grace and Ginger would be...well, fooling around with each other."

"Really?"

Isabella sat up a little straighter. "You never told me that."

He shrugged. "Didn't seem important. I mean, sometimes Bill would sit in the middle, but often the girls would be just—well, it wasn't full out anything, you know. But they'd be all over each other. Like teenagers, necking."

"Okay, I get it." I thought for a moment. "And that didn't make Bill or Frederick uncomfortable?"

Travis gave me a small smile, and I saw a glimpse of the sexy, compelling presence he must have projected outside the walls of the Q. "Men love to watch women together. They like a little show, and that's what it seemed like the girls were doing. Men get off on that, or haven't you heard?"

"Yes, I've heard," I said. "But still," I persisted, "you didn't have the impression that it might have bothered one of them, Bill or Frederick?"

"Not really," he said. "Frederick didn't even seem very bothered when it was Bill who was getting handsy in the back," he observed.

"Why'd Frederick always sit in the front, anyway?"

Travis shrugged. "He'd get on his phone and read e-mail or

text back and forth. He pretty much ignored what went on back there. It was like, he got back in the car, turned off the fun, and went right back to work."

"But this was very late at night, right?"

"Mostly, yeah. But his business is 24/7, as he always said. There's some money market open somewhere in the world, every hour of every day."

"Compulsive."

"You got that right," he said.

I looked at him. He stared back at me. "You're thinking that's what started the whole thing between Grace and me?"

"Gives a girl pause," I said. "And Bill?"

"Hard to tell with that guy," he said. "He's one closed-off, uptight, intense drink of water. I know people joke about how much he looks like a whippet, and he does. But he always reminded me of a rattler, cold-blooded and all coiled up, waiting to strike."

"But he'd get frolicsome in the backseat?"

"Sure, but it wasn't very personal. More like, I don't know, somebody had challenged him to a handball game—there was a partner and a court and a ball, and he already had on a glove, so what the hell?"

Isabella and I sat silent. Did this mean anything?

"Plus..." Travis began. We waited. "Plus, it was like Brand knew that Frederick was the alpha dog in the pack, and it was fun to handle the alpha dog's property." He shrugged. "Probably didn't matter, though, since the alpha dog hardly looked up from his BlackBerry or iPhone or whatever he was glued to."

"That would have driven me crazy if I were Grace," I said.

"But it's like it wasn't Grace," said Travis.

"Meaning what?"

"Well, here's something I've never thought of. The nights that Bill would get frisky with the girls in the backseat were usually nights one of them would be doing some alter ego thing."

"I don't get it."

"They'd dress up like other people once in a while. Ginger

used to wear wigs on occasion—you know, one of those electric blue or white, white blond ones. Sometimes they'd both do it, sometimes just one—but they were good. You had to get pretty up close and personal to recognize them."

"What did that have to do with Bill in the backseat?"

"I don't know exactly," said Travis. "But I think he got off on pretending to fool around with these two 'other women.' Or maybe being in disguise made them feel more free about flirting with him—as a stranger."

"Curiouser and curiouser," I said.

"*Alice in Wonderland*," said Travis.

"*Through the Looking-Glass*, actually," I said. "But you've got the idea."

CHAPTER 42

When I stopped at the intersection, I heard a faint, insistent beep-beep-beep coming out of my purse. My cell phone had been announcing messages, and between traffic and my distracted state, I hadn't heard anything. I pulled over, put on my flashers, and rummaged for my makeup bag. This was my new solution to being able to retrieve my phone quickly from my purse, since I'd always know exactly where it was, zipped into my oversize makeup bag, bright pink, visible even in a black-bottomed purse. I unzipped the bag—which held two ancient lipsticks, some sugarless chewing gum for the boys, parking receipts, and a pair of folding opera glasses. What were they doing here? And then I remembered, Josh had borrowed them for birding—or so he said. I suspected he'd used them to spy on the nymphet across the street, which was probably why I'd found them discarded on the front-porch bench, and tossed them in my bag on my way out the door, so they didn't sit outside. I plucked the beeping cell out of the bottom of the bag. "You have eight messages."

I felt that little clutch of fear. Eight! Too many, someone's trying very hard, very continually to get hold of me. Hospital! Accident! Disaster! I'm sure someone else might think eight calls could mean they'd won the lottery and someone was trying to reach them with the good news—but those "some people" were neither Jewish nor married to a Catholic. I punched in my retrieval code, so nervous I hit a wrong number in the sequence. Calm down, Maggie. Deep breath, tried the number again. I clicked through the messages, one routine call from Michael about pick-up duty, then five hang-ups in a row. Then a message from Ivory, "Maggie, call me please. As soon as you can. I feel like, well, like the fog is lifting." She sounded breathless. I hit the last message. It was Ivory again. "Hi, Maggie. You can ignore my last call. Everything's...fine. I just wanted to say thank you for everything you've been trying to do for Travis." She paused. "That's it. Just, thanks so much."

The sun beating through the windshield had made the car uncomfortably warm. Now it felt chilly, all of a sudden. I hit redial and got Ivory's cell message. "Ivory, it's Maggie. What's up? I got both your messages and I'd really like to talk to you. Please call me as soon as you get this message."

I sat in the car, watching downtown lunch foot traffic hurry back and forth across the busy Union Square intersection. Two horn blasts from behind made me jump. I glanced in the rearview mirror and saw a giant SUV in back of me. I needed to move the car if I was going to stay here. I looked across Union Square to the St. Francis. Maybe Ivory was still there. She hadn't said she'd moved yet. I turned the corner and whipped into the Union Square garage, took the elevator up to the ground level, and trotted up the street to the hotel.

At the front desk, I asked for Ivory Gifford. No one registered by that name, said the clerk, shaking his head. "How about Augustus Reeves?"

The clerk looked at the computer. "Yes, we do have a Mr. Reeves registered."

I hesitated. "Can you ring the room?" I asked.

The clerk glanced at the screen. "Sorry, there's a 'do not disturb' request from the guest."

"Really?" I said. "Because I just got a call that sounded somewhat urgent."

Two other people were waiting next to me. They didn't look happy and were clearly impatient to talk with the clerk. I saw him glance over at them and raise his finger, signaling "just a minute while I get rid of the pushy lady."

"I'm sorry," he said. "Perhaps you'd like to leave a note for your friends. We'll deliver it to the room." He pushed notepaper and an envelope to me.

"I will," I said, "but is there a manager I can speak with?"

The desk clerk narrowed his eyes. "I assure you our manager has to honor the guest's request as well," he said. "And he's at lunch right now, but if you care to wait..."

"Oh, I understand," I said. "I'll leave a note, and check back in half an hour or so? He'll be back from lunch then?" The clerk nodded, distracted, and turned to the couple behind me. I stepped aside, wrote a note to Ivory, letting her know I was in the hotel, and left it on the counter. Okay, I knew how these things were done, or at least how they were done in the movies. I reached out my hand to the desk clerk, reading his name tag at the same moment, "Sorry to interrupt, Brian," I said. "But I wanted to thank you for your help, and for making sure this gets to my friends as soon as possible." He shook my hand, which enabled a twenty-dollar bill to change hands. His face didn't change expression. "I'll make sure," he said. "And check back in a while, our manager should return from lunch shortly." Brian the desk clerk picked up the envelope, wrote something underneath Ivory's name, and held it in his hand, tapping it absently against his pocket while he listened to the couple explain the problem housekeeping had been unable to fix in their shower.

I walked briskly away, heading toward the door, and then doubled back behind the square, green-veined, mirrored pillars, and disappeared into a wingback chair in the lobby bar. Brian was not having a good day—though I couldn't hear the conversation well from this distance, I could sense the escalating complaint level from the plumbing-challenged couple.

I reached into my purse, retrieved the makeup bag and pulled out the opera glasses, and casually raised them to my eyes. The clerk still had the envelope, twisting and tapping it in his nervousness while he tried to placate the guests. I could read a big 9, the first number of the three-digit room number he'd scribbled on the envelope, but no more. Suddenly, his arm snaked out and grabbed a bellman going by. He handed the envelope to the bellman, who glanced at it, and then headed toward the elevators. I dropped the opera glasses in my bag, and strolled after him, picking up my pace once I was out of sight of Brian, the gatekeeper.

I caught up to the bellman, just as he stepped into the elevator. I leaned against the glass-walled elevator and smiled at him. He gave me a friendly nod back. "Enjoying your stay?" he asked.

"Oh, yes," I said. "Lovely city, lovely hotel." I tried to sneak a look at the envelope, but he held it in his hand, flat against his leg, only the sealed-flap side showing. I turned to face the glass side of the elevator. I knew the St. Francis elevators the way Southern California moms know Space Mountain. They provide the best cheap-thrill ride in town. For the first six floors, the glass is dark, the elevator shaft still inside the building. Suddenly, at the sixth floor, the glass wall hits the outside, and with a suddenness that always startles, no matter how many times you've experienced it, the City view opens up, and you feel as if you're rushing straight up in thin air, with the floor falling away from beneath your feet. If you're in the elevator with kids, you hear them exclaim "oooh" and see them cautiously move back from the glass, a little dizzy and disoriented. My kids always insisted we bring out-of-town visitors to "ride" the St. Francis elevators.

I braced myself for the "reveal," and as soon as it happened, I swayed and bumped, hard, right into the bellman. He dropped the envelope, grabbed my arms to steady me. "Lady, are you okay?"

I leaned against him, and looked at the carpeted elevator floor, where the envelope had dropped, face up. Room 926, it read. I straightened and gently disengaged. "Oh, thank you, I'm fine." I gestured to the glass wall. "That view just startled me."

He laughed. "Always gets the first-timers," he said. He bent and picked up the envelope, then looked at the buttons. "Where are you headed? You forgot to press your floor."

"Sorry," I said, "I'm not staying here, just meeting a friend for lunch at the top." He pressed the Penthouse level. The car stopped at nine and he got out.

I rode to the top, killed a few minutes standing at the windows, looking at the City below, then stepped back into the car and rode back down to the ninth floor.

I stepped into the long, carpeted hall, and waited a moment. No sign of the bellman. I glanced at the room number directions on the wall, and walked quickly toward 926.

I could see the corner of the envelope sticking out from under the door. I tapped on the door. Nothing. "Ivory," I called, and knocked a little more insistently. I waited a moment more, puzzled. Ivory or Gus or both of them had to be inside; otherwise, why would they have called down a "do not disturb" message to the switchboard? Though, oddly, there wasn't a "do not disturb" sign on the door. Faintly, from the inside, I heard something. I renewed my knocking, louder, calling "Hello? Anyone there?" I stopped and heard what sounded like a groan, and someone mumbled, "Go away."

"Ivory," I tried one more time. "It's Maggie. I have something to tell you about Travis's case."

I heard another moan, and then a crash, then silence. I tried knocking again, then pounding. I turned on my cell to call the front desk, but the little screen said, "No signal." The door to the right flew open, and a middle-aged man in a bathrobe stuck his head into the hall. "What the hell is going on?" he barked. "I'm trying to take a nap."

"I'm sorry," I said, starting to feel a little frantic. "My friend is inside, and I think there's something wrong with her. I knocked and knocked, called her, and I heard her moan and then there was this crash, like something fell or she fell or I don't know."

He shook his head, "For Christ's sake, she's probably trying to take a nap, too," he growled.

"I don't think so," I said. "Could I use your phone to call down to the front desk? I think this is an emergency, and I can't get cell service."

It took some persuading at the front desk, but finally, the young woman who answered the phone agreed to call security. In a few minutes a bulky guy wearing a blue blazer with a breast pocket badge strode down the corridor, followed by a slight bellman in a uniform that looked at least two sizes too big. When they got to the door, I could read what the patch said on the big guy's breast pocket: Security, Dan Clover.

Clover said, "What's the problem, miss?" I retold the story. The wannabe napper was hanging out in the hall by now. I'd ruined his siesta, so he'd become interested in the possibility a drama might unfold.

Clover listened impassively, gestured me to step aside from the door, and gave three forceful raps on the door, "Mr. Reeves? Ms. Gifford? Is everyone okay in there?"

Silence. Clover nodded at the bellman, who inserted his cardkey into the door and pushed it open.

As soon as the door swung open, I heard Clover say, "Oh, crap." I peered around him, so I could see into the room—and then I saw Ivory. She was crumpled on the floor, her arm outstretched in front of her, her legs scissored underneath, looking like a swimmer yanked from the water, and tossed on dry land, still trying to do an overhand stroke. I froze and in a rush plunged back to the terrible moment when I had discovered my friend and editor, Quentin Hart, dead in his apartment. "Please, no," I whispered to whoever might listen, in that room or any other.

Clover rushed into the room, moving quickly for a guy who looked like a football player gone to seed. He bent to Ivory, leaned close to her face, and spoke loudly, "Ms. Gifford?" He turned to the bellman, who danced nervously from foot to foot. "Call the house doc," he barked. "And tell the front desk to call 911."

While he was issuing orders, I made myself move, sidestepping past him, and knelt on the floor next to Ivory. She was breathing, I could see the uneven, up and down of her chest. "Thank you,"

I whispered. There was a fresh-looking cut on her forehead, with a trickle of blood running down, and pooling in the fine hairs of her eyebrow.

Then he turned to me, "You know her, right?"

I looked up, "Yes, I do."

"Know of any medical condition that might cause her to pass out—diabetes, seizures, anything?" he asked over his shoulder, as he disappeared into the bathroom. He came out with a towel.

"She's had a stroke before," I offered.

He knelt next to me, and pressed the towel to the cut, "Doesn't look like a blow," he said. "Looks like she grazed her head, maybe when she fell, trying to get to the door."

I sat on the floor, and picked up her hand. I leaned on one elbow, almost prone, next to her body, leaning in, putting my mouth as close as possible to her ear.

"Ivory," I said. "Please be okay, please."

The bellman had edged his way toward us, eager to see, half-excited, half-frightened by this unexpected turn of events. I sensed more than saw him, as he crept around the room. "Hey," he said suddenly. Clover and I both looked up. The young bellman stood next to the desk, just in back of Ivory, and pointed. On the desk, next to an ice bucket, and a short, high-ball-style glass, sat a gun.

"Don't touch anything," barked Clover. He struggled to his feet. "In fact, get out of here, and just wait outside for the doc and the 911 crew. Don't let anybody else in here." The bellman was shaking now, and backing toward the door. "And don't run your mouth about this, either," said Clover.

"I'm staying," I said firmly. "I don't want to leave her alone." He shook his head. "Not to be rude," I said, "but you're not a police officer. You can't order me to leave."

He scowled. "Stay right where you are," he said. "So I can watch you. And don't touch anything."

I nodded meekly, and leaned back down to be close to Ivory.

Time took on that awful quality, slowed down, so that each minute felt as if it would never pass. I watched Ivory's chest go up and down, willing those small, precious movements to go on, and continued to press the towel to her forehead. On an impulse, I put my mouth right to her ear, and whispered, "Ivory?" Her eyes opened wide, then closed. I put my face right next to hers. "Ivory, it's Maggie. You're going to be okay."

Without opening her eyes, she said, "I heard that music."

"What music?"

"That...klezmer music," she said. Suddenly, a rap at the door, and a deep voice called "Dr. Stewart. Open, please."

Clover opened the door, and the house doctor strode in, bag in hand. "Excuse me," he said, gesturing me out of the way.

"She just came to for a minute," I said. "She was trying to talk."

"Let's have a look." I scrambled to my feet too quickly, and felt dizzy. I leaned against the desk, and watched while the doctor examined Ivory and the paramedics arrived. Stewart stepped back and they lifted Ivory onto a gurney. I picked up my purse and followed the stretcher down the hall. "Where's she going?" I called after the EMT.

"St. Francis Hospital," he called over his shoulder.

"If she wakes up," I called back, "tell her Maggie is on her way."

I followed them to the freight elevator, and watched the doors close. "Maggie," said a voice at my elbow, and I turned to see John Moon, and then I burst into tears.

He took me by the arm, walked me to a nearby plush bench, ordered me to stay put, and disappeared. In a few minutes he was back with a cup of hot tea. I took a sip. It was piping hot and sickeningly sweet. "Yuck, John. It's got sugar in it."

He nodded. "Good for you when you've had a shock. Drink up."

Between sips, he made me walk him back through the last hour—from retrieving Ivory's calls to the awful moment when the door was opened, and I saw her on the floor.

"That's it?" he asked, when I finished.

"That's all I remember."

"You save that message from Ivory?"

Without a word, I dug the cell phone out of my purse and dialed up the voice mail. I skipped forward to Ivory's message and handed it over to him. He put the phone to his ear, listened, then pressed replay and listened again.

"What does it sound like to you?" he asked.

I hesitated. "I don't know, for sure. But it sounded as if she was struggling with something, and then had decided what to do."

"Suicide?"

I frowned. "I can't imagine that she'd leave Travis behind," I said. "And that's what suicide would have meant. That makes absolutely no sense to me. However terrible all this has been—his arrest, the trial, the sentencing—not to mention what's happened to her—the stroke and the fire—I find it incomprehensible that she'd leave Travis to fend for himself."

"Unless she'd decided it was hopeless and thought it would be a relief to him not to have to worry about her any more," suggested Moon. "In addition, there are a number of confusing things at the scene. It appeared that Ivory could have fallen ill from drugs in her drink—but who put the drugs in her drink? And why a gun? Women who kill themselves almost never use a gun."

"I don't know," I faltered. "This seems impossible to me, but could *Ivory* have killed Grace and been ready to confess, to save Travis? And she was drinking to get her nerve up? Or, she felt threatened, and that's why the gun was there. But who would threaten her? And if someone did, wouldn't Gus the fierce protector have wrestled that person to the ground? And where is Gus, anyway?"

"We're trying to find him," said Moon. "Anything is possible. That's what I've learned from being a cop. Absolutely anything."

"Are all of the possibilities terrible?" I asked.

"Usually," he said. "But not always. Some day I'll tell you a few good stories."

But not then. Then, it was time to collect myself, to call Michael, to call Anya and check in on the boys, and leave one St.

Francis (the hotel) and head over to the other, the hospital, just a little west and north, but miles away in spirit and purpose. In the City of Saint Francis, the man who asked God to "make me an instrument of thy peace," there seemed precious little of that commodity to be had.

CHAPTER 43

When Travis was a kid, he used to make up stories about his father. About how he must be a captain of something—a ship, an airplane, soldiers in a unit. That gave him a pressing reason not to show up. He stopped asking Ivory about him when he heard her describe herself as "a very happy single mother" to the father of one of his friends. As an adult, he realized that guy must have been hitting on his mother. But at the time, all he thought was—if she calls herself a single mother, that must mean my father is never coming back. Now, he wished his father had come back. Or Ivory had given in to one of her other suitors—who was that lawyer she'd dated? Welsh or Welch or something? Instead, here she was, still unsteady after the stroke, and with no one but... Travis winced a little at the thought: no one but Gus to look after her.

CHAPTER 44

Moon insisted that I shouldn't drive myself over to the hospital, and made me promise to wait for one of his detectives to give me a lift. I protested, and then abruptly shut up when Moon began threatening to send me directly home. "I've ordered an officer to guard Ivory's room," he said, "and it's just as easy for me to take you off the cleared-visitor list."

"She called *me*," I protested. "Ivory wanted to talk to me."

"Fine," said Moon. "Then do what I tell you. My guy's waiting for you by the front desk, his name's Pollock."

"How will I recognize him?"

Moon laughed. "Don't worry, you'll spot him. He'll be the only guy in the lobby of the St. Francis wearing a bolo tie. How many of those do you see in the City?"

"You'd be surprised," I said, thinking of Doc, Mr. Delta Oscar Charlie with his bolo and lame come-on patter at the Crimson Club.

I took the elevator down to the lobby and walked over to the front desk. It seemed like hours since I had stood in exactly the same spot, trying to fast-talk my way into getting Gus and Ivory's room number, but the same clerk was behind the desk, showing some tourists how to find something on an open San Francisco map. He glanced at me, and pursed his lips with displeasure. I ignored him and scanned the people on either side of me, looking for a detective in a bolo tie. And then I spotted him, none other than Delta Oscar Charlie himself, snakehead bolo tie and all. His eyes met mine, and then continued to glance around, scanning the room as I had been. I walked up to him, "Detective Pollock?" I asked.

He narrowed his eyes at me, "Who's asking?"

I held out my hand. "Maggie Fiori," I said. "We've danced, I believe, but we've never been properly introduced. John Moon told me you'd take me over to St. Francis Hospital."

A series of expressions washed over his face—suspicion, annoyance, sideways glances that made me think he was looking for a quick escape, and then he shrugged. "Yeah, fine. Whatever. Let's go." He took me by the arm and began walking me toward the parking garage entrance. I began to feel a little panic. I'd gotten in a car I shouldn't have a year ago and it had been nothing but trouble. I stopped cold in my tracks.

"Let's walk," I said. "It's just a few blocks away, and I'd like to get some fresh air."

"The lieutenant told me to drive you over to the hospital," he said. "It's more than a few blocks and it's uphill."

"Uh-huh," I said. "Well, I'm walking, and you can walk with me or you can drive without me. But I'm not getting in a car with you."

He tightened his grip on my arm. "You are not issuing the orders around here, little lady."

I inched my heel over to his instep, while leaning in a little closer. "Let's remember that the ladies issue the invitations in the places we hang out together," I whispered. "And that maybe your boss and my friend, John Moon, would be interested to know where you spend your free time."

He let go of my arm. "I could have been undercover," he said.

"Really? Wearing the exact same tie you have on today?" I asked. "Doesn't seem likely to me."

We walked through the lobby and toward the revolving door. Despite the confusion and chaos of the events up on the ninth floor, despite the presence of more than a few police officers, and an injured Ivory being whisked via gurney down the freight elevator and out to the waiting ambulance, life in the lobby continued as if nothing unusual had happened. Conventioneers wearing name badges greeted each other and networked madly; elegantly dressed couples lingered in the bar over Flirtinis and dark-amber Scotch in heavy, cut-crystal glasses. Just a few steps up from the lobby, the staff in the hot restaurant *du jour*, coffee, cream, and celery-toned Michael Mina, quietly rushed from table to table making preparations for hungry people with well-padded wallets who would be dining there when evening fell.

"*Life goes on*," I muttered. "*I forget just why*."

Pollack looked puzzled. "How's that?"

"Line from a very sad poem by Emily Dickinson," I said. "Never mind."

Pollack allowed me to go through the revolving door out to the street. As I waited for him, I glanced over at the glassed-in display cases at the entrance. One held the menu from Michael Mina, and next to it was a poster promoting the musical group performing in the rooftop bar. I took a step closer, "Klezmer Katz & Their Musical Kapers," read the poster. I sighed. Suddenly, I realized Pollack was at my elbow.

"What are you staring at?" he asked.

I pointed to the poster. "Something Ivory said when she woke up for a moment," I said. "She was trying to tell me something about hearing klezmer music."

"I hate that stuff," said Pollack. "Makes me feel like I'm trapped in a long, boring Jew wedding."

I regarded him with new distaste. "Let's go," I said.

We turned north up Powell, away from Union Square and up the hill toward the hospital.

"You weren't undercover, were you?" I asked Pollack. We were both breathing a little harder, as the hill grew steeper. A cable car clanged and passed us, going back down the hill, toward the cable car turnaround. It was crammed, as usual, with tourists leaning far out, their cell phones in one hand, shooting friends and family, as they obediently waved from the steps.

Pollack shrugged, "Nope. I like that place," he said. "Nothing illegal in that."

"Guess not," I said.

"Hey," he shot back, "let's remember you were there, too, Missy."

"I was investigating," I said.

He snorted. "Yeah, I remember, that's what you said. Not too skillfully, if memory serves. I made you as a party crasher in about two minutes."

We came to Sutter, and turned west. Rush hour was beginning, and the streets were filling up.

"So," he continued, "is that what you're still doing? Nosing around in things that don't concern you?"

I bridled, then took comfort in the thought that this nasty little guy probably never got all that lucky at the Crimson Club.

I was panting too much to sound very dignified, but I tried. "First, we are doing a magazine piece on Grace, so this is my business. And second, Ivory Gifford has become a friend, so I was naturally concerned."

He shot me a skeptical look. "Is that so? That's why you conned your way into her hotel room?" I looked surprised. "You think we don't talk to the front-desk staff? How dumb do you think cops really are?"

"I don't think *all* cops are dumb," I said pointedly. "I think Lt. Moon is very, very smart."

"Yeah, well, he's just like the rest of us. Once there's a conviction in a capital case, it's a trophy on our wall, too. Nobody wants to be responsible for taking that trophy down—least of all the cops."

We glared at each other, companionable in our mutual dislike. We pushed open the doors to the St. Francis Hospital lobby in silence.

CHAPTER 45

It was dark outside by the time they brought Ivory up to her hospital room. The young doctor who came to talk to us said that they'd pumped her stomach and were hydrating her. The cut on her head was minor and had been stitched up. She was conscious, and we could go see her in an hour or so. She had been asking for me and for Isabella. I left voice mails for Isabella at home, work, and on her cell. Moon and I continued to sit in the waiting room near the nurses' station, checking our watches every few minutes or so to see if we couldn't make that hour go a little more quickly. It didn't work. Pollack had gone to stand watch at Ivory's room with the young, uniformed officer.

My phone was turned off, so I didn't disturb people in the waiting room, but I'd turn it on periodically and check messages. Michael. Anya. And a message from Lulu: "Maggie, call me. I've been thinking about our conversation at the soccer game. What did you mean when you said Gus and a friend had 'restrained' that young woman in Vietnam? How did they restrain her?"

Moon and I sipped more disgustingly sweet tea together. The taste was not growing on me. He reached into his side pocket and pulled out a flat plastic bag and passed it over. "Don't open it," he said. "I've got a copy of what's inside for you to read. But just look at the envelope through the plastic." I held the bag gingerly in one hand. Through the plastic I could see the envelope was addressed to Isabella and me.

"Where'd you find this?"

"On the floor, by the bed. Pollack found it. Is it her handwriting?"

I frowned. "I have no idea. I don't think I've ever seen anything she's written."

"Doesn't matter," said Moon. "We can get samples."

"Can you?" I said. "Everything burned up at Ivory's place."

"Room service check," he said.

"You're killing me," I said. "Did you open it? What did it say? And by the way, it wasn't addressed to you."

"Potential crime scene," he said. "Gives us certain privileges."

He slipped the bag back into his pocket, and pulled out a piece of paper and handed it to me. "Here you go."

It was a photocopy, written on hotel letterhead, with the distinctive, cursive Westin St. Francis mark at the top.

Dear Isabella and Maggie,

Thank you for everything. I've remembered some things that make me very, very sorry. Tell Travis I will see him soon.

I turned the piece of paper over. "That's it?"

Moon nodded. "Doesn't that seem odd? No signature?"

"A little," he said.

"So is it a suicide note or not? Did she mean she'd see him when..." I shuddered. "They're both dead? That seems horrifying. And as if she's giving up on Travis."

"Or—" Moon started, then stopped.

"Or," I said grimly, "it means that Ivory remembers killing Grace, and that's why she's sorry. And what, then? How would she see him? If she confessed..." I broke off. "But this isn't a confession. Why would she leave things hanging like this?"

Moon shrugged. "Maybe whatever she put in that glass worked faster than she thought, and she couldn't finish."

"Something for sure in the glass?"

"We'll know tomorrow," he said. "There's a rush on at the lab, and the hospital can analyze what they pumped out of her. But I'd be willing to put money on it. There was something that looked undissolved at the bottom of the glass."

"Envelope sealed?"

"Nope. But the note was tucked inside."

"So, she didn't have time to finish the note? But she did have time to fold it and slip it in the envelope. That makes no sense. And the gun?"

"Not hers. She did have one at the bar, and it was in a fireproof safe, so it's probably still there."

I looked at Moon. "Numbers gone on this one?"

"Precisely. Just like the weapon that killed Grace."

"Who has access to guns without numbers?"

"Any bad guy—or gal—who wants to file them off."

"Who else?"

Moon looked puzzled. "I don't know what you mean."

"The cops," I said. "I bet your evidence rooms are filled with weapons that don't have numbers."

"They are, but so what? Every weapon is logged in, tagged, and tied to an investigation. And how would Ivory get a gun from a cop anyway?"

"I don't think she did," I said. "I think Gus got one from a cop."

"A specific cop—or are you just speculating?"

I shook my head, trying to clear the fog. I muttered, "*Quis custodiet ipsos custodies*?"

Moon glanced at his watch again, and stood. "Restroom break. Want anything while I'm up? More tea?"

I made a face, and watched him walk down the hall toward the cafeteria and the restrooms. As soon as he was out of sight, I stood and raced down the hall.

CHAPTER 46

The door to Ivory's room was closed. No sign of the young uniformed officer or of Pollack. I hesitated a moment, then tapped and pushed the door open. The lights were out, and the room was dim. But the shades were up, and some light came from the street outside. The closet door was wide open, and the yellowish fluorescent light inside fell directly on the bed, where I could make out Ivory, lying very, very still. I took a step closer, nervously looking over my shoulder at the closed door to the bathroom. Now I could see Ivory more clearly, her eyes fluttering, as if she were torn between waking to rejoin the world or staying tucked in the merciful oblivion of sleep.

I crept over to the side of her bed. The call-button cord was looped around the metal rail at the side, with the button itself right next to her left hand. I sat down next to the bed, and tentatively put my hand on hers. Suddenly, the room got darker, as the closet door squeaked closed and Pollack stepped out from behind the door. He had a pillow tucked under his arm. We regarded each other, the glittery little eyes in the snakehead catching the light from the open closet door.

"No visitors yet," he said. "What are you doing here?"

"What are *you* doing here?" I asked. "You're supposed to be guarding the door. And where's the cop who was with you?"

"Officer," he said, taking a step closer. "We call them officers. And, he's in the men's room, not that it's any concern of yours." He turned to glance at the door, and while he did, I slipped my hand from atop Ivory's to the call button and pushed it quickly three times. He looked back at me. "Where's the Lieutenant?"

"On his way here," I said, hoping that was the truth. "What's the pillow for?"

He looked down at the pillow, as if he'd forgotten he had it under his arm. "Oh, this? I heard Ms. Gifford call out, and she was struggling to sit up." I looked down at Ivory. That seemed unlikely. "I thought another pillow behind her back would help her be more comfortable."

"A regular Florence Nightingale," I said. "Sure you weren't trying to do something else with that pillow?" I watched as he tossed the pillow on the bed, first with relief, and then with concern, as I realized that both his hands were now free.

"You know Gus Reeves, don't you?" I said.

He smiled, and tapped the snakehead at his throat. "Smart little thing, aren't you? Old Gus saved my life in Nam. Killed a very nasty, slithery, poisonous thing for me one night while we were out on patrol. That's why I'm here. Looking out for the lady Gus loves."

"The 'silver fox' he loves," I said. "You're the *officer* who said you saw Gus and Ivory at that movie, aren't you?"

And then the door to the room flew open, as a nurse, Moon and the missing-in-action cop bustled in. Everyone started talking at once, and the nurse rushed over to Ivory's bedside. From the opposite side, I watched in relief as she checked her pulse, the monitors, and put a stethoscope to her chest. She looked up and said, "Sounds good."

And then, Moon pointed at Pollack and said, "Outside. Now."

Pollack shot me a look and edged toward the door, with the young officer at his side. "I'm staying," I said. I glanced at the nurse, "If it's okay."

She nodded. Moon crooked his finger at me. "Maggie, give me five minutes, please." I started to protest, and then followed him outside. You've got to know when to compromise, or at least, that's what I think I was starting to learn from Dr. Mephisto.

CHAPTER 47

After briefing Moon on my theories, and my fears, I returned to Ivory's bedside. Periodically, she'd wake up, look over, talk for a few minutes about the klezmer music, and drift off again. Around ten o'clock that night, Michael and Isabella arrived. I could hear Isabella's heels tapping toward the door, before I heard the knock. Ivory was sleeping again, so I went into the hall and shooed them all into one of the visiting-room lounges. I'd seen a shift change of nurses, introduced myself, knew the name of the nurse assigned to Ivory, and the names and ages of all her kids. We'd even traded hat-shopping tips. She leaned more to contemporary, wearable art; I favored vintage. But we were becoming pals. Michael had stopped at Everett and Jones on the way to the City and brought me a big, messy barbecue sandwich and a milkshake. I hadn't known I was hungry 'til I smelled the familiar aroma of burned brisket edges and smoky sauce. Comfort food, which I devoured while we talked, and I licked stray dribbles of sauce off my fingers.

Isabella was so wired, she could hardly sit still. Between bites, I told them what I had learned from Ivory. That the shock of losing The Devil's Interval, sifting through the rubble, and coming face-to-face with the possibility Travis would never come home to the place they both loved, had shaken something loose in her. She'd started to remember—and Gus had tried to help with those memories. At her insistence, Gus had driven her to the movie theater where *Mitzvah in Mali* had played. She'd walked inside, sat in the seats, and realized that she'd never set foot in the place.

"Where was I if I wasn't at the movie?" she'd asked Gus.

And he had told her. That she'd come home late at night, dirty, distraught, and with a gun stashed in her purse. She'd sobbed and babbled incoherently about protecting Travis from "that woman." Gus cleaned her up, gave her a sleeping pill, and put her to bed. He'd been to the movies, he said. Later, he found a tape of *Mitzvah in Mali* and brought it home, and convinced Ivory she'd actually seen it that night, and liked it enough that they needed to own a copy.

Michael and Isabella listened. A few times Isabella tried to interrupt with questions, but Michael put his hand on her forearm, and kept saying, "Go on, Maggie. Finish."

"The next day, Gus told her he had taken care of everything and not to worry. Ivory was frantic to go to the police, but Gus insisted that she think things over. Travis would never forgive her when he found out what she'd done. And what good would it do anybody for her to go to prison?"

"She agreed to wait. And then, a few days later..."

"Travis was arrested," Isabella completed the sentence. She sank back into the rump-sprung armchair. "I can't believe she was going to let Travis take the rap for a crime she committed. What the hell kind of parent would do that? Where's this famous do-anything-for-my-kid love?"

"The kind of love..." said Michael slowly, "that can't remember anything about what happened."

"That's right," I said. "Ivory had a stroke right after Travis was arrested. When she regained consciousness, she remembered nothing—about the crime, about Gus's cover-up, zip. It's as if the hard drive in her brain had been erased about that night."

Michael was looking at me. "It wasn't erased, was it, Maggie? It was altered. And Ivory just realized how."

"The klezmer group playing upstairs," I said. "It shook a lot more stuff loose."

CHAPTER 48

In fact, Isabella was right. The whole thing was about protective parental love gone very wrong—but it wasn't Ivory protecting Travis. It was Gus protecting his daughter, Ginger, from what he perceived as her hopelessly immoral and corrupt best friend. It was Gus who had crashed the Crimson that night and dragged Ginger, disguised in one of her dress-up moments, outside into the night. And, of course, Doc had reported that story to me because he knew I'd hear it anyway, and he could cover for Gus.

"That is so random," said Krissy, through a mouthful of pizza, the night we gathered the AWE duo and some other selected guests—Moon, Lulu Brown, Andrea, Calvin, Hoyt, and Carol Ann. Beer and wine for the grownups, along with an informal agreement among everyone that we'd keep the details of what went on at the Crimson at the PG level, lemonade for Josh and for Esme, who seemed to be logging more time at our house than hers. Zach, mercifully, was spending the night at a soccer buddy's house. Krissy continued, "I mean, I've heard of overprotective parents, but Ginger's an adult. Get a grip!" She shook her head.

Lulu, now at work on the blue and gold booties to accompany the sweater, looked up. "You haven't met my mother-in-law. She would have murdered anyone to keep me from marrying Prince Hal. Fortunately," she allowed herself a small smile, "the senior Mrs. Brown realized there was a new sheriff in town just in the nick of time. So, I didn't have to off her."

I shot Michael a glance. More things Lulu and I had in common. The senior Mrs. Fiori had been something less than pleased to see "her Mikey" lie down on the nuptial couch with a Jewish harlot. Or wait, had she called me a Whoring Daughter of Zion? I'll have to ask Michael; I seemed to have blocked those particular memories out of my personal hard drive.

Michael and I opened beer bottles, passed pizza, and shared the floor, bringing everyone up to date. About how creepy, old, snakehead Doc Pollack had alerted Gus he'd seen his precious Ginger at the Crimson Club, frolicking with Grace, their husbands, and a few others. How Gus had pled with Ginger to end her friendship with Grace—and Ginger had refused. How serendipitous it seemed that Travis and Grace became involved, and how handy to have the keys to Travis's car and apartment, hanging on a hook in the bar.

"And my mom was smart enough to figure out how that weirdo cop Pollack was connected to Gus," bragged Josh. He beamed at me. Dear Lord, take me now, I thought. I've impressed my kid—it will never get better than this. In fact, Josh looked delighted with the whole scene. Krissy had brought him a "Hastings Hunk" T-shirt, and though it drowned his still-slender chest, he wore it proudly. And there was that little Esme, glued to his side, and oh, my goodness, were they holding hands?

"Mom," said Josh, "Mom? Tell 'em how you figured it out."

"Oh, well," I said, distracted, tearing my eyes away from the completely fascinating-in-a-disturbing-way sight of my son holding hands. With a girl. In front of his parents!

"They both spelled something out in front of me and they used the military alphabet—when I couldn't understand Doc's nickname at the nightclub, he spelled it: Delta Oscar Charlie. And then, the night of the fire, Gus told us not to worry about Ivory, because he had a gun, and he spelled it out for us: Golf Uniform November. Plus, I knew Gus had been in Vietnam, and Pollack was about the same age. And then, when I saw Doc hanging around the crime scene, it just seemed like too much of a coincidence all around."

"And Gus is who I saw at Grace's that night?" asked Carol Ann. "And Doc was the short guy hiding in the backseat?"

"That was our big break," said Isabella. "That gave all of us some hope that there was some mysterious somebody or somebodies out there."

Krissy let out a sigh. "Well, all our terrific AWE ideas didn't pan out, did they?"

"Actually, they did," I corrected her. "You were chasing down financial information to find out who might have benefited from Grace's death. And benefiting from her death turned out to be exactly the right answer—just not for financial reasons. And then," I added, taking a lovely gulp of Merlot, "Lulu pointed out that what we really needed to figure out was who would benefit from Grace's death, and also benefit from getting Travis out of the way."

"The elusive Mr. Reeves," said Moon. "He saves his daughter from what he perceives as Grace's evil clutches, and is suddenly able to be the 'main man' in Ivory's life, with her son conveniently locked away. Her son, who doesn't really approve of Mom's long-time beau, anyway, is now a nonfactor."

"At the end, he wasn't so elusive, though," pointed out Michael. "The cops found him, *cara.*"

I couldn't help a little self-satisfied smile creeping across my face. "Thanks to Maggie," said Moon, "who remembered Gus mentioning some cabin he had in the woods, and the name of the place he went for bait and supplies, which enabled us to narrow the search."

"Proust had his madeleines," I said. "I have my trout po'boy."

"And I have to admit that was extraordinary good fortune," said Moon. "Ivory had no idea where Gus had gone. He left her with a glass of Scotch and several Vicodins dissolving in the bottom. And a gun with no pedigree, kindly supplied to him by Doc Pollack, who had, just as Maggie suspected, removed it from an evidence locker. He realized that with Ivory's memory coming back, the goose was cooked one way or another. He figured he'd let Ivory continue thinking she did it, and just see what happened."

"Ain't love grand?" said Michael.

"Oh, I believe he loves her," said Moon. "He told us he was holed up, waiting to hear what happened, If she killed herself, he was prepared to eat his gun and join her in the sweet hereafter. If she confessed, he swore he'd come back and tell the truth."

There was silence in the room.

I glanced at Josh and Esme. Now things had escalated. He had his arm around her. I looked from them to Moon.

"Poor choice of words," said Moon. "I apologize."

"So," said Michael, giving me the 'should we throw Josh and Esme out of the room right now' look?

"Who wants dessert? Brownies on the counter in the kitchen, and coffee in the urn."

We watched the group stream into the kitchen. "What do you think?" Michael asked. "This seems pretty intense for Josh and Esme. On the other hand, it's all been in the papers."

"Oh, they're already intense," I said dryly. "They're flooded with hormones. It's *Spring Awakening* right here in the 'burbs."

Michael put his arm around me. "Lighten up. Don't you remember what it was like to be that age?"

"I do," I said. "Oh, I do." We agreed that the worst was behind us in the debrief, and that we might as well let the two of them stay. "And you'll be calling Esme's mom to give her a heads-up about the topics of conversation tonight?" I asked.

"Not my job," said Michael. "Mom-to-mom. Absolutely your department. Not negotiable."

When everyone was resettled, Moon picked up the thread.

"When we brought Gus in, he confessed. Frankly, he was so relieved to know that Ivory was all right, I think he'd have confessed to the earthquake and fire of '06."

"He did set that fire at The Devil's Interval, didn't he?" asked Calvin.

"Indeed he did. Part of his continued efforts to make Ivory

completely dependent on him," Moon responded. "And he had, foolishly, mentioned to Maggie that he'd been a volunteer firefighter in the past. So he clearly knew enough to set a fire that would burn hot and move fast."

I threaded my way to the DVD player and inserted a disc.

"Here's the thing," I said. "On some level, I think Gus actually wanted somebody to figure all this out. He told me that there was a 'Top Winners' of all time compilation of old *Jeopardy* episodes. And I just got around to watching it the other night."

I pressed play, and a much younger Alex Trebek and Gus Reeves showed up on the screen. I fast-forwarded to the right spot. " 'Illegal Hot Stuff' for $800," said Gus. And as we watched, the window opened and revealed the words: *Carbon Disulfide.* Gus went for the buzzer, "What is a common accelerant used in arson?"

I hit pause, catching Alex in midacknowledgment, that once again, Gus knew his 'hot stuff.'

"And, according to the arson forensics, there were traces of carbon disulfide at The Devil's Interval." I hit stop, and ejected the DVD. "Of course, Gus told me about the Top Winners compilation DVD before he torched the club. I just wish I'd taken it out of its little Netflix sleeve a lot sooner."

"Even the great detective, Maggie Fiori, isn't a psychic," said Lulu briskly. "If you'd seen the tape, would you have been able to predict Gus would set a fire?"

"Of course not," I said. "Okay, just wanted to share that little scene with you all."

"So we know exactly what happened the night Grace was murdered?" asked Hoyt. "I've pulled the story from the next issue, so we can do an update. That means it would be helpful to actually *have* an update."

"Here's what we know," said Moon. "Gus was becoming increasingly distraught about what he thought Ginger was up to, and was convinced that if she were only free of Grace's influence, she'd become the paragon he knew her to be. Travis had been at the bar that afternoon and had mentioned to his mother that he was going out that night. Gus boosted the spare keys, drove out to the Plummers' home, waited 'til Grace got back from her date with Travis, knocked on the door, and told her some story about Ginger having been in a car accident, and that she was asking for Grace."

"That's why I saw her racing out the door," said Carol Ann.

"Exactly. She gets in the van, and off they go toward SF General, or at least, that's what Gus tells her. And he introduces Doc, who's in the back seat, as a friend who knows Ginger, too."

"And that's the shorter person I glimpsed in the backseat?" asked Carol Ann.

"Yes," I said. "And here's what's weird, I remember thinking about Doc's height when we danced together at..." I paused, glancing at Josh. "When we danced together. He was really a good dancer, and I wondered at the time if it's easier to dance with someone your own height. But it does seem odd that Grace didn't recognize Doc from the club."

"Not really," says Moon. "She's distracted enough, worrying about Ginger, and it's dark in the car, so she doesn't look at Doc closely enough to recognize him as someone she might have seen somewhere else."

"And did they go to the hospital?" asked Krissy.

"They headed in that general direction," said Moon. "SF General is hardly Grace's usual stomping grounds, so she's disoriented about where they're headed. She's not suspicious when Gus pulls into an empty parking lot. Doc reaches over from the backseat, pulls a gun on her. Together, they force her into the backseat and tie her up." He stops, looks around the room. "According to Gus, they didn't mean to kill her. They meant to scare her to death, and give her an ultimatum about ending her friendship with Ginger."

"What went wrong?" asked Krissy.

Moon shrugged. "Who knows? Gus said things got out of hand. They were taunting her about how she enjoyed being tied up. Pollack leaned in really close to her, and she spit in his face. Pollack grabbed her head and wrenched—and broke her neck."

"On my God," whispered Krissy.

"That's more or less what Gus kept shouting, when we found him," said Moon. "He alternated between rage about how things went wrong and remorse, that he'd only meant to protect Ginger and take care of Ivory."

"Pollack confessed, too?" asked Seth.

"Nope. He's lawyered up. This is Gus's version. He says they panicked. Pollack decided it would make things harder to figure out if they shot her. And conveniently enough, Gus had a plastic tarp in the back of the car."

I shuddered. "This is so creepy to imagine," I said. "But it makes more sense. Somehow I couldn't picture Gus shooting someone in cold blood."

"Don't romanticize the guy," said Moon. "Murder is murder."

"I'm not," I said. "In fact, Lulu had figured out something important while we were sitting there in the waiting room. That's what her call was about."

Lulu shook her head, as if she was still trying to get clear on things. "It occurred to me there was a lot of 'tying up' in this story. More than you run into on an ordinary day. And I wondered what the details were about the girl Gus and Doc had 'restrained' in Vietnam."

"That's going to help us nail Pollack," said Moon. "We're getting more details about their misadventure all those years ago in Vietnam. In fact, they had tied the girl up when they threatened her."

"So awful," said Krissy.

Moon continued, "At some level, these are guys who think they get to play by their own rules. Anyway, you know the rest. The irony is, Gus had taken keys to Travis's apartment, thinking he might have to wrestle the body inside. Instead, the door to the limo was conveniently unlocked."

"What happened to the gun?" asked Calvin.

"We don't know where he hid it all this time, but it turned up again," said Michael. "That's the gun he left in the hotel room for

Ivory. Eventually, the ballistics would be run—and it would be tied back to the gun used on Grace."

"This," said Hoyt, "is such a sad story."

"It's a long line of sad stories in Grace's life," I said. "That's the worst part."

"On a more cheerful note," said Isabella. "Ivory is recovering, Travis was released last week, and someone has underwritten six months of rent on a new spot for The Devil's Interval 2.0."

"And," added Hoyt, "it's a heckuva cover story for *Small Town.*"

The evening wound down after that. By 11 p.m., Michael had driven Esme home, Josh was in bed, and I was collecting glasses for the dishwasher. Moon was helping.

"This drives me nuts," he said.

"Oh, me too," I said. "No matter where I put the glasses, Michael will rearrange them."

"Don't be obtuse, Maggie," said Moon. "What I meant was, I think tonight's tie-it-up-with-a-bow denouement is a dangerous reinforcement for your detecting career."

"Not career," I said. "Just the occasional avocation. And lovely pronunciation of denouement, by the way."

"Try not to be so patronizing," he said. "And why can't you take up knitting, like your friend, Lulu?"

"Lulu's knitting is like Madame Defarge's," I countered. "You can only speculate what it's a cover for."

CHAPTER 49

Sometimes Travis dreamed about Grace. He'd awaken with a bitter taste in his mouth, knowing already that she was gone, remembering very little of the dream. But here was the strangest thing. Sometimes while he was still in that just-awakened state, some word he didn't even know would pop into his head. Excimer. Langerhans. *And he'd pick up the Webster's on his nightstand, and just like Grace, say the word aloud, trying to sound out the spelling so he could look it up.* Elision *was the word this morning, right around daybreak. He had to try a couple of spellings to find it, but there it was. Meant something in poetry, but also in music. "A note that serves as the last note of a phrase and the first note of a new phrase." Travis let the dictionary fall on his chest and glanced up at the mirror over the bureau facing his bed. It was as if he was looking in the rearview mirror again in the limo, glancing into the backseat to catch Grace's eye. "Amazing Gracie," he said. "You're talking to me."*

AFTERWORD: THE GIRL IN THE BLACK HAT

Three months after Travis was released, Michael and I celebrated our sixteenth anniversary with a night out on the town. I wore a gift Frederick Plummer gave me, the frothy black evening hat I had coveted the moment I saw it perched on Grace's sleek head in a photograph. True to my word, I had called Plummer as soon as the pieces came together to tell him what we had discovered and elaborate on the cryptic explanation he'd received from the cops. We sat at his kitchen counter, drinking coffee, and he told me more about Grace. We both wept.

As we said goodbye, he asked if he could give me something of hers. "She had beautiful jewelry," he said. "I know, because I bought it for her."

I shook my head to the jewelry. "There's one thing," I said, and told him about lusting after that evening hat. "I'm sure you've given her clothes away to charity," I said. "But if that little hat were around..."

He disappeared into the back of the house and returned with a simple red hatbox. The hat rested inside like a perfect, ebony egg in a spun-sugar nest.

I didn't look anything like Grace in the hat—but I didn't put it to shame, either. And it seemed lovely to be taking it out for an elegant evening. We were splurging on dinner at the too-cool-for-words eponymously named Michael Mina for two reasons. First, it was located in the lobby of the St. Francis, and it was good to replace the memory of finding Ivory there with something entirely positive. Second, we could afford a lavish dinner out because we'd cut back on our therapy budget so dramatically.

Dr. Mephisto had fired us. Or released us back into the wild. Or something. Instead of weekly sessions, she'd suggested we check in with her every three months or so. Or, if something critical came up. "Which does not include," she said, "your endless negotiations about unloading the dishwasher."

Turns out a really good dinner with the man you love is excellent therapy in and of itself. After dinner, we walked up Powell to Pine, ignoring a threatening sky and moisture in the air. We climbed the stairs to a new, tucked-away spot over the lobby in a worn but still classy apartment building. It was now the location for The Devil's Interval, and we showed up just in time to hear the late set. We joined Lulu and Hal at a small table in the back. "Nice space," said Michael, looking around.

"Isn't it?" said Hal. "Lulu shook some of her old finance trees and scared up some investors."

Lulu patted his hand. "Just listen to the music, darling."

At the end of the set, the pianist—Travis Gifford by name—waved to his mother to come join him on the bench. They sat side by side and began a simple, stripped-down version of "Come Rain or Come Shine." At the end of the piece, Ivory sat with her right hand in her lap, and her left hand on Travis's shoulder. We all waited for Travis to sign off with The Devil's Interval. Oddest thing, though. He resolved the final chord. In a major key.

And then we all went out into the starry night. The clouds had dissipated, the moon was perched high above the Starlight Roof at the Sir Francis Drake Hotel. It seemed unseasonably mild for a San Francisco summer night. Hal and Lulu were meeting friends for a late drink, so we parted ways.

Michael tucked my hand into his arm, and we started the walk to BART. "By my estimation," he said, "we're not more than a ten-minute stroll from the Crimson Club." He glanced at me. "Want to drop by?"

I was silent for a moment. "You remember that story we did on the chefs who were experimenting with exotic game dishes?" I said.

"I remember."

"So, I tried everything—including the rattlesnake."

"And?"

"It wasn't bad. But once was enough."

Michael dug in his pocket and pulled out our BART tickets. He handed me one. "Home?"

"Home," I said.

ACKNOWLEDGMENTS

Writing may be a lonely gig, but I always feel surrounded by what my mother called my "amen corner." To all of you in that corner, I send love and gratitude.

This book would not have been possible without my friend Evan Young, who provided an insider's guide to the death-penalty appeal process and San Quentin, and who patiently answered many dim-witted questions. The fact that she's a great reader as well was lagniappe. Despite Evan's excellent coaching, errors may have crept into the book. Evan is responsible for what's right. I'm responsible for what's wrong. And it's possible that Evan's given first name, Eugenie (which also belongs to her mother), inspired some aspects of Travis's mother. The Women Defenders are a real-life group (womendefenders.net), and they are doing God's work, in whatever way you care to define that. The backstory of Grace Plummer's childhood was inspired by heartbreaking tales I heard during my work as a mentor and board member at Youth Homes, an agency that cares for young people in foster care (youthhomes.org).

Early readers Tom Clarke, Fred D'Orazio, Scott Hafner, Sue Handa, Randy Hyde, Maria Hjelm, Phyllis Peacock, and Steve Tollefson provided encouragement and important feedback.

My Bay Area writing group—Ronnie Caplane, Greg Ellis, Gloria Lenhart, Susan Parker, and Christine Schoefer—were the perfect mix of heartless and helpful. Other writer pals were generous boosters; Barbara Austin, Bob Dugoni, Margret Elson,

Jonnie Jacobs, Jon Jefferson, Karen Mulvaney, Susan Shea, and Wendy Lichtman, thank you! Bill Dunk, fine writer and husband to another fine writer, Courtney Beinhorn, is always willing to spread the word. He gave me the opportunity to write about many passions, including baseball, shameless promotion, and Portlandia.

What do writers do when they're not writing? We read, and so a shout-out to my Bay Area book club (Johanna Clark, Janis Medina, Pam Miller, and Ellen Zucker) and to my Portlandia book club (Peggy Almon, Karen Halloran, Joni Hartmann, Susan Hartnett, Laurene Mullen, Nanwei Su, Sandra Tetzloff, and Joyce Wilson).

As always, I am indebted to my friend and designer, Jacqueline Jones (www.jacquelinejonesdesign), for her fine eye and generous spirit.

I have appropriated some friends' names for various purposes in this book. While I hope you find the characters of Lulu Brown, Susan Hawk, and Hal and Joyce Hothan engaging, the real-life versions are way better. And thank you, dear friend and colleague Kathy Halland, for giving me insight into the grace and power of Scandinavian grandparents.

There are some real folks in this book, notably musicians Karen Blixt, Alex Acuna, Frank Martin, and Sheldon Brown. If you want to hear the kind of jazz I imagined playing at The Devil's Interval, go directly to iTunes or to karenblixt.com and you can listen to Karen's music and decide she needs to be in your collection.

I am indebted to my friends and work colleagues who make writing possible: Ann Appert, Kathy Bowles, Betsy Brown, Caity Burrows, Ben Peterson, and Bob Rucker. Copyeditor Roz Kulick cleaned up my act.

As always, I am grateful for David Skolnick, my business partner and friend, and the guy who (a) sent me to the Book Passage mystery writers' conference years ago and (b) was the originator of most of the best lines in the book.

Amy Rennert is the best________. You can fill in the blank however you want. She's the best literary agent, of course, but also the best reader, cheerleader, and more. Dear Amy, hard to believe, but words fail me.

Amy brought me together with Prospect Park Books. Publishers Colleen Dunn Bates and Patty O'Sullivan and their colleague Jennifer Bastien make a great team, and I am grateful for all their support.

I come from a family of readers and writers, and have learned from all of them. My siblings Laurie Winthrop and Larry Winthrop and sib-in-law Pat Winthrop are not only fine writers themselves, they also see promoting my work as a personal mission. My sister, who once ran my informal New York chapter, now lives in Geneva and is an advocate for my work in multiple European locations. My immediate literary Peterson posse—Ken, Ben, and Kate—provide cheer every day. Will Peterson, age seven and the newest Peterson wordsmith, may one day be the first right-handed slugger in the majors to recite poetry at bat.

Finally, I am grateful to my parents, Vauneta and Murray Winthrop, who taught me that while cleanliness is well and good, it is really bookishness that is next to Godliness. Like all the rest of us in miraculously long marriages, Maggie and Michael will continue to pursue the kind of relationship Neta and Murray created. Mom and Dad, you still inspire all of us.

ABOUT THE AUTHOR

Linda Lee Peterson is the managing partner of Peterson Skolnick & Dodge, a creative services agency based in San Francisco, Philadelphia, and Portland, Oregon. A longtime resident of the San Francisco Bay Area, she was inspired to set her mysteries in the city that inspired Dashiell Hammett. Linda and her family now live in Portland, Oregon.